Hyksos Boo Conquest

By Max Overton

Writers Exchange E-Publishing
http://www.writers-exchange.com

Publisher note:
Due to formatting issues symbols such as ü, ä, é and ö have been replaced with the simple letter u, a, e and o. We apologise for this necessity.

Hyksos Series, Book 2: Conquest, A Novel of Ancient Egypt
Copyright 2020 Max Overton
Writers Exchange E-Publishing
PO Box 372
ATHERTON QLD 4883

Cover Art by: Julie Napier

Published by Writers Exchange E-Publishing
http://www.writers-exchange.com

ISBN **ebook**: 978-1-925574-71-5
Print: 978-1-925574-78-4

Hyksos (/ˈhɪksɒs/; Egyptian ḥq□(w)-ḫ□swt,
Egyptological pronunciation: *heqa khasut*, "ruler(s) of foreign lands"

Setting the Scene

This is a work of fiction, but fiction based on fact. The closest parallel I can draw is of a dramatised re-enactment of actual events in history.

I have tried to be historically accurate within this series of books, but I did not want it to read like a history lesson. I have invented dialogue, and many incidents that fill in the stories of men and women, both fictional and real, that lived and died in these trouble-filled years. I have also tried to make sense of tangled and sometimes contradictory lists of kings and relationships between real characters.

I am indebted to Professor Kim Ryholt of the University of Copenhagen for his book *The Political Situation in Egypt during the Second Intermediate Period*, which provided me with the bones upon which to hang the flesh of my novels.

I would also like to thank Sara Jane Sesay who is my first reader. She takes the time to go through my manuscript and is quick to point out any mistakes and places where my ideas need clarification.

My cover art is by Julie Napier. I have long admired her work and over the years she has designed all my book covers.

I am grateful too to my many readers. Without readers, a writer's efforts are just a personal exercise in telling a story. I would probably write them anyway, even if nobody read them, but I like to think I am bringing enjoyment to someone.

The Second Intermediate Period in Ancient Egyptian history is the time between the Middle and New Kingdoms. It encompassed the

Twelfth to the Eighteenth Dynasty between about 1800 and 1550 B.C.E. Despite knowing the dynasties involved, the details of the period are obscure at best, and often lacking altogether. There are lists of kings but they are incomplete and sometimes they are names only with no information on what they did or how long they reigned.

The Twelfth dynasty merged with the Thirteenth and can only really be distinguished by the later presence of a rival dynasty of Canaanite kings ruling from Avaris in the Delta (Fourteenth Dynasty). The Thirteenth ruled from the city of Memphis, known as Ankh-Tawy in those days. The Fourteenth arose from Canaanite settlers who gradually drew apart from the rest of Egypt during the Twelfth and then declared their own kings.

The Fifteenth Dynasty was that group known as the Hyksos (*heqa khasut*) or 'rulers of the foreign countries'. They invaded the Delta and conquered Avaris, ending the dynasty of Canaanite rulers there. They subsequently invaded the Nile Valley and defeated the native rulers of the Thirteenth Dynasty, and after them the Sixteenth and Abydos Dynasties.

The Sixteenth Dynasty arose in the city of Thebes (Waset) in the south, as a result of the weakening and eventual collapse of the Thirteenth. They were conquered by the Hyksos after about fifty years. The Abydos Dynasty was an ephemeral one that arose at the same time as the Sixteenth, in the southern city of Abydos (Abdju), and fell quickly to the northern invaders.

The Seventeenth Dynasty arose in the south of Egypt as the Hyksos invaders of the Fifteenth withdrew to the north. The native kings followed them, and eventually reunited the Two Kingdoms under the reign of Ahmose in the Eighteenth Dynasty.

The ancient Egyptians believed that a name was more than just an identifying label. A name meant something, it was descriptive, and a part of a person's being. For instance, Sobekhotep means 'Sobek is satisfied', and the mouthful Sekhemre-sewdjtawy means something like 'A powerful one who allows the Two Lands to thrive'. The names of the kings have been simplified. Egyptian pharaohs had five names, two of which are important as far as these stories go--the prenomen and the nomen. Only the nomen was given at birth, the prenomen being a coronation name. I have generally used the birth names on informal occasions and limited the use of the prenomen to more formal occasions or when referring to past kings. Another reason to use a

2

prenomen is that kings did not have a numbering system like us (Henry III, Henry IV), so Sobekhotep III had the prenomen Sekhemre-sewdjtawy, and Sobekhotep IV had the prenomen Khaneferre.

Most of the names we know from Egypt, including the name of the country itself, come from the Greek. Ancient Egyptians called their country Kemet, the Black Land, but the Greeks named it Aigyptos. Similarly, they gave their own names to the king (Pharaoh), to the names of cities like Waset (Thebes) and Abdju (Abydos), and many of the names of the gods. Asar became Osiris, Auset became Isis, and Heru became Horus. I had to make a decision whether to use the real names as the ancient Kemetu (Egyptians) knew them, or to use the more familiar Greek names. Some people may disagree with my choice, but it just felt wrong to put Greek words in Ancient Egyptian mouths.

The Hyksos name itself derives from the Greeks also, many years after the events detailed here. In the ancient Egyptian language they were called *heqa khasut*, meaning 'rulers of the foreign countries'. Nobody really knows who they were, but the consensus is that they came from the region known as Retjenu, which comprises modern-day Israel, Lebanon and Syria. They possessed superior military skills and equipment, and introduced the chariot to Egypt. Later generations of Egyptians turned these skills and equipment back on the Hyksos and defeated them.

Now, enough of notes. On with the story....

Family Tree of Hyksos 2: Conquest

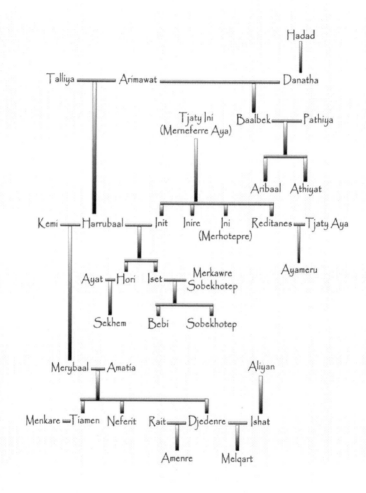

Prologue
1670 B.C.E.

The King of Hattush liked nothing more than spending his days in the small orchard attached to the palace, sitting in the sun and thinking about days past. Arimawat had ruled his little kingdom in southern Kanaan for nearly thirty years now, and though his bones were old and his muscles weak, his mind was still sharp in the winter of his life, and he knew what was coming.

"There's nothing I can do about it though," he murmured.

"Do about what?" the young man sitting beside him asked.

"The consumption of our little kingdom. It is only a matter of time."

The young man, who was the king's son, knew exactly what his father meant as he had lived with the threat all his life. He was heir to the throne of Hattush, but the kingdom was only a client kingdom, a stepping-off point for the army of Anep-Aper, the ruler of most of Amurru, Lebanon and Kanaan. Thinking about it soured his stomach, but there was nothing he could do about it, anymore than could his father.

"I won't be alive much longer to worry about it, Baalbek, but you will be, and you must find a way to protect the family."

"Don't say such things, father. You have ruled Hattush well and all men speak of Arimawat with respect."

"Graves are full of respected men," Arimawat said. "It comes to us all, my son, but you must find a way to ensure our family survives the coming war."

"You are certain it is coming?"

"War always comes, and I've talked about this before." Arimawat took a deep breath of the cool spring air delicately perfumed by the scents of the flowering orchard. "I won't see this year's harvest..." He held up a hand as Baalbek opened his mouth to protest. "You know it as well as I. No, next year or the year after...five years even, or ten... Anep-Aper will decide the time has come to invade the Delta. Unless the Delta army has improved drastically in the last thirty years, Anep-Aper will sweep over them, dealing death and destruction."

"That's not going to affect our family though," Baalbek said. "Pathiya and Aribaal will be safe enough in Hattush and...and if I'm king by then, I can protect them anyway."

Arimawat nodded. "Yes, they will be safe enough, but your family is larger than that."

"My mother, you mean?" Baalbek frowned. "Pathiya's parents are dead, and I care nothing for her brother."

"Your mother will be safe and your wife's brother is worthless. I mean your half-brother Harrubaal and his son Merybaal. I left them in Avaris and Merybaal at least still lives there. He has children of his own, I think. Anyway, they are all your family and stand in the way of danger when Anep-Aper invades the Delta."

Baalbek shrugged. "I know of them though I don't know them. I can send a message if you want."

"Don't you think I've already done that?" Arimawat asked. "They do not reply. It is possible they hold me in low regard and so ignore my warnings."

"Then I don't see what more you can do."

"I want you to go to Avaris and persuade them of the danger."

"What?"

"Go to Avaris and talk to your nephew Merybaal. Convince him of the danger Anep-Aper represents."

"If the Amurran king finds out I have done so..."

Arimawat gave a wry smile. "Then don't let him find out."

"I am the heir of Hattush; I can scarcely go there without him finding out."

"My minister Eltan is going down there soon. I am sending him on a trade mission to try and shore up some business transactions. That sort of thing happens all the time, and nobody will think anything of it.

If you go with him, disguised as one of his assistants, you won't be recognised."

Baalbek considered his father's words. "You trust Eltan with the life of your son?"

"He knows I have his family in the palm of my hand. He will not risk them."

Baalbek shrugged. "Then if it is your wish, father, I will go. I am not particularly interested in these other relatives of mine, but I've always wanted to see the Delta lands."

Harrubaal liked to sit on a small hillock overlooking the river and contemplate the waters, equating the flow of the current with the passage of time in his life. The river was currently in flood and this always depressed him, seeing the days of his life slipping away faster and faster. Still, he could not look away as the flood waters brought their yearly gift of silt to his lands. The flood was receding now, and the pastures by the river edge emerging from the waters, the tips of the grass poking up through the ebbing flow. He sat on a chair, under a cloth canopy set up by his servants, sipped wine made on his estate, and contemplated his life.

"The gods have mixed good with bad in my life," he murmured. "But which gods? Hattushi or Kemetu?"

His attendant frowned, unsure whether he had been addressed by his master. "Your pardon, master?"

Harrubaal shook his head. "Just thinking aloud, Bennu." He glanced at his attentive servant. "Who rules my life, Bennu? The Hattushi gods because I was born Hattushi, or Kemetu gods because I live in Kemet?"

"That is a question for the priests," Bennu said carefully.

"Yes, but which priests?"

Bennu kept silent, letting his master think his own thoughts. He refilled Harrubaal's cup as it emptied.

Harrubaal turned in his chair to view the rest of his sprawling estate. Toward the higher land in the west lay the house, painted mud brick and surrounded by orchards. To the south lay fields waiting to be sown with wheat and barley, melons and cucumbers, onions and lettuce, and to the north grassy pastures littered with cattle and sheep spread down to the receding waters of the river. Farther away, he could just glimpse the sun dazzling off the white walls of Ankh-Tawy. Closer, in the direction of the house, he saw a man waiting beneath the sparse shade of a thorn tree. He leaned forward, trying to make out who it was.

"Who is that?" he asked. "I can't quite make him out."

"Master, it is your son Hori. I think he desires speech with you."

Harrubaal sighed and shifted in his chair, feeling every one of his seventy-three years. "Let him approach."

Bennu gestured to the waiting man and then discreetly withdrew as Hori approached.

Hori knelt at his father's feet. "Greetings, father."

Harrubaal looked down at the youth fidgeting at his feet. "Sit beside me," he ordered.

Hori dutifully sat on the grass beside his father, but it did not stop him fidgeting. "Father..." he said tentatively.

"What troubles you?"

"Father, Uncle Inire wants to take me to Hut-waret."

Harrubaal could not think where Hut-waret was until he remembered it was the Kemetu name for Avaris. "Does he indeed? Why?"

"Why is he going? I think he has business there."

"No, why has he invited you?"

"He said it would be an opportunity. I've never been to the Delta, father, nor seen these foreign Kanaanites."

"Nonsense. I'm one of them...or was. And you are half Hattushi yourself."

"Yes, father, but can I go?"

Harrubaal sat in thought for several minutes while Hori sat squirming in anticipation.

"You have a brother in Avar... in Hut-waret, you know."

Hori looked at his father in surprise. "I do?"

"A half-brother. His name is Merybaal and he must be...what? Fifty years old?"

"Who is his mother?"

"Kemi, daughter of Neferhotep of Ankh-Tawy."

"A king's daughter?" Hori frowned. "I remember her, I think. She died about three years ago..." His voice trailed off as the import of this fact registered in his mind. "If you were married to her, then what does that make mother? Is your marriage to her invalid?"

"Kemi left me and married King Maaibre Sheshi of the Delta. Your mother Init and I are properly married."

Hori breathed a sigh of relief and sat in thought for a few moments. "That means you have married a king's daughter twice. How is that, father? Forgive me, but what makes you so important?"

"Important?" Harrubaal's eyes unfocused for a moment. "Not important, but I served my kings well. Sheshi rewarded me with marriage to Kemi, and after she left me and I fled to Ankh-Tawy, I served Merneferre Aya and he rewarded me with marriage to his daughter Init...your mother."

There was another period of silence, while Harrubaal remembered and Hori considered his father's past actions.

"So I have a brother as well as a sister?"

"Yes. Will you see him when you go to Hut-waret?"

"I don't know. Yes, I suppose so. Would he want to see me?"

"I doubt he'd want to see me, for reasons you already know. He probably regards me as a traitor, but you are innocent of my actions."

"If I do try to see him, how will I know him?"

"He is the Treasurer of the Kingdom; one of the most important people after the king. I will ask Inire to make sure you meet him."

Merybaal still owned the house in Avaris that had belonged to his father and grandfather before him, though years of holding the position of Treasurer had enriched him greatly. Rather than buy or build another house more befitting his status in the Delta, he had opted to expand the old house, buying up and knocking down surrounding structures. Walls now turned the house into a miniature walled city, with a large population of servants living within it to look after his family.

Kings came and went in Avaris, a few by father to son succession, more by non-violent coup, but the Treasurer was the constant factor that kept the government running smoothly. Merybaal had come to the position in the reign of his half-brother Sehibre Sobek-Har some thirty years before and had seen twenty ephemeral kings come and go, regarding their presence as no more than a temporary disturbance in his normal duties. He married, raised a family, and amassed wealth, and kept his fingers on everything that happened in the Delta kingdom. So it was that in the reign of Anati Djedkare, two letters crossed his desk that gave him pause. One was from the court of Hattush, and the other from Ankh-Tawy.

"What do we know about this Lord Eltan from Hattush?" he asked his scribe.

"Very little, my lord. He is Arimawat's minister in charge of trade."

Merybaal harrumphed, not welcoming the mention of his grandfather's name. "He says he wants to see me in a personal audience as well as officially."

"Perhaps because he desires a favour of you, my lord."

"Perhaps. All right, tell him I will grant him a personal audience." He passed the letter across to the scribe and picked up the other one. "This one is from Inire, son of Merneferre Aya of Ankh-Tawy. He too requests an informal audience, though he makes no mention of trade."

"Will you see him, my lord?"

"I cannot very well refuse the son of the King of Kemet, even if he is a younger son and unlikely to inherit." Merybaal tapped the folded letter against his chin as he considered the best course of action. "He wants an informal meeting, so invite him to my house rather than to the palace. I shall entertain him and find out what he wants."

"I will reply immediately, my lord."

"Come to think of it, invite this Eltan of Hattush at the same time. It won't hurt to show each of them that we maintain good relations with all our neighbours."

A month later, as the last of the flood waters drained from the land and growing shoots burst out of the fresh, dark silt, the two delegations arrived in Avaris. One came from the northeast, overland, on horses, while the other arrived from the south by ship. The one from Ankh-Tawy came in greater state, Lord Inire making no secret of the fact that he was the son of a reigning king. King Anati Djedkare of Avaris welcomed him and gave him rooms within the palace, but was a little put out that Inire was more interested in meeting his Treasurer than him. Lord Eltan of Hattush was offered accommodation within the city, the king being happy to ignore the details of a trade agreement. Hunting and the pleasures of the flesh were of greater interest to him than wearisome talks. Officials from the Treasury found both visitors and invited them to a banquet in the Treasurer's own house.

Inire and Eltan arrived within minutes of each other and were greeted personally by Merybaal. He was not surprised that each man brought companions, but was a little astonished by the age of them. Inire was accompanied by a youth who could surely have no experience in trade, and the young man with Eltan was not much older. He decided that perhaps these men enjoyed the attentions of other men and had brought young men who interested them. Merybaal had no interests in that regard, but as long as they behaved with decorum, he had no objections.

"Welcome, Lord Inire. Welcome, Lord Eltan. I am delighted that you could both join me, and that I can offer some informal entertainment before we get down to the serious business of trade agreements."

Both lords made polite replies, and though the young men were introduced--simply as Hori and Baalbek--no mention was made of who they were or what duties they performed. This tended to confirm Merybaal's opinion of their status. He led them into an inner room where a feast had been laid out.

"Your family will not be joining us?" Inire asked.

"No, Lord Inire. They will dine separately so that we may have the opportunity to talk freely if that is your wish."

Servants appeared, bearing dishes of beef, lamb, and goose dripping with fat, a large array of vegetables and fruits, and fresh-baked bread. Jars of wine and beer, as well as milk and cool river water, quenched their thirst. They talked of inconsequential things while they ate and Merybaal grew more and more puzzled as to why each ambassador had requested an informal audience but was now avoiding any mention of a reason. It could only be that each man required privacy and was reticent about talking in the presence of the other.

After the meal, servants brought bowls of scented water for the guests to wash their fingers, and clean linen cloths to dry them. Then Merybaal led them out into a walled courtyard and offered sweetmeats and spiced wine, while musicians entertained them. He managed to get Inire alone. Despite prompting, Inire only smiled and complimented Merybaal on his hospitality. Eltan, when alone, was no more forthcoming, thanking his host and saying he looked forward to fruitful discussion in the days to come.

"Forgive me. Lord Eltan," Merybaal said at last. "You asked for a private meeting, yet you have said nothing. Do you no longer wish to talk informally?"

"Forgive me in turn, Lord Merybaal, if I have been less than honest. It was not I who desired a private meeting but my king, Arimawat, who is your grandfather."

"I see," Merybaal replied coolly. "I am prepared to talk with you on trade matters, but I have no desire to concern myself with your king's wishes."

"He asks only that you talk to the young man I brought with me tonight."

"Baalbek? Why, who is he?"

"I would rather he told you that himself."

"You are being very mysterious, Lord Eltan." Merybaal considered the request. "Send for this Baalbek then. I will speak to him."

"With your permission, I will withdraw, Lord Treasurer. We will have ample opportunity to talk in the days ahead. Tonight, it would be better for you to talk to the young man."

"I am intrigued."

When Eltan took his leave, Inire declared that he would leave also, but that the youth Hori should stay behind, for he too desired private speech with their host. Merybaal was thoroughly perplexed by this time, but bade his visitors farewell, and ushered the young men back into the courtyard.

"Now, what's all this about?"

Hori looked down at his feet and shuffled them, but Baalbek shrugged and knelt before Merybaal.

"Your grandfather Arimawat is my father."

"What?"

Hori cleared his throat. "And...and your father Harrubaal is my father also," he said. "He married Init, daughter of Merneferre Aya and had me and my sister Iset."

Merybaal stared from one to the other for several minutes, before shaking his head. "Why are you telling me this?"

"My father thought I should meet my family," Hori said. "I... I didn't know I had one."

12

"And my father charged me with a message for my family here in Avaris and in Ankh-Tawy," Baalbek said.

"Your family?" Merybaal asked. He sighed and shook his head again. "Sit," he ordered, before leaving the courtyard.

Hori looked at Baalbek with interest. "We are related?"

"So it seems. Your father is my brother by a different mother."

"You are much younger than my father."

"And your brother Merybaal is much older than you."

"It is all very strange to me. I had no idea."

Baalbek nodded. "Harrubaal is in Ankh-Tawy?"

"Yes." Hori hesitated. "I'm not really sure why there is such tension within the family, or why my father should be regarded with suspicion."

Baalbek shrugged. "My father lived in Avaris before he returned home and became king of Hattush. Your father lived in Avaris too, but had his differences and gave his allegiance to Ankh-Tawy. Merybaal, on the other hand, remained loyal to Avaris. Political differences have split our family, it seems."

"Your father is king? Do you have brothers?"

"No."

"Are you the heir?"

"Yes."

There did not seem much to say to that, so Hori poured himself a cup of beer and sipped it, frowning as he considered this startling information.

"I wonder what Merybaal is doing," Baalbek said. "He's just gone and left us, but there are things I'm supposed to tell him."

"What things?"

"A warning for him...and for your father."

"A warning about what?"

Baalbek just shook his head. "Later," he murmured. "When Merybaal returns."

Merybaal came back a little later with several other people whom he introduced as his family. "My wife Amatia, My son Djedenre, my daughters Tiamen and Neferit. Tiamen's husband Menkare, Djedenre's wife Rait, and their child Amenre. This young man is a son of my grandfather Arimawat, the Hattushi traitor. The boy is Hori, son of my traitor father; apparently he is my half-brother from Ankh-Tawy."

"Gods!" Djedenre exclaimed. "I have heard stories of my grandfather and great-grandfather, but never thought they had other families."

Amenre, a small child, tugged at his father's kilt and Djedenre picked him up. His wife Rait smiled and bobbed her head, though she said nothing. Menkare coolly studied the two strangers but also said nothing, while his wife Tiamen murmured a greeting.

"You are family indeed, and welcome," Amatia said. "The night air grows cool, though. Will you not all come inside so we can talk and get to know each other?"

"I thank you, madam, for your kind invitation," Baalbek said, bowing stiffly. "However, I can no longer enjoy the hospitality of a household where my father is considered a traitor. I shall take my leave."

"What about your warning?" Hori asked.

"What warning?" Merybaal queried. "And, Baalbek, calm down. If I have given offence, I apologise, but your father warred against Avaris after the king had taken him in and shown him great kindness and naturally, I take exception to that."

"My father is King of Hattush and he has always been loyal to our nation."

"And yet he sought refuge in Avaris; fleeing from those in Hattush who wished to kill him. During those years he swore an oath of loyalty to King Sheshi. Was he dissembling?"

Baalbek scowled. "In truth, I only know what I have been told as, I suspect, have you. Exactly what happened in those days has been lost, known only to a few, like my father Arimawat and your father Harrubaal."

"I was there," Merybaal said. "I know what transpired. Neither of our fathers was loyal to Avaris, which is why they both fled and remade their lives elsewhere."

"Please," Amatia said. "Come inside and let us talk in comfort. We are all one family, and any rancour you feel can only be based on a lack of knowledge. These things happened in your father's and grandfather's day. Let us all talk calmly together in peace and settle any differences."

"How can you talk of us as family, wife?" Merybaal said. "These men are strangers to me."

"Baalbek is the brother of your father," Amatia replied, "and Hori is your brother. Forget their ages and accept their relationships, my husband. Of course they are family."

Merybaal shrugged and turned to go inside. Amatia ushered the others in, though Baalbek went reluctantly, and then the women instructed the servants to bring wine.

"And milk for the children."

"I'll have wine, mama," Neferit said.

"You'll have milk," Amatia said firmly. "You're only five."

Neferit scowled but turned her attention to Baalbek.

"Why do you have a beard? Nobody else I know has one."

"It is a custom in Hattush, little one. Men have beards because they can. It's regarded as a sign of manliness."

"Can I touch it?"

"Neferit, mind your manners," Amarit said sharply. "My apologies, Baalbek. The children should be going to bed."

"I don't mind," Baalbek said. He squatted so his face was on the same level as the girl's. "There."

Neferit gingerly fingered Baalbek's short beard. "It's prickly. Don't women in your country mind?"

"Indeed not," Baalbek said with a smile. "Perhaps when you grow up you'll meet a nice bearded man from Hattush and get married."

"Ugh, no. I'm never getting married."

"Don't mind her," Tiamen said, laughing. "Neferit's a goose. Da will arrange a good husband for her in a few years, just like my Menkare." She squeezed her husband's arm. "Are you married, Baalbek?"

"I am, yes. Her name is Pathiya and I have a three-year-old son called Aribaal."

"I'm three too," Amenre said.

"Perhaps you'll be playmates one day," Baalbek said.

"I think that is unlikely," Merybaal said. "Hattush and Avaris do not mix. Say goodnight now, Amenre...you too, Neferit. Time for bed."

Protesting, the two children were ushered away by the servants, and when the door had closed on them Merybaal turned to Baalbek again.

"What is this about a warning?"

"My father charged me with its delivery to you and your father." Baalbek looked at the others in the room. "Harrubaal is not here, so I

15

suppose I can warn his son Hori, but what about these others? Do you want them to hear it too?"

"My family has my complete confidence."

"Very well. What do you know about the political situation in Kanaan?"

"Kanaan is relatively stable at the moment. I suppose we have your father's policies to thank for that," Merybaal added grudgingly.

Baalbek nodded. "My father tries to maintain the peace in the south anyway, but he is in an impossible position. You know of the Kings of Amurru, Lebanon and Syria?"

"The ones the Kemetu refer to as *heqa khasut?* Rulers of foreign lands?"

"The same. Their king is Anep-Aper and for the last thirty years these kings have kept a military presence in Hattush."

"Why does your father allow it?"

"We have no choice in the matter," Baalbek said grimly. "We allow it or we perish."

"So wherein lies the warning?" Hori asked. "This Anep-Aper is a threat to Hattush, not to Kemet."

"Anep-Aper has his eyes on the Delta lands. He cannot yet afford to move south, but that day is coming. Make no mistake, Anep-Aper desires the lands of the river greatly."

"I don't know how strong the army of the Delta is," Hori said, "but that of Kemet is mighty. This threat, if it exists, is only to Avaris. If the foreigners come down to Kemet, they will meet with ignominious defeat."

"Thus speaks youth," Merybaal murmured. "Kemet and Avaris are equally strong. If one falls, so will the other."

"Unless we unite," Hori said.

"I think that is unlikely given the degree of enmity between the kingdoms. If you don't believe me, ask your father."

Hori frowned, but in the face of scorn from his older brother, he fell silent.

Merybaal turned his attention back to Baalbek. "How ready is Anep-Aper? Will he invade this year? Next?"

"Who knows?" Baalbek said. "My father thinks it could be next year or in five years. Ten even. All he can be certain of is that it will come."

"You have said that Anep-Aper holds Hattush hostage," Djedenre said. "Will Hattush fight on our side when the day arrives? Will you?"

"My father is very old and increasingly frail. It is with the gods, of course, but I will likely be King of Hattush then. As such, I will fight for my people."

"On our side then?"

"No. Anep-Aper would crush Hattush if we opposed him."

"Then if you will not fight with us, why have you come to give us this warning?" Djedenre demanded.

"You are family, all being descended from my father Arimawat. I would be lacking in family loyalty if I did not carry the warning to you."

"And what are we to make of this warning? Are we to persuade the king of Avaris to mobilise the army and oppose Anep-Aper? You expect us to wage war on him?"

Baalbek shook his head. "You could not win, even now when the armies of Amurru are unready. No, my advice is to use the time you have to flee. Seek refuge in Ankh-Tawy or even further south, for who knows how far Anep-Aper's arm will stretch."

"That is not going to happen."

Baalbek shrugged. "I have given you my father's warning. If you will not heed it willingly, I cannot make you." He rose to his feet and made a courteous bow to Amatia. "Thank you for your hospitality. I will take my leave now."

The members of Merybaal's family looked at one another after Baalbek had left, and then at Hori.

"Perhaps it would be better if you leave too," Merybaal said. "I bear you no ill will as you cannot help being the son of Harrubaal any more than I can, but I need to discuss this with my family...with people of Avaris."

Hori looked upset, but got to his feet. "If what Baalbek said is right, we are in this together. We are all one family, after all."

"No. I am sorry if it upsets you, Hori, but Harrubaal is dead to me, and I cannot acknowledge any person who claims a relationship with him."

"Even in the face of this threat from the north."

"I am sure that is exaggerated. And even if it's not, the armies of Avaris will be sufficient to repel any invaders. Now go, Hori. Warn your father if you think it is necessary."

Hori had no recourse but to leave. After they were alone, Merybaal's family looked troubled.

"You truly believe there is no danger, father?" Djedenre asked. "Baalbek seemed quite sure there was."

"I didn't say there was no danger, only that is has been exaggerated. It is nothing for any of you to be concerned about. I will talk to the king and we will find out what, if anything, is going on in Hattush."

"Our army is strong enough?" Djedenre persisted.

"Ask your sister's husband if you don't believe me."

Menkare nodded. "It is as your father says, Djedenre. The army of Avaris is ready for anything our enemies can throw at us, whether tomorrow or in ten years' time."

Chapter 1
1655 B.C.E.

A nep-Aper called his son and heir Samuqenu to him and greeted him with a warm smile. This relieved Samuqenu considerably as he could never be sure what was in his father's mind. It was entirely possible someone had betrayed him, and although his plans to take over the kingdom were no more than talk at this stage, that would not stay his father's hand. Others had died for such perceived acts of betrayal, including one of Samuqenu's brothers a few years before. No, his life was as nothing when the king sent for him so peremptorily.

The king picked up a scroll from the table next to him and brandished it. "It has happened at last; a treaty with Mitanni. You know what this means?"

"Our eastern borders are safe?"

"Yes, yes, of course that, but it frees up our army. I can turn my attention to the south."

"Avaris."

"Yes, and Kemet beyond that. Who knows, even the gold lands of Kush if the gods favour us. The riches of the river valley are ours for the taking."

"When?"

"Immediately. You will take a thousand men down to Hattush and secure it. Make sure that King Baalbek does not get any ideas about betraying us. Disarm their fighting men until we can be sure of their loyalty. I'll follow on with the main army in half a month."

Samuqenu grinned. "It's really happening, isn't it? I wasn't sure it was ever going to happen."

"I know you have been impatient for it. I was the same with my father, but it would be folly to invade the south while Hatti and Mitanni were waiting for the first sign of weakness on our part. Go get your men ready; you'll leave tomorrow."

Samuqenu hurried away, his mind working furiously on the best advantage he could squeeze from this turn of events. He could pick men loyal to him personally for this advance force and maybe use them to secure a position of unassailable power down in Hattush.

"I will not go the way of my brothers," he muttered.

The advance force left at dawn the next day, Samuqenu riding in his chariot at the head of a squad of chariots, leading a hundred horsemen and nearly a thousand men on foot. His army had the solid bulk to defend itself against attack, as well as the swift mobility of horse and chariot. No-one would dare stand in his way between there and Hattush, and King Baalbek would not have the strength to interfere either.

The journey down to Hattush was uneventful and the advance force crossed over the borders in strength and advanced on the capital. Baalbek met them half a day out at the head of five hundred of his own men and waited, pale with worry, as Samuqenu arrayed his force before the Hattushi men.

"Why are you here with so many men, Samuqenu?"

"That is no concern of yours, Baalbek. As a client king, your duty is to make us welcome and supply us with what we need."

"I may be a client king, as you put it, but I am still the sovereign of Hattush and it would be reasonable to expect a measure of respect from the heir of Amurru."

Samuqenu scowled at this reference to his lesser status. "I represent my father Anep-Aper, and you would do well to remember that."

"What do you want, Samuqenu?"

"I come to prepare the way for my father. In half a month, he will be here with ten thousand men and a thousand chariots. Will you dare to stand in his way with your paltry army?"

"He is coming here? Does he mean to invade Avaris at last then?"

"Yes. You need to decide if you fight with Amurru or against us. I would be very happy to do away with the inconvenience of a reluctant ally."

"As always, Hattush stands ready to do what is right."

"Then why are you here at the head of five hundred soldiers, Baalbek? Do you think that opposing us in the right thing to do?"

"I had to be sure who marched on Hattush. Now that I know who and why, there is no need to oppose anyone." Baalbek rapped out commands to his officers and his soldiers drew aside, opening the road to the capital. "You are welcome, Lord Samuqenu, you and all your men."

Samuqenu marched into Hattush and effectively occupied it. Together with the five hundred men that had been stationed there for years, he almost outnumbered the army of Hattush. He called a meeting of the high officers of Hattush and had them hand over command to his own officers, securing every important position within the kingdom. Baalbek acquiesced as there was no way he could oppose Samuqenu with the main army of Amurru under Anep-Aper almost on their borders. There was one thing he could do, and he did it, calling to his side Maltu, a trusted servant.

"Take this letter and ride to Avaris. Deliver it to the House of Merybaal or to his son Djedenre. No-one else, mind, and no-one must see you leave Hattush. Can you do that?"

"I can, master."

"If you are caught, destroy the letter."

"I will, master."

Just to be sure that even if the letter was intercepted, it would not reveal the writer, it said very simply, 'The troubles I forecast fifteen years ago are upon us. Flee for your lives.' Baalbek hoped that his extended family would remember his warning of fifteen years before and pay heed to it. If they did not, their lives were in danger.

The army of Amurru flooded into Hattush, setting up camps around the city and stripping the countryside of its produce. Baalbek sought an audience with Anep-Aper, in his own palace, and complained about the shortages and deprivations his people were even now undergoing.

"Have you ever had experienced an army conquer a country, Baalbek? No, I thought not. If you had you wouldn't be complaining. The shortages your people suffer are as nothing compared to what my troops would inflict if we did not come in friendship."

"This is friendship?"

"Of course. You are a client king, and we are using your country as a staging post for our invasion of the Delta. If you were not a friend, we would sack and pillage your farms, raze your cities to the ground, and put your men and grown boys to the sword. Are we doing that?"

"No."

"No, we are not, but we can if you do not accept our hand of friendship. So what is it to be? Your father Arimawat accepted the friendship of Amurru, welcoming our presence. I rather thought you were doing the same. Am I wrong?"

"No."

"Good. Then you will tell your people not to resist and to surrender any goods and provisions we need."

"Are my people to be left destitute?"

Anep-Aper leaned back in Baalbek's throne and contemplated the man standing before him. "As always, you have a choice. You can be a reluctant friend and pray to the gods that we show you mercy, or you can be a generous friend and share in the wealth of the Delta kingdom."

"Share how?"

"Join us. Your Hattush army is small and we don't need it, but in friendship...for the sake of the friendship your father Arimawat showed to me and my father before me...I am willing to let you join me in invading the Delta."

Baalbek frowned as he considered Anep-Aper's words. "That would leave my own kingdom undefended."

"I rule from the northern mountains of Hatti and the eastern plains of Mitanni, and soon down to the great river of Kemet. Who would dare attack you knowing they also attacked me?" Anep-Aper shrugged and yawned. "I am bored with this conversation. I have been generous, Baalbek of Hattush. Will you throw my generosity back in my face?"

Baalbek knew his answer was literally one of life or death for himself and also for his country. "Forgive me, King Anep-Aper. I did not mean to sound ungrateful, but it had never occurred to me that you would include my kingdom in your plans. My country stands ready to do what is needed. Tell me what you wish, and I will do it."

Anep-Aper laughed, and smote the arms of Baalbek's throne. "Well said, Baalbek of Hattush. Gather your men together. We have an invasion to launch."

Baalbek sent orders out to his officers to gather the men together and to arm them. Hattush relied on foot-soldiers and on mounted warriors, utilising only a few light chariots as scouts. A little over a thousand men joined the army of Amurru, but his officers reported to their king that the men of Hattush were to be spread out within the northern army rather than fighting in their own units. Baalbek knew he had to protest this or risk losing any semblance of command.

"My men must be allowed to fight together," he said. "They are trained to fight in their units, each trusting the man with them on either side. More often than not, they grew up together or are related. If you separate them, they will be no better than raw recruits, not knowing how to trust the men fighting alongside them, and being less than they could be."

"I suppose you will ask for their own officers to command them too?"

"Yes."

"Then let it be so," Anep-Aper said. "You shall command the men of Hattush in the assault on Avaris."

Baalbek was appalled at the thought that he would personally attack Avaris and his family within it, and was on the point of raising an objection when he realised that this was perhaps the best outcome. If he was there, commanding the troops, he might be able to protect his family if they had not fled south.

"Thank you for that honour, Lord Anep-Aper."

The king of Amurru called together his generals and lords to work with the latest information from the border and plan the attack on Avaris. Baalbek listened, and did not offer up his own suggestions, beyond volunteering his men for the assault on the city. Samuqenu and many of the other leaders favoured a frontal assault through the hills though others pointed out that the trails and narrow roads did not favour the passage of chariots.

"The coast road is the only way," General Anati said. "It is longer, but the road is used for trading caravans and is broader and flatter."

"How many men can Avaris put in the field?" someone asked.

"No more than four thousand."

"And are their generals capable?"

"They will be led by King Seneferenre, who ascended to the throne from the ranks of the army. We have to assume he has a measure of ability."

"It will avail him nothing," Samuqenu said. "We will overwhelm them."

Anep-Aper considered the words of his generals and lords before calling his son out in front of the meeting.

"My son and heir, Samuqenu, will lead the first assault on the enemy. Make your dispositions, my son."

Samuqenu's pleasure was evident. He preened and regarded the others present with contempt, rattling off a few of the names of his favourites among the generals.

"These men will lead their units in the frontal assault on Avaris. When their defences have crumbled, I will bring the rest to the city."

Anep-Aper studied the reactions of the generals, letting no trace of his thoughts appear on his face.

"Only five thousand men?" he asked Samuqenu. "You have a reason for not taking the whole army?"

"Ten thousand will be cumbersome. I only need a smaller force to utterly destroy the enemy."

"What of the chariot squadrons?" Anep-Aper asked.

"They will not be needed, but I will send General Anati north by the coast road to sweep down behind the enemy." Samuqenu shrugged. "There will be little for them to do, but I will find a meaningful task for them later."

"And the men of Hattush?" Baalbek asked.

"I see no reason why they should share in the initial glory of conquest. Let them follow with the baggage train."

Baalbek turned to Anep-Aper. "My lord king, you promised me my men would assault Avaris."

"And so they shall, Baalbek of Hattush, but my son Samuqenu leads the initial assault. It is for him to say where you fight."

The rest of the meeting was given up to discussing the logistics of the invasions, how the supplies would be transported, and how much the troops could live off the land. War always led to misery and deprivation for the conquered people, and no-one saw any reason why the people of the Delta should be exempt. The invading troops would largely live off the land, and after the conquest, the surviving population would yield up the resources of the kingdom to their new overlords.

"Take no chances," was Anep-Aper's final advice for his son. "If Avaris resists, make an example of it. Destroy the city if need be, and its people."

Baalbek came away from the meeting feeling depressed. War was coming and his relatives in Avaris stood in the way. The situation was more serious and immediate than he had first thought. Even if Merybaal or Djedenre had received his first cryptic warning, they might not treat it with the urgency it deserved. King Seneferenre was likely to resist the invaders and that meant the destruction of the city and its inhabitants. The question that faced Baalbek now was whether he should risk his life and kingdom to send another warning. His wife decided him.

"They are your other family, my husband. You cannot abandon them," Pathiya said.

"And what of you and our son Aribaal? What will Anep-Aper do if he finds out I have warned the enemy?"

"Do you imagine the enemy does not already know? Their spies will have told them of the army in our midst, and of the preparations being made to invade them."

"If that is so, then I don't need to warn them."

"Yes, you do. You have a responsibility to warn them. You cannot rely on others doing it for you."

Baalbek knew his wife was right, and if the circumstances were reversed, he hoped that others would see fit to warn him. The messenger he had used for the first letter had not returned though, and Baalbek did not know whether this was because he had been killed or captured by Amurru scouts or perhaps even imprisoned as a spy in Avaris. He could not even know if his warning had reached the intended target. This time he would have to be more forthright in what he said, and send it by more than one route. First, he penned the message by his own hand.

'The invasion we talked about fifteen years ago is happening and Avaris is the target. Flee the city as soon as you get this.' Baalbek tried to think of a way of signing it so they would know it came from him, but not in such a blatant way as to identify himself. 'From one whom Neferit thought had a prickly beard.'

He sighed, and made two copies, sealing them and hiding them in small cloth pouches. One he gave to another of his servants who had no cause to love the Amurru, and the other to a merchant on his way down the coast road into the Delta. The merchant route was considerably slower than the direct one across the hills, but was perhaps less likely to be intercepted.

The borderlands were in uproar for days as the army of Anep-Aper set about the great venture that had been generations in preparation. Anep-Aper's father Anatisil had longed to conquer the lands to the south, but had spent his life stabilising his northern and eastern neighbours. Anep-Aper inherited his father's problem but solved it as an old man. It was likely that Samuqenu would be the one to reign over Kemet, but Anep-Aper greatly desired to see the conquest start in his lifetime.

The units of the northern army set off for the border, the columns of soldiers snaking up into the hills, slowed by the narrow trails but still inexorably moving toward the Delta. At the same time, General Anati marshalled his thousand chariots and set them off on the coast road, the cloud of dust raised by hooves and wheels billowing into the clear blue sky. Traders plying the road with their mule caravans of farmers moving flocks of goats moved aside to watch in awe this great invasion. All who watched gave thanks to their gods that this army was not interested in them.

Baalbek and the men of Hattush were one of the units heading into the hills, though Samuqenu had delegated to them the dishonourable task of guarding the enormous baggage train that accompanied the army. He fumed as he rode with his men, knowing that he would not be able to influence the attack on Avaris from his position at the rear. His son Aribaal rode with him, equally frustrated, though for a different reason. This young man desired only to excel in warfare, to make a name for himself. He had never met his relatives in Avaris, and their plight meant little to him.

Chapter 2

P anic gripped Avaris as the first reports from the border came in. King Seneferenre called an emergency meeting of his advisers to discuss the reports and decide what was to be done about them.

Treasurer Merybaal figured prominently among those advisers and, as he had held the position for most of his adult life, was considered something of an expert. Other ministers represented a multitude of other trades and interests, from shipping to farming and fishing, from guilds for the creation of images of gods to the guilds that governed the carting away of nightsoil, from traders and shopkeepers to armourers and horse trainers. Nobles swelled the ranks of the advisers; men who held positions of trust inherited from their fathers but displayed no inherent abilities. Others represented the army, and though several scions of noble families held high positions, there were still able officers among them.

General Inkhare commanded the border forces, and as soon as he had seen the strength of the army arrayed against him, had withdrawn toward Avaris. Messages sent to the king had elicited an angry response, Inkhare being ordered to stand firm and repel the invaders. He had replied that he was badly outnumbered and unless the king was prepared to sacrifice trained men to no purpose, reinforcements would be needed forthwith. Seneferenre gave his permission to withdraw as far as the plains to the east of Avaris.

Menkare, the husband of Merybaal's daughter Tiamen, was an offer in Inkhare's army, and he had seen for himself the advance of the Amurran army. Now that they had withdrawn to the vicinity of the capital city, he was allowed a brief respite with his family. He lost no time in greeting his wife and children and then hurrying to Merybaal's house where he found the Treasurer getting ready to attend the king's council.

"My lord Treasurer, a moment of your time, I beg," Menkare said.

Merybaal shook his head good-naturedly and clapped his daughter's husband on the shoulder. "Less of the 'my lord' if you please. We are both grown men."

"As you will, my...Merybaal. I have news of great import."

Merybaal nodded. "You were with Inkhare."

"Indeed. Amurru emerges from the hills like a river in flood."

"Comparable to the invasion by Urubek in my father's day?"

"I would say greater. Estimates put them as five to ten thousand."

Merybaal whistled through his teeth. "No wonder Inkhare fell back before them. A pity Baalbek could not give us more warning."

"Another few months would not have helped much. We only have so many men and resources within the kingdom."

"I meant only that you could have evacuated the women and children."

"They would not have gone without us, and we could not flee. What sort of example would that have set?"

"So what is to be done?"

"The king has called his Council. We'll know soon enough."

The mood at the meeting was subdued as Inkhare gave his report and scouts who had ventured close to the oncoming horde spoke of the numbers and their state of preparedness.

"That's all very well," King Seneferenre said, "but this sort of thing has happened before. We have raiders perhaps one year in three, and I'm told there was a major incursion fifty years ago. The army threw that back without any problem, so why can't they do it again?"

"I remember that time, Majesty," Merybaal said. "I was only a youth when Urubek invaded from Hattush. He was killed and the enemy ejected, but it was not just by force of arms. My grandfather Arimawat, who later became king of Hattush, killed Urubek when he tried to kill my father Harrubaal. It was those actions, as much as the actions of the Delta army, which saved Avaris. The army that faces us today is very different."

"Different in what way?"

"Hattush is a small kingdom in southern Kanaan, and while they produce some good fighters, they are as nothing compared to the

28

seasoned soldiers of Amurru, Lebanon and Syria. These soldiers, under the leadership of King Anep-Aper, are the ones invading us." Merybaal sighed. "Urubek's army was about a thousand strong, while Anep-Aper's is five or ten times as large. How many men can we muster? Inkhare?"

"I have a thousand camped east of Avaris. There are others though. General Menenre? What can you tell us?"

"The southern army is about the same size...perhaps a thousand men, and another few hundred in garrisons scattered through the kingdom."

"That few?"

"We can call up more men from the farms and cities," Menenre said. "They'll be mostly untrained, of course."

"So we can perhaps match their numbers with our own," King Seneferenre said.

General Inkhare nodded. "In numbers, yes, but maybe not in skill. We won't be able to test that until we meet them in battle."

King Seneferenre looked worried, and Merybaal could understand why. The military men on the Council were experienced, and Merybaal knew to the last *deben* how much the kingdom could afford in its defence, but the king was new and lacked skill in military matters and possibly more importantly, also lacked judgement.

"But you can defeat them?" Seneferenre asked.

"Perhaps, but we must decide on a strategy."

"What do you mean? The enemy lies there, we are here. You march out and engage them in battle."

"It is not quite that simple, Majesty," Inkhare said. "First, we have to decide if this is a defensive war or an offensive one. Do we wait for the enemy to come to us, or attack?"

"Attack, of course," said the king.

"Let them come to us," General Menenre said.

"That is not honourable."

"Forgive me, Majesty, but what does honour have to do with survival? We face a strong enemy and defeat could be the end of Avaris. I would urge caution until we have the advantage."

"Menenre is right in this," Inkhare said, "but if we let them come to us, do we then fight or do we withdraw further while we wait for this advantage?"

Several of the advisers concerned with their businesses and properties clamoured for the army to fight and prevent further losses. As one merchant put it, "What is the point of letting the enemy do as he pleases? If we do not meet them in battle, the wealth of the kingdom will be drained."

"You are welcome to come and stand with us," Menenre said. "I'll find you an axe and you can protect your property with your life."

The merchant harrumphed. "My life is too valuable to just throw away."

"I regard every man's life as too valuable to throw away. That is why I counsel extreme caution. This is an Amurran army and should not be taken lightly."

"So you favour drawing back to the city and when the enemy follows, withdrawing further?" Inkhare asked. "Where to, exactly?"

Menenre shrugged. "That is what we are here to decide."

"I say we pull back to the city, but choose our ground and fight them there," Inkhare declared. "Good flat ground where we can manoeuvre at will."

"He makes sense," Menkare whispered to Merybaal. Merybaal signed to his daughter's husband to keep quiet.

"Flat ground is hazardous," he said. "No-one has yet spoken of chariots and the danger they represent."

"There are no chariots," Inkhare said. "My scouts have only reported foot soldiers and horsemen."

"Horsemen we can counter with our own," Merybaal said, "but the absence of chariots surprises me."

"With all due respect, Treasurer Merybaal," Menenre said. "You are an old man with limited experience of warfare. I suggest you leave such things to those who know of them."

"You don't find the absence of chariots curious?"

"No, I don't, and why would I? What have we to fear from what is little more than a box on wheels drawn by horses? Horses by themselves are more manoeuvrable and useful."

"You've never faced chariots, have you, General?"

"No, and neither have you. In fact, has anyone here?"

"I haven't," Merybaal admitted, "but I have heard my father and grandfather speak of them. They are a weapon not to be taken lightly."

Menenre shook his head, and Inkhare smiled knowingly.

"The only use I can imagine for a chariot in battle is to carry men to where the fighting is, and how many men can a chariot carry? Two? Three?"

"Besides," Menenre added, "the enemy doesn't have any, so why are we discussing them at all?"

"Because if the chariots are part of the Amurran army, then where are they?" Merybaal asked.

"They could not reasonably be brought through the hills," said the captain of Inkhare's scouts. "The trails are narrow and there are stretches where you'd have to lead a horse. I can't imagine a box on wheels being feasible."

"So rule out chariots," Inkhare said. He turned to King Seneferenre. "Majesty, it is my recommendation, as senior army general, that we draw up our army on the plains beside Avaris and defeat the enemy there."

"I still favour drawing them further into the Delta," Menenre said. "We know the land; they don't."

"Majesty, may I speak?"

Heads turned, and Merybaal's eyebrows rose in surprise that his son Djedenre would speak in such company.

"You have my leave," King Seneferenre said.

"Majesty, I have listened to the opinions voiced here," Djedenre said, "and there have been valid arguments expressed by all parties..."

"You seek to agree with everyone and bring nothing to the discussion," Menenre growled. "You are only a Troop Commander and have no understanding of strategy."

"I may not have experience of higher command, but I can still see the flaws in a plan and make suggestions," Djedenre retorted. "General Inkhare would have us risk everything on a battleground that favours the enemy as much as it does us, while General Menenre would have us wander aimlessly with the enemy on our heels."

"What would you have us do, Djedenre son of Merybaal?" Seneferenre asked.

"I would have us cross the river and take our stand on the far side, Majesty."

Menenre laughed, and Inkhare shook his head pityingly.

"What would be the point of that?"

"Majesty, two armies meet on a field, equal in every way, and the outcome is decided by who has the fiercer spirit. On any normal field,

31

with equally matched armies, the matter will be in doubt, but interposing the river between the armies can give us the decisive advantage."

King Seneferenre stroked his chin with one hand as he considered the junior officer's words. "How would it give us the advantage?"

"Majesty, we take up defensive positions and invite the enemy to attack us. To do so he must cross the water and by doing so, he is at a disadvantage. Our men can slaughter them as they land on the far side."

"An interesting proposal," Seneferenre said.

"And highly impractical," Inkhare said. "Faced with a river crossing, why would the enemy do so?"

"If they want to destroy our army, they have to. He cannot leave an undefeated army in the field. This combines aspects of the plans of both your generals, Majesty. We withdraw, enticing the enemy deeper into the kingdom, and then destroy them on a field of our choosing."

"I like it," Seneferenre said.

"What happens to Avaris?" Inkhare asked. "You would leave the city undefended."

Djedenre frowned. "It has walls."

"Without an army to defend it, those walls would soon fall."

"Inkhare is right; we cannot leave Avaris undefended," Seneferenre said.

"Then let the army stay outside Avaris and defend it by bringing the enemy to battle here," Inkhare said.

Menenre felt contempt for his junior officer's suggestion, but if Inkhare looked like he was to triumph, he would ally himself to whoever was necessary.

"On the other hand," he said. "Djedenre's idea has some merit. Avaris would be better protected by drawing the enemy away from it. Let us choose a field of battle and bring the enemy to it."

"On the other side of the river?" Inkhare jeered. "That is madness. Far from protecting Avaris, that would incite the enemy to destroy it."

"And your plan is ridiculous," Menenre yelled. "You are..."

"Silence! Both of you." Seneferenre glared at both generals as people held their breath at the king's anger. "I have heard enough. We will gather the army beneath the walls of Avaris and defeat them there. General Inkhare will command."

While Inkhare preened and Menenre glowered, a messenger entered the chamber and offered a letter to the king's scribe. He opened it and handed it to the king.

"A complication from the north," Seneferenre said. "It seems your question has been answered, Treasurer Merybaal. Chariots are moving toward us along the coast road."

"Does the report say how many, Majesty?" Merybaal asked.

Seneferenre shook his head. "It doesn't say."

"Are they a force in themselves, or just reinforcements for the main army?" Inkhare asked.

"How many chariots can a kingdom like Amurru have?" Menenre asked.

"Who knows? It could be several score or many hundreds," Merybaal said. "Either way, this is a danger that must be faced."

Menenre shrugged. "Suppose they have as many as five hundred chariots. Each contains two or three men being transported to battle. That's a thousand or a bit more. Let me take a thousand men north, Majesty. I will attack this northern invasion and throw it back in confusion."

"You don't know chariots," Merybaal protested. "The stories I have heard..."

"Are just that; stories." Menenre laughed. "They bring men to the battle quite efficiently, I suppose, but they still have to fight on foot. If I, with a thousand men, await them on the north road, I will attack as they dismount, catching them unawares, and destroy them. You have my word on it, Majesty."

"I'm not sure we can afford to send a thousand men north," Seneferenre said. "That will leave our army depleted."

"Let Menenre run off and attack his pony carts," Inkhare said. "Even with a thousand men fewer I will have no trouble defeating the enemy on a field of my choosing."

Menenre scowled but having given his word to his king, could not back down. Merybaal tried once more to impress on the king and the generals the danger a chariot force might represent, but as neither he nor anyone else there had seen chariots in action, his words lacked force.

The king made his decision and gave the generals their orders. Inkhare was to command the main army on the plains to the east of Avaris, while Menenre was to take a thousand men and ambush the chariots on the north road. Menkare, as one of the senior officers, was to take command of the city garrison and defend the city itself.

"And I, Majesty?" Djedenre asked.

"You will be an observer," Seneferenre said. "Your father has made much of the terrors that chariots excite. Now you will observe the destruction of the enemy chariots by General Menenre, and report back to him and to me."

The meeting broke up and Djedenre turned on his father with recriminations. "Why am I being singled out for such a shameful assignment? It can only be because I am your son and you go on and on about the supposed dangers of these chariots."

"That is because they are dangerous."

"How do you know? Have you ever seen them in use?"

"No," Merybaal admitted, "but my father told me what his father told him--that chariots are to be feared."

"If they are so fearsome, then how is it that Amurru has apparently spent years subduing their northern neighbours?"

"I don't know. Perhaps the Hatti and Mitanni have chariots too."

"Or perhaps chariots really are just a means of carrying soldiers to battle, like Menenre says."

Merybaal sighed. "I pray that is the case, but son, be mindful of our king's instructions, however shameful you think them to be. He charged you with observing the battle and reporting back, not taking part in it."

"I am a grown man and a Troop Commander in the army of Avaris. I should be there taking part in the defence of my country, not standing aside and taking notes like some weak-livered scribe."

"Then as a Troop Commander and mature man you know the importance of a soldier obeying orders. Obey your orders, Djedenre. You will have plenty of opportunity for fighting later."

Djedenre scowled, but he nodded and left his father's presence, hurrying to catch up with Menenre as the officers of the army shouted orders to prepare for the march northward.

Chapter 3

Tjaty Aya hurried to find the king as he offered up early morning prayers in the Great Temple of Ptah in Ankh-Tawy. He would have preferred not to disturb him while communing with the god, but the news he had was too important to wait. The guards in the gateways passed him through, and a mid-level priest appeared to lead Aya into the inner sanctum of the god, where King Sewedjare Monthhotep assisted the Hem-netjer of Ptah in offering up fresh food and raiment for the statue of the god.

Aya started to walk toward the king to impart the news but stopped at Monthhotep's imperious gesture. The king's attention was fixed on the meal laid out on virgin linen cloths on the tiled floor of the temple, and on the naked statue of the creator god. Ptah's erection was impressive, despite being of carved stone, and highlighted the function of Ptah as a creator. Later, when fresh raiment was draped over the statue, his priapic state would be less obvious. In the meantime, the delicious aromas arising from the choicest cuts of meat, from fresh-baked bread, and from newly-brewed barley beer seemed at odds with the god's sexual readiness.

Ptah did not move, though the flickering torchlight gave the statue a semblance of life. The physicality of the food and drink did not interest an inanimate carving, but the spiritual dimensions, as evidenced by the sight and smell would excite the aspect of the deity within the stone statue. After waiting a suitable period of time for the god to have his fill, the food was cleared away and taken to the priests' quarters where they would later partake of the holy leavings. The linen was folded and put away for later disposal. Although still in pristine condition, it would never be used for any lesser purpose, having once served the god. Clothes were now brought out, held up for the god's inspection, and then draped over the lithic limbs. Prepared once more for the day, the heavy statue was carried back into the pitch-black inner chamber where the god resided. Here he would dwell having, by his acceptance of food and raiment, given his blessing to the city of Ankh-Tawy and to the kingdom of Kemet.

King Sewedjare Monthhotep turned to his Tjaty with a petulant expression.

"What do you want, Tjaty Aya, that could not wait until I had finished my holy communion with the god?"

"Forgive me, Son of Re, but important news has arrived from Avaris, and I felt it warranted your immediate attention."

"Avaris? Ah, you mean my province of Hut-waret. What is your news?"

Aya inwardly cursed the fiction beloved of the kings of Kemet that the northern kingdom of the Delta was still governed from Ankh-Tawy. Monthhotep was only the most recent of a long line of kings reluctant to accept that interlopers from the northern tribes of Retjenu (or Kanaan as they called their land) had wrested the Delta from their control and had renamed their cities. The northern city of Hut-waret had become Avaris, and having been that for over a hundred years, was unlikely to change back anytime soon. If the kings of Ankh-Tawy would only accept the reality of the situation, it would make things a lot easier.

"Son of Re, the Delta has been invaded by those called the *heqa khasut*. They are marching on Avaris... Hut-waret."

"Does our governor there have the matter in hand?"

Monthhotep, like his predecessors, did not recognise the Retjenu rulers as legitimate kings, but rather as governors, albeit rather unruly and unresponsive ones. Aya did not regard this as a useful attitude, but Monthhotep was the king, and his views had to be agreed with.

"He is mobilising his soldiers to counter the invasion, Son of Re."

"Good, then there is nothing to be worried about."

"Regrettably, Son of Re, I think there is. Seneferenre has perhaps five thousand men at his disposal, but he faces an invasion on two fronts. The latest word I have is that a large body of men approach Hut-waret from the hills, while chariots approach from the coast. His army might be able to counter one but not both."

"Chariots? I have heard mention of these, but I know little about them."

"I'm told they are a box on wheels, drawn by horses, that carries soldiers into battle."

"Like an ox-cart or a wagon?"

"Yes, Son of Re, but faster. I have heard that Lord Harrubaal knows of them. Should I send for him?"

Monthhotep waved his hand dismissively. "I doubt they are that important. Men are what count in a battle; men firmly planted on their own two feet and armed with an axe or a sword. None of this trundling about on wheels."

"Undoubtedly, Son of Re. However, there will be other reports in from my spies in the north and it might be as well to be fully apprised of what is happening. Shall I call a meeting of your Council?"

"Is it really necessary?"

"I think it is, Son of Re."

"Oh, very well."

"And Lord Harrubaal?"

"If you must."

Monthhotep stalked off and Aya followed more slowly, thinking about what was happening in the Delta. The king might be right and the invaders already repulsed, but Aya preferred to wait until the latest information came in from his spies. They should be in in the next day or so, so he would schedule a meeting of the Council for three days hence. That would give Harrubaal time to get there from his estates to the south. Aya did not particularly like Harrubaal, for all that he was a relative by marriage, but he recognised that he was one of few men of high status who had first-hand knowledge of both Retjenu and Hut-waret.

King Merneferre Ay had ruled Kemet for over twenty years before he handed over the throne to his son Merhotepre Ini. This same Ini had a brother Inire (since deceased) and two sisters--Init and Reditanes. The former daughter had married Harrubaal and the latter Aya, and it was as a result of this royal connection that he had risen to the position of Tjaty, and that Harrubaal gained wealth and land. Royalty had passed from the family though, and now others, unrelated to the former kings, ruled over Kemet. Aya remained, serving faithfully, while Harrubaal retired to his estates.

As soon as he got back to his office, Aya dictated a letter to be sent to Lord Harrubaal, summoning him to Ankh-Tawy. Harrubaal was old and he would be reluctant to make the journey north, but three days gave him time. Aya also sent out commands in the king's name to the military and the Overseer of the Treasury. Reports came in from the north over the next two days as expected, and Aya organised the Council meeting in the small audience chamber.

Harrubaal, now bald and toothless, stooped and stiff-jointed, spent his days in the courtyard of his estate, leaving the running of it to his son Hori. His daughter Iset also lived there with her sons Bebi and Sobekhotep and their youthful enthusiasm delighted him. The years had brought physical frailness to Harrubaal, leaving him weak and waiting for the day when death would claim him, but his mind was still active. He had servants bring him the news from the estate, the surrounding countryside, Ankh-Tawy, and occasionally further afield, and he would often discuss topics of interest with his children and grandchildren.

When the messenger from Tjaty Aya brought the king's summons, Harrubaal was surprised as he had long been out of the corridors of power. He had retired twenty years before and had last travelled to Ankh-Tawy in the days of Merkawre Sobekhotep seven years in the past. Those had been dangerous days as his daughter Iset had married Merkawre before he became king, and her sons by him, Bebi and Sobekhotep, could have attracted the attention of the king's successor, but they had been children at the time and were no threat. Then the line of succession had brought Monthhotep to the throne and left the young princes as no more than an afterthought.

In the days of Merkawre, Harrubaal had travelled to Ankh-Tawy in a litter and now, seven years later, even that looked unlikely. Harrubaal's eyes were weak, along with the rest of his body, and a scribe had read the letter out to him. He thought about the contents for a while, letting the warmth of the sun soothe him, and then he told a servant to bring his son to him.

"I am called to Ankh-Tawy," he said simply when his son arrived.

"Well, you can't go. The journey would kill you."

"I'm not that infirm...well, perhaps I am, but I can't refuse." Harrubaal held out the letter. "It's from the king."

"I'll refuse on your behalf, father. He'll listen to me when I explain how weak you are. You're eighty-eight and...and..."

"And should be dead? I agree, most men my age would be." Harrubaal forced a wheezing laugh from between thin, dry lips. "The gods must have something in mind for me yet."

"No, father, that's not what I meant, but you are too weak to travel. Even seven years ago the trip to Ankh-Tawy almost killed you. Remember? Jolted in that litter for three days?"

"I remember, but I have to go. Read the letter."

Hori looked hard at his father and then bent his head to the letter, murmuring each word as he deciphered it.

"It was remiss of me, Hori," Harrubaal said softly. "I should have kept you to your lessons."

Hori looked up. "I'm a military officer; why should I have to read well? I have scribes to do that. Besides, I can manage this well enough." He flicked the letter with his fingers. "Does this say what I think it says? The Delta is being invaded? And who are these *heqa khasut*?"

"Terror out of the north. That's why I have to go to Ankh-Tawy. Few people know what we are facing, but I do."

"You, father? How?"

"I wasn't always an old man of Ankh-Tawy and this estate. Have you forgotten I was born in the land you call Retjenu? I fled south with my father Arimawat who is... or was...he might be dead by now...probably is as he's twenty something years older than me. Anyway, he was king in Hattush. He told me about the kings in the north; lords of Amurru and Syria. They were a threat to Hattush, a threat to the Delta, and a threat to Kemet. I never thought I'd live to see that threat become real, but here we are. I have to go."

"All right, say you do, but how? You can't walk, you can't ride a horse, and even a litter would be too rough on you. You could try an oxcart, I suppose, but at the pace they move it'll take six or seven days."

"I'll take a boat."

"A boat?"

"Yes, those things that float upon the water. One could carry me to Ankh-Tawy in a day."

Hori stared. "Why didn't I think of that?"

Harrubaal wheezed with laughter again. "You're a good son and a passable army officer from what I hear, but you can't see what's in front of your nose. Now, arrange a boat for me, that's a good boy. I want to leave at dawn tomorrow."

Tjaty Aya opened the meeting by reading out the latest reports that had come in from his spies in Hut-waret. The situation had not changed much in the last few days; Seneferenre was massing his army near the city to meet the northern army streaming out of the hills, and General Menenre was moving slowly toward the coast with a thousand men.

"That's where these so-called chariots are supposed to be, is it?" Commander Sewahenre asked.

"That's where they are," Aya said. "We know very little about them or their capabilities..."

"You'll find out," Harrubaal murmured.

"Thank you for coming to the meeting, Lord Harrubaal. I appreciate the journey is tiring for an old man, but your advice may be useful. But before we tap into that fund of knowledge, we should discuss the army bearing down on Hut-waret."

"Men are men," General Neferhotep said. "All you need to ask is who leads them and how many there are."

"What about armaments?" Treasurer Maia asked.

"Options are limited, and they're likely to bear the same arms as our soldiers--axe, sword, spear, bow."

"But how many of each?" Maia asked. "Archers can strike from a distance, for instance. Wouldn't it be important to know how many they have?"

"Indeed it would," Aya said, "but we don't know."

"We'll know soon enough," Neferhotep said. "As soon as they attack the Delta Army. Providing our spies are there, of course."

"They will be."

"Son of Re, are we just going to sit and wait while these foreigners attack Hut-waret?" Sewahenre asked. "I mean, aren't they just as much our enemies as theirs?"

King Monthhotep said nothing, waving his hand toward his Tjaty.

"Basically, yes, we're going to sit and wait," Aya said. "First, the attack will take place in the next day or so, if it hasn't already, so we have no way of getting our army up there in time. Second, with our spies in place, this is a wonderful opportunity to study the capabilities of the foreigners. Anything we can find out without loss to ourselves will be invaluable."

"We abandon them to their fate," Sewahenre said.

"There's no abandonment," Neferhotep snapped. "They haven't asked for our help...have they?" Aya shook his head. "So," Neferhotep went on, "whatever happens to them is with the gods."

"Let me frame this in words we can all understand," Monthhotep said. "Hut-waret is on its own. They have been invaded by the *heqa khasut*, and we are going to watch carefully to see who prevails. If the foreigners win, we will have some knowledge of their strategy and tactics and, if they look to us, they will face a mightier foe. If, on the other hand, Seneferenre wins, the..." the king smiled, "...much the same applies. Either way, we will have a measure of the enemy that lies to our north."

"Admirably put, Son of Re," Tjaty Aya said.

"Then if everything is decided..." Monthhotep started to rise, but Harrubaal cleared his throat, and heads turned in the old man's direction.

"Son of Re, you called on me to attend this meeting and I have made the effort to be here. Are you just going to ignore me now?"

Monthhotep scowled and sat back down. "You are as much a foreigner as these *heqa khasut* and have the same manners. It signifies nothing that you have obeyed your king, so you can turn around and go home."

"Yet, Son of Re, it would be a pity to waste an asset," Aya said quietly. "Harrubaal is the only man we can call upon who knows about chariots. They have the reputation of being fearsome weapons of war, and if that is the case, then we should learn what we can before we have to face them."

"You have faced chariots, Harrubaal?" General Neferhotep asked.

"No, not personally."

"Then what use are you?" Monthhotep demanded.

"Son of Re, please listen," Hori said. "My father has often told us tales told to him by his father Arimawat, and my grandfather knew chariots."

"Yes, he knew," Harrubaal added. "You would do well to listen."

"How can boxes on wheels be a weapon of war?" Sewahenre demanded. "Even drawn by horses, they must be slow and cumbersome."

Neferhotep nodded. "Useful for carrying men to a battle, perhaps, but I'd rather trust on my own two feet."

"Perhaps if you all stopped barking like jackals and listened..." Hori suddenly stopped dead as he realised he was reprimanding his military superiors. "Forgive me sirs, I did not mean to cause offence."

Tjaty Aya looked at the anger and amazement on the faces of the General and Commander and struggled to hide a smile.

"This is a war discussion and sometimes passionate words are spoken in them," Aya said. "Let no-one take offence for we can all learn from the thoughts of others. Lord Harrubaal, we asked you here to speak to us. Please do so."

Harrubaal struggled to stand, and Aya looked toward the king before saying, "I don't think anyone will take it amiss if you remain seated."

Monthhotep nodded. "Yes, there is no need for you to stand."

Harrubaal settled back into his chair. "Thank you, Son of Re." He took a deep breath and marshalled his thoughts. "Son of Re, Noble Lords, Officers of the Army of Kemet, as I have stated before, I have no firsthand knowledge of chariots, but my father Arimawat had and he told me enough about them for me to be thankful that I never had to face them. My lords, disabuse yourselves of this notion that a chariot is just a box on wheels drawn by horses. When you conjure up this image you immediately think of an oxcart hauling a wagon, and you find it hard to see a threat in it. Such a thing might be useful for carrying troops to a battle but could play no part in the actual battle as it is too slow and cumbersome."

"We know all this," Neferhotep grumbled. "Get on with it."

Hori handed his father a cup of water and Harrubaal drank gratefully before continuing.

"A single chariot can inspire wonder and awe. Forget a wooden cart; think instead of a lightweight wicker frame strengthened with supple rods. There are two wheels, with six spokes and a thin rim covered with beaten bronze rather than the heavy solid wheels of a cart. A yoke pushes forward from the chariot and two horses are harnessed to it--high-spirited beasts unlike the placid animals we sometimes see people riding. Standing in the chariot is a driver, with the reins to control the horses around his arms, bare to the waist with his long hair flowing. Alongside him you have an archer, practised at loosing arrows from a racing chariot, and often a third man in armour with a spear and a shield."

"A squad of archers would cut them down in moments," Commander Sewahenre said.

"No doubt," Harrubaal said, "but it is a completely different matter when facing massed chariots. The wonder of a single chariot is multiplied many times, and when a wall of horses and wheeled chariots, bristling with spearmen and archers is rushing toward you, well..." he shrugged his thin shoulders. "I've never faced it, but I'm told brave men's bowels have loosened at the sight. My father saw a Troop of men, about two hundred, trampled and destroyed by no more than fifty massed chariots. He saw men try to stand against them, but go down into death under hooves and wheels, arrows and spears."

Harrubaal looked at the shocked and thoughtful expressions on the faces of his listeners. "Whatever else you do, Noble Lords," he said softly. "Do not underestimate chariots. It might be the last thing you do."

There was silence as he finished speaking, and then Aya cleared his throat. "Well er...thank you, Lord Harrubaal. You have given us much to think about. I am mindful that this experience has been tiring for you, so we will allow you to retire."

Harrubaal and Hori bowed to the king and left the Council chamber.

"He has obviously lost his nerve," General Neferhotep said. "Not surprising in such an old man, I suppose."

"Indeed," Sewahenre agreed. "A man like that cannot control his own emotions, as evidenced by the disrespect he allowed in his son."

"The picture he painted of a massed chariot charge was alarming," Treasurer Maia said.

"That is only because you are not a military man," Neferhotep replied.

"But Lord Harrubaal is...or was."

"Yes, but by his own admission has never faced chariots. No doubt he was fed all sorts of exciting stories at his father's knee, but his imagination has got the better of him. These chariots are just

43

wickerwork boxes with men in them. Disciplined men will have no trouble neutralising them."

"I hope you are right," Tjaty Aya said.

"I know I am," Neferhotep said. "Mark my words, the threat these chariots represent has been greatly exaggerated."

"I rely on your military experience," Monthhotep said. "It is reassuring that you see no especial threat in these *heqa khasut*. Aya, make sure your spies are present at the battles in the north. I am greatly interested in finding out the relative strengths of these two foes. That knowledge could well shape our foreign policy."

"Let it be so, Son of Re," Tjaty Aya said.

Chapter 4

S amuqenu looked on in satisfaction as his men streamed down from the hills into the flat lands bordering the branching river system of Kemet. The sight of the well-watered land took his breath away as he imagined the wealth that this kingdom claimed as its own. He could see herds of cattle in the distance, with herdsmen hurrying them away from his oncoming army, and knew that horses would do equally well on those lush pastures. Dragging his mind away from the calculation of coming riches, he looked at the city of Avaris nearer at hand, and at the army that waited on the plains beneath its walls. From where he stood, it looked to be smaller than his own army, and he anticipated an easy victory.

His officers scurried among the men, creating some sort of order from the streams of soldiers, organising them into units, and drawing them up on the first level ground they could find. As the soldiers waited, fiddling with their gear, adjusting belts and buckles, testing the edge of an axe, or fidgeting, they looked toward the city and the motionless Delta Army. Mutterings arose from those that had anticipated the enemy would just run away, but the officers strode amongst them, quelling any unease with words and the occasional blow from the batons of office they carried. The orders came to move forward, and the cavalry rode out first, arcing out to the south, while bands of archers trotted out to the north, leaving the main body of foot soldiers to advance straight toward the waiting enemy.

Behind the Amurran army, Baalbek watched them move forward while he and his men did nothing but guard the extensive baggage train. He waited for Samuqenu or one of the other high officers to

45

relent and allow him to join the attack, but no messages were dispatched in his direction. Finally, he could bear it no longer and strode off to the command outpost where Samuqenu stood atop a rise, surrounded by his personal officers.

"My lord Samuqenu, let my men join in the assault."

Samuqenu turned and stared at Baalbek. "Why have you left your post, Baalbek?"

"The baggage train is safe, my lord, but you waste five hundred men of Hattush by not letting them take part."

"Are you telling me you have a greater knowledge of tactics than me?"

"No, my lord, but my men are eager to fight and..."

"They will get their chance. Now return to your post, Baalbek of Hattush, before I decide you are being obstructive."

Samuqenu turned away dismissively, giving Baalbek no option but to withdraw. He wore an expression of anger as he marched back to the baggage train. His son Aribaal saw him coming and guessed from his father's demeanour that the Commander's answer had not been favourable.

"We remain here?"

"Yes," Baalbek snapped.

He gestured to his son and they climbed a low ridge nearby which gave them a good view of the battlefield.

"Let us at least see how Amurru goes about winning a battle."

"Is that certain, father?"

"It's hard to see how they could lose."

From where they stood on the ridge, they could look over the heads of the Amurru soldiers to the city walls and the army gathered beneath them. The Amurrans stopped a few hundred paces from the enemy and spread out, thinning their ranks as the wings of the army extended past the other army.

"Interesting," Baalbek said. "I would have massed my men and punched through the enemy. Samuqenu seems to want to envelop them."

Horns sounded, first from the command hilltop and then picked up from others in the ranks of the army and officers shouted, urging their men to attack. The Amurrans surged forward, swiftly losing cohesion as faster runners outpaced their fellows, and a few heartbeats later the Avaris army charged in their turn. By the time they met, both armies had been reduced to a loose mass of men. Each soldier chose an opponent and attacked, swinging sword or axe, probing with spears and interposing leather shields. Dust churned high, obscuring vision and the battle became a melee of struggling men.

"It's chaos," Aribaal said. "Are all battles like this?"

"More or less. You can attack in good order, but as soon as you make contact with the enemy, each man must look out for himself."

The mass of fighting men in the plain heaved back and forth, first one side and then the other gaining a temporary ascendancy. Arrows arced into the Avaris men from the north, but if their aim was too close to the actual fighting, as many Amurrans died as did the enemy. After a while, the archers were released and ran closer, loosing arrows at individual targets rather than en masse. The Avaris soldiers turned their attention to the archers, cutting many down and forcing others to withdraw.

"Archers have their uses," Baalbek observed, "but give me a spear or an axe and I'll match any man on the field."

"What are the cavalry doing?" Aribaal asked.

"I don't...there!"

Dust boiled up on the southern flank and the two men could glimpse horses galloping toward the battle, their riders bearing couched spears or wielding bows. Aribaal yelled in excitement, urging them on as they bore down on the ranks of Avaris men who had yet to join the fight, but at the last moment, instead of bursting into the ranks they swung to either side. Spears were thrown and arrows loosed, inflicting many casualties, and then they were off, retreating into the dust cloud.

"That's it?" Aribaal demanded. "They hardly did anything."

"They'll be back," Baalbek said. "But that's how cavalry are used. They pick off soldiers on the flanks."

"They should just ride them down. They'd be unstoppable."

"That's the work of chariots. Horses are unprotected and their riders cannot keep a seat firm enough to withstand the shock of hitting a mass of men."

"Where are the chariots?"

"They couldn't come through the hills, so they'll be coming by the coast road. Not soon enough for this battle, though."

The cavalry returned, again inflicting light damage, but now the Avaris archers brought their numbers to bear and loosing their arrows from a stable base, killed many horses and threw the Amurrans into chaos. Their commander ordered their withdrawal and a cheer went up from the Avaris soldiers. Heartened, they surged forward and the Amurran army, spread thin by their enveloping tactics, were thrown back several paces.

"Anchor your men on a feature of the land," Baalbek growled. "Gods, look at them. They're too spread out and they have no rallying point."

As he spoke, the Avaris men broke through the thinning ranks of Amurru, splitting the army into two unequal portions. The larger one now drew back on itself, but the smaller shattered and ran for the shelter of the rough ground and scrubland. A great cheer went up from the Avaris soldiers and many ran after the fleeing men, cutting them down. Now, with both armies suddenly bereft of a part of their force, the contest turned again as the Avaris army was forced to spread out around the bunched Amurrans, now cast into the role of defenders.

"Now is when we should hit them with a fresh force," Baalbek said. "The battle is evenly poised."

"We have nearly five hundred men, father," Aribaal said. "Will you order them into the attack?"

Baalbek shook his head. "That is not for me to say." He called up one of his Hattush men and told him to run to the command post. "Ask of Prince Samuqenu whether I may attack with my men."

The man ran off, and they watched his progress as he shouldered his way through the press of men around Samuqenu. He was lost to sight for several moments and then he reappeared, running toward them with great vigour and waving wildly.

"Run back to the baggage train and get the men ready," Baalbek told his son. "It looks like we might see some action after all."

Baalbek watched his son scramble back down the ridge toward the baggage train and then cast another look toward the battle. The even contest had turned again as the Amurran army was now driven back, pace by pace as the Avaris force was reinforced by men pouring out of the city.

"Too late," he muttered and headed down to intercept the messenger.

"Prince Samuqenu bids you attack, my lord," the man of Hattush gasped.

"Good. Get back to your unit."

The two men ran back together and by the time they got back, Aribaal had roused the men and they were forming up into a rough column. Baalbek waved them forward and took up a position at their head, Aribaal joining him a few minutes later. They advanced quickly, each Hattushi eager to get to grips with the enemy and prove their worth to their commander. Amurrans were the first ones encountered, however, battle-weary men streaming back, dusty and sweat-stained, many nursing wounds either slight or severe, and often with fear in their eyes. The sight of Baalbek's men, fresh and ready for battle, reenergised many of them and their officers managed to turn many around. Baalbek's little force swelled to twice its number by the time contact was made with the enemy.

The men of Avaris were buoyed up by their victory, but were weary and hoping that the enemy had been routed. When Baalbek's fresh men appeared, they hesitated and the first hundred or so were quickly overrun and cut down. Others following on behind formed a defensive formation and the men of Hattush found themselves battling in earnest. Baalbek concentrated his men with shields and spears to the front, and led his men at a charge straight into the ranks of the enemy. They pierced deep into the enemy formation before they lost impetus and fighting became general.

Baalbek, with his son Aribaal beside him, traded blows with the soldiers of the Delta, beating down his opponent's defence and hacking at arm or neck or chest, ignoring the spray of blood. As one man fell, another took his place, and Baalbek felt his battle ardour rise. It would have been easy to give in to the thrill of killing but he laid a hand on his anger and controlled himself. He had his son to look out for, his men also, and ultimately his kingdom. It would serve no purpose to give himself up to the fray and risk death unnecessarily. Instead, he fought with all his skill and strength, leading his men. The pulse of the battle flowed and ebbed, the struggling mass of men swaying back and forth, and gradually Baalbek and his men edged forward, stumbling over fallen men, slipping in reeking blood and faeces, as the men of Avaris started a slow retreat.

"The day is ours," Baalbek called. "Forward now, and let us drive them back to their city."

The Hattushi surged forward in response, raising cries of victory as many Delta men turned and ran. Their pursuit was slow, hindered by the fallen, and though many of Samuqenu's men had now joined them, so too had reinforcements arrived from Avaris. What started as a triumphant advance broke on the swelling ranks of the Delta soldiers. Hattushi men crashed into Avaris men and once more the mass of men slashed and hacked and stabbed at each other, pushing with their shields, their breath rasping as their chests heaved from the effort. Sweat ran into their eyes, blinding them, and dust churned up by their feet blocked noses and mouths, while blood slicked their weapons and weariness overwhelmed them.

The armies drew back, each too exhausted to follow up an advantage and for long minutes stood about twenty paces apart, chests heaving and limbs trembling from the effort. Faces obscured by blood and streaked with dust and sweat stared across the small gap and each man wondered when the enemy would come at him again and he would die. Officers called out, exhorting their men to further violence, but neither army responded and then, without conscious thought, the men of Amurru took a step back...and another...until the men started shuffling back, retreating back into the hills.

The Avaris men raised a weak cheer, but did not pursue. In part, their exhaustion disinclined them for further heroics, and in part they could not quite believe this was not some clever ruse by the enemy. They stayed where they were, surrounded by the dead and dying, and watched the invaders melt back into the scrub and rocky ground of the foothills. It was not until it was nearly dark that they dared stir from their position and slowly make their way back to Avaris.

The men camped outside the city while the senior commanders, General Inkhare and Troop Commander Menkare reported to the king. Merybaal was on hand to hear the words of the General and shook his head at his claims of victory.

"You have driven them off, General," he said, "but did you destroy them? Did you kill their Commander? Their king?"

"They fled and are probably halfway to Hattush by now," Inkhare said. "As for their commander...well, we have not searched among the piles of their dead, but I imagine he could well lie there."

"You really think they have gone?" King Seneferenre asked. "We have won?"

"Yes, Son of Re. The enemy fled and left us in possession of the field of battle. What else can you call that but a victory?"

"Does one victory mean the war is won?" Merybaal asked.

"It is a good start," Inkhare replied. "If they come again, we know how to beat them."

"I think you are being overly optimistic, General, but I hope you are right. Your men fought well and saved Avaris today. You are to be congratulated."

After the meeting, Merybaal drew his daughter's husband Menkare aside and would have taken him home with him, except the General required him in the camp. Instead, they snatched a few moments of privacy and exchanged words within the palace.

"Whatever the General says," Menkare said. "This war is far from over. The enemy withdrew in reasonably good order rather than running. My guess is they'll regroup and return, particularly if they can get reinforcements."

Merybaal nodded. "That was my thought too. I find it hard to believe that the great Amurran threat was so easily beaten off."

"Perhaps we should tell General Menenre to return with the thousand men he took north. We may have need of those men here."

"That depends on how much of a threat those chariots are. A few hundred of them could disgorge a thousand men, and Menenre will be needed to counter them." Merybaal thought for a few moments. "The king would probably say there is no need, but I think I might send a messenger north to apprise him of what has happened here today. Let him make up his own mind."

Menkare returned to the camp outside the walls, and Merybaal walked home deep in thought. He was greeted at the door by his wife Amatia with alarming news.

"Neferit is missing, husband."

"What? Explain yourself."

Amatia drew him inside and into a private room where they could not be overheard by the servants. "She has not been home at all today."

"Then she is with friends."

"No, I sent servants round to all her female friends today, but none of them had seen her since yesterday."

"What happened yesterday? Apart from Djedenre leaving with the last of the men for the north?"

"Just that. She and some others went to the north gate to wave goodbye to the soldiers, and when they were gone, so was Neferit."

"She went with them?" Merybaal was incredulous.

"No. No, of course not, but that's when the young women who were there noticed her missing."

"So you've known since yesterday?"

"No. I only found that out today, when I made enquiries." Amatia clutched her husband's arm. "Where has she gone? I'm so worried."

Merybaal thought for a few moments. "Think about the possibilities. You've talked to all her women friends..."

"Yes."

"...and her sister Tiamen..."

Amatia nodded. "First thing."

"...and we know she has no male friends she might have visited..."

"Of course not. You know Neferit does not like men in that way."

"I know. I'm thinking aloud. So if she has not visited relatives or friends then there can only be one other solution."

Amatia gasped and covered her mouth, her eyes wide and filled with tears. "She... she's been abducted..."

"What? No! Gods, woman, what made you think of that? Avaris is not so lawless a man would dare kidnap the daughter of the Treasurer. No, I meant the horse lines. You know she loves horses."

"You really think she's there?"

"It is most likely. I will send men there immediately."

Merybaal did just that, and his men scoured the horse lines, questioning every man they found, but Neferit was not there.

"She was, though, my lord," said the overseer the men had reported to. "She was at the horse lines yesterday, where she was seen talking to her favourite mare."

"So where is she now?" Merybaal demanded.

"Nobody knows, my lord...but the mare is missing too."

Merybaal dismissed the servants and went to see his wife. He did not hide the news from her, trusting in her strength.

"I believe she has ridden after Djedenre and the men he took north."

"But why? What could have possessed her? Surely she cannot believe she can be a soldier like her brother?"

"Has she ever wanted anything else?" Merybaal sighed. "She should have been born a boy."

"What will you do?"

"I will send riders north to find her, but she is no longer a child. I cannot easily command her..."

"You are her father."

"Yes, but in this I think she would not obey me."

Chapter 5

Neferit watched her brother Djedenre march away with the last of the troops sent north to bolster general Menenre's little army. Unlike her female friends who had posed and preened, flirting with the young soldiers, calling out to them and throwing flowers, she had stared in envy, wishing that she was marching with them. At an age when all her friends were married and some even had children, she had resisted any attempt to match her with the sons of the nobles of Avaris. Her mother had given up making suggestions or hinting that she would love some more grandchildren, and her father just smiled and let her do whatever she wanted--as long as it was seemly.

The problem was that what she really wanted to do was not seemly at all, particularly for the well-brought-up daughter of the Treasurer. Ever since she had been a small child she had been enamoured of the military life. As she grew older she found that girls were not allowed to play at being soldiers and the use of arms was frowned upon. Nevertheless, she sought out the company of boys prepared to play with her, and taught herself the rudiments of weapons training.

With puberty came an interest in horses and whenever the opportunity arose she frequented the horse lines. The grooms were happy to talk with her, but the overseer was appalled that this daughter of an important official was putting herself in harm's way. He talked to Merybaal and he talked to Neferit.

"The Overseer of Horses tells me you are often in the lines. Why are you there? Have you some romantic interest in one of the grooms?"

"Men do not interest me, father, only the horses."

"You like horses?"

"Yes, and they like me. The grooms let me look after them and even sit on them. I hope they will let me ride them soon."

"Daughter, you cannot just wander the horse lines. There are many young men there...and older ones...that would take advantage of a girl."

"I hear you, father, but I can take care of myself." Neferit showed him the dagger she kept in her belt.

Nothing Merybaal said would dissuade her and though he confined her to the house for half a month, eventually he had to let her out. She immediately returned to the horse lines. Faced with her disobedience, Merybaal took what steps he could to protect her. He called the Overseer of Horses to him.

"Senen, my daughter Neferit will be frequenting the horse lines."

Senen frowned. "My lord, I brought her to your notice because I feared for her safety."

Merybaal grimaced. "She is a strong-willed girl and unless I keep her locked up I cannot prevent her."

Senen said nothing but looked unhappy.

"Therefore, you will set a guard upon her when she visits the horse lines. Someone with a bit of authority who can guard her against any unwelcome attentions from the grooms." Merybaal thought for a moment before adding, "Any welcome attentions too. Let me speak plainly, Senen, my daughter is young and has formed an infatuation with horses. I am prepared to indulge her fancy, but if any harm comes to her within the horse lines, I will hold you responsible and you will feel the full weight of my wrath."

Senen looked even unhappier. "My lord, the horse lines are extensive and...and in a bad area of the city. I cannot guarantee her safety outside the lines, and even within..."

"I will have her escorted to and from the lines, but you have power within and I expect you to use it. Keep her safe, Senen. Your life depends on it."

Neferit objected to an escort, but reluctantly accepted one provided he was unobtrusive. So she resumed her association with the horses and, under the stern instructions of Senen, the grooms behaved themselves and instructed her in all aspects of their work. Within a year, they let her ride the horses and she proved to have a knack for it, though some adjustments had to be made for her gender.

Women in Avaris typically wore long light-weight dresses if they were of the nobility and shorter linen kilts if they were of the working classes, and usually nothing underneath. The only exceptions were made at the time of the *hesmen*, when they wore a loincloth, often with a pad of folded linen. Noble ladies tended not to venture outdoors at this time of month, but working girls had to. Neferit found that a padded loincloth had other uses when it came to horse riding, protecting both her modesty and her tender parts. As she grew older, Neferit found that her physical development called for other adjustments to her clothing and she adopted a tight band across her chest. Luckily for her, she was small-breasted anyway, and with her loincloth and chest band in place was sometimes taken for a youth, which suited her.

On the day that Djedenre marched away, she wore her normal clothes as she intended to wave goodbye with the other young women of her acquaintance and then go home. She was surprised to be overcome by a desire to ride with her brother, though, and as she made her way back into the city she wondered whether she could actually take charge of her life.

"I am twenty years old," she muttered to herself as she walked, "and I have done nothing with my life. How long will it be before father loses patience with me and forces me into marriage?"

She knew it was unlikely that her father would do any such thing. As fathers went, he was very understanding and doted on his youngest child, but she felt that she was somehow letting him down, and how long could that state of affairs continue?

"I don't want to get married; I really don't; but what is the alternative? If I was a man, I'd be a soldier, but I'm not skilled enough with weapons. I don't have the strength to wield an axe or spear, though I'm reasonably good with a bow. I could be an archer...but how likely is that? I can't imagine father ever allowing me to fight in a battle."

She reached a point where she could either continue on home or turn aside to the horse lines and she stopped, looking both ways.

"All I'm really good at is riding a horse. Looking after them too; and horses like me. But of what use is that? If I was better at weapons...and a man...I could join the cavalry." Neferit sighed and was about to resume her way home when she noticed a man running down the street holding a letter in his hand. He did not look like he was the kind of man to be able to read, so he was likely a messenger. She started to wonder where he was going when the answer to her problem struck her.

"I could be a messenger. I know how to ride a horse...better than many...and...and I could be useful. I could carry messages between the army in the field and the king."

She felt excitement rising in her as she contemplated a glorious future as the swiftest and bravest messenger in the kingdom, and then she realised her father would never let her do it. He was a wonderful father, but he would never agree...unless...

"I need to show him I can do it, but how?" She stood in the middle of the hot and dusty street, her forehead furrowed as she thought. "I could...I could carry news of Menenre's victory over the chariots back to the king faster than anyone else. That would show everyone I can do it."

She grinned and turned toward the horse lines.

The grooms had learned to obey her instantly in all things, and even when they suspected she was not supposed to do something, to just look the other way. Her guardian within the horse lines was nowhere to be seen, so she hurried toward the stall where her favourite mount was housed. A pale grey mare, she had named her Wenet, the swift one, and the mare responded well to her voice and her touch. When he heard that Neferit had a special relationship with the mare, the Overseer of Horses had ruled that no-one else was to ride her.

Now, Neferit sought out her riding clothes that she kept in Wenet's stable and, after checking that she was unobserved, changed into her padded loincloth and chest band. Taking the halter and bit, she stroked the mare, soothing her and murmuring phrases of praise until she accepted the bronze in her mouth and the leather straps and reins. She led the mare out of her stable and down the broad avenue toward the gate that opened out into pastures to the north of the city. The old man who kept an eye on her saw her and called out, so she replied calmly.

"I am just taking her out for a run. I won't be long."

"Let me find someone to ride with you. The enemy are approaching the city and you shouldn't be out alone."

"No need," Neferit called back.

She leapt up onto Wenet's back and urged her toward the gate. The gatekeeper saw her and swung the gate open, letting her pass through and out into the open land beyond. An immense feeling of well-being overcame her and she yelled incoherently, letting Wenet run. Ahead, she saw the soldiers who had left an hour or so earlier and suddenly realised that if she galloped straight up to them, Djedenre would be sure to send her straight home. She pulled on the reins and checked her mare's progress, and started to think about her best course.

The geography of the north-eastern delta was a mystery to her. She was unsure whether there were any cities or towns in the north, but she knew the Coast Road started (or ended) somewhere near the coast, and as the army was making for this point to intercept the enemy chariots, she would have to make for it too. The problem was that the enemy was out there somewhere and it was too much of a risk to just circle round the marching army. There was nothing for it; she would just have to tail her brother until she felt she was too far from Avaris to be sent home.

Neferit had set out on the spur of the moment and had no supplies with her, having vaguely thought she could share her brother's tent and rations. Now, she would have to fend for herself. She slowed her mare to a walk and followed in the beaten path of the army. Toward nightfall, she started thinking in terms of finding some shelter for the night, and came upon one of the unfortunate aspects of following an army across open countryside. Several hundred men had passed this way recently and it seemed as if every man had relieved himself beside the marching column. It was unpleasant to come across scattered waste products every few paces, so she mounted Wenet once more and rode out to one side of the path where she could find unsoiled grass.

The night was chilly, and without warm clothing or the luxury of a fire, Neferit lay awake with her teeth chattering. At last, not being able to stand the chill breeze from the north, she got up and stood in the lee of her horse, grateful both for her warm body and the shelter from the wind it provided. She was stiff, hungry and thirsty in the morning, so her first action was to ride west to find the river and quench her thirst. A little bit of fossicking in the reed beds turned up a nest with three eggs. Cautiously cracking them, she found they were fresh with only a partially formed chick in them, so she swallowed them down as quickly as she could.

The warmth of the sun soon eased her chilled limbs, and she walked her mare slowly after the army the rest of that day. Faced with another cold and hungry night, she decided she was far enough from Avaris to risk contact with her brother. She rode into the army camp just before nightfall, attracting a lot of notice and not all of it favourable. Despite her efforts to flatten her chest it was hard to disguise her figure and several men called out, making obscene suggestions before an officer could intervene.

"What are you doing here, young woman? We are too busy to accommodate your trade."

Neferit blushed at the suggestion that she was a camp follower or prostitute. "I have come to see Troop Commander Djedenre. I have news from his family."

The officer looked doubtful, but escorted her through the camp to the command tent. Djedenre was amazed to see her, and sent for wine and food, as well as ordering that her horse be attended to.

"What in the name of all the gods are you doing here, Neferit? And dressed like that?" He stared so hard, she blushed again.

"I have to dress like that to ride a horse."

"You look... I don't know what you look like." Djedenre looked in the small chest in his tent and found a warm cloak. "Here, put this on."

Neferit wrapped herself in the cloak and tucked into the food and drink the officer brought.

"So why are you here?" Djedenre asked. "Is there trouble at home? Why couldn't a messenger come?"

"Nothing like that, brother. I want to..." Neferit hesitated, realising her desires were going to sound ridiculous. "I want to fight. I want to be a soldier."

Djedenre opened his mouth to laugh, but turned it into a cough when he saw his sister's expression.

"It is... er, commendable that you want to help, but Nefer, you're a woman."

"I know. I can't help that; and it doesn't matter anyway. I can handle a bow quite well and I can ride a horse. I can be useful."

"I have no doubt, but sister...this camp is full of men."

"So? I have no interest in any of them."

"But they might have an interest in you."

"I can take care of myself." Neferit showed him the dagger in her belt.

"I believe you, sister, but it would be better if you didn't have to. Look, most soldiers believe a woman in camp is there for...er, well...pleasure. Say one of them propositions you and you refuse. He doesn't take no for an answer and you cut him..."

"I'd kill him."

"Either way, it would cause trouble, and having to face our enemies in the field I'd rather not have trouble in the camp as well."

"I don't want to cause trouble."

"Good, then at first light you can ride back to Avaris."

"I'm not going back, brother. If you won't let me stay, I'll follow the army and when we find the enemy I'll do what I can by myself."

Djedenre groaned. "Do I have to tie you up and send you back with an escort? I can't spare the men to do that, but if you're going to be difficult, I'll have to."

Neferit scowled but said nothing. She knew her brother was on the brink of deciding against her.

"How did you persuade our parents to let you come?" Djedenre looked at his sister but she avoided his eyes. "You didn't? They don't know? Gods, Nefer, they must be worried sick."

"They wouldn't have let me come, but they'll know that I came after you and that you would..." she grimaced, "...look after me."

"You see the trouble you cause? If you refuse to go back alone, I have to send you back with an escort. At the very least, I have to send a messenger back to let them know where you are. I really can't spare the men for such foolishness."

"Then don't. Father will guess where I am, and look, brother, I came here to fight. Regard me as being another soldier in your army. Find a use for me. It won't be for long. Another few days and you'll meet and defeat the enemy and we can all go home in triumph."

Djedenre paced, his fists clenching and unclenching, and then he sighed. "Well, it's too late to do anything tonight. I'll decide in the morning. You can sleep in here."

"Thank you, brother. If you think on it, you'll find that I have my uses. Surely someone who can ride a horse as well as me..."

"Enough, Nefer. I'll decide in the morning."

A scout returned just before daybreak with news that the enemy had been sighted, and Djedenre knew that the problem his sister represented would have to be thrust aside. There was still the problem of her state of dress--or undress--but he remembered that he had a few Ribu archers who had volunteered for duty. He sent for one of them and procured some garments that were foreign to both him and Neferit--baggy woollen tunic and leggings that would hide her gender.

"I can't wear those," Neferit objected. "I'll look like a barbarian."

"It's that or go home," Djedenre said. "Decide."

Neferit shrugged. "I'll wear them."

She felt self-conscious in the baggy tunic and leggings, but after a while she had to admit that they felt comfortable, and she no longer had to worry that parts of her anatomy were becoming visible when she walked or ran or vaulted onto the back of her horse. The men in Djedenre's little army knew now who she was, but politely ignored her, treating her as if she was truly another Ribu tribesman.

"I can't call you Neferit while you are with us," Djedenre said. "My men will overlook our little fiction, but General Menenre would be suspicious of a tribesman bearing a woman's name."

"What then?"

"We need a Ribu-sounding name." Djedenre consulted the archer who had lent her the clothing. "Neterre, then. It's close enough to your real name that if someone forgets and addresses you as Neferit, you can just say it was mispronounced."

"I am to be an archer in your army then?"

"You'd have to march with the other Ribu. No, I'll keep you close to me as my personal messenger."

Shortly after dawn, Djedenre ordered his men to march in battle formation, ready to meet the enemy if they should appear. Scouts added more information during the course of the morning--General Menenre and the main army were no more than an hour or so away and the dust of the approaching chariot force could be seen on the horizon beyond them.

Djedenre urged his men to pick up the pace and before long made contact with the southern parts of Menenre's army. He took Neferit with him and went to see the General.

"Is it wise to thrust me into his presence?" Neferit asked. "Won't he be suspicious?"

"He'll be more suspicious if I keep you hidden and word gets back to him. Stay behind me, keep your head down and say nothing."

They were shown into Menenre's command tent where he was going over the latest reports from the scouts.

"Ah, there you are, Djedenre. About time you showed up. How many men have you brought me?"

"Two hundred sir, and a handful of Ribu archers. Volunteers."

Menenre grunted. "That brings our total strength to thirteen hundred. My latest information is that there are close on a thousand of these chariots, so if they each hold even two men we'll be outnumbered. Still, the odds are in our favour. We're fighting for our homes and that doubles our strength."

"Are we certain that that is how they will fight, sir? On foot?"

"How else? They'll be at a disadvantage when their men are dismounting, so we'll hit them hard then." Menenre looked past Djedenre, noticing his companion for the first time. "Who is that outlandishly clothed person?"

"This is Neterre, sir. He is a prince among the Ribu and a skilled horseman, so I have taken him on as my personal aide and messenger."

"He looks effeminate. Can he be trusted?"

"Yes, sir. He is young, but has readily sworn an oath of fealty to the king at Avaris."

The General nodded and turned back to his reports. "The enemy are following the road south, so we will meet them here, where there is good flat land. We will be drawn up across their path, so they will have to stand and fight. I'll put you and your men on the river side, Djedenre. Keep an ear out for the horns. A double blast and you charge the chariots as they halt and disgorge their men. We'll take them unprepared and destroy them."

Djedenre and Neferit moved to the left flank of the army with their men, occupying the edge of the bare ground close to the road and the pasture that dropped gently down to the reed beds and marshes along the river. By now, the dust cloud kicked up by the approaching chariots hung over them and they could detect motion in the distance.

"Here they come," Neferit said.

"You sound excited to see them."

"Well, of course I am. I've never seen chariots before."

"None of us have," Djedenre said. "Just remember that this is going to be a savage battle. If things look bad for us--if the enemy proves too strong--I want you to mount up and ride back home as fast as you can."

"I'm not running away and leaving you."

"You will do as you're told...soldier." Djedenre grinned. "Seriously though, if things go wrong, the king must hear of it immediately. You have a fast horse; who better to carry the news?"

The army of Avaris stood ready to meet the invader, a little over a thousand men spread across the way south from the coast, each one determined to throw back the enemy. Individual chariots could be seen now, a column of horse-drawn carts churning up a huge cloud of dust that drifted over the waiting men on the northerly breeze. It seemed the enemy had not bothered to send out scouts, for their surprise at encountering the waiting men was evident. The leading chariots checked and then wheeled to one side, the following column spreading out on either side of the road and came to a halt, the horses pawing the ground. Shouted commands in a foreign tongue could be heard.

Djedenre stared at the line of chariots only a few hundred paces away and frowned. "They look a lot more mobile than mere carts," he said, "and the men in them don't look as if they're dismounting."

"They do look dangerous," Neferit agreed. "Dangerous and beautiful."

A rams' horn sounded from General Menenre's command post, two long blasts and his army beat their swords and axes against their leather shields. Then they cheered and broke ranks, charging forward to carry out their duty. Djedenre's men followed suit, but as Djedenre himself started forward, Neferit clutched his arm.

"Why isn't the enemy doing anything?" she asked. "Shouldn't their men be leaping down to face our men?"

Djedenre stared, letting his men slip past him to join the rest of the Avaris army. "You're right. Why aren't..." His voice trailed away as the enemy responded to the charge.

There must have some signal, either by sound or sight, which set the enemy chariots in motion, but it was not evident from that distance. Far from disgorging their men, the chariots started forward as one, rapidly picking up speed, and now the thunder of their approach drowned out the cheers and shouts of Menenre's men. The distance between the two armies closed rapidly, and then Djedenre and Neferit were watching in horror as the Amurran chariots tore through the Avaris army as if it was no more than wet paper. Shouts and cheers changed to screams, and now the Avaris men strove to get away, turning and throwing up their arms in surrender or stumbling back the way they came.

Djedenre was reminded of a field of ripe barley when a northerly storm broke upon it, flattening and breaking the stems, throwing the ears aside and rendering the crop useless. Within a few short minutes, the Avaris army had been all but destroyed, and now consisted of little more than scattered groups of fleeing men pursued by remorseless chariots. Dead men lay tumbled and torn upon the dusty ground. It was hard to see that the invaders had been harmed in any way.

"Come away, brother," Neferit said. "There is nothing we can do here."

Djedenre stared at his sister. She was pale and she stood wide-eyed, but her lips were parted and her eyes shone as if in excitement.

"I must fight with my men...rally them."

"There is no-one left to rally."

"Then I will die with them."

"That would serve no purpose. You are an army officer who can bear witness to the power of a chariot charge. The king must hear of this."

"Then...then you must ride and tell him...as I instructed you before."

"The king will not listen to a woman, but he will listen to you." Neferit pulled her brother round and took his face in her hands. "Look at me, brother. You can do nothing here, but you can serve your king well by surviving and bearing witness of this defeat. And look...already the enemy have seen us standing to one side. They are coming."

A squad of chariots had turned aside from the pursuit of the shattered army and were approaching the two figures in the pasture to the river side of the rout. Neferit turned Wenet and soothed her before leaping lightly onto her back. She held her hand out and helped Djedenre scramble up behind her.

"Hold on tight," she muttered, urging her horse into motion.

Arrows hissed by, but she guided her mare closer to the river, skirting the marshy, water-logged areas.

"We should be heading south," Djedenre said, holding her in an anxious stranglehold.

"If we try it, they will likely overtake us. It's only a guess, but I think their wheels will be too narrow for soft ground."

"What if you're wrong?"

"Then we're dead."

Neferit was not wrong, and the chariots soon gave up the pursuit, though they released a shower of arrows in their direction. They all fell short, and they turned back to search for easier prey. After a while, Neferit turned Wenet's head toward home and slowed her pace to a walk. Neither of them spoke, each filled with memories of the battle and the future, though each would have been surprised by the other's thoughts. Djedenre feared that Avaris could not stand against this foe, whereas Neferit was excited. The chariots were something new, and rather than filling her with dread, made her heart beat faster as she contemplated the new world that beckoned her.

Chapter 6

S amuqenu raged at his officers, and had a few executed on the spot for daring to run from the enemy. The others grovelled, though one or two daring souls voiced the opinion that facing an unknown foe, it would have been better to utilise the full force of Amurru. Luckily for them, Samuqenu's anger had largely been assuaged by the executions and he allowed these officers to live. He knew they were right, and dreaded the thought of appearing before his father, Anep-Aper, without capturing Avaris.

He issued a string of orders that sent his officers scurrying. Most concentrated on rounding up the remnants of his army from their refuges in the hills. There were more there than he had anticipated, given the debacle beneath the walls of Avaris. Fully four thousand men still survived, and more were trickling in shame-faced as the days passed. They were chastised and any who could be identified as cowards made an example of.

Samuqenu also sent for reinforcements from Hattush. Nearly half of the Amurran army had been left behind when he underestimated the strength of the enemy, but now he called these fresh troops to him, determined to crush the Delta Army once and for all, and by doing so, expunge the shame of his defeat. Somewhere to the north lay the chariot force under the command of General Anati, but no word had been received concerning his progress. Several riders were sent out to find the chariots and order them to make for Avaris at once.

Half a month passed before the reinforcements from Hattush arrived, and Samuqenu nodded in satisfaction as their numbers swelled his army to more than double its previous size. A letter came from his father, and that was less welcome. King Anep-Aper chastised his son for his miscalculation and encouraged him to do better by reminding him he was not indispensible.

"Fulfill your boasts, my son, and remember you have brothers eager for a share of the glory."

Samuqenu ground his teeth and crumpled the letter in his fist, vowing that he would die before he allowed himself to be supplanted as heir to Amurru, Lebanon and Syria. The city of Avaris would suffer for making him fail. He had a far larger army now and he would allow no more failure. Avaris would fall within the month and the Delta kingdom would fall within a year.

His determination received a boost when the messengers he had sent to General Anati returned, reporting that the chariot squadrons had annihilated an enemy army and was now advancing southward toward Avaris. Ordering Anati to make all speed south, Samuqenu marshalled his inflated army and sallied out from the cover of the foothills.

He found that the Delta Army had withdrawn back to the shelter of the city walls, but now, as they spread out into the dry plains to the east the men of Avaris came out once more to meet them. This time, the invaders held the numerical advantage and after the initial sorties, the Delta men withdrew. Samuqenu advanced more confidently, but found his officers still reluctant to close with the enemy in the shadow of the city. He executed those he considered most cowardly and ordered the others to attack or die.

The men of Amurru rushed forward like an avalanche down a steep hillside, hoping to overwhelm the enemy by sheer numbers, but Avaris fought back savagely, making Amurru pay for every step they advanced. Once more, thousands of men struggled for ascendancy in a welter of dirt, blood and sweat, but this time the invaders achieved a slow ascendancy, pushing the men of Avaris back.

Then into this struggling mass surged Anati's chariots. After the victory in the north, the chariot squadrons sped south, sweeping any opposition aside. Messengers from Samuqenu directed their course and now they impacted on the northerly flank of the defenders, crushing them beneath hooves and wheels. The Delta men had no answer for this type of warfare, having always fought on foot or occasionally on horseback. They died by the score and the left flank of their army collapsed, tipping the balance of the battle. Defenders scrambled for the safety of the city, and many of the invaders followed so hard on their heels that they poured into the city too. Fighting became general in the streets around the eastern and southern gates, and things might have gone badly for the defenders had not the king found his courage.

The streets around the gates were relatively narrow and restricted the numbers of men who could press forward at any one time. Defenders could take refuge in buildings, throwing bricks down from the rooftops and even the women of Avaris threw furniture at the invaders. Archers picked off many soldiers, ducking back into cover whenever the enemy tried to kill them. Then King Seneferenre gathered his palace guards and threw them at the invaders, leading them in a charge that pushed them out through the eastern gate. Other defenders took heart from the king's example and cleared the southern streets, closing the last gate against the invader.

Samuqenu roared with anger when he saw the Avaris army safely inside the city and the gates closed against him. He saw now that he had made another mistake. Rather than allowing superior numbers to grind down Avaris and force their way into the city, he had ordered his chariots into the attack. The chariots had provoked a panicked reaction from Avaris and they fled into the city in numbers too large to overcome in the cramped conditions within the city. The chariots were useless to him now, so he ordered them away and had his engineers and officers examine the city walls for the best way of breaching them.

"A general assault with ladders to scale the wall," said one.

"A battering ram to break down the gate," said another.

"Fire," declared a third. "Burn down the gate."

"Dig beneath the walls and collapse them."

"Starve them out."

"Sail around to the river side and storm the dock area."

"We don't have ships."

"Entice them out and destroy them in battle."

"They will not come out for fear of being cut to pieces by my chariots," Samuqenu declared. "Neither am I willing to wait half a year or longer for them to surrender." He glared around at his army officers. "Advise me. I desire to take this city within the month. Which method will deliver it into my hand?"

"None...and all," General Kanak said.

"Explain yourself."

"Give the four tasks to four leaders and let them compete for the honour of breaking in. They can each take a different section of wall or gate and launch simultaneous attacks. You will soon see which is most likely to succeed."

Samuqenu considered the words of his General and smiled. "Yes. I shall reward the successful one greatly, and the others will wish they had succeeded. For making the suggestion, General Kanak, I will let you choose the way you attack."

"I will take fire," Kanak said.

Samuqenu assigned three other generals to try the other methods. Generals Yannass, Siaan and Qub-Har groaned inwardly, but offered up thanks to their leader for giving them the chance of proving themselves. They had no choice with their assignments, it being given to Yannass to storm the walls with two thousand men; Siaan to construct a battering ram and break down the southern gate; and Qub-Har was given the task of undermining the walls. The Generals left to gather their men and organise just how it was going to be accomplished. Siaan discovered that he would have to send back to Hattush to find a tree-trunk massive enough to knock down a gate, and Yannass chopped down most of the trees in the foothills to construct assault ladders. Kanak had the easiest task as all he needed was dry scrub and fallen branches for fuel, though he found himself in competition with ordinary soldiers needing fuel with which to cook their meat.

Baalbek watched the preparations being made to take the city and knew that a city taken in violence meant dire things for the survivors. Some members of his family lived in Avaris and while he had no greatly developed feelings for any of them, having only met them briefly fifteen years before, he had no desire to see their bloodied corpses. He went to see Samuqenu.

"Ah, King Baalbek, I wondered when you'd turn up. I suppose you want an active part for your men in the reduction of Avaris."

"Whatever pleases you, my lord, but I was wondering what your intentions were for the city once you have taken it."

"I intend to make them rue the day they opposed me in the field," Samuqenu said. "Blood and fire, though maybe I'll spare and enslave the young women."

Baalbek knew that the Amurran heir would not be swayed by arguments of mercy, so he appealed to greed.

"It seems a pity to waste such a valuable resource, my lord."

"What do you mean?"

"Just that the Delta kingdom is rich, and the bulk of its wealth is in Avaris."

"Quite so; and I mean to make it my own. For my father, of course.'

"Of course, my lord, but a city destroyed, a population slaughtered, is not as valuable as one left intact, functioning. A city's wealth is measured in more than just gold. Avaris has been a wealthy trading nation for many years and could continue to produce wealth for you for many years to come, but to do this; its financial structures must be left intact. Its financial people too. For instance, Lord Merybaal within Avaris has been the king's treasurer for over forty years, serving one king after another. He will readily serve another king, I'm sure, and if any man has his fingers on the wealth of the Delta, it is him. Wouldn't it be in your interest to treasure this man and let him serve you?"

"Hmm, you make a persuasive argument, Baalbek, but how is it that you know so much about Avaris and its treasurer?"

Baalbek suspected Samuqenu already knew the answer to this, but even if he did not, it was too risky to try hiding it from him.

"Merybaal is the grandson of my father, Arimawat."

"Really? He must have come to his post as an infant if he has served forty years as Treasurer."

"He is an old man, my lord, whereas I am a child of my father's old age."

"How do you know Merybaal?"

"I met him and his family fifteen years ago when my father sent a deputation to Avaris seeking trade."

"You believe he will serve whoever is king in Avaris? Faithfully, without deceit?"

"I do, my lord."

"Then I will issue a command that when the city is taken, he is to be spared. I will even extend my mercy to his immediate family if they can be identified quickly enough."

"You are generous, my lord, but you know how chaotic it can be when an army fights to take a city. What if I could persuade Avaris to surrender? Wouldn't that serve you better?"

Samuqenu frowned. "How would you do that, when even my Generals disagree on the most effective method?"

"I would seek to be admitted to the city and speak with King Seneferenre, Merybaal, and his high officials. It may be that I can persuade them to lay down their arms and submit."

The Amurran heir considered Baalbek's words. "On the other hand, they may just execute you."

"It is possible," Baalbek admitted, "but I don't think so. Merybaal, at least, is an honourable man. My lord, you lose nothing by letting me try."

"Very well, then, King Baalbek, you may attempt to secure the surrender of Avaris."

The first thing Baalbek did was talk to his son Aribaal about what he was going to do.

"Hattush rests in your hands if I do not survive. Rule with justice and mercy, and take care of your mother and sister."

"I'm coming with you, father. That's my family in there as well."

"No, you're not. I cannot risk Hattush by putting you in jeopardy."

Baalbek talked to General Kanak about his intentions and asked him to pull the troops back from the eastern gate. Kanak thought he had lost his senses, but as he was not to be persuaded, ordered the men to fall back. The King of Hattush walked out into the open ground in front of the gate dressed in a simple tunic and with his arms held out to the side. He hoped that being obviously unarmed would give him the opportunity to talk, but he faltered when he saw archers rush up onto the wall. A few moments later, two arrows thudded into the ground only a few paces in front of him. He stopped.

"I am the King of Hattush," he called. "I seek audience with your king and his Council."

There was silence from the walls for a minute, and then a voice called out.

"How do we know you tell the truth?"

"Why would I lie?" Baalbek gestured back toward the Amurran army. "You can see they defer to me. But if you need proof, send for your Treasurer Merybaal. He knows me by sight."

Another silence, then,

"Lord Merybaal has been summoned. Advance to the gate alone."

Baalbek started forward again, a little hesitantly, wondering if the archers would take the opportunity to claim another victim. He passed the arrows sticking in the ground and walked closer, but no further arrows were sent in his direction. Faces peered over the parapet at him as he drew closer, and he saw several archers with drawn bows, no violence was offered him. The gate opened a crack and an old man peered through.

"You are Baalbek, King of Hattush?"

"I am. And you are Merybaal. I recognise you, though you are now an old man."

"Old age will come to you too, Baalbek, if you are lucky enough to live. I recognise you too, though you are no longer a young man yourself. As you are king, I assume your father has died?"

Baalbek nodded. "Nearly ten years ago. Are you going to let me in?"

"You want to talk to King Seneferenre?"

"And you. I want to try and prevent unnecessary bloodshed."

"A noble aim." Merybaal thought for a few moments and nodded. "I will escort you to the king myself. I cannot promise he will listen to you, but I will do my best to protect you."

"Thank you."

"Are you sure you want to do this? You can still walk away."

Baalbek grinned. "And risk an arrow in my back? No, I'll try my luck with your king."

"Then follow me."

Merybaal sent a messenger ahead of them and ordered an escort of soldiers to accompany them, leading the way into the city. Men and women flocked to see the stranger and many called out insults and exhorted the soldiers to kill the man with them. Baalbek kept close to Merybaal, hoping that his authority would protect him. When a gang of toughs bearing staves and knives blocked their way, Merybaal ordered the soldiers to clear the way, but the soldiers were reluctant.

"This man has come to speak to the king, and I know the king will want to speak with him. Do you dare oppose the king?"

Grumbling and making muttered threats, the toughs stood aside and let them through, and soon they reached the palace. The palace guard waited for them on the steps and took charge of Baalbek, allowing the soldiers to return to their duties. Merybaal accompanied them through to the Small Audience Chamber, where the king waited with General Inkhare.

Baalbek bowed respectfully to King Seneferenre, recognising him as the ruler of a great kingdom. Merybaal introduced him as King Baalbek of Hattush.

"I am surprised to see you, Baalbek," Seneferenre said. "It is not usual for enemies to seek an audience. Are you here to surrender or to demand terms? If the former, I am inclined to be generous; if the latter I am minded to hang your body from the wall as an example."

"I have come in the hopes that we might broker a peace where both sides may live in amity, King Seneferenre. The rulers of the Delta are our kin, having conquered this land a hundred years ago."

"I do not see how we can live in peace, Baalbek of Hattush, unless your great army withdraws beyond our borders and remains there."

Baalbek sighed. "Ah, Lord King; would that that was possible. Nothing would give me greater pleasure than to live in peace, but Anep-Aper of Amurru, Lebanon and Syria is my overlord, and his son and heir Samuqenu commands his army. He will not withdraw."

"Then I fail to see what we have to talk about," Seneferenre said.

"Can there be a compromise, Lord King? As matters stand, hundreds if not thousands of men must die, mothers and wives grieve, and the wealth of both nations get eaten up. Is there something that will give satisfaction to both sides?"

"You espouse an interesting way of waging war, King Baalbek," General Inkhare said. "If every man spoke like this, we would have no need of armies."

"Perhaps that would be a good thing," Merybaal said. "Certainly the Treasury would be in better shape."

Inkhare snorted. "Men will always find cause to fight."

"Precisely," Seneferenre agreed. "Greed will provide a motive where all else fails. Why else does Anep-Aper seek to invade our lands, King Baalbek?"

"He has long desired the well-watered lands of the Delta. In similar fashion he desired Hattush and my father found he could not resist him. Amurru sent men to our land, but allowed Hattush to keep its own king and govern its own affairs."

"You became a vassal king?" Seneferenre asked. "Where is the honour in that?"

"Not every nation can be foremost, and weaker nations must make any necessary accommodations in order to survive. Hattush has done that and we survive. Maybe the Delta kingdom could do likewise."

"Bend my knee to Anep-Aper?" Seneferenre asked softly.

"If it meant survival..."

"Never!" King Seneferenre leapt to his feet. "Merybaal, take this man out of here before I have him hanged."

Baalbek opened his mouth to speak, but Merybaal grasped his arm and pulled him away. "Nothing is served by you losing your life," he said.

The palace guard escorted him back to the palace entrance and handed him over to the soldiers. Merybaal went with him to ensure his safety and as the crowds had dispersed, walked back to the gate without interruption.

"I am sorry it did not work out," Merybaal said. "This war will mean ruination for the Delta and will hurt you as well, I think."

Baalbek nodded. "Avaris cannot stand against the might of Amurru, you know."

"I know, but what can any of us do?"

"Survive."

"I fear that will be easier for you than for me," Merybaal said with a wry smile. "When the city falls, there will be murder and rape, looting and burning. It is the way of war."

"I would have you avoid that."

"So would I, but how?"

Baalbek thought about that until they were almost at the gate.

"You still live in the same house in the city? The one built like a fortress?"

"Yes."

Baalbek stopped and squatted, drawing in the dust with his forefinger. "When the attack starts in earnest, take your family with you and lock yourself in your house..."

"I have my duty to perform. I can't go and hide."

"What is more important, your family or your duty to a king who cannot hope to win?"

Merybaal grimaced, but nodded.

"So, when the attack starts, lock you and your family in your house and paint the sign of the Hawk of Hattush on your doors and gates. It looks like this." Baalbek sketched a stylised hawk in the dust. "Can you remember that?" He scuffed out the drawing and started on toward the gate. "Paint that sign on your doors and gates and I will make sure the soldiers know to spare those under the protection of the Hawk."

Baalbek slipped out through the gate and made the long walk back to his lines, his shoulders hunched for the first part of his journey as he half expected an arrow in his back. It would not have surprised him if Seneferenre gave the orders for the archers to kill him. Nothing happened though and he reached the Amurran army and his own men. He made his way to Samuqenu's command tent to report on his attempt.

"So, are they going to surrender?" Samuqenu demanded.

"No, my lord, they are not."

"I didn't think so. It was a wasted effort."

"Not entirely. There are those within the city who favour a peaceful transfer of power. Treasurer Merybaal for one."

"Is he in a position to hand over the city? Does he have that much influence?"

"No, my lord."

"Then of what use is he?"

"It is men like that who will ensure the economy of the city and kingdom does not collapse when you conquer them. Such men are worth protecting."

"Then let us hope he survives the sack of the city."

"I have promised him his life, my lord," Baalbek said.

"How can you do that? Will you be everywhere when my men break down the gates and put the city to the torch? Will you stand in front of the swords and axes of my men and protect this man?"

"I have told him that if he shelters in his home and paints the Hawk of Hattush on his door, then none will enter there and he will be spared."

"You take a lot upon yourself, Baalbek of Hattush."

"I judged it to be in the interests of all involved, my lord."

Samuqenu regarded his subject king thoughtfully. "Because he is of your family, I will allow it, but I cannot answer for the enthusiasm of my soldiers. If, caught up in battle fever and with blood lust in their hearts, they break down his door and kill him; I will not punish them for it."

"If you make your wishes known in this regard, my lord, you will be obeyed."

"Then tell the generals, the officers, and any you deem fit, of your promise and of the sign of the Hawk."

"I have limited authority in your army, my lord, but if you issue the command, all will obey."

"You may tell everyone that this is my wish."

"You will not issue the command yourself?"

"No."

With that, Baalbek had to be content. He issued strict orders to all his own men and let it be known to the other commanders that those orders were in line with Samuqenu's wishes, but he got the feeling that they did not fully believe him.

"Protection of our family must rely on our own efforts," he told his son Aribaal. "When we breach the city, our men must head straight for Merybaal's house and put a guard on it."

Chapter 7

King Seneferenre watched Baalbek and Merybaal leave before turning to General Inkhare.

"I should have followed through on my threat and hanged him from the city walls. The arrogance of the man, suggesting I surrender from a position of strength. Has he already forgotten we beat them? Sent them running to the hills?"

The General frowned, stroking his chin with one hand. "The situation has changed, Lord King. The enemy has returned with renewed strength and our army was slaughtered in the north by their chariots."

"Remind me of our casualties there."

"Menenre survived, but lost eight hundred men. He returned several days later, his men scattered, with an almost incoherent description of the battle. It will be many days before he can resume his duties. If it had not been for Troop Commander Djedenre, who arrived on horseback only two days after the battle, we would know very little about it."

"How is it that he survived so opportunely? Is he a coward? Did he run?"

"No, Lord King," Inkhare said. "Menenre placed him on the far left wing, in soft ground near the river where their chariots were less effective. He was able to ride back with one of his Ribu scouts, to whom he owes his life."

"Not a coward then?"

"No, my lord."

"And the Ribu scout?"

Inkhare shrugged. "He did his duty and has returned whence he came, I suppose."

"A pity. I would have rewarded him." The king looked thoughtful. "Menenre is wounded and unfit for duty?"

"Yes, my lord King. For a month, at least."

"Give him duties within the city, where he will not be taxed unduly. Who should replace him?"

"I have several men worthy of being elevated in rank," Inkhare said confidently. "Atumre perhaps...or Khamose."

"No, I don't like either of those."

"There are others among my commanders."

"I thought Djedenre. He should be rewarded."

Inkhare held his annoyance in check. "He has little experience beyond being lucky enough to survive the destruction of Menenre's army."

"He always struck me as a competent officer."

Inkhare nodded, wondering what he could say to turn the king from Djedenre to one of his own candidates.

"He has only ever been a junior officer; not long raised to Troop Commander."

"I only mean to give him a command, not make him General."

"Even so. And he is the son of your Treasurer, whose loyalty is...perhaps suspect."

"I have no reason to suspect Merybaal," Seneferenre said. "And if Djedenre is indeed his son, then he will have every reason to defend Avaris diligently. Also, as you said yourself, General, he is lucky. I think we need luck on our side."

Inkhare had served the kings of the Delta long enough to know when he had lost a battle. 'For the time being' he told himself.

"Good, then that is settled," Seneferenre said. "Now, what do we do about the army outside our walls? Do we sit and wait them out or do we go on the offensive?"

"We cannot hope to outlast them, Lord King," Inkhare said. "We are limited to what we have stored in the city, while they can roam throughout the land, taking what they please."

"How long could we last?"

"We have all the water we need, and we can perhaps catch fish from the river, but we will run out of other food in six months, fuel a little longer. By then, rebellion by the city's populace will become a danger."

"You favour attacking the enemy then?" Seneferenre asked.

"I do."

"Despite being outnumbered?"

"Better than sitting in a trap waiting for the end. I say we gather every able-bodied man and attack the enemy. They won't be expecting us to come out, and if we hit them suddenly and hard, we might even kill this Samuqenu."

"What of their chariots? They destroyed Menenre's army."

"And where are they now? Not around here, though they may return. If our attack is to succeed, my lord King, we must strike immediately, before the chariots return."

Seneferenre considered the words of his General and agreed. They talked further on the aims of their attack, and who would lead each part of their army. There would be three parts to their attack, they decided-- a quick sortie to remove the guards in the enemy camp just on daybreak, the main attack by the bulk of their army, and a third group composed largely of townsfolk, whose duty would be to kill any of the wounded they found.

"That is work suited to the men of the city, the old men and youths. They may be untrained in arms, but they can handle a knife or a club to finish off the wounded.

"I will lead the greater part myself," Inkhare said, "as is my right as senior General. Djedenre can lead the sortie that kills the scouts, and perhaps one of my other officers might be permitted to lead the men of the city."

"I will lead the main army myself," Seneferenre said. "It is only right that their king leads them at such an important time."

Inkhare marvelled to himself that the king would lead the attack but there was nothing he could say that would dissuade him. Having been dispossessed of the main command, he took command of the sortie for himself and gave Djedenre the lower status command of the townsfolk. It fell to Inkhare to organise the attack, and he immediately started to bring together the best officers and give them command of small units, drilling them in the battle plan for dawn two days hence.

Djedenre, unaware that he had been touted as a possible leader for a more important position, accepted his command of the men of Avaris and organised them into small groups of ten or so individuals, setting them in competition with other groups by issuing a challenge for which group could kill more of the wounded enemy.

Merybaal came to see him the day before the attack and told him of Baalbek's idea to spare his Avaris relatives.

"There are other places around Avaris we could paint the Hawk sign, father. More people we could protect."

"That is true," Merybaal said, "but if too many signs are out, none may be observed. Baalbek has offered protection for his family only, and we should respect that. Can you get away and stay home while the attack takes place?"

"I have been given a command; it would be dishonourable to forsake my duty."

"I understand; but you will send your wife and son to my house, so that I might offer them protection?"

"Gladly, father. Tiamen too, as her husband Menkare will likely be fighting."

Watchers on the walls of Avaris kept a close eye on what happened within the invaders camp, noting down the positions of troops, of chariots, and where the command tents lay. Archers of both sides peppered each other with arrows, but neither side achieved anything worthwhile. It served more to keep their spirits up. One thing was observed that decided Seneferenre to attack the next day was the movement of the enemy chariots. There were always a few in evidence, and a day before a squadron had come in from the south. Now the chariots all sped out of camp, heading south, and this meant that those fearsome vehicles would not be present if the city men attacked their enemy. The enemy was plainly planning something as quantities of rough-hewn timber were in evidence, and huge piles of brushwood were dragged down from the hillsides.

"Tomorrow," the king decided. "You will lead your men out while it is still dark, Inkhare, and remove the guard posts quietly, without causing alarm. Then I will lead out the main army and overwhelm their camp before the alarm can be raised. In my wake you, Djedenre, will lead out the city men to finish off the wounded. With the gods on our side, how can we lose?"

"What about the chariots, Lord King?" Djedenre asked. "They are a devastating weapon."

"There are no chariots left in the camp," Inkhare said. "Watchers report they journeyed south from the city earlier today."

"They could come back."

"They won't travel at night. If there are none here at sunset, there won't be any at dawn."

With that, the commanders went to settle their men and make last minute adjustments to their targets for the next day. The sun sank in the west, with no sign of the enemy chariots and Djedenre for one breathed easier. Camp fires sprinkled the plains outside the city as if all the stars in the body of Nut had fallen to earth, and a muted hum arose from the camp as thousands of men prepared their evening meal. From within the city, too, arose the aromas of fresh baked bread and frying fish, as the men of the city fortified themselves with a good meal before the trials of the coming day.

Djedenre made sure his units of townsfolk were resting, and went round to his father's house. A stylised hawk was emblazoned on every door and gate of the sprawling building, and inside he found the courtyard and rooms swarming with people.

"Who are they all?" he asked his father.

"Servants, friends and their families." Merybaal shrugged. "How could I save my own family and consign others to possible death? I tried to keep my offer quiet...twenty of my closest friends...but word got out and there are over a hundred here, eating and drinking everything I have." He sighed. "Never mind, it's only for a day or so. You attack tomorrow and we either win and everything goes back to normal, or we lose and just maybe we've saved a few lives."

Djedenre took his leave of his family, and Neferit drew him aside, seeking a bit of privacy in one of the rooms.

"Take me with you," Neferit pleaded. "I was of use before. I can be again. I still have my Ribu clothes."

"I'll be on foot tomorrow, as will all my men," Djedenre replied. "Honestly, Nefer, it's no place for a woman. We'll be clubbing and stabbing wounded men."

"I can do that."

"Really? You've killed a man before?"

"No, but how hard can it be?"

"Harder than you'd think. Not just the act, but looking in a man's eyes as his life departs and knowing you have done it."

"I want to be a warrior. I...I should learn how to kill."

"Don't even think about it, sister. Stay here, and wait until we see the outcome of the battle. If it goes against us, the best thing you can do is protect our family."

"If you won't take me, I'll go by myself."

"Must I tell father to keep you locked up?"

Neferit glared at her brother. "No."

"You'll stay here? Until the battle is decided?"

"If that is your wish, brother."

"Good." Djedenre smiled and embraced his sister, and then took his leave of his family, hastening back to his command.

Neferit watched him go and made her own plans. No man, she told herself, whether father or brother was going to decide her fate.

Clouds scudded across the eastern skies before dawn, darkening the new day, and the gates of the city; both east and south lay in deep shadow. They creaked only slightly as they parted just enough to let men through. A hundred men slipped through, gathering themselves silently beneath the walls before setting off toward the dimly discerned enemy camp. Behind them, the gates yawned wider and disgorged hundreds more men. Each soldier of Avaris bore a weapon, either sword or axe, clothed in linen, and a small leather shield. Their feet were bare and they made no more than a whisper of sound as they formed up in their ranks, staring toward the enemy who still lay in darkness. The men had been warned against making any noise, and even the accidental bumping of weapon against shield was muffled by the cloth.

King Seneferenre dressed plainly, his *nemes* headdress and kilt only revealing a glimmer of paleness in the dark, and he whispered to his officers to stand ready. They stood staring toward the enemy as the dawn, masked by the clouds, gleamed softly over the eastern hills. Blackness became grey, and objects could be made out ten, twenty, fifty paces away. The air was chilly, and so still that the waiting men could hear snores in the enemy camp, a cough, a yawn, and the clink of metal as some guard shifted.

"What is Inkhare waiting for?" Seneferenre whispered. "Any longer and they'll see us."

Hardly had he spoken than there was a clash of arms to the east, shouts of alarm, and a ram's horn cut off abruptly. Cries arose from the sleeping camp and Seneferenre knew the time had come. He signed to the officers near him and they shouted the advance, the army of Avaris surging forward. Cloth was dropped from weapons and bronze gleamed in the gathering light. Seneferenre saw the enemy milling about in front of him, in confusion as Inkhare's men laid about them with axes, and with a shout of encouragement, led his men into battle.

The men of Avaris crashed into the disorganised invaders, hacking down with blades, bowling them over with blows of shield and shoulder, and trampling them with bare feet. Behind them, almost unnoticed, streamed men from the city under the command of Djedenre, and though the common men of Avaris--shopkeepers, street sweepers, potter, bakers and a dozen other trades--knew little of weapons, yet they could handle a knife or a club. Fallen men, many groaning from wounds that were not fatal, died where they lay and others, struggling to their feet were beaten down again and killed.

Horns sounded in the east, from the main body of the camp, and now hundreds of men joined the fray, striving to counter the surprise attack. Seneferenre rallied the men around him and fought back, stemming the advance of the invaders and now General Inkhare joined the struggling mass of men around the king. He grinned, his bloodied *khopesh* sword gleaming in the first rays of the sun that squeezed out from under the eastern clouds.

"We have them, my lord," he panted. "We took them completely by surprise."

"The day is not yet won, Inkhare," the king said grimly. "Keep your congratulations for when we have Samuqenu's head."

83

Daylight seeped over the battlefield, and the light brought with it the realisation of the scale of the victory that was almost within the grasp of King Seneferenre. The Amurran army was fragmented and the men fought individually, without any plan, though their actions displayed bravery and commitment. It would not be enough to stave off defeat from a numerically inferior foe though, for the men of Avaris fought for survival and were concentrated around their king and general.

The sun broke through the cloud cover, illuminating a battlefield strewn with the dead and wounded. Men fought in a surging tide back and forth across the ruins of the Amurran camp and the level ground nearer the walls, while the gates of the city stayed open allowing more and more citizens out to join Djedenre's army.

"One more push," Inkhare called across to King Seneferenre. "There is Samuqenu..." he pointed to a concentration of the enemy a hundred paces away. "Kill him and the battle is won."

Away from the clash of bronze, Djedenre's world was made up of the cries of the wounded, the bubbling screams of dying men, and the wet thudding of clubs impacting the fallen enemy. Women from the city had joined his men, tending to their own fallen, dragging them back toward the city where physicians and priests were starting to treat them. He became aware of a faint trembling in the ground beneath his feet, a distant rumble as if a storm was gathering in the hills. Looking up at the clouds, he wondered if a rare storm was going to break over the Delta. Rain was uncommon, but not unheard of, and he wondered what effect it would have on the battle. If it was heavy, the ground would become slippery, making combat more dangerous for friend and foe alike. The clouds above him did not look like rain clouds, yet the sound was getting louder, and now he could detect a direction in the low rumble--from the south where there were no clouds. There was a familiarity to the sound, something he had heard recently.

"Chariots," he muttered. He grabbed a young man and shoved him in the direction of the fighting. "Find the king...or General Inkhare. Tell him the chariots are coming."

The young man sped off, and Djedenre started shouting for his own men to stop what they were doing and go back to the city. They started to obey, and he saw too that the tenor of the main battle had changed. Avaris men were in retreat--evidently the king was now aware of the approach of enemy chariots. Djedenre had seen the devastation a chariot charge could create and urged his men onward.

"Back to the city," he yelled. "For your very lives."

He was nearly halfway back, his men streaming ahead of him and the main army fighting a rearguard action with the reinvigorated Amurran men, when the chariots came in sight. They surged out of the south on a broad front, sweeping between the position of the Amurran camp and the city walls. The thunder of their wheels and drumming hooves filled his ears, soon overlain by cries of terror and screams as the first of the chariots trampled the retreating men and women of Avaris. Djedenre saw he could not hope to get back to the shelter of the gates, nor was there safety to the east, amongst the advancing enemy, so with heart beating faster he waited to die.

He saw the chariots racing toward him, the wheeled vehicles bucking and leaping as they were bounced high by the bodies on the ground, and he saw his only chance of survival. Throwing himself to the ground, he squirmed into the shelter of a tumble of bodies, and moments later had the breath knocked out of him as a huge blow sent him tumbling. A hoof smashed into the ground near his head and another stunning blow made his vision fade.

King Seneferenre saw the surge of chariots and knew the battle was lost. It was as that troop commander had said--nothing could stand against such a charge. He was determined to keep fighting though, and knew that to do so, as many of his men as possible must survive.

"Take your men and head north," he told General Inkhare. "Keep to the rougher ground where the chariots cannot go and seek safety."

"I am not deserting my king," Inkhare said. "Let us make a stand here and sell our lives dearly."

"No, it would be a useless sacrifice. We have lost today, but if we survive we can fight again. Go north quickly, Inkhare. I shall head south and if the gods will it we shall meet again."

The move took Samuqenu and his army by surprise. They had herded the retreating Avaris men toward the open area where the chariots were raging, believing that they could leave the final destruction to them. Instead, the enemy suddenly split in two, running north and south in ground too broken up for chariots to follow easily. It took some minutes for new orders to reach the common soldiers and the men of Avaris opened up a small lead before they could start in pursuit.

"Let them go!" Samuqenu roared. "They are a rabble and flee for their lives. Search the fallen; I want the head of their king."

Baalbek held his men back from this purpose as he could see something else happening in the distance--something that was of far greater importance.

While the Amurran men obeyed their commander, the chariots had all but obliterated the fleeing Avaris men and had captured the open gates of the city, pouring down the wider streets. Baalbek ordered his Hattushi men forward, pouring across the bloody destruction of the chariot charge and into the city. The Amurran army followed his lead, casting aside their search for the fallen king, and hurrying to occupy the city that lay open and defenceless before them.

Telling his men to respect the integrity of any house bearing the mark of the Hawk, Baalbek took his son Aribaal and a squad of men, hurrying through the streets toward where he knew Merybaal's house lay. All around them rose shouts and screams as the battle for Avaris raged within the city, but they paid no attention to anyone who did not trouble them. They found the great house of Merybaal and saw that every door and gate bore the royal sigil of Hattush. The doors and gates were intact and Baalbek posted men on each to guard it, before leading his men toward the palace.

Avaris burned. Soldiers caught up in battle lust cut down men, women and children indiscriminately, setting fire to houses and shops, looting and raping. Samuqenu had given up on both the search of the dead and the pursuit of what he regarded as the shattered remnants of Seneferenre's army. Instead, he ordered his men into Avaris and allowed them free rein.

"They have fought well," he declared. "Let them enjoy themselves."

Baalbek found Samuqenu at the palace and implored him to stop the destruction of the city.

"Avaris belongs to you now, my lord. These men are destroying your property."

"We discussed this before," Samuqenu said. "I promised blood and fire if they opposed me, and I am a man of my word."

"Nobody doubts it, my lord, yet mercy is also a prized attribute. You have let the men have their way, but unless you stop them you will rule over no more than a smoking pile of rubble filled with corpses."

Samuqenu frowned as he considered Baalbek's words. "It may be as you say. Did you protect your relative? The Treasurer of Avaris?"

"I have men guarding his house. My lord...the city?"

"Oh, very well." He called in his senior officers and gave the orders for the fiery destruction to stop. "There is to be no more killing except in self-defence. Also, organise the surviving populace into teams to fetch water from the river and put out the fires."

"Thank you, my lord," Baalbek said. "Your mercy will earn praise from everyone."

It took two days for Samuqenu to subjugate Avaris and to control the fires and looting, but at last relative quiet settled over the city. Sections of the city were burnt out and others were badly damaged, with hundreds dead. The people themselves, long used to being ruled by foreigners, shrugged their shoulders, buried their dead, and set about getting on with the business of life under their new overlords.

Chapter 8

Tjaty Aya received the report from his agents in the north and idly opened it one morning while he broke his fast. He scanned the report, stopped chewing and read it again, then swallowed convulsively. A morsel of bread lodged in his throat and he felt panic as his breath locked up. He stumbled to his feet, knocking chair and dishes flying and servants rushed in. They stared aghast at Aya, leaning against the table with the blood rushing to his face, but one with a little more presence of mind dared to lay hands on his master. The servant thumped Aya between the shoulder blades and as the Tjaty fell forward he caught the edge of the table on his belly. Air rushed out of his lungs and a piece of bread shot out of his mouth. Aya drew a shuddering breath and sat down on the chair that another servant hastily set for him. Another servant poured water for him and he sipped, calming himself. Then, dismissing the servants, he picked up the letter from where it lay in a puddle of grease and wiped it with a cloth, reading it again.

He immediately sent word to General Neferhotep and to the king, suggesting that they meet to discuss important news from the north. Neferhotep, Commander Sewahenre, and his recently appointed aide Hori son of Harrubaal, all sent word that they could attend upon the king's pleasure, but it was half a day before King Monthhotep agreed to a meeting. He was feeling increasingly indisposed, complaining of pains within his bowel that were unrelieved by emetics and enemas administered by the court physician. On bad days, when it felt like a vulture ripped at his guts, Monthhotep relied on infusions of poppy in honeyed wine to relieve the gnawing pain. Now the king sat miserably on a padded throne in the small Audience Hall and looked morosely at his Tjaty and military commanders.

"You have news that could not wait until I felt better?" the king asked.

"Regrettably no, Son of Re," Aya said. "You remember those we call the *heqa khasut* invaded the north with a large army and a thousand chariots? Well..." he brandished the report, "my agents have sent me news of the battle outside Avaris...that's Hut-waret, Son of Re."

"Yes, yes, get on with it." Monthhotep grimaced and shifted on his throne, seeking an easement of the dull ache inside him.

"You put it very nicely, Son of Re, when you said we would get a measure of the enemy. That is exactly what we have." Aya caught the expression on his king's face and hurried on. "Seneferenre sent a thousand men north to intercept the enemy chariots and was utterly destroyed by them."

"How is that possible?" General Neferhotep demanded. "Chariots are just boxes on wheels useful for transporting soldiers to battle. Was the officer in charge incompetent?"

"It is as my father said," Hori murmured. "Chariots are a fearsome weapon."

"I'm inclined to think there must be some extenuating circumstances," Neferhotep said. "I cannot conceive how boxes on wheels can prevail against disciplined men."

"Perhaps Seneferenre's men were not disciplined," Commander Sewahenre said.

"We have no reason to think they were any more undisciplined than most soldiers," Hori said. "Given that likelihood, we must take this report seriously."

"Young men are prone to assuming the worst," General Neferhotep said. "Take no notice of Hori's words, Son of Re. Take it from a soldier experienced in the ways of war; chariots are just another tool in an army. No more dangerous than archers or axemen."

Commander Sewahenre nodded sagely. "I concur, Son of Re."

"What do you think, Tjaty?" Monthhotep asked. "You know the men who made this report. Are they exaggerating the danger?"

"I don't believe so, Son of Re." Aya saw the anger on Neferhotep's face and sought to placate the powerful General. "Whatever the truth of it, it would be foolish to accept or dismiss the report unverified. It points toward a danger, but we need more information before we can properly judge the veracity of my agents."

Monthhotep nodded. "We shall await further reports then."

"There is more to the report from the north, Son of Re. There was a pitched battle beneath the walls of Hut-waret in which the *heqa khasut* proved victorious. Hut-waret has been captured."

Monthhotep looked stunned, and the army men troubled.

"That is ill news indeed," Neferhotep said. "Are you certain?"

"There is no doubt," Aya replied. "Sections of the city were set ablaze and hundreds of its people killed. The pall of smoke hung above the city for two days."

"And King Seneferenre?" Hori asked.

"Governor Seneferenre," Monthhotep growled. "He is no more than a provincial governor."

Aya bowed, willing to go along with the fiction that the Kings in Ankh-Tawy liked to believe, that the foreign kings who had conquered and ruled the Delta were still governors within the old Double Kingdom of Kemet.

"Seneferenre appears to have escaped," the Tjaty said. "When the chariot charge broke his army, Seneferenre guided part of his surviving army into the desert to the southeast, and one of his generals, Inkhare I think his name is, took another part to the north. It is presumed they are still alive."

"What of Merybaal?" Hori asked. "Is there news of him?"

"Who?"

"The Treasurer."

"I have no news on who else survived. Why are you interested?"

"Merybaal is my brother by another mother," Hori said.

"Is he indeed?" Aya mused. "Well, if he survives we shall have to see what use we can make of that fact."

"In the meantime, what are we to make of the situation in the north?" Monthhotep asked. "You all assured me that the *heqa khasut* were no threat."

The king's ministers were silent for a few moments.

"In fairness, Son of Re, none of us were aware of the uh...capabilities of chariots."

"Agreed," said Aya, "but how do we counter them?"

"Do we need to?" Monthhotep asked. "Are we actually in any danger down here? The present self-proclaimed rulers of the Delta were satisfied with the rich farmlands of the north. Is there any reason to suppose these *heqa khasethet* will be any different?"

"I believe we can contain them," Neferhotep said.

Sewahenre nodded, but cautiously.

"With respect, the fighting style of the Delta is akin to ours," Hori said. "That is why they have never been able to conquer us, or we them. These invaders are something else. In a month or less they have overrun Hut-waret and routed the army of the Delta. That is down to their chariots. If we cannot find a way to neutralise them, they will conquer us too."

Neferhotep hissed his anger that a junior officer should espouse such defeatist ideas. "Do not listen to him, Son of Re," Sewahenre said.

"Exactly how would you contain the chariots, General?" Aya asked.

"That is something I must discuss with other military people," Neferhotep said.

"In other words, you don't know."

"Enough of this bickering," Monthhotep said. He shifted uncomfortably on his throne, his face displaying the pain he felt. "I want you, as my principal advisers, to tell me what we can do...what we must do."

"I shall gather the army and march them north to the border," Neferhotep declared. "A show of force will dissuade the invader from pushing south."

"How will we stand against them if they bring a thousand chariots south?" Hori asked. "A thousand chariots were enough to rout the army of the north."

"If you are so knowledgeable, then suggest a solution yourself," Sewahenre said.

Hori looked thoughtful, but said nothing.

"Perhaps we could put a barrier between us and the chariots," Aya said. "A trench or something that would provide an obstacle."

"They'd just drive around it," Hori said.

"The Great River then," the king said. "We are safe in Ankh-Tawy surely, for they would have to cross the river to get to us and we could sink their ships."

"A very good idea, Son of Re," Neferhotep said.

"They'd cross elsewhere and approach the city by land," Hori said.

"Must you be so negative?" Sewahenre asked. "If you can't suggest something useful, say nothing."

"No, Commander," Aya said. "We should hear all ideas. How else are we to discern what we can and cannot do? Somewhere among all these words is the solution to our problem."

"The only solution is force of arms," General Neferhotep said. "These chariots only succeeded because there were insufficient men to oppose them. A thousand men under their General Menenre were not enough, and even a few thousand men were not enough under the walls of Hut-waret because they were undisciplined. Give me five thousand disciplined men and I will undertake to break this chariot force of the invader."

"By the gods, you shall have them, Neferhotep," Monthhotep declared.

"Son of Re, we only have about three thousand near Ankh-Tawy," Aya said.

Monthhotep waved a hand negligently. "Find the others, Aya. I have promised Neferhotep he shall have them."

Aya grimaced. "Perhaps we could no longer pursue our aims of putting down rebels in the south, Son of Re. That would free up a thousand men."

"Then do so, and quickly."

"Yes, Son of Re."

"Good, then all is in hand. When Neferhotep has his men he will march them north and oppose the invader should he turn his eyes to the south. These chariots will prove to be nothing."

Monthhotep indicated that the meeting was at an end and everyone bowed as he left the room, one hand held against his belly and a look of intense discomfort on his face. General Neferhotep and Commander Sewahenre also left, already talking over their plans of what needed to be done. Both men ignored the junior officer Hori, so he stayed behind, waiting until he was alone with Aya.

"It won't work, you know," Hori said.

"Why not?"

"Because you are asking a man on foot to stand and face a wooden chariot drawn by two swift horses bearing down on him. One is enough to make any man quail, and they have a thousand...maybe more."

"There'll be five thousand men, though," Aya said, "if I can find them."

"It won't matter. Five thousand men armed with spears or bows might withstand a charge, but warfare is not a stationary pastime. As soon as they move, they break up into a mob, fighting individually. It's how we've always fought--how every army has always fought."

"Sewahenre was right; you are negative."

"I prefer to think of myself as realistic."

"Is there nothing we can do, then?"

"I can't think of anything, but maybe if we had a chariot to study, we might think of something."

Aya smiled tiredly. "If you are right, we'll have ample opportunity as soon as the *heqa khasut* get down here. Of course, it'll be too late then."

Hori left the Tjaty to his duties and went back to his home in Ankh-Tawy which he shared with his son Sekhem, and his sister Iset and her sons Bebi and Sobekhotep. Iset had risen high in the world, marrying Merkawre Sobekhotep, a man who had, for a brief time, become King of Kemet. With his passing, power had been grasped by other men and his young sons relegated to obscurity. Hori's sister had tried to stand up for their rights, but Harrubaal had dissuaded her, telling her that if she pushed their claim to the throne she would endanger them. Fear had overcome ambition, and now they all lived quietly, attracting little attention. They kept a small household, no more than ten servants at any one time, and Hori had a small room set aside where he could sit and think.

After spending some time with his son and nephews, he retired to his room with a jug of wine to consider the problem of the chariots. He drew pictures on a wax tablet he kept for such purposes, made notes and scraped them away, eventually throwing his stylus down in disgust.

"Do I owe Neferhotep an apology?" he muttered. "I was so sure I could find a solution, but maybe just standing up to them is the only way."

A knock came on his door, soft and hinting at hesitation. Hori got up and opened it, staring down at his young nephew Sobekhotep.

"What is it, 'Hotep? I'm a bit busy."

"Sorry, Uncle. I just wanted your help with my bow." Sobekhotep drew a curved piece of wood out from behind his back and held it out.

"I'm trying to make it more powerful, but no matter what I do, it doesn't work."

"I'm no archer, lad."

"You're in the army though. I thought you must know."

"A man cannot know every aspect of soldiering, 'Hotep. I know some things, but not how to make a bow."

"So what do I do?"

"Ah, 'Hotep, use your mind. If you don't know something, find out. Ask an archer for advice. If he's too busy, then see if you can examine a bow. Examine it to see how it's made..." Hori's voice trailed off as an idea niggled at the edges of his mind.

Sobekhotep waited for Hori to say something more, but when he just stood there, his eyes unfocused, he shuffled his feet and started edging away.

"Er...thank you, Uncle. I'll er...go and er...do that then."

Hori was unaware his nephew had left, his thoughts returning time and again to the last thing he had said.

"Examine it to see how it's made," he muttered. "That's exactly what we have to do. Examine a chariot; see how it's made and how we can fight against it."

Easier said than done, though, he thought. Still, the idea of going into enemy-held territory and examining a chariot excited him. He thought about it some more and then took his idea to Tjaty Aya.

"A daring idea," Aya said, "but how are you going to have the leisure to examine a chariot in enemy territory? And if you're looking for weaknesses, will you know what to look for?"

"Well, I wouldn't go alone."

"So you already know what sort of expert you'll need to find its weaknesses? No, I thought not." Aya clapped Hori on the shoulder in a friendly fashion. "You can't possibly go north and examine one, Hori; you'll have to capture one and bring it back to Ankh-Tawy where the job can be done thoroughly."

Chapter 9

The city of Avaris was in shock. Large parts of it lay in ruins and the men and women walked or stood around in a daze. Business had come to a standstill for a few days, but was starting to stir once more as everybody had to eat. The invaders were present in force, armed men roaming the streets or occupying positions of importance within the city, like the palace, the granaries, stables, docks and barracks. Some of the leading citizens had plucked up the courage to approach Samuqenu to complain about the treatment they had received during the occupation.

"Women have been raped and men killed when they tried to intervene," Mayor Muthotep said. "Businesses have been burnt and looted, and daily men are accosted on the streets and forced into labour."

"What do you expect?" Samuqenu demanded. "You opposed my army, and can hardly blame my men if they got a bit carried away."

Some of Muthotep's companions murmured something about compensation.

Samuqenu laughed. "Be thankful I do not tax you for the cost of the war. You are getting off lightly as it is, but if you want to make further complaint, do so to my father Anep-Aper, who will arrive in a few days. Be warned though, I have seen him impale men who complained to him."

Muthotep went pale. "No, no, my lord. We do not wish to make further complaint."

"Good. Now get out; I have work to do."

A temporary stockade had been erected outside the city walls to enclose hundreds of captured enemy soldiers, and it was here that Djedenre regained consciousness. He found himself lying on the bare ground, his head still ringing from the blows he had taken, his body bruised and aching. Raising himself up on one elbow, he groaned aloud as the pain in his head flared. A man who had been sitting nearby rose and forced his way through a knot of men, returning a few minutes later with a cup containing a little tepid water.

"Here, sir. They don't give us much water, but you'll need this."

Djedenre took the cup with a trembling hand and drained it thirstily. "Thank you. It's Min, isn't it?"

"Yes, sir. I saw you fall in the battle. They was going to kill you but I managed to convince them to take you prisoner instead."

"Where are we?"

Min told him. "It's crowded, sir. Many are wounded and we don't get treatment for our wounds. A bit of bread and a little water."

"What are their intentions? Do you know?"

Min shrugged. "No, sir, begging your pardon, but...well, would they feed us if they was just going to kill us?"

It was an interesting question, but not one Djedenre wanted to pursue. Instead, he lay back and closed his eyes, waiting for the throbbing in his head to subside. The sounds of the stockade intruded, wounded men moaning and a few screaming with the agony of untreated injuries. Despite it all, Djedenre managed to sleep and woke at dusk. His headache had receded to a dull ache, but his stomach growled with hunger and his mouth tasted foul. He got to his feet gingerly and looked around; Min was nowhere to be seen; though he recognised a few other men.

"Where are the guards?" he asked.

None of the men said anything, but one of them pointed. Djedenre murmured his thanks and eased his way through the throng to where a chained gate offered access to the outside. Armed guards looked round as he approached.

"No further," growled one, lowering his spear threateningly.

"What are your intentions toward us?" Djedenre asked.

"You'll find out soon enough."

"We have wounded here in need of treatment. Where are the physicians? And food and water? We need both."

One guard laughed, and the other grinned. "Why waste food on dead men?"

That seemed ominous, so Djedenre did not pursue it further. He made his way back to where he had been before, but found another man sitting there. Min turned up and found Djedenre a place. Hungry and thirsty, and filled with trepidation as to their fate, Djedenre lay awake most of the night.

Baalbek's men guarded Merybaal's house conscientiously for two days, only allowing the people inside to come out when things had settled down in the city. Merybaal went to the palace as soon as he could to introduce himself to Samuqenu and to offer his services as Treasurer.

"I have men of my own who can manage the Treasury of the Delta," Samuqenu said, "men I can trust. Why would I want to rely on a man whose loyalty lies elsewhere?"

"I understand your reluctance, my lord," Merybaal replied. "I have served the kings of the Delta for over forty years; over twenty kings. Some of those men were bitter enemies of the ones whom they succeeded, but none of them doubted me, because they knew that my loyalty lay with the kingdom rather than any one king. I know this kingdom like I know my wife's body, my lord, and I can keep it running smoothly, producing maximum profits. Nothing has changed except the king. I will serve you and King Anep-Aper as faithfully as I served Seneferenre and the kings who came before him."

Samuqenu took a bit of convincing, but he inclined toward trusting Merybaal because of things Baalbek had told him. He was not about to tell Merybaal that, however, so merely said that he would give him a trial period to prove his worth. Merybaal was well pleased with this and asked only some token that would offer protection for the women in his household as the city was still in a state of unrest. Samuqenu ordered a document drawn up to that effect and copies made.

"There is one other thing I must ask, my lord. My son Djedenre and son-in-law Menkare have not returned home. May I have your permission to search for them? My wife and daughters are worried."

"They may be dead," Samuqenu observed.

"Even so, my lord. If the worst has happened, I would give them a decent burial."

"You have my permission but make haste, for my men are gathering the enemy fallen together and will likely throw them in a common pit or in the river."

Merybaal returned to his house with the written passes and handed them out to his servants, bidding them search the battlefield and the dead for any sign of Djedenre and Menkare. They returned toward the end of the day, bringing the good news that neither man was to be counted among the dead, though the major-domo told his master that some corpses were unrecognisable and others may have fled the battle only to succumb later.

"There is one other place you could try, Lord Merybaal," the major-domo said. "A number of men were made captive and are imprisoned in a stockade under the walls. I went there, but the guards would not let me near."

Merybaal went immediately, though the hour was late. The guards were reluctant to let him near, but he persuaded one of them to send for a scribe who verified what the pass allowed. They then let him call through the wooden stockade and the chained gate. The prisoners told him that Djedenre was within and sent him word that his father was there. One of the men also had other news.

"I served under Commander Menkare, sir. He was with the king, last I saw of him."

"Thank you," Merybaal replied, "but what became of the king?"

"He went south, sir, with many men when he saw the battle was lost. He likely escaped as he was not pursued long, and if he did, then Commander Menkare likely did too."

Djedenre arrived, but the most father and son could do was clasp hands between the wooden palisades of the stockade. Tears were shed, and Merybaal assured his son that everyone in the family was safe.

"Save only Menkare. He went south with the king, I'm told, and may still live."

"Assure Tiamen he still lives, father. She will need to be strong in the coming days. Give my love to Rait and Amenre too."

Merybaal assured him he would. "I'll talk to Samuqenu again, and see if I can get you freed."

"There are more urgent concerns, father. Men are dying of their wounds here, and we have no food and little water. Nobody knows what is to happen to us."

"I'll see what I can do," Merybaal promised.

Samuqenu refused to do anything. "Another night will make no difference. If the wounded die, they will escape my judgement."

"What do you mean? They fought you honourably, my lord."

"I will make them an offer. Life or death."

Samuqenu would say no more, and neither would he allow Merybaal to return to the stockade. Instead, he had men escort him home and make sure he stayed there.

Merybaal gathered the family together and told them that Menkare had escaped south with the king, but that Djedenre was captive and facing Samuqenu's judgement in the morning.

"What does that mean, husband?" Amatia asked.

"I don't know, but I fear the worst."

"You must go to Samuqenu again and plead for our son's life."

"I was escorted home and I am unable to leave tonight. As soon as I can, I will go to him."

"I could go, father," Neferit said. "Samuqenu has forbidden you to stir from our home, but not me. Let me go to Samuqenu and plead with him, or at least let me go to the stockade and tell Djedenre what will happen."

"Silly girl," Amatia said.

"There is no way I would allow a daughter of mine to go out at night on the streets of Avaris, let alone to the stockade," Merybaal said. "Things have become dangerous for women lately."

"But father, I can..."

"No!" Merybaal snapped. "I will not allow it, and that is an end to it. Go to your room."

Neferit shrugged and excused herself. In the privacy of her room, she sat in thought and before long, reached a decision. She could not plead for her brother's life, and though she could warn him, of what use was that? The only useful thing she could do was free him...somehow. She thought about how she could achieve that and came to realise that the only way she could do it as a woman was to bribe the guards with her body, but she would die before she allowed any man to do that.

"There's only one way," she muttered. "I must become a man again and if it is necessary to free my brother, to kill."

She opened her clothes chest and lifted out several dresses, laying them on her bed. At the bottom of the chest lay the woollen Ribu garments she had worn before. Moving quickly, she stripped off and donned the garments, buckling a belt around her waist and slipping a dagger into it. She tucked her hair up under a loose cap. Lacking any reflective surface save a small polished copper plate in which to examine herself, she had to guess what she looked like, but thought she probably looked like a youth, albeit one dressed strangely. Waiting until the house settled into sleep, she left her room and crept quietly to one of the side gates and let herself out.

"Halt!" A man came out of the shadows with a levelled spear. He stared at the figure in woollen tunic and leggings. "Who in Baal's name are you?"

Neferit hesitated, sure her voice would come out as a squeak unless she calmed herself. She cleared her throat and tried to make her voice sound deeper. "I... I am Neterre, a prince of Ribu and guest of Lord Merybaal. How dare you accost me like that?"

The man peered closer, his eyes travelling over the strange garments and back to the beardless face.

"Ribu? Where's that?"

"In the west. Now are you going to let me pass or must I complain to Lord Merybaal?"

The man hesitated, and then lowered his spear. "Sorry, sir. Can't be too careful. Er...the city's a bit troubled at the moment. Shall I call for an escort?"

"No need." Neferit patted the dagger in her belt. "But thank you."

She strode away, trying to appear manly in her walk, and was grateful for the shadows that quickly hid her. The docks were to be avoided as a place where criminal elements often congregated at night, but neither did she want to go near the palace. Security would be tighter there and she was not sure if she could continue to pass herself off as a young man. Any hint that she was a woman could see her returned to her father's house or worse. It really was not fair, she thought to herself. *If I was a man, no-one would question my right to go where I pleased.*

The stockade where Djedenre was held was close to the eastern gate, she knew, but that gate and the southern one, being major routes in and out of the city, would be closely watched. She would have to go out through a lesser gate and work her way round under cover of darkness. The gates would be closed now, and guarded, so it would require some planning. Thinking it over, she decided that the easiest route of egress might be the horse gates. As Neferit, she was known in the horse lines, and although she was dressed in an outlandish fashion, she might still be able to convince someone to let her out.

The horse lines were almost deserted when she got there, a few lamps burning in the Overseer's rooms and a single one in the stables. Horses nickered softly when she let herself in, and she stopped for a minute to stroke Wenet. She wished she had brought her a treat, and that she could ride her out that night. It would be so much easier to flee the city on horseback. Neferit reminded herself why she was there--to free Djedenre--and the next day she could perhaps take her mare out again.

She crept to the broad gate whereby the horses were taken out but found soldiers on guard there. Had they been men she knew, she might have tried her luck, but they were Amurran, so she eased back into the shadows and tried the narrow gate instead. This hardly rated as a gate and had originally been a fissure in the mud brick city walls. Rather than fill it in, it had been turned into a narrow gate that was easily barred from within. The exterior land was rocky and did not favour an easy approach, so armed men were unlikely to approach from that direction. If they did, they would have to turn sideways and scrape through to enter, even if the stout wooden gate was unbarred. Now, a single elderly man was on guard, sitting nursing a fire pot and no doubt wishing he was tucked up in bed. Neferit eased closer and saw that she recognised the man. Without revealing herself, she spoke from the shadows.

"A cold night, Simen. You should be home with your wife."

"Eh?" The old man scrambled slowly to his feet and peered about him. "Who's that? Show yourself." When nobody stepped out of the shadows, he added, "Your voice is familiar, and I am old, no danger to you."

"I'm not supposed to be here, Simen. Will you betray me?" Neferit moved out of the shadows and came closer.

"Lady Neferit? But dressed in such a fashion? You look like a barbarian...and a man. What...?"

"Well you keep my secret, Simen?"

"Of course, my lady...er, what secret?"

"That I am here, dressed like this...and that I am leaving the city tonight."

"You're leaving...oh, you want to use this gate? Why, my lady? It's not safe now that we are overrun by Amurrans."

"I must, Simen. I have just heard that my brother Djedenre is held captive outside and I cannot rest until I know he is safe."

"Your father is a powerful man, my lady. Won't he know?"

"He knows, but he is content to wait for Samuqenu to spare him. I am not so trustful of Amurru."

Simen nodded. "Nor should you be, my lady, but surely your brother has friends who could help him? It is a heavy burden to thrust on the shoulders of a girl."

"You do not believe me strong enough, Simen...or dedicated enough?" She showed him her dagger. "I will use it if I must."

Simen shook his head. "In my day, women were not so forthright. Well, you will do as you must do. I suppose you want me to open the gate and not tell anyone you passed through?"

"Thank you, Simen. That is exactly what I must do."

The old man grumbled a bit more about what the world was coming to when girls dressed as barbarian men and wandered around at night, but he unbarred the narrow gate and opened it enough for her to slip through. As she disappeared into the shadows, he asked once more if she would be safe.

"I'd feel terrible if anything happened to you, my lady."

"I'll be alright, Simen, but thank you for your concern."

Simen waited a few moments more, but there was no further sound from the darkness of the passage through the wall, so he sighed and closed the gate again, barring it securely before returning to the warmth of his fire pot.

Neferit moved along the outside of the city wall, hugging the shadows and moving cautiously. She had no idea whether there were patrols out there, and had no desire to be accosted by one. It proved to be relatively quiet, though she heard howling in the darkness that made the hairs on her arms prickle with apprehension. She told herself it was only jackals or wolves, no doubt drawn to the stench of blood and dead bodies on the battlefield.

"They won't bother with me," she told herself, trying to bolster her courage. "And I have my dagger if they do."

Neferit worked her way around the city and smelled the prisoner's stockade before she saw it. Men had been held captive for over two days and they lay in their filth, dead and dying among the living and the miasma of their suffering spread out like a cloud from their prison. Her eyes were used to the darkness by the time she got there and the starlight enabled her to see the tall stakes that had been rammed into the earth, roofed over with others, and bound by ropes and copper bands. There were gaps between the palings and she could see and hear bodies on the other side. She moved closer and was about to call out softly when she heard voices and the clink of metal from her left.

Guards, she thought, and cowered into the shadows at the base of the stockade wall. Of course there will be patrols, else the prisoners might escape.

Two soldiers hove into view, walking casually, obviously regarding their job as routine. They did not even glance at Neferit, huddled by the wall, and went their way. She went back to the gap and whispered.

"I am looking for Djedenre. Is he there?"

Silence greeted her, and then, just as she readied herself to risk a louder call, a man stirred and replied, "Who is that?"

"I am...a friend of Djedenre." Neferit decided to maintain her Neterre persona. "Is he there? Can you bring him to me?"

There was a prolonged silence, broken only by murmurings and surreptitious movement and then, "I am here. Who is that?"

"Djedenre, is that you?"

"Yes, who is...Neferit?"

"Neterre. I am Neterre."

"Of course. It is good to hear your voice. How are mother and father?"

"They are well, but I fear for your safety. Samuqenu has hinted that he will deal severely with the captured soldiers of Avaris."

"That is with the gods."

"I thought the gods might like a little help." Neferit took out her dagger and started sawing at the ropes that bound the palings together.

As each strand parted, hands from within the stockade pulled at the rope, tugged on the wood, easing a small hole in the wall. Djedenre took the dagger and worked at ropes out of Neferit's reach, and then with a screech of wood, the palings parted.

"Quickly now," Djedenre hissed. "Out for your lives."

To Neferit's dismay, Djedenre stood back and allowed others to escape, and several men squeezed through and ran for the covering darkness. At last, he came out himself and stood with another man, helping some of the wounded through the opening.

"Hurry, brother, there are guards patrolling out here."

"Brother?" queried the man with Djedenre. "I did not know you had a brother."

"A brother in spirit, Min. Neterre the Ribu."

"We are in your debt, Neterre," Min said.

"Then repay me by getting away...both of you."

They started away into the darkness, but shouts arose, and running men with flaring torches bore down on them. Separated from her brother, Neferit ran back in the direction she had come, hoping and praying that her brother would evade the pursuers. She made it to the city wall and edged her way round, hoping to find the narrow gate again. If Simen was still there, he might open it for her. Footsteps sounded behind her and someone shouted in Amurran. She heard the anger in the voice and knelt, stretching her arms out in surrender; but she was hurled to the ground and she felt cold bronze at her throat.

"Who in the name of all the gods is this?"

A torch flared and Neferit looked up at three men holding spears and swords.

"What manner of man is this?" one of them asked. "A youth? Some outlander by the look of it. Do we kill him or take him back?"

"I am Neterre," Neferit said. "I am a prince of Ribu."

"A prince, eh? Might be worth gold alive then."

The men agreed they should take their captive to the stockade, evidently thinking he had escaped from there. Neferit was thrust into the prison, and pushed her way through the mass of dead and dying men to sit with the able-bodied ones against one of the walls. It was dark, and she could not be certain, but it seemed to her that Djedenre and his friend Min had not been recaptured.

What do I do now? she asked herself. I wanted to free Djedenre and did that, but now I am the captive. What will happen tomorrow? Must I reveal myself and plead for mercy from Samuqenu?

The more she thought about it, the more she realised the derision in which she would be held. Just spending the night in a cage with a hundred or so men would tarnish her status in the eyes of Avaris.

"As if I care about that," she muttered, though her face burned at the thought that the city might blame her parents for her decisions.

Dawn came soon enough, though sleep had eluded her. With the increasing daylight, she saw the squalor of her surroundings, and the corpses of prisoners who had died of their wounds. They were not fed, though a little water was made available. Neferit drank nothing, not wanting to stress her bladder further. It was starting to signal its presence and she knew answering its call would reveal her gender.

Guards threw open the stockade gates and ushered the prisoners still capable of walking out onto the plain beneath the city walls. The dead were dragged away, and any wounded who were still alive and could not stand were dispatched where they lay. Neferit and the other living were lined up with many guards around them, and they waited in the growing heat. Halfway through the morning, as men started to stagger from the heat and weakness, a chariot emerged from the eastern gate, bearing Samuqenu.

Despite her weariness and anxiety, she stared at the chariot, admiring the way the charioteer controlled the two high-spirited horses and the immobility of the Amurran Commander despite the movement of the chariot.

"Now that is a weapon of war," she murmured.

"You obviously didn't face the charge," muttered a man next to her. "I soiled myself when I saw them bearing down on us."

One of the guards silenced the man with the butt of his spear, and Samuqenu started to talk.

"Men of Avaris, you have lost the battle, you will lose the war, for nothing can stop my army, but you have a choice before you--will you lose your lives as well in a hopeless cause? You should have died in battle but you did not, and my father Anep-Aper intends to be merciful as he will rule Avaris and the whole of Kemet. He says that any man who will foreswear his allegiance to King Seneferenre and join my army will be rewarded with his life and the opportunity to serve my father and me."

The men shuffled their feet and looked at one another. "And if we won't?" one man called out.

"Then I have no use for you. It is your choice, men of Avaris. How many of you feel like this? How many refuse to join my army?"

About a quarter of the prisoners raised their fists in the air, and when they saw so many others refusing to stand by Seneferenre, they muttered threats and imprecations against them. Others reluctantly raised their fists.

Samuqenu shrugged. "Come out then. Stand apart from your fellows."

They stepped out cautiously, sneering at their companions who stayed behind. Neferit knew that if Djedenre had still been there, he would have refused to betray his king, and she wondered if she should be similarly principled. As a woman, she had never sworn allegiance to anyone as it was generally assumed that her father's word encompassed everyone in his household. It annoyed her that any man should speak for her and she wondered if this was her opportunity to declare her independence.

So Neferit hesitated and her hesitation saved her life. Samuqenu gave a signal and the guards surrounded the men who had refused to join his army and butchered them. It was over so quickly, Neferit could only gasp in horror.

"The same fate awaits any man who swears allegiance to me and goes back on their word," Samuqenu said. He waited in silence for several minutes, letting the full import of his words sink in. "You will pass before my officers and let them know your particular skill or past experience. They will assign you to units in my army. Stay loyal and work hard and who knows to what heights you might rise."

Neferit lined up with the other prisoners, her eyes avoiding the blood-soaked corpses of the men who had so recently been standing with her. When her time came, she identified herself once more as Prince Neterre of the Ribu. The officer stared at the beardless face and shook his head.

"What skill or experience can you bring, Neterre of Ribu? You are obviously too young to have learned anything."

"You are wrong, sir," Neferit said. "I have skill with horses, having been with them from an early age."

"Horses, eh? That could be useful. Very well, you are assigned to the chariot squadrons. Take this token to Semtak, Captain of Chariotry, and he will assign you your duties."

Neferit hardly noticed the scrap of pottery incised with Amurran lettering that was thrust at her by the army scribe as her heart had leapt within her breast at the news. She was going to join the chariot squadrons, the most beautiful and terrifying weapon of war she had ever seen.

Chapter 10

King Seneferenre took nearly a thousand men and slipped southward, away from Avaris, and keeping to the rocky ground of the eastern foothills. He was very conscious that the morale of his men was low, and as the men kept up a steady pace, he moved up and down the column, talking to them and trying to keep their spirits up.

"You are brave men, one and all. No-one doubts your courage, your loyalty, your determination, but I am not willing to throw your lives away on a pointless last stand against a more numerous enemy. We will fight again, I promise you, and we will prevail. You are men of Avaris and each of you is worth three of Amurru. We would have won today if it had not been for their chariots. I know, you are asking how we can stand against them, but I know how we can do it. All we need is a little time to prepare."

If the men did not cheer the king's words, neither did they lose all heart, but under the urgings of their officers they pulled clear of all pursuit, and as darkness fell, started angling back toward the river. Back on the edge of the farmlands of the Delta, they came to the broad road that connected Avaris with Iunu and beyond. Created over half a century before, it was still in good condition, being repaired as necessary by work crews sent out by local towns and villages. Part of the tax they paid each year was in labour for such works.

"We make for Iunu," Seneferenre told his officers. "We can make good time on the road and Iunu has walls we can fortify."

His thousand men streamed south along the road, eager to reach the perceived safety of the holy city. Neferkhare, Mayor of Iunu, was the son of Menneferkhare, and his family had ruled Iunu in all but name for nearly a hundred years. A few days before, chariots had appeared on the road leading to his city and he thought that war had come to him. They had turned back though, disappearing into the north in a cloud of dust, and now here was the king and a battered remnant of his army marching to the gates of Iunu.

Neferkhare brought out his councillors, the leading men of the city, to greet the king at the head of his army. He was all agog to find out who the chariots had been and why the king's army showed such signs of damage. Seneferenre took up residence in the Mayor's palace and had his officers look after the needs of his men, drawing upon the city's granaries. The city treasurer, Pitenre, opened up the books, revealing that a bad harvest had depleted the food stocks and that short rations would have to be instituted very shortly.

"It...er, all depends on how long you envisage your army staying within the walls of Iunu, Mighty King."

"King Seneferenre will stay as long as he needs to stay, Pitenre," Mayor Neferkhare said. "It is our duty to make sure he has everything we need."

"Of course," Pitenre said. "I only meant that everyone will be hungry within a month, and starving not long thereafter."

"Then we must seek a quick victory," Seneferenre said. "Send out men to find General Inkhare. He went north with another thousand men. Bid him bring them down to Iunu, for I have need of them."

General Inkhare had not fared as well as his king. Heading north from Avaris, he had encountered many more of the enemy still streaming down from the hills and had to fight a running battle to win clear of the city environs. He won free into the open land in the north, and the losses he sustained in that trial were partly made up by the scattered survivors of the chariot charge that had devastated Menenre's army days before. Slowed by many wounded men, Inkhare stopped on the site of that massacre to rest his men and debate what he was to do. He called his two most senior officers, Nebdjedre and Awibkhare, and put the problem to them.

"King Seneferenre ordered me to flee north with my men and this I have done. I have brought eight hundred men, many of them wounded, to temporary safety, but the question is what do I do next?"

"The king fled south, didn't he?" Awibkhare asked. "Where would he go?"

"Iunu would be the logical choice--if the enemy has not reached it first."

"Then surely he meant for us to join him there."

"Of course," Inkhare replied, "but how? Avaris and the Amurran army lie between us. It would be death to attempt that passage."

"If we cannot go directly there, then we must go around," Nebdjedre said. "The east is blocked by Amurru, so we cannot go by that route."

"And the west by the river, I know," Inkhare said. "I asked for your advice in the hope you had something to offer."

"If we had boats, we could sail past Avaris on the river," Awibkhare said.

"But we don't."

"What, none? There are fishermen around here, aren't there?"

"Yes, but only a score or less. There are no villages nearby. We would need two hundred boats at least."

"Then we must seek another solution," Inkhare said.

"Not necessarily," Awibkhare said. "We could sail across the river and then march south to Iunu. A score of boats could ferry our little army to the far bank without too much trouble."

It proved a little harder than that as fishermen resented their boats being used for such a long period of time when they could more usefully be used for fishing. They had a much greater mobility than men confined to the riverbank and Inkhare's men could only find twelve boats. The officers immediately started shipping men across the river and by the end of the day had moved some two hundred men across. It took them another day and a half to complete the process.

Once across, Inkhare organised his men into a column and, with the able-bodied carrying the wounded on litters, marched them south through the pastures and farmland of the delta. The ground was soft beneath their feet, the grass lush, and their pace was slow, with many breaks for rest. On one of these breaks, as men went to get water from the river, they saw enemy soldiers on the eastern bank, and Inkhare hurriedly moved his men away from the river.

"There are many boats in Avaris, and if the enemy has captured the city, they will have access to them all. If they suspect we are over here, it will be a simple matter for them to send an army across to destroy us."

"We could fight them off from dry land," Nebdjedre said. "We would have the advantage and could kill them as they waded ashore."

"And how long before they sent fleets north and south, or sent an army in darkness?" Inkhare asked. "Better that they don't know we are here."

They marched away from the river for a time before turning south again. The land was inhabited and several herdsmen and many farmers saw the column of men. It was possible that any one of them might carry news of their presence to the invader, but Inkhare thought not. First, they would have to be aware of the presence of the Amurran army and second, he doubted the common people cared who their master was. As long as the ruling classes did not prey too heavily on them, it was safer just to let them go their way and attend to the daily task of survival. Either way, they were not betrayed in the five days it took them to march south far enough to be close to where Iunu stood. Inkhare sent scouts eastward to ascertain where they were and to look out for the enemy. They were still a little north of where they wanted to be, but the scouts were met by others sent out by King Seneferenre. Two days later, Inkhare's army was across the river from Iunu.

Many boats put out from the city to ferry Inkhare's army across, and the general was one of the first across, leaving the transport of the rest of the men in the charge of his senior officers. Once in Iunu, Inkhare reported immediately to the king, informing him of the numbers of men he had, and their capabilities.

"You have done well," Seneferenre said. "Though eight hundred extra men will strain the city's resources."

"It will not be for long, Lord King. Together, we shall retake Avaris and put Amurru to flight."

The king said nothing. He applauded Inkhare's fervour but knew the task was greater than the both of them. The damage wrought by the chariot squadrons would be too great for open warfare. Something else was needed and for now he had no idea what that might be.

Inkhare prattled on for a few minutes, seemingly unaware of his king's thoughts, and then said, "I suppose the question is whether we feel strong enough to march on Avaris or whether we should remain here in Iunu and let the enemy come to us."

"Neither is feasible in the face of their chariotry," Seneferenre said.

Inkhare frowned at the seeming pessimism of his monarch. "We have to do something, Lord King."

Seneferenre led his General to the palace window that looked to the north, and pointed to the broad road and the level ground on either side of it.

"As soon as we set foot upon it, we are vulnerable to their chariots. We have nothing to counter them. They would sweep over us and cut us down as they did Menenre's men."

"There must be a way to contain the chariots. Even destroy them."

"Perhaps," Seneferenre said, "but for now we have nothing."

"So what do we do, Lord King?"

"The only thing we can do is defend Iunu."

"I hear you, Lord King, but if we could not defend Avaris, how can we defend Iunu? We have far fewer men and Iunu's walls are not built to repel a determined enemy."

"What else can we do? Surrender?"

"Never."

They ferried the rest of Inkhare's men across the river and set the city's priests and physicians to work healing as many as they could and giving a decent burial to those beyond earthly help. Refugees from the north drifted into Iunu over those days, including Djedenre. He reported to the king as soon as had cleaned himself up enough to be presentable.

"You are welcome indeed, Djedenre," Seneferenre said. "We can use every man and every competent officer."

"Thank you, my lord. I was accompanied by Min, a junior officer, and by six other men we found on our way."

"How did you escape?" Inkhare asked. "The city men were right in the path of the chariot charge."

Djedenre nodded, remembering. "I fell, and it seems I was protected by dead men for the hooves and the wheels passed over, leaving me untouched. I was captured but my sister Neferit freed me and Min."

"Your sister? Do even the women of Avaris fight against the invader?" The king smiled. "How can we lose?"

"She has the heart of a lion, my lord. She would willingly fight within your army were she allowed."

Seneferenre chuckled. "I commend her spirit, but fighting should be left to men, who have a knack for it. Let her remain at home and rear sons for my army."

Djedenre bowed to the king's will, though he had no doubt Neferit would have words to utter if she was present.

Talk turned to more general matters and the king and General quizzed Djedenre on what he had seen in the aftermath of the battle. He confirmed that the city had in fact fallen, and told them that although smoke had risen from fires within the walls, the destruction had not encompassed the whole city.

"It seems that Samuqenu wishes to keep Avaris intact, my lord."

Inkhare nodded. "He keeps it safe for the king's return."

"So tell me, Djedenre, as you have survived two chariot charges now--in the north under Menenre, and beneath the city walls--how are they to be overcome?"

"I was lucky on both occasions, my lord. In the north I ran away. My sist...my aide Neterre bore me on his horse, and beneath Avaris I was as a dead man and the chariots passed over me."

"Luck in warfare is not to be taken lightly," Inkhare observed.

"No, indeed," the king agreed. "Yours is a tale that will inspire the men, Djedenre. I gave you a command once before; this time I will make you a General."

Inkhare winced but said nothing. He too was aware of the effect of a 'Lucky General' on the morale of the men.

"You did not answer my question, Djedenre," Seneferenre said. "How can the chariots be overcome?"

Djedenre considered his answer. A simple denial, though honest, would not satisfy the king. "They are a fearsome weapon, my lord, but I have observed two limitations to their use. The first is that they cannot travel easily on soft ground as their wheels sink. The second is that they prefer not to travel over rocky ground. I suspect it is because the wheels would be damaged."

"Interesting observations," Inkhare said. "How do they help us?"

"If we were to fight in the stony desert or the well-watered lands of the delta, their advantage would be negated."

"They still enjoy a numerical advantage in men."

"Yes."

"So even in the stony desert or farmland they could still overwhelm us, even without the chariots."

"It would appear so," Djedenre conceded.

"So your astute observations are meaningless," Inkhare said with a hint of triumph.

Seneferenre shook his head glumly. "How can we retake Avaris?"

Djedenre looked at Inkhare, but the senior General just shrugged, leaving it to him to answer the king.

"I don't think we can, my lord, at least not yet. As you and General Inkhare have noted, we cannot yet defeat their chariots and we are outnumbered by their soldiers."

"You admit defeat?" Inkhare asked.

"Never that while I have life," Djedenre replied, "but we must be realistic. We cannot face a chariot charge, and neither can we face a frontal assault by their army."

"That doesn't leave much."

"No." Djedenre hesitated. "There is a way, but it might seem less than honourable. My grandfather Harrubaal fought the numerically superior Hattushi when they invaded half a hundred years ago. He kept a small, mobile force that struck at the enemy under cover of darkness and fled as soon as they tried to strike back. By all accounts, he was very successful."

"As you say, not an honourable way of waging war," Inkhare said.

"How would you translate that into the present circumstances?" Seneferenre asked.

"My lord, you cannot seriously be considering such a thing?" Inkhare protested.

"I will consider anything that defeats the enemy. What do you say, Djedenre?"

"My lord, Iunu is indefensible. The walls would stop the chariots but not their army. If you stay here you risk losing everything. Rather than do that, you should strip Iunu of its fighting men and disappear into the delta lowlands. Split into groups of no more than five hundred men and harass the enemy."

"Do that and they will just ignore us," Inkhare said. "Then you have these invaders occupying every notable city in the kingdom, reaping the benefits, and our king reduced to a voice crying in the wilderness."

"They cannot ignore us, General," Djedenre said. "While the king lives and fights, they cannot rest easy, and every day we will wear them down by our attacks."

"Pin-pricks," Inkhare scoffed.

"But pin-pricks by the hundred, by the thousand. And if we are troublesome enough, they will have to come after us, into land where the chariot is useless. Then if we can raise the men of the countryside, we can fall upon them and destroy them."

The king dismissed both his Generals and considered his options. He speedily realised that it was only a matter of time before Iunu was attacked and even if they repulsed the invaders, further attacks would follow, weakening them every time. Accordingly, he gave the command to evacuate the city. Inkhare could not disobey his king, but he gave a convincing argument for concentrating their men and moving south along the road rather than tramping into the farmland.

Seneferenre found an extra five hundred men by stripping Iunu and surrounding villages of every able-bodied man, and started shipping them across the river. It took several days as the army would need essential provisions that might be hard to glean from farms--metals, leather, and wood. As the last of the farmland force left Iunu, Inkhare marched a thousand men out of the city and marched them slowly southward. Djedenre was not sure what he hoped to achieve by this, except drawing the enemy after him. The king was willing to let him do it though, so Djedenre could not object. The only thing he could do was to send the fleet of boats they had used to cross the river, to shadow Inkhare's army. If the worst occurred, they could perhaps evacuate his men.

Samuqenu greeted his father Anep-Aper into Avaris with great ceremony, honouring him as the king who had conquered the Delta Kingdom. The fact that only the city of Avaris had been conquered was overlooked. In private, though, Anep-Aper made it quite clear to his son that the task he had been set was incomplete.

"You will complete the conquest of the northern kingdom by the year's end."

Samuqenu knew better than to expect praise from his father for taking Avaris. Praise engendered complacency, and the King of Amurru, Lebanon and Syria kept his sons vying against each other for the royal favour.

"Seneferenre has gone to ground in Iunu," he told his father. "He and his generals fled from Avaris with remnants of his army. It makes no difference. My men will take Iunu if he stays behind its walls, and the chariots will destroy him if he ventures out."

"Then make sure of him. The longer he remains at large, the more incompetent you look. Don't make me change my mind about making you heir."

Samuqenu bowed and kept his expression non-committal. He knew it was unlikely his father would change his mind, but it would be foolish to take the risk. Only a little longer, he thought. His father was old and might be gathered to his ancestors at any time. Then he would go through any relatives who disputed his right to rule like a summer storm in the wheat fields.

He took his leave of his father and went to organise the final campaign that would destroy Seneferenre once and for all. Leaving a token force in Avaris, he sent General Anati and his chariot squadrons down the great road toward Iunu, with five thousand men following on foot. Samuqenu went with his army, fully prepared for a hard battle to take Iunu, for he was determined to see the final victory for himself. It surprised him that the gates of Iunu stood open, the mayor and principal priests waiting nervously for his arrival.

"Where is Seneferenre?" he demanded.

"Gone, Great Lord," Mayor Neferkhare said.

"Gone where?"

"Over the river, Great Lord...except General Inkhare. He has gone south with a thousand men."

Samuqenu sent Anati onward with the task of bringing him the head of Inkhare. The chariot squadrons swept around the city and raced south on the broad firm road. The Amurran heir knew that the road owed its existence to the efforts of Arimawat, one time ruler of Hattush, and to his son Harrubaal. Back when his father Anep-Aper had been a young man, the Hattushi had fled to the south and worked secretly for Amurru, creating roads that would aid the invasion when it eventually happened. The preparations had taken longer than anticipated, and though neither father nor son saw the fruit of their labours, they had been rewarded. And now the Delta would fall in part because of their work. Samuqenu would never publicly acknowledge the Hattushi, but he offered up a private prayer of thanks anyway.

He sent his men in to occupy the city but gave strict orders that the city was not to be damaged or the populace harassed. Then he walked down to the edge of the river and stared across at reed beds and pasture flattened and trampled where the army had crossed. There was no sign of them now, nor any sign of the boats that had taken them across. Only a few fishing boats remained in the city. He would have to find more if he was to cross the river and bring Seneferenre to account.

General Anati gloried in the chase. His chariot squadrons swept around Iunu and reconnected with the Great Road before pounding southward in pursuit of Inkhare and his army. He was completely confident that he could obliterate these men in the same way he had the army in the north and around Avaris. Anati was an ambitious man and was aware that his chariots were his king's premiere weapon. He dreamed of the heights he might achieve if he continued to be the one who won battles. The throne itself was not an impossibility.

From his position in the leading chariot, Anati looked ahead and saw the dust churned up by the enemy and shortly thereafter saw the men beneath it. He tapped his charioteer on the arm and pointed. The charioteer had already seen them but nodded.

"Do we slow in preparation, my lord?"

"No. Drive straight into their rear. I shall destroy them right here."

Anati turned and instructed the signaller standing behind him in the three-man chariot to signal his intent to the following chariots. He took out two brightly coloured flags and whipped them into a series of positions that conveyed his master's wishes. The following chariots spread out over the width of the road and the hard ground to either side and bore down on the enemy.

Now the enemy seemed to glimpse them for the first time. They paused, then turned and ranged out on either side of the road, but more toward the river.

Anati grinned and yelled, "Will they never learn that men cannot face a chariot charge?"

A cloud of arrows rose into the air, seemed to hover high above, and plunged toward the on-rushing chariots. Cries arose around him as arrows found their mark and he saw one horse stumble and bring its chariot to ruin, creating a swirl in the ranks as other drivers sought to avoid destruction. Then they were past the fall of arrows, closing rapidly with the ranks of the enemy, but some fifty paces from the ranks a shadow marred the surface of the road, from edge to edge. It was not until Anati's chariot was almost upon it that he saw what it was. A trench had been dug, narrow and shallow, but an impediment to wheeled vehicles nonetheless. It was too late to stop or avoid it, so all Anati could do was hold tight.

The horses leapt the gap easily enough, but the weight of the chariot pulled them back. The wheels plunged into the trench and met the far embankment with a crash that shook Anati to the bone. His teeth ripped into his lips and he spat blood as the chariot lifted into the air before crashing down again. The signaller uttered a forlorn cry and fell from the chariot, his body disappearing amidst the pounding hooves and wheels of the following vehicles.

Then they were past and though the line of chariots was in disarray, there were enough left and they crashed into the enemy line. Faces looked up at him, eyes wide and mouths gaping in terror before falling beneath the chariot charge. The crush of men slowed the chariots, but their impetus was too great to halt and they burst through the lines into open road beyond.

Anati resorted to hand signals and shouting to turn his chariots and there were several minutes of confusion before they were turned and facing the enemy once more; but now they were streaming away from the road toward the pastures along the river. He could see white sails on the water now as scores of little boats converged on the place where the enemy fled to.

"This was planned," Anati said. "They set a trap for my chariots."

The Amurru chariots swung toward the river and plunged off the road, hurrying after the fleeing men, rapidly overhauling them. They passed the wreckage of other chariots and wounded men and screaming horses; and their own archers peppered the men of the Delta. But then they reached the soft land bordering the river and the chariot wheels sank into the soil, slowing them. The enemy turned to face them, the line bristling with spears and swords, and the chariots lacked the speed to punch through them. Amurru and Avaris stood paces apart, each trying to inflict damage on the other with spears and arrows, while on the river the host of little boats picked men up and ferried them over the water before returning for more.

Anati ground his teeth when he saw the enemy getting away, but there was little he could do. He ordered his men to dismount and carry the fight to the enemy on foot, while the chariots, relieved of some of their burden, were more mobile. Together, they pushed the enemy back, but they fought more fiercely as their numbers dwindled. At the last, when no more than a hundred or so of Inkhare's men remained, and the chariots and men of Anati's squadrons pressed them hard, the enemy threw down their weapons and threw themselves into the water. Most struck out for nearby boats, clinging to the sides, but others tried for the far bank. Blood stained the water, though, and swirls in the water betrayed the presence of crocodiles.

Anati watched in fascination as these great scaly beasts, which he had never seen before, closed on their struggling victims, cutting off their terrified cries by dragging them underwater. Before long, the enemy had made it to the far side and, lacking boats, Anati could not follow. Instead, he turned back to count the cost of the battle.

He had his men salvage what they could from the wreckage of the score of chariots that had foundered on the trench across the road. Dismounting, Anati examined the trench and saw that it was no more than knee-deep and perhaps three times as wide, the edges crumbled in under the impact of hooves and wheels. He thought that if he had not pressed them so hard, the trench might have been deeper and wider and then the outcome of the battle might have been different. It was a sobering thought, and one that needed countering.

Inkhare's army had lost nearly two hundred men in the assault, against a handful of horses and some fifty men. Anati counted it a victory, having taken possession of the field of battle, but he knew it should have been much more one-sided. Gathering together the dead and the salvaged chariots, Anati turned back to Iunu. Samuqenu would demand an accounting, and Anati was determined to put the most favourable face on his encounter.

Chapter 11

Hori was careful to get permission from Tjaty Aya for his foray into the north. Nervousness over the proximity of the heqa khasut could easily lead to suspicions of disloyalty or spying unless protected by somebody influential. The Tjaty was persuaded to supply Hori with a document saying he and his companions travelled with the blessing of the king, but Aya had a word of warning too.

"You realise if you get caught by the enemy with this document on you, it will be a death sentence."

"If there is any danger of that, I will destroy it," Hori said.

"Who will you take with you? A large force of armed men will attract notice."

"I had thought of that, sir, so I'll take two friends only. I've talked to them and they are willing."

"What supplies do you need? Donkeys?"

"No, sir, we'll go by water. I thought a fishing boat would be less conspicuous."

"Can you sail a boat?" Aya asked. "An incompetent fisherman will stand out."

"I know a fisherman prepared to earn a little gold, sir."

"Well, keep it cheap. I can extract some gold from Maia, but I don't want too many questions asked until we have something to show for it. When will you leave?"

"Sooner gone, sooner back. I had planned on tomorrow morning."

"And what's your plan?"

Hori shrugged. "I thought I'd keep my options open, sir. The aim is to capture a chariot somehow, but I'm hoping we don't have to sail all the way to Hut-waret to find one and liberate it from its owners."

"What about the horses?"

"We'll never get them on board a fishing boat. We'll have to settle for just the chariot."

"I suppose you could drive the chariot back," Aya suggested.

"If we had time to learn how to drive one, but we'd have to drive it well enough to evade everyone the length of the delta. No, we'll get one and load it aboard the boat; in pieces if necessary."

Hori gathered his companions at the boat at dawn the next morning. They were Piye, the youngest son of a minor noble who was also an Overseer of Cordage on the docks, and Ibi, another younger son of a scribe of the army. As younger sons, they would not inherit family estates and sought to make their own way in the world. This expedition of Hori's looked like it could be exciting and, if successful, could be a gateway to further adventures. Neither of them had journeyed beyond the borders of Kemet and was eager for the experience. The boat owner was Khui, an elderly-looking man who had lived a life on the river as a fisherman and messenger, and his son Neb. Neither father nor son was known to Hori personally, but he knew the man who recommended them and trusted him. The gold that would be coming their way after a successful trip would help ensure their loyalty and silence.

After introductions were made, Khui instructed the young nobles on how to act if they were to pass themselves off as fishermen, and assigned them places and duties in the vessel.

"I don't know why you want such a large boat, sir," Khui asked. "A smaller one would be more manageable."

"But five can sail it?" Hori asked.

Khui nodded and spat over the side. "As long as they can obey orders."

Hori considered the weather-beaten man, aged before his time by hard work. "I am in command of this expedition, but in all matters concerning the boat, you are captain, and all will obey you."

Under Khui's instructions, they cast off and rowed clumsily out into the river current. The breeze was from the north, so they did not raise the sail. Instead, Khui gave further instruction on how to row efficiently, how to steer with the rear-mounted steering paddle, and how to fish. This provided much hilarity, though Piye and Ibi glowered at the comments that were made by Khui and Neb.

"I did not come to be insulted," Piye declared. "Tell this man to apologise, Hori, or I'm going home."

"He has said nothing for which he has to apologise," Hori said. "Your antics are indeed amusing, but the reason behind them is more serious. If we are to pass ourselves off as fishermen, then we may have to apply this trade under the eyes of other fisherman. If we cannot do this, then we might as well stay at home."

Piye grumbled, but saw the sense of Hori's words. "He should still apologise though."

"If I have given offence, young sir, then I do indeed apologise," Khui said. "I only meant to instruct, and if I made comment that my son Neb could throw a net by the time he was five, then I was forgetting that the sons of nobility are not raised to such standards."

"Nobly said, Captain Khui," Hori said, hiding a smile. "Will you not accept his apology, Piye, and put this to rest between you?"

Piye grumbled some more that the apology could be interpreted as another insult, but nodded his agreement.

"Then let me take my turn," Hori said. He stood and picked up the net, holding it as Khui had shown, took a step forward and threw. The weighted net caught at his foot, where he had not been careful enough to keep it free, and he stumbled and fell overboard. Everyone roared with laughter as Hori rose sputtering to the surface. They hauled him aboard and made many jibes at his expense as he lay soaking wet in the bottom of the boat. Khui hauled the net aboard making the comment that they were unlikely to catch many fish if he made a habit of falling in every time he cast the net.

The current carried them northward and except for Neb at the steering oar, they lay back and relaxed, the hot sun beating down on them and a cool breeze ruffling their hair. It seemed they were almost standing still in the water, though if they looked carefully at the shores, the landmarks could be seen to be slowly moving.

Khui shifted and leaned close to Hori. "It is a rare man who will deflect anger in others by taking it upon himself."

Hori raised his eyebrows. "You mean falling overboard? I did not mean to do that. Put it down to plain clumsiness."

"As you will, sir, but I saw you shift your foot so the net would catch it."

"You thought you saw it."

Khui grinned, the gaps in his teeth apparent. "And you could have easily fallen inboard, but you leaned out and fell in."

"You credit me with too much," Hori said.

Khui just grinned again.

Half a day later, after they had eaten bread and dried fish for the midday meal, Khui pointed to where the river branched.

"The first arm, young sirs, and we will be taking it, for it leads to Hut-waret."

Khui, who was on the steering oar, guided the boat into the right-hand side of the current, allowing it to carry them into it. Reed beds, which had been sparse in the stretch of river near to Ankh-Tawy, became more common.

"Have we left Kemet yet?" Ibi asked.

"Depends who you ask, young sir," Khui replied. "Some say the Delta spreads down to where the river splits; others say it is marked by the border stelae, though you can't see them from the water."

"And what do you say?"

Khui ruminated on this for a few moments and spat over the side. "I say it depends upon whom we meet. If we find Kemetu fishermen, then we are in Kemet; if not, then we are not."

The boat continued its slow way downriver, floating easily on the current. As the sun sank in the west, Khui directed Neb to guide the boat into the eastern shore.

"A little bit of fishing for our supper, and a good night's sleep beside a warm fire," he said.

The boat was hauled up close to the bank and anchored with a long wooden hook and then, while Neb foraged around the reed beds for dead and dry reeds for the fire, Khui and Ibi cast the net in the shallows, hoping to catch their supper. There was still ample light in the sky, so Hori took Piye and they walked inland, away from the water's edge.

"What are we looking for?" Piye asked.

"My father Harrubaal constructed a road all the way down the eastern arm of the river to the border between the kingdoms. If we find it, it will tell us were are within the Delta."

They found a road, but it was no more than a dirt track that had been cleared of stones. It stretched northeast and southwest, and showed no evidence of having been constructed. Hori found it difficult to hide his disappointment.

"We're either still south of the border or my father was exaggerating."

"Assume the former for now," Piye advised. "From everything I have heard, your father is an honourable man, not one who would lie."

Hori nodded. "It is good of you to say so, but old men sometimes exaggerate the exploits of their youth."

They returned to the camp and found fish roasting on green reed sticks over a small fire. When cooked, Khui added a tiny pinch of sea salt from a pouch and they ate with gusto, washing the food down with draughts of cool river water. Piye was sent down to the river to refill the jar with water and returned grumbling again.

"Why do we have to camp so far from the water's edge?" he asked. "There are plenty of good sites a lot closer."

"Indeed there are, young sir," Khui said with a smile, "but I have no desire to end up in the belly of a crocodile. They don't often venture this far from the water, but any closer would put us at risk."

Piye and Ibi pointedly bedded down on the landward side of the fire and lay awake longer than the others, flinching at the cry of a night bird, the scream of a hunting owl, the howl of a desert wolf, and the croaking of frogs in the reed bed. Finally, overcome by exhaustion, they drifted off to sleep and awakened at dawn to find Khui and Neb already up, feeding the fire. Piye seemed almost surprised to wake up at all.

They continued their journey downriver before the sun had risen more than four fingers above the eastern horizon. Fishing boats were sighted that morning and Khui had his crew going through their exercises with the net. None of the other boats paid any attention to them as they drifted with the current, and soon left them behind.

"We could have found out if we are in the Delta kingdom if we'd steered for them," Piye said.

"And they might have wondered why we asked," Hori replied. "No, we'll keep our own counsel for the time being."

They put ashore again that night, and once more Hori and Piye trekked inland to find the road, and once more found just a dirt track, though it was apparently well-travelled. The next day, they found some activity on the eastern shore with armed men roaming around so decided for safety's sake to camp on the western shore, but half a day later found evidence of violence on both shores. Flattened reeds and pasture spoke of the recent presence of large bodies of men, and some broken spears were caught in the vegetation. Putting in to the eastern shore, Neb found a body caught in the reeds. It bore several wounds which caused Hori to declare that there must have been a battle close by.

"But between whom?" Ibi asked.

"He's not saying," Hori said, nudging the corpse with his foot. "We don't even know which side he fought for."

"I thought the *heqa khasut* were utter barbarians," Piye said. "This man looks quite normal."

"So he might be a man of Avaris."

They camped early that day a little north of the battle scars, intending to investigate it a little more. Leaving Khui and his son to guard the boat, Hori walked inland with Piye and Ibi and was amazed to discover a broad well-constructed road of packed gravel and earth raised above the surrounding countryside. It stretched north and south as far as they could see, and was deserted except for a man driving a heavily laden donkey. The man urged the beast away as quickly as possible, so Hori paid him no attention. Instead, they walked southward; in the direction they knew the battle had taken place.

They came across it soon enough, and stared at the scene of destruction where it was apparent many men had died. Hori was appalled by the trench dug across the road, destroying a wonderful construction for no good purpose.

"This, more than anything, tells me it is the work of barbarians," he said.

"Look," Ibi said. "A dead horse and...and those must be chariots. Parts of chariots," he amended.

Three dead horses had been dragged to one side of the road, and sundry debris piled up beside them. The bodies were bloated and stinking, alive with flies and maggots, so with cloths over their noses, they only gave the horses a cursory examination. Broken chariots were of more interest, and Hori's hopes rose when he saw the mound of broken wood and leather. His hopes faded as they examined the debris.

"They must have removed anything useful," Piye said. He held up a piece of wickerwork attached by a torn leather strap to a piece of wood. "Is this even a piece of chariot?"

124

Hori found a segment of wheel, curved wood and a single intact spoke; then another piece with two broken spokes. He laid them on the ground and studied the configuration. "Six spokes, I think, with a wheel maybe a pace across."

"How do they fit to the chariot?" Piye asked.

Digging into the mound unearthed a shattered axle with a hub still attached to one end. Fragments of the box that sat atop them were sorted out and laid out on the ground in an attempt to understand the construction. Gradually, the outline of a chariot took shape, though the details of construction were still a mystery.

"What do you think?" Ibi asked. "Is this a chariot or not?"

"I think it must be," Hori said. "Look, here is the box in which men stand...the floor and one...two...three sides. An axle runs underneath..." He bent down and lifted the putative floor to show a bent brass hoop and a rip in the wood where another had been torn out. "...near the back of the box. Two wheels with six spokes each...and a yoke at the front." He looked at the remains of fittings on the yoke. "Two horses, one on each side, but how the horses are guided is anyone's guess."

The three men stared at the pieces as the light faded.

"The question is," Piye said, "is this enough to find out how they make a chariot or must we try and find an intact one?"

"An intact one would be good," Hori conceded, "but the fact that every reusable piece of these ones has been scavenged, shows how valuable they are. They will be well-guarded."

"So tell us what you want to do," Ibi said.

"I don't know, but for now, take a piece you can carry and we'll take it back to the boat."

The three of them carried fragments back to where Khui and Neb had set up camp. They talked it over in the darkness after supper and decided they could not ignore what they had in favour of a possibility. So, the next day, they moved the boat back to where they had seen the trampled ground and followed the path back to the mound of debris and the laid out framework. They spent much of that day loading everything that looked useful aboard their craft, and only then did Hori make his decision.

"We carry on downriver," he said. "While there is a possibility of finding an intact one, we must try."

"Having the parts of a chariot on board might make people think we are spies," Piye pointed out.

"Or we are just innocent fisherman scavenging some firewood," Khui said. He spat into the river as if to punctuate his thought.

"We must take the chance," Hori said. "What we have is valuable but what we could gain is priceless."

They pressed on the next day, moving awkwardly around the remains of the shattered chariot. They saw other fishing boats, but apart from a little fishing for their supper, Hori forsook any more pretence. Two days more brought them within sight of a walled city.

"Iunu," Khui said. "A holy city dedicated to the Nine gods."

"Which nine?" Ibi asked.

"The creator gods. It is the foremost city within the Delta after Hutwaret."

"You know a lot about it," Piye said, more than a trace of suspicion in his voice.

"I've travelled a lot," the old fisherman said. "I was born in the Delta and have fished on most of the river arms at one time or another."

"And we appreciate your knowledge and expertise," Hori said. "No-one doubts your loyalty to Ankh-Tawy."

"Nor should they," Khui snapped. "I've lived most of my life there. Once upon a time, both kingdoms were ruled from Ankh-Tawy and I long for the day when they are again."

"As if that's going to happen anytime soon," Piye muttered.

"Maybe sooner than we think if the *heqa khasut* have their way," Hori said. "They seem well on their way to claiming the Delta and if once they rule there, do you think they will be content? Unless we can find a way to counter them, we will fall too."

"Then we should get these chariot parts back to Ankh-Tawy," Ibi said. "They may be important."

Hori nodded absently, his eyes staring at the walled city of Iunu. "We have the parts of a chariot, and can guess at how they work together, but what I'd really like to see is how they move, how they're controlled."

"I don't see how we're going to learn that without...what are you thinking, Hori? Going into the city?"

"We could."

"Gods, we'd be taking our lives in our hands. If we got caught..."

"What do you mean, get caught? We're simple fishermen, nothing more. Khui, could we catch enough fish to take and sell in Iunu?"

126

"You'd get nothing for them. There are too many fishermen here."

"We don't need to actually sell them. It's just an excuse to go into the city."

"Then you don't need fish. Take a bit of copper and buy some rope. Fishermen always need rope."

Piye grinned. "That'll be me then. My father is Overseer of Cordage, so I suppose I know more about rope than any of you."

They put into Iunu, though not into the official docks there, anchoring a little south of the main area and wading ashore. Hori gave Piye enough copper to buy the rope and allowed him to take the lead in the markets, while Ibi and he struck up conversations with nearby stall-holders and customers. The city was full of the news of King Seneferenre fleeing across the river, and the defeat of General Inkhare to the south.

"I heard about that," Hori said. "It was the chariots, wasn't it?"

"Where have you been that you even have to ask?" said one man.

"Fishing. Near Per-Bast. Our captain here is buying rope." Hori waved a hand in Piye's direction before continuing. "We only heard rumours. Is it true then?"

"True enough, but Inkhare gave a good account of himself, I'm told."

"Those chariots must be marvellous things. I've never even seen one."

"Then you're in luck, stranger. There's still a squadron or two in Iunu and they do there exercises outside the walls most days."

Hori found out where with a little more judicious probing, and after Piye had bought the coil of rope that was their excuse, they made their way to the northern walls, where they mingled with a crowd of other curious onlookers. They moved to one side and found a spot near the battlements that gave them an unobstructed view of the level area inland from the road that the chariot squadrons used for practice. Further round, on the eastern side, a low hill rose, with several temples on its slopes and another at the top. The hill was outside the walls and it excited Hori's interest.

"Why are your temples outside the city walls?" he asked a bystander.

The man looked at him curiously. "The gods don't need the protection of walls," he said. "No-one would dare desecrate them."

"Whose temples are they?"

"You must be a stranger in Iunu. The top one is that of Atum, and the others of the Nine are arranged below it."

Hori remembered what Khui had said about the creator gods worshipped here above all others. He thanked the man and turned back as a buzz of excitement arose from the other watchers.

Chariots emerged from the city gate, one after another with a pair of horses seeming to effortlessly draw the wickerwork and wooden boxes behind them, and Hori leaned over the wall, excited to see what he knew only as scraps of shattered chariots come together and almost come to life below him.

"They are beautiful," he murmured.

The officers in charge ordered the chariots into a double line, ten on a side and strode between them, inspecting horses, tack, and the framework of the vehicles. Then they were off, the horses urged into a gallop, the chariots themselves seeming to float above the desert sand, manes and tails and the long hair of the charioteers blowing in the wind of their passing. They were almost out of sight when they turned, each line of ten intersecting the other, streaming together as they raced back to the city where they performed the same manoeuver. Hori could now see how skilfully the chariots were handled as the horses hooves struck the sand only a pace behind the chariot wheels in front and sand peppered the faces of the charioteers. The reins from each horse were wrapped around the forearms of the driver, left horse to left arm and right to right, and as they passed close under the walls, Hori could see the movements of the drivers' arms that were translated into the motions of each horse.

"Incredible," he murmured to Piye. "That must take months to learn."

"Years even," Piye agreed. "If we bring back the parts of a chariot and actually manage to make one, can we ever learn to control them like this?"

"We have to," Hori said, "or we won't be able to stand against them."

The chariots continued to weave back and forth on the plain beside Iunu, a dazzling display of skill and armed might designed to instil pride in those who supported Amurru, and despair in their enemies. Men ran out with figures made of clay and straw, setting them out as an army of a hundred figures facing the chariots which came together a few hundred paces away. The chariots spread out in a line facing the straw men and, at a signal, leapt forward. Even Hori, safe on top of the wall, could imagine himself as one of the straw men facing this chariot charge, and felt his heartbeat increase.

Straw and clay flew into the air and disappeared beneath hooves and wheels as the twenty chariots overwhelmed their targets, and after they passed, there was just wreckage on the ground. The watchers on the walls broke into applause, cheering and stamping their feet, which surprised Hori so much, he asked the man he had spoken to before.

"Are these all men of Amurru? I had thought they were citizens of Iunu."

"Oh, they are," the man said. "But how can we not appreciate such power and skill? In truth, does it matter who rules us as long as we can all get enough to eat and be happy?"

"Surely war is not good for the people?"

"Why not? It provides work for many, and as long as we are left alone to worship our gods and live our lives as we are accustomed, then we are content."

"Then Amurru has won already," Hori said. The man just shrugged and turned away to watch the chariots file back into the city.

"I think we have seen enough," Hori said. "Time to return to Ankh-Tawy and try to impress on our rulers how much danger really faces us."

Chapter 12

Merybaal and Amatia were despondent in the days following the fall of Avaris; not so much for their lives, for it seemed their relative King Baalbek had offered them his protection, but because they had no idea of the fate of two of their children. Tiamen was safe enough, but her husband Menkare was missing; Djedenre had disappeared in the battle for the city; and Neferit had vanished from their house in the night. They had organised searches for her, and even the new Amurru overlords had been helpful in this regard, but it seemed she had stepped out of their house one night and been swallowed up by the ground. Only one man came forward with any information, but his account was rambling and disjointed and spoke of a girl dressed as a man going out through the narrow gate. Merybaal investigated further, willing to follow up any thread, no matter how unlikely, but there was no trail to follow.

Few days had passed since the battle and the events following it, but Amatia was giving way to despair, and Merybaal's heart was heavy. Using his position as Treasurer and drawing on the goodwill lent him by Baalbek's favour; he had men scour the battlefield, searching for any sign of his son and son-in-law among the fallen. For a time, he hoped that they might have been taken prisoner, incarcerated in the prison outside the walls, but there were only two exits from that prison. One led to the Amurran army and the other to death. Merybaal was torn between a desire to discover that Djedenre and Menkare had switched sides and survived; and that they had held fast to their principles in death. Unfortunately, either choice was only too easy to check. Those that refused to compromise were laid out in death, and neither young man's body was on view. He had access to the list of names of those who had changed their allegiance, but neither man was registered there.

It could only be that his son and Tiamen's husband had been so badly disfigured that their bodies could not be identified. Merybaal ordered the family hearth fires put out as a sign of mourning, and he and Amatia, Tiamen, Riat and Amenre, made offerings to the gods for their loved ones safe passage through the afterlife. It was all they could do in the absence of bodies for the proper rites and burial rituals. And then a man arrived on their doorstep with incredible news.

"I am Renmire, a carpenter of Iunu, and I was told to bring a message to Merybaal, who used to be Treasurer in Avaris."

"I am Merybaal, and I am still Treasurer in Avaris. From whom does your message come?"

"He did not give a name, perhaps for fear of being discovered."

"What is your message?"

"I am to say, 'Father, I live, as does my sister's husband. We are well and continue in our loyalty to the king.'"

Merybaal stared and then beckoned the man into the courtyard, where he sat him under the shade of a tree, had servants bring him beer and honey cakes.

"Who told you this?"

"As I said, he did not give a name."

Merybaal grimaced and wrung his hands. "I cannot raise the hopes of my family on so little. What did he look like? The man who gave you the message?"

Renmire described him and Merybaal was in no doubt that he described Djedenre.

"It is him," Merybaal gasped, and wiped away tears. "And...and the other man...what did he look like?"

"I saw no other man, sir."

"Yet he referred to him as his sister's husband...it can only be Menkare. They continue in their loyalty to the king?"

"That is what he said, sir. I took that to mean they were with King Seneferenre. He fled westward from Iunu as the foreigners approached."

Merybaal nodded, and poured more beer for Renmire. He could think of nothing else to ask, but he was reluctant to let him depart, when he was the only link to his missing son.

"He said nothing more?"

"One other thing, but it was addressed to his sister."

"Which sister?"

"He didn't say, sir. Only that I was to speak to her."

"She is not here. Speak the words to me."

Renmire hesitated and then nodded. "I was to say, 'Thank you, sister, for giving me my life."

Merybaal frowned. "What did he mean by that?"

"I don't know, sir," Renmire replied. He drained his cup of beer and popped the last honey cake into his mouth, before standing. "I have done as I was instructed, sir, so I will take my leave of you. I see you are in mourning."

"No more, good Renmire, for you have brought me the best of news. You shall be rewarded."

"No need. I was given gold to carry the news to you, sir."

"And you shall have more from me, for the news you bring has lightened my heart and banished sorrow from this house."

Merybaal had his major-domo bring gold from the storeroom and insisted Renmire take it. After the man had left, he gathered his family together and broke the good news to them. They were disbelieving at first, and plied Merybaal with more questions than he could answer.

"I don't know," was his common refrain. "Renmire brought no proof with him, but his description of Djedenre allows for no mistake."

"And Menkare?" Tiamen asked. "Is there no word of him?"

"Only that he is alive and well. Renmire intimated that both men were with the king still, fighting loyally for our land."

"Gods be praised," Amatia said. "But...no word of Neferit?"

"No...though I wonder about the last thing Renmire said. Djedenre thanked his sister for giving him life. What did that mean? Does this relate to you in any way, Tiamen?"

"I cannot think of any way, Father."

"Then could it relate to Neferit? Could she have helped him in some way?"

"How can we know?"

They could think of no way of reconciling Renmire's words with a message of hope for Neferit's survival, but the very next day it came from an unexpected quarter. Amentep, the major-domo, reported that a strange foreigner dressed in outlandish garb was at the door requesting audience with Merybaal. He ordered the foreigner brought to him in a private room, and marvelled at the appearance of the youth--for he was obviously a youth, slim and with no evidence of facial hair. The youth was dressed in leggings and a loose-fitting tunic with a hood that fell forward, obscuring his face.

"I am Merybaal, treasurer of the city. You asked to see me?"

The youth pushed back the hood and grinned. "Do you not know me, father?"

Merybaal stared, open-mouthed. "Neferit? By all the gods...it is you. Where have you been? Your mother has been frantic with worry and..." Abruptly, he frowned. "Why are you dressed in that outlandish fashion? It is not seemly for a young woman."

"It's...uh...a long story."

Merybaal turned and strode to the door and flung it open. "Amentep! Get in here immediately!"

Amentep arrived, his face full of alarm at his master's tone. Merybaal ordered him to fetch his family at once. The major-domo glanced at the other person in the room and his mouth fell open as he recognised Neferit.

"And you'll say nothing about this," Merybaal growled. "On your life."

"No, sir," Amentep muttered before scurrying off to fetch the family.

Amatia burst into tears and hugged her daughter tightly, while Tiamen, Rait and Amenre goggled at the strange apparition posing as Neferit. After several minutes, Amatia held her daughter at arm's length and stared at her.

"What is this, and where have you been?" Amatia demanded. "I've...we've been so worried."

"I had to help," Neferit said. "I think they got away, but I was captured instead."

"You're not making sense," Merybaal said. "Start from the beginning."

"Why are you wearing those strange clothes?" Amenre asked. "You look like a man...sort of."

Neferit smiled briefly. "That's the idea." She frowned, trying to collect her thoughts. "Remember when I rode north to find Djedenre? Before his men were routed by the chariots? He disguised me in the camp by making me wear these clothes and passing me off as a Ribu prince in the king's service..."

"What's a Ribu?" Amenre asked.

"I'm not sure exactly," Neferit confessed. "Except they live in the west somewhere."

"They inhabit the land to the west of the Delta," Merybaal said. "Fierce warriors, mostly archers. Anyway, leave that for now. Why is it relevant?"

"I was accepted as a Ribu prince," Neferit went on, "and I liked the freedom of riding my horse and being with the army, so I kept the clothes when I came back to Avaris."

"Shameful," muttered her mother. "Openly wearing men's clothes, and...and flaunting your legs like that."

"Hush, my love," Merybaal murmured. "Neferit is our daughter and has done nothing to shame either us or her."

"When Djedenre and Menkare went missing, I wanted to find them, so I dressed up like this again and went out of the city to look for them..."

"How did you get out of the city? Even dressed as a man, the guards would be more likely to arrest you than let you out."

"I used the narrow gate near the stables. The only guard was an old man who knew me and let me out."

"Simen," Merybaal said. "He came to me with some garbled story but I dismissed his tale as ridiculous. Go on."

"I found the prison outside the walls, and both Djedenre and Menkare within. I released them, but was captured, and I don't know if they got away."

"Be easy on that account, daughter. We have heard from your brother. He and Menkare are in Iunu with the king."

"Thank the gods," Neferit said. "I was so worried."

"Thank you for freeing Djedenre," Rait said.

"And for Menkare's freedom," Tiamen added.

"You were captured?" Merybaal asked. "Did you then reveal your identity to secure your release? There were only two other ways to leave the Amurru prison--death or service."

Neferit smiled. "Well, I'm not dead...and everyone still believes I am a man."

"Then how...?" Merybaal stared at his daughter. "You haven't accepted service with the Amurru?"

"Is that such a bad thing?"

"They are invaders who have captured Avaris, who war against our king and who mean to subjugate us all. Your brother and brother-in-law fight against them like every loyal man. How could you even contemplate such an action?"

"You are working with them, father. You are still Treasurer of the city. How is that any different?"

"It is very different. I am Treasurer so that our kingdom will not go down into ruin. I keep the city and the kingdom operating so that Seneferenre, when he has driven back the Amurru, will have an intact kingdom to return to."

"Forgive me, father, but is that likely? Can the king prevail against the Amurru? Did you see the chariot charge that shattered our army?"

Merybaal frowned. "No, but I saw its aftermath. All the more reason Seneferenre must prevail."

"Then you missed out on a spectacle, father." Neferit became pensive and fell silent for a few moments. "I am mindful of the many good men who died, but I saw the charge in the north that destroyed the army of General Menenre." She shook her head, but her eyes sparkled. "It was deadly and...and oh, so beautiful. I have never even imagined anything like it. I tell you, the chariot squadrons of the Amurru are an irresistible force, and we cannot hope to win against them."

"I will have none of that defeatist talk in this house, Neferit. We are loyal to the Delta and to Seneferenre and that's an end to it. I am glad you are safe and have managed to find your way home. Go with your mother now and change out of those dreadful clothes. Happily, you still have some decent dresses to wear."

Amatia held out her hand to her daughter, but Neferit shook her head.

"No." She saw the anger in her father's face and knelt before him. "Hear me, father, for I cannot do as you ask."

"By all the gods of Kemet and Hattush, you will obey me, daughter. I see that I have allowed you too much freedom. It is time I found you a husband who can control you."

"I do not want a husband, and I refuse to marry. You cannot make me."

"But Neferit darling," Amatia said. "Every girl wants to marry and have a family. We'll find you a good man whom you'll grow to love."

Neferit got to her feet. "I don't want a man; any man. I have no interest in men. I never have."

Tiamen smiled and Rait raised her eyebrows, while Amenre merely looked puzzled. Amatia looked shocked at her daughter's revelation, but Merybaal merely frowned and nodded his head slowly.

"That explains a lot," he muttered. "If you do not intend to marry and have children, what will you do? There are few opportunities for a woman alone unless you mean to be a lady of leisure."

"I want to be a charioteer."

Merybaal stared. "And just how are you going to do that? We don't have chariots...gods...you mean with the Amurrans."

"Yes."

"So you betrayed your nation and joined the enemy."

"I don't see it as a betrayal, any more than you did, father. Amurru is going to win, for nobody can stand against their chariot squadrons."

"If you are right and these chariots mean our destruction, then how can you bear to look at them?"

Neferit looked at each member of her family. "Have you never looked at the sunrise or the sunset and noticed the beauty of it? Have you never looked at a storm over the hills and marvelled at the flashes of white fire in the sky? Heard the thunder that beats at your ears? Felt the irresistible power of the storm winds? No? It is those things that I liken to the chariot charge. Great beauty and great danger. I cannot think of anything I would rather do than be a part of it."

"You are a woman," Merybaal pointed out. "How can you be a charioteer?"

"I already am."

"What? How can you be?"

"Well, not a charioteer yet, but I have been accepted into the chariot squadron as a horse groom."

"There are no women in the Amurran army."

Neferit scowled. "Not yet, but they don't know I am a woman dressed like this. In their eyes I am a Ribu prince called Neterre. I will prove myself and then it will not matter."

"Neferit, you are putting yourself in great danger," Tiamen said. "My husband has told me tales of what happens even in the Delta army, and I'm sure the Amurrans are worse. What will happen to you in the camps? You will be regarded as a camp follower and your fate..." she shuddered, "...does not bear thinking about."

"They will not find out I am a woman. Already I am accepted as a Ribu prince by the men in my squad."

"Forbid her to return to the stables, husband," Amatia pleaded. "I cannot bear to think of my youngest daughter in such danger."

"Must I lock you in your room, Neferit? Place a guard upon your door?" Merybaal asked.

"You have the power to imprison me, father," Neferit admitted. "But I beg you, if you love me, let me do this."

Merybaal sighed deeply. "Ah, daughter, you know I love you, but how can I let you walk into dishonour and danger? What sort of a father would allow that?"

Neferit considered her father's words. "I am in no danger at present, as they believe me to be the young man Neterre. Let me remain there as long as I am undiscovered. If my disguise is pierced, they will probably not let me remain anyway, so I will then return home and give up my dream. Would that satisfy you?"

Now it was Merybaal's turn to consider his daughter's words. "Satisfy me? No. Yet if you promise to guard yourself diligently, remembering whose daughter you are, I will let you remain for as long as they think you a man."

"Husband, you cannot let her do this," Amatia protested.

"Are we to keep our beloved daughter a prisoner in her home? I have no doubt she would seek to escape, putting herself in greater danger than she faces now."

"Thank you, father," Neferit said. "Mother, you will see that I will be safe."

"Can I come and watch you drive a chariot?" Amenre asked.

"When I do, nephew, you will ride with me if you wish."

"We'll see about that," Rait murmured. "It may never happen."

Neferit took her leave, embracing her family before slipping out of the house. Amatia bewailed what she saw as the certain fate of her daughter, but Merybaal offered some comfort.

"I will talk to King Baalbek. I am sure that he will arrange for the leader of the chariot squadrons to offer protection to Neferit."

"Wonderful. Tell them she's a girl and they'll send her home immediately."

"I will not do that; it would betray the trust she has placed in me."

"What will you say then?"

"I will tell them that Neterre, Prince of Ribu, is as a family member to me and that I desire that no harm comes to him."

"I still think it would be better to reveal her identity," Amatia said.

"Let me do it my way," Merybaal replied. "I am quite sure she will be unable to maintain her disguise for long. It has only been a few days so far. When she is discovered, the chariot commander will protect her and she will return home."

Chapter 13

Ankh-Tawy was in mourning. King Monthhotep succumbed to an abscess on his jaw that resulted from a cracked tooth. Somehow, a fragment of the bowl used to grind the flour made its way into his bread. He bit down and cried out in agony, but the pain was as nothing compared to that which awaited him less than a month later. Despite the best efforts of the court physicians, the king died and his body was sent to the Place of Embalming. When his earthly body was prepared and wrapped, it would be solemnly interred in a tomb prepared beneath a flat-topped brick Per-djet situated in the region south of the city called Mer, or Place of Ascendance, after the great structures erected there by kings half a thousand years before.

Meanwhile, there was turmoil within the white-walled city. Monthhotep lacked a credible heir, and the various factions were manoeuvring for ascendancy. One of the stronger claims to the throne came from the family of Harrubaal. His daughter Iset had married Merkawre Sobekhotep long before he briefly occupied the throne some years before, and had two sons--Bebi and Sobekhotep--now fifteen and thirteen floods old respectively. They were a touch on the young side to claim the throne but as sons of a previous king had their share of supporters. The greatest argument against them was their Hattushi blood through Harrubaal, and many Kemetu viewed them with suspicion because of this.

Into the turmoil stepped Khasekhare, an army officer popular with the local soldiers. Backed by their arms, Khasekhare hinted that anyone who opposed him would regret it, and was a little more straight forward with the family of Harrubaal, sending for the present head of the family, Hori.

"Let me speak plainly, Hori son of Harrubaal. I mean to be king and I will brook no challenges."

Hori realised that the survival of his nephews Bebi and Sobekhotep might depend on his next words, so he gave it some thought while bowing politely and murmuring some stock phrases. As a mere army officer, Khasekhare did not warrant such deference, but Hori thought it worth the gesture.

"Commander Khasekhare, I hear your words and wish you well in your endeavours."

"You do? I thought that you might press your own claim. You are the son of Init, the daughter of Merneferre Aya."

"I have no ambitions beyond my present status, Commander."

"Then the claims of your sister's sons."

"Ah, Commander, you are as aware as I that my nephews do not have that strong a claim."

"They are sons of Merkawre Sobekhotep," Khasekhare said. "As well as sharing your connection to the family of Aya."

"True, but they are young. Too young to take on the burdens of ruling Kemet."

"Youth by itself is no great impediment as long as they have experienced advisers."

"Again you speak the truth, Commander, but there is a greater impediment. They have the blood of Hattush within their veins and given the present threat to Kemet from the northern invaders, that kinship would not inspire confidence." Hori pretended to consider the problem, but he knew already what he must say, as did Commander Khasekhare. The army officer needed to hear the words and waited patiently for Hori's capitulation.

"Commander Khasekhare, I can think of no-one who is better suited to take the throne of Kemet in these troubled times. I can assure you of my family's complete approval and support, and will state this publicly if you so desire."

"I shall require that of you, and your nephews must be among the first to kneel before me."

"It shall be done, Son of Re."

The title belonged only to the anointed king, but Hori could see the pleasure in Khasekhere's face when addressed in that manner. He bowed and left the Commander's presence.

The old king was buried in due course and Khasekhare mounted the throne amidst restrained celebrations from the populace. Khasekhare was not popular outside of the army, but the common people dreaded civil war above anything, and it appeared that the new king had the strength to rule the kingdoms. The people of Kemet still believed the fiction that they ruled the Delta, but that belief was becoming harder by the day as news came down from the north of the setbacks and defeats inflicted on the defenders of the Delta by the northern invaders. Khasekhare doubted Kemet had the strength to defeat either Seneferenre of the Delta or the Amurran invaders, but hoped they might weaken each other sufficiently in time so he could take over. He was content to wait and do nothing.

His army commanders believed that the best course too, but Hori believed some preparation was essential. He had persuaded his superiors to authorise a raid north, and he had brought back many fragments of that deadly weapon wielded by the *heqa khasut*--the chariot. Now, he and his companions Piye and Ibi were faced with the task of reconstructing a working chariot from the salvaged pieces.

Ibi, as son of an army scribe, had artistic pretentions, and had made a series of sketches of the chariot fragments, together with what he could remember of an intact one seen near Iunu. He now tried to use these sketches to identify the parts and reconstruct one, at least on papyrus. Piye, as son of an Overseer of Cordage, had no special skills to bring to the task, but had taken up the challenge of finding skilled carpenters to make the reconstituted parts of a new chariot. Hori needed someone with authority to oversee his project, and found it in the person of the Tjaty's son Ayameru. His mother Init was the sister of Reditanes who had married Tjaty Aya, so Ayameru was Hori's cousin, and he made full use of this familial relationship.

"I heard about your expedition to capture a chariot," Ayameru said. "A pity you did not succeed."

"I think we did very well, considering," Hori replied. "We may not have one of their precious chariots, but we have the parts of several wrecked ones. I'm sure we can reconstruct one."

"Well, if you do, I'd be interested to see it."

"I hoped you might take a more active part in our project...cousin."

Ayameru kept a straight face, but his eyes twinkled. "I have no expertise in either chariots or carpentry."

"You have status, cousin, and people pay attention to you."

"Only because my father is Tjaty."

"Whereas my father is tainted by his Hattushi blood. I need someone beyond reproach who can intercede for us."

Ayameru thought for a few moments. "Tell me why you think this project is so important."

"All the reports filtering down to us from the Delta show the chariot to be an invincible weapon. Whenever the army of Seneferenre has met a chariot force, he has gone down in defeat. So what will the *heqa khasut* do when they hold the Delta in their hands?"

"Turn their eyes to Kemet," Ayameru said.

"Can Kemet's army succeed where the Delta has failed? I doubt it. They still have their chariots and we have nothing that can withstand them."

"So we build our own." Ayameru nodded. "I can appreciate your argument, but the invaders have used chariots for who knows how long...generations. Can we possibly build enough in a few short years and learn how to use them?"

"We have to," Hori said. "The alternative is surrender and life under the invaders."

"I'd rather die," Ayameru agreed. "All right, I will help where I can. What do you need?"

"Thank you, cousin. For a start, we must have carpenters put together intact parts of a chariot working from the fragments we have and the sketches Ibi has made. Piye has identified the best carpenters, but they will not work without the promise of payment."

"I'll see what I can do," Ayameru said.

True to his word, Ayameru spoke to his father, who could also see the importance of being prepared. Tjaty Aya authorised the release of a small sum of gold from the Treasury, and had a scribe draw up a document commanding certain unnamed carpenters to offer such assistance as they could provide. Ayameru took this to Hori and Hori's group started work.

Initially, Piye had a single carpenter make all the parts needed, but it soon became apparent that the worker in wood was making assumptions regarding the final use of the parts, and the finished products only superficially resembled the salvaged parts. After that, they divided up the work between several artisans--one making the wheels, another constructing the framework of the chariot, a third making the yoke, and a fourth shaping the axle--all to the specifications Ibi provided. Within a month, Hori and his men were looking at a heap of freshly carved and shaped timbers ready to be put together.

"Have we truly duplicated a chariot?" Ibi asked. "Is this heap of timber the answer?"

"Why not?" Piye asked. "The carpenters have faithfully duplicated every part."

"Every part we know about," Ibi said. "What if we missed some bits?"

"Then we'll find out when we put it together, won't we?" Hori said.

They found that having the parts made separately had not worked as well as they hoped. The wheels would not fit on the axles without modification, but a little further work enabled this. Smooth shiny wood gleamed as the axle was attached to the wicker and wood carriage, the wheels lending it a feeling of energy, and the long forward-reaching yoke anchoring the whole thing. Ayameru stared at the finished product in awe.

"Is that a proper chariot?" he asked. "Do the ones of the *heqa khasut* look like that?"

"Yes," Ibi declared.

"I think so," Hori said more cautiously.

"So what's next?"

"We yoke up two horses and try it out."

That was not as straight forward as it seemed. Hori had access to many fine horses from the family estates, but they ran into problems immediately. Horses were ridden in Kemet, but seldom used to pull vehicles. Oxen pulled carts or sleds, but horses almost never. Those that were used to pulling a cart were strong but slow, useless for drawing a chariot into battle at speed, while the smaller, more agile horses balked at being hitched to a yoke.

"What do we do?" Piye asked.

"We train horses to the yoke," Hori said.

"How long is that going to take?" Ayameru asked.

Hori shrugged. "I don't know."

Harrubaal was ninety summers old and spent his days dreaming, but roused himself on hearing of Hori's problem.

"I have seen chariots in use," he quavered, "though not in war. I have also spoken with charioteers."

"Can you tell me how to train horses to pull a chariot, father?"

"I might be able to help with a few things, but I lack the strength to do anything."

"Tell me what to do and I will be your strength," Hori declared.

"Start with horses that carry riders," Harrubaal said. "They are already used to people, and to wearing the metal bit that controls them. Then you must fit them with leather straps that fit around the chest behind the front legs. Riders often use one to slip their feet into so they can sit astride their mount. Fit another one from that strap across the front of the chest."

"I thought that we could just use the same leather collars we use for oxen. We have them ready made."

Harrubaal coughed and wheezed from the effort of talking. "That won't do. In case you haven't noticed, horses and oxen have a different body shape. I'm not even sure simple straps will do...I honestly can't remember every detail...but it's a good place to start."

"I'll see to it, father. What else?"

"That will do for now. Let the horses get used to that before doing anything more."

Hori selected ten of the best horses from his father's stables and had the grooms stitch leather bands for the girth and breast. It took a bit of work getting the horses used to wearing these straps, but after they calmed down, he had the grooms lead them on long reins, letting them move and get comfortable with the feel of the straps. He let his father know the progress they were making, and Harrubaal remembered another piece of equipment.

"You need a breech strap running back from the girth around the horse's backside...not so high that it stops them defecating, but not so low that it interferes with the movement of the legs."

"Why do they need that?"

"I'm not exactly sure," Harrubaal said. He thought for a few moments. "Remember that it has been over fifty years since I saw a chariot being used, but you've got two horses attached to a central shaft. They pull the chariot using the breast strap, but you want to stop them turning their hindquarters away from the shaft, so I think it is because you need the horse connected to the shaft at the back. That's what the breech strap does...I think."

"This is getting very complex," Hori said. "Are you sure all this is necessary?"

"Do you want to do it properly, or just play at it?"

"Yes, you're right. Sorry, father."

Hori returned to his work with the grooms, making adjustments to the leather fittings and training the horses until they were comfortable wearing the accoutrements of control and could exercise fully while wearing them. Of the ten horses they had started with, only seven proved suitable, but Hori knew that only two were needed to pull a chariot so he was happy with their progress. He sent word to Ayameru in Ankh-Tawy that it was time to bring the chariot to his father's estate, and to his surprise the Tjaty's son told him they had constructed a second chariot. Ibi would set off immediately to bring them to Hori.

Harrubaal was on hand to see the two ox-carts as they rumbled into the estate several days later, each bearing a new chariot. The vehicles gleamed in the sunlight, pale wood unadorned and without a speck of dirt on them. Nodding and mumbling beneath his breath, Harrubaal had the chariots unloaded and brought before him for an inspection.

"They are not as I remember them," he mumbled.

"Perhaps the *heqa khasut* have changed the design in the last fifty years," Hori suggested.

"Maybe...or maybe it is because they look so new. The ones I remember were old and battle-worn, stained and ornamented with flags and pennants, silver studs and painted panels. These ones have no character, no history of great deeds."

"Then we will have to make sure these earn honours on the battlefield," Hori said.

Harrubaal retired to his bed then, exhausted, so Hori and Ibi had the chariots wheeled over to the stables. They were eager to hitch the horses to the chariots and watch them in action. It was then that Hori realised there was a lot he had yet to learn. The horse being led up to the chariot shied at the unfamiliar object, rearing and lashing out with its hooves. Much the same happened with the other six horses and it was only after they had been led around and calmed that they could approach the chariot. Finally, after much coaxing and offering of treats, two horses were cajoled into position on either side of the central shaft, and fastened to it by clips on the strap running the length of the animals. The two horses stood trembling beside each other while reins were fitted and one of the grooms climbed up into the body of the chariot. He gave Hori a confident grin and assured him that he knew how to guide the beasts.

"All right, but keep it slow and steady," Hori instructed. "No more than a walk at first." He signed to the grooms holding the horses' bridles to let go and stand back.

They did so, and the driver clicked his tongue and twitched the reins. The horses started forward, though they tended to try and pull apart, each being unused to the close proximity of the other, until they caught sight of the chariot following close behind. One of them reared, while the other tried to leap forward. Both panicked when neither found they could rid themselves of the wheeled vehicle and they took flight, bursting into a gallop. The driver was bounced around, lost his grip and was thrown out, landing on the ground with a cry of agony, while the horses bolted, desperate to escape the thing following them. As fast as they ran, the chariot kept pace, urging them to greater and more frantic efforts.

They raced through the pastures until they came to a drainage ditch and such was their terror that instead of turning away they tried to jump it, but the jump was uncoordinated and one horse failed to clear the ditch, dragging the other one down with it. Both animals screamed, and the chariot caromed into them, shattering under the impact, tearing the leather straps and clips, and freeing one of them. It raced into the scrub bordering the farm, dragging the remnants of the chariot with it, while the other horse, two legs broken and its body impaled by a timber, screamed in agony in the drainage ditch.

Hori clutched his head, while the other grooms ran to help the fallen driver, who had hit his head and lay still. Others ran to put the stricken horse out of its misery, and a few set off after the runaway. Ibi had watched open-mouthed, and now groaned as he saw that one of the precious chariots had been smashed into bits.

"What frightened the horses?" Ibi asked.

"The chariot itself," Hori said. "I thought they were ready, but how will they ever be if they are fearful of the very thing they are pulling?"

"Your father seems to know a bit about chariots. At least, he talks as if he does."

Hori nodded. "He's old though, and forgetful. He gave no warning that this might happen." He sighed. "I suppose I will have to ask him and show my ignorance of such matters once again."

The grooms returned to say that the fallen driver was bruised and shaken but otherwise unhurt, but that one horse had had to be killed and the other one had been injured.

"We still have five good horses," Hori said. "We can't afford to lose any more, so from tomorrow we start getting them used to pulling together. Have them yoked in pairs to a pole between them and just lead them around quietly. Get them used to the presence of the other chariot, but don't hitch them to it. That's not going to happen until they feel comfortable around it."

"What do you want me to do?" Ibi asked.

"See what you can salvage from the wreckage of the chariot, and then talk to the carpenter we have on the estate. With a complete chariot to examine, they should be able to rebuild it swiftly."

Harrubaal, when he heard about the disaster, shook his head in dismay. "Train the horses in pairs. I would have thought that was obvious. If they are going to be working in pairs they must get used to doing so."

"I have instructed my men to do just that, father."

"And it seems they were scared by the chariot following close behind them. You'll have to limit their vision so they can't see it. Let them see straight ahead so they know where they are going, but they don't need to see to the side or behind them."

Hori and Ibi returned to the problem and came up with a program of introducing small changes to the horses' routines. Stiff leather was affixed to their bridles that limited their vision, blocking out the sight of anything that might startle them, and they rapidly became calmer. Horses were now trained in pairs. Some pairings did not work, as the animals took a dislike to their partner, but trial and error led to successful unions and before too long they had two sets of horses that worked well together, even with a chariot bumping and rattling around behind them. Grooms worked with them as charioteers, becoming accustomed to how the horses reacted, and devising ways of controlling them with a word, a flick of the reins or a touch with a willow wand. Months passed, but the day came when Hori could show off his two chariots, his father watching as they drove by at a smart clip, performing some simple manoeuvres.

"Good," Harrubaal said. "You have the basics. Now you start the real work."

"It has taken us nearly a year to get just two workable chariots," Ibi said. "We need hundreds if we are to counter the northern threat. How long is that going to take? Years?"

"Not as long as that," Hori said. "We know what we're doing now."

"Always providing the king supports us. Every carpenter in the kingdom will be needed, and many more horses than your estate can provide."

"I have every confidence we'll be given what we need. We leave for Ankh-Tawy soon to show off our chariots. When the king sees what we have achieved, he'll order chariots to be made by the hundred. They are the only thing that will counter the *heqa khasut* threat."

Chapter 14

Merybaal requested an audience with King Baalbek at the palace and was granted one almost immediately. Everyone knew that the king of Hattush and the Treasurer of the City were related, but few commented on the fact. It was accepted that a certain amount of corruption occurred within the higher (and lower) echelons of government, but as long as it remained within the bounds of propriety, no-one objected.

"I have a small problem, Majesty," Merybaal said, after the initial pleasantries had been concluded. Baalbek had sent for watered wine and the two men relaxed on a palace veranda overlooking the gardens.

"Official or unofficial?" Baalbek asked. "And there's no need for the title," he added. "We are family."

Merybaal inclined his head at the gesture. "Unofficial." He paused, sipping his wine. "In fact, it relates to family and is...um, somewhat delicate."

"If it is to do with Djedenre, there is probably nothing I can do. It is known that he is with Seneferenre."

"No, no...nothing to do with him. Officially I am critical of his ill-thought out and hasty decision, but he is my son, so I avoid the subject. No, this concerns my daughter Neferit."

"Sweet girl. How is she?"

"Well enough, but she too has made an unfortunate choice."

"She has loved unwisely? You want me to draft the importunate lad into the army? Put him in the front lines perhaps?"

"Nothing like that, Maj...er, Baalbek. She has fallen in love with chariots."

"A charioteer?"

"No, the vehicles themselves. She saw how devastatingly efficient they were when Menenre's army was annihilated, and has fallen in love with the concept. She wants to be a charioteer herself."

"But she's a girl...a young woman. Her thoughts should be on marriage and family."

"I have tried to persuade her of this, but she is adamant."

"My dear Merybaal, this can come to nothing. She is a woman and unacceptable in the chariot squadrons."

"She has already been accepted."

Baalbek stared at his elderly cousin. "What? How?"

"She disguised herself as a man."

The king burst out with laughter, but his humour dried up as he saw Merybaal was serious. "How?" he asked again.

"Few people know this, but she followed Djedenre when he went north with General Menenre. She was there at the battle, disguised as one Neterre, a Ribu princeling in the king's service. She wore a loose tunic, barbarian leggings and a cap." Merybaal shrugged. "She looks enough like a youth...an unbearded youth...to pass cursory inspection, and of course, no-one would think to see a woman in such a position."

"No...no, I suppose not. Still...where is she? At the Avaris stables?"

Merybaal nodded.

"So you want me to unmask her and return her to the family home."

"No. She would know it came from me and would never forgive me."

"Then what exactly do you want from me, Merybaal?"

Merybaal sighed. "Imagine how I feel, cousin. My youngest daughter deliberately puts herself in harm's way. I'm not talking about battle; she'll never get there, I'm sure, but she is a young girl in the company of hundreds of men and I wouldn't trust one of them. She needs protecting but I'm just her father...what can I do? You know the man in charge of the stables. Can you intercede with him?"

"The Overseer of the Stables does not have authority over the chariot squadrons. You need Anas-Har, the Supervisor of Chariots."

"Anas-Har then. Can you ask him to protect Neferit?"

"You know what will happen when I ask him to watch over Neferit, daughter of Treasurer Merybaal, who has recently enrolled as one of his trainee charioteers, don't you? She'll be out on her ear and no doubt he'll complain to the king."

Merybaal shook his head. "No, we've got to stop him finding out who she is."

"You can't have it both ways, cousin. Either she is revealed and protected, or has to take her chances as a man."

"Then...then ask him to protect her as a man."

"Why would he do that? If he was your son, perhaps, but your son would not be disguised as a Ribu princeling."

"Then ask him to look after Neterre, Prince of the Ribu, as a special favour to me. You may tell him he is a close friend of the family."

"You want me to lie for you?"

"I want you to help protect a member of your family, Baalbek. That is not too much to ask, is it?"

"And when this little subterfuge is discovered? It will be, you know."

"Then you blame me. You say you never met this Neterre, just passed on a request from me." Merybaal waited, examining the conflict in the younger man's eyes. "Will you do it?"

"Have you considered that your daughter may one day meet your son in battle? They are now on opposite sides of this conflict."

"It'll never happen. She'll be discovered and sent home long before she's trained."

"I hope so."

"Will you do it?"

Baalbek shrugged. "All right."

Neferit was, in turn, excited and terrified in her early days within the training school of the chariot squadrons. Being so close to these beautiful and deadly instruments of war thrilled her, but the proximity of so many young men made her heart beat faster. It was not that she was attracted to any of them, but she had not really thought out what it would mean to live and work with men. For one thing, they lived in a state of near nudity, and thought nothing about stripping off in front of her. Although growing up in the Delta had accustomed her to seeing half-naked men going about their everyday lives, she had lived in a household that observed all the proper proprieties. She had blushed and turned away at the start, but some men had noticed her shyness and took her to task on it, so she had to adapt quickly and learn to ignore the spectacles around her.

"I am Ribu," she told those who laughed at her. "In my country we are more modest. That is all there is to it."

"Well, get used to it, Neterre. You'll soon be working naked alongside us."

Bodily maintenance was another problem. Amurrans were not as obsessed with cleanliness as were Kemetu or the mixture of races that inhabited the Delta, but they still enjoyed swimming and washing after a day's hard work. Neferit was forced to declare she could not swim (though she could) so as to avoid stripping off for this communal pastime, and her ablutions were often carried out after everyone else had finished. Using the common middens were an agony at first, but she developed habits that allowed her to use these facilities when most other people were at work or swimming. Again, she used her supposed origins in Ribu to explain her modesty.

The work itself was hard and time-consuming. They rose before dawn and spent hours cleaning out the stables, feeding grooming and exercising the horses, before attending to the leather parts of the chariots and learning every part of the equipment. Instructors would take delight in hiding tiny flaws in the leather or stitching and waiting for a trainee to miss them. Punishment was swift and often painful and the men learned swiftly or dropped out. Neferit had a good eye and was painstaking, so only failed once. She was lucky that time as the instructor put her to mucking out the middens. Other instructors made their luckless victims strip naked and run circuits of the horse lines, so Neferit was at pains to avoid a punishment that would instantly reveal her gender.

It was not all grinding work though. Neferit had a genuine love of horses and managed to find time to take horses out, ostensibly to exercise them, but more often than not to ride out into the countryside or into the foothills for hours at a time and delight in the freedom and solitude of the sky and the grass, scrub and wildlife, and the feel of a horse running free beneath her. Other times she would seek out a place where she could watch the senior charioteers as they drilled and put their teams through their paces. Their actions reaffirmed her desire to become a charioteer herself. It was on a day only about a month after she started as a trainee that one of the other trainees found her watching the daily chariot manoeuvres.

"There you are, Neterre. Look lively, Commander Anas-Har wants to see you."

Neferit looked up in surprise. "What's it about, Nedjem?"

"You think the Commander takes me into his confidence? I was just told to find you and pass on the order. I don't care if you ignore it."

Neferit nodded and made her way back to the stables and presented herself at the Commander's office, wondering what she had done wrong. She was made to wait for the best part of an hour before being admitted, and she then saluted the Commander and stood in silence while Anas-Har looked her over carefully.

"You are Neterre, a prince of the Ribu?"

"Yes, sir."

"Formerly in service to King Seneferenre of the Delta?"

"Yes, sir."

"I can find no record of you in the army rolls we captured. There are other Ribu...a few at least...but none are a prince or go by the name of Neterre. How would you explain that?"

Neferit swallowed. Caught in a lie of Djedenre's making, she could either admit who she was or continue the lie and hope she was not found out.

"I joined General Menenre's army just a day before it was destroyed, sir. Possibly he had not yet entered me on the army roll. I was with Commander Djedenre during the battle and rode with him to safety on my horse."

"I was there," Anas-Har said. "Very few escaped; you were lucky." He looked at Neferit contemplatively. "Having seen the destruction of your army by chariots, you still want to join the squadrons? Why?"

"They are the most beautiful and deadly things I have ever seen, sir. I can think of nothing I could ever do that would match being a charioteer."

Anas-Har grunted. "Only the best are chosen to be charioteers." The Commander leaned back in his chair and stared at Neferit for several minutes, making her shift uncomfortably under his scrutiny.

"You have a certain beauty about you, Neterre. How old are you?"

Neferit was twenty-one, but knew that her slight figure and hairless face might attract suspicion. She would have to compound her lie, and hope that Anas-Har was not attracted to youths. "Seventeen, sir."

"Are all Ribu youths unbearded?"

"Some are, sir, though the royal family are traditionally clean-shaven."

Anas-Har grunted again. "How do you find the training course?"

"It's good, sir."

"Not too hard for you?"

"No, sir."

"I imagine living in close proximity to common men can't be easy for a prince."

"Nothing I can't get used to, sir."

"It has been suggested to me that a prince of Ribu should be afforded privileges."

Neferit hesitated. Some amelioration of her living conditions would be most welcome, but she knew that she could not ask for them, or appear to welcome them.

"I don't need privileges, sir, just the opportunity to learn."

The Commander nodded. "Good. I would hate to think that you thought your birth gave you rights others did not enjoy."

"No, sir."

"Yet I know what it is like to live amongst others not born to privilege. We share a common heritage, Prince Neterre. My mother was daughter of one of the kings of Lebanon and when I trained I found it a comfort that others knew of my position. It did not make my life as a soldier any easier...I still had to train and learn my trade...but my commander allowed me certain small benefits. In what part of your life here do you suffer the most?"

Neferit groaned inwardly. Did she dare hint at any dissatisfaction? Anas-Har could punish her for complaining, but if there was any chance of easing some aspects of her life, she had to take it.

"I find it difficult to use the middens, sir."

Neferit expected a scathing response from the Commander, so was surprised when he nodded.

"Understandable, though we all need to use them. What I can do is allow you to use the officer's facilities. They are cleaner, being less frequented."

"That is good of you, sir, but won't the officers object? I'm only a trainee."

"I think they will see the advantage of associating with a member of royalty." Anas-Har thought for a moment. "I think I'll move you in with one of the junior officers. You'll still perform your usual duties and be expected to train like the others, but you'll have a little more privacy. Not as a special privilege, you understand, but it is no more than your due. We can't have the Ribu royal family and your friends in Avaris thinking we hold you in low regard."

Friends in Avaris? Neferit thought. *I don't have friends...this is father's doing.* She opened her mouth to object and then thought what this privilege would mean. Anything that delayed the day when her gender was discovered was to be welcomed. But with whom would she now have to share quarters? She could hardly refuse the Commander's generosity.

"Thank you, Commander Anas-Har."

"Return to your duties, Prince Neterre. I will send word to you shortly, after I have arranged matters."

Neferit saluted and left the Commander's office, happy to be putting her days in the common barracks behind her but apprehensive about her future accommodation. Living in a barrack full of young men threatened imminent discovery, she thought, but surely her privacy would be more respected by an officer in the squadrons.

Later that day she received word that she was to be housed with Sadiki, a young captain of chariots. Apprehensively, she took her meagre belongings and took herself off to the assigned rooms in the officer's quarters, climbing a flight of stairs to an upstairs suite, where she introduced herself to Sadiki.

"So you're the Ribu princeling I've heard about?" Sadiki looked Neferit up and down, his lip curling as he took in the outlandish clothes she wore. "Anas-Har said he was going to foist a companion on me, but I thought he was joking when he said it was going to be a foreigner."

"I'm sorry to be an imposition, Captain Sadiki. I did not ask for this reassignment."

Sadiki shrugged. "We all share rooms, and the man who would have lived here with me died a while ago in battle. Up north somewhere, fighting against those god-cursed Avarans."

This isn't going to work. Why even bother? "I was there, Captain Sadiki, on the side of those god-cursed Avarans."

"Were you, by the thunder god's balls?" Sadiki looked at Neferit with renewed interest. "You must tell me about it sometime over a cup of wine. I'm always interested in tales of battle but I so rarely get to hear it from the point of view of the enemy. Now, where are my manners? Come inside, young Neterre of the Ribu. Let me show you your place."

Neferit entered the room carefully, unsure exactly what her welcome would be. Sadiki initially seemed unsure himself whether he was a friend or an enemy, but suddenly the young captain seemed to now overlook any reserve he had had, and became friendlier. He draped his arm about her shoulders as he led her around the two rooms they had at their disposal.

"Two rooms," Sadiki said. "This is the room in which we live. If we want we can eat here, though I like the barrack dining area...you get to meet people and talk...but it's nice to have a quiet drink of an evening. Through there is the bedroom. Two simple cots...no great luxuries and a bit cramped. You don't object to a little familiarity, I hope?" He laughed. "I'm joking, Neterre...though I needn't be. Might be fun, you know. Anyway, through here is a flight of external stairs that lead down to the dining area and general barracks. And that's it, I suppose. What do you think?"

"It looks all right," Neferit murmured. "But I don't want to be an imposition. I can go and ask the Commander to put me somewhere else."

"Nonsense. We'll get along just fine, I'm sure. Drop your belongings on your bed and get back to your work if you like. We'll have some wine and get to know each other better this evening."

Neferit saw no option but to do as Sadiki suggested. She almost ran back to her duties where she spent the day worrying about the interest the young captain had shown in her. *Has he seen through my disguise?* she asked herself. *Has he guessed I'm a woman?*

She returned to her rooms that evening, ready to defend her honour with her life, if necessary. A single oil lamp burned as she entered the rooms, and she found Sadiki waiting, sprawled in a chair with a jug of wine and two cups on the table in front of him. He grinned as she entered and gestured toward the other chair.

"Sit, young Neterre. Have some wine and relax. It is high time we became better acquainted." Sadiki poured the wine and pushed one cup across the table.

"I am tired," Neferit said. "Perhaps another time."

"If not wine, then at least sit and converse for a little while. I will not keep you from your bed long, but if we are to share these rooms, we must become better acquainted."

Neferit hesitated and then pulled the chair round the opposite side of the table from Sadiki. She sat and sipped at the wine.

"That's better," Sadiki said with a smile. "So...tell me about yourself, Neterre. How is it that a Ribu prince finds himself in the army of Samuqenu?"

Neferit shrugged. "I came to serve the king of Avaris, but when you northerners took over; I decided to stay on in your chariot force. That simple."

"Nothing is that simple," Sadiki said. "You know horses; I can see that much. But why come to Avaris where you a simply another man in the northern army? Had you remained in the land of Ribu, your status as a prince would surely have meant wealth and position."

"I er...wanted to see more of the world."

Sadiki smiled and poured a little more wine in Neferit's cup. "Drink up, beautiful boy. You have come to the right place if you seek to broaden your experiences. I can introduce you to many wonderful things."

"Learning to be a charioteer is all I want."

"How do you know what else you might desire if you don't try them?"

"I'm not sure what you mean."

"Come, Neterre, such things cannot be unknown to you. You are a beautiful youth and men must have paid attention to you before. Do not deny it."

"Yet I do deny it, Sadiki. I am not interested in such things."

Sadiki leaned across the table and grasped one of Neferit's hands. She tried to draw back, but he was strong and held on.

"Do not resist, Neterre, for I mean you no harm. Place yourself in my hands and you will find that I am a gentle and considerate lover."

"I...I am not interested in men, Sadiki. Please let me go."

Sadiki kept hold of Neferit's hand. "Have you ever been with a man?"

"No."

"Then how do you know you won't like it? It is perfectly natural that two men may enjoy each other's company, be intimate together.

You have that fragile and tender quality, Neterre, which tells me you are made to enjoy a man's bed."

Neferit drew back her hand firmly, and Sadiki let go. "Sadiki, it may be natural to you, but it is not to me. I know within myself, as I have known since I was a child, that I am not interested in men...in any way. I am sorry if you thought otherwise."

"Try me, Neterre," Sadiki cajoled. "If you haven't experienced a man..."

"I do not have to experience the flux to know I would not enjoy it."

Sadiki sucked in his breath. "Ah, you wound me, beautiful youth." He shook his head sadly. "I have never been compared to a flux before, but if that is your earnest wish..."

"It is."

"Then I will seek my pleasures elsewhere."

Neferit rose to her feet. "I suppose I must ask for different quarters then."

"No need, Neterre. You have made your preferences plain and I will not seek to persuade you otherwise. We can still be friends, can we not?"

Neferit was not at all sure that she could trust him, but complaining to the Chariot Commander might not serve her well. If she remained on her guard, she might be all right, and if all else failed, she had a knife and would use it to defend her honour. The thought made her smile inwardly as Sadiki would discover exactly what he did not desire should he ever try anything physical.

Chapter 15

K ing Seneferenre quickly found that the farmlands of the Delta were not the best place to maintain an army, particularly an army that lacked the normal supply pathways and lacked a secure base of operations. There was a lack of structure to the maintenance of a fighting force that had recently tasted defeat and morale was low. He had moved some five thousand men across the river from Iunu in the face of the *heqa khasut* chariot squadrons, and then moved them further west without any clear destination in mind. He ultimately intended to retake Avaris and oust the invaders, but he could think of no easy way to do this. Rather than remain indecisive, he called together his principal officers and asked them for their advice.

The senior officer was General Inkhare and he resented any other opinion being asked. It was his view that General Menenre had lost all credibility after his defeat by the chariots in the north. As for the other officers present, Djedenre and Menkare were mere Commanders, young men without experience. No, his was the only opinion that mattered and the king was making a mistake consulting anyone but him.

"There is only one course of action, Majesty," Inkhare declared. "We must conserve our strength and avoid conflict until we can be certain of victory."

For his part, General Menenre felt his defeat deeply, though he was sure it had not been his fault. His own advisers had offered him faulty information as to the capabilities of the enemy chariots. If only he had not arrayed his men on flat firm ground and stood waiting for the chariot charge. It was a wonder anyone had escaped and it was only chance that ensured his own survival. He would not make the same mistake the next time he faced the enemy, and yearned to cleanse his name of the stigma of defeat by bathing in the fires of battle.

"We gain nothing by hanging back, Majesty," Menenre countered. "The longer we wait the stronger and more secure the enemy becomes. I say we strike back immediately and recapture your throne."

Djedenre and Menkare were under no illusions as to their abilities. They were both young and had little experience of battle, though Menkare had been a member of the Delta army for half his forty years. His brother-in-law had only recently taken up a military life, yet their experience was about equal as the army had had little to occupy itself with before the invasion. Now that they were with the king's army in flight from the enemy, they knew they had a responsibility to temper both the caution of one general and the recklessness of the other.

"Majesty," Djedenre said. "We are not strong enough to strike back with any hope of success, yet we cannot afford to just do nothing."

"The longer we go without a victory," Menkare added, "the harder it will be to inspire the men. Already men are deserting us."

"They dare to do this?" Seneferenre asked. "You must stamp out this disloyalty."

"I agree, Majesty," Inkhare said. "Better to have a hundred loyal men than a thousand weak-livered ones."

"That attitude will see us defeated," Menenre said. "Forget about getting rid of cowards. Throw them into battle and they will quickly remember their loyalty."

"Or betray us by throwing down their weapons," Inkhare said. "We need to withdraw into the far reaches of the Delta and strengthen our army by casting out undesirables."

"Attack the enemy and let the cowards serve some purpose by dying," Menenre said.

"I very much desire to recapture Avaris and cast out the invaders," Seneferenre said, "and in this I favour General Menenre." Inkhare scowled at his beaming colleague. "But I can see the wisdom of General Inkhare." Now Menenre scowled. "What am I to do? Menkare, Djedenre, advise me."

"We do not have enough men to face the enemy, Majesty," Djedenre said, "even if they were all eager to fight."

"Five thousand is not an inconsiderable force," Seneferenre countered. "Perhaps we could improve morale somehow."

"Five thousand might face the enemy infantry, but they could not triumph over a thousand chariots."

"So we need more men?"

"Many more, Majesty."

"Or chariots of our own," Menkare added.

Menenre laughed. "And just where are we to get chariots?" he asked. "Capture them or make them? And even if we could, do you know how to drive one or guide it in battle? I have seen them in use and I doubt that skill is easily learned."

Menkare shrugged. "More men, then."

"It doesn't matter how many we have if we cannot face their chariot squadrons," Inkhare said.

"So you are advocating we just give up?" Djedenre asked.

"Don't be foolish. I'm just saying we cannot, at present, face the enemy chariots. That may change in the future, but for now we must fall back and avoid battle."

"Coward," Menenre muttered, but Inkhare ignored him.

"Fall back where?" Menkare asked. "For how long?"

Inkhare shrugged. "One of the other Delta cities."

"Can any city in the Delta support five thousand extra men?" Djedenre asked.

"Well, they're going to have to. It's their duty."

"It would be adding a tremendous burden to any community. Food would be totally inadequate, as would accommodation, even just the destruction of the surrounding farmland by ten thousand trampling feet."

"Five thousand you mean...ah, yes...sorry."

"What is the alternative?" Seneferenre asked. "There must be something we can do."

"There is," Inkhare said. "What I've been saying all along. We've lost Avaris for now, so choose another city in the Delta and make it your capital. Fight the invader from there. Djedu would be a suitable city."

"Why give up on Avaris?" Menenre asked. "Attack at once and take it back. They won't be expecting that."

"Neither course is feasible, Majesty," Djedenre said, "but both have elements of the right course."

161

"How so?"

"Men on foot cannot face chariots, but our men are the match of any infantry the invader can throw at us. Pull back into the well-watered lands of the Delta and draw the enemy after us. They won't bring their chariots because the wheels would sink into the soft soil. Infantry only, Majesty, and we deal with each foray, destroying them."

"It could work, Majesty," Menkare said. "Make the enemy pay in blood for every span of Delta land."

"A force that large is too cumbersome to wield in that fashion," Inkhare said.

"Exactly," Menenre said. "We should use it to attack instead."

"I wouldn't try and do it with five thousand men, but with a thousand or fewer it could work," Djedenre said.

"It is an interesting proposal," King Seneferenre said, "but could you actually achieve anything with a thousand men or fewer?"

"I believe so, Majesty. A small mobile force could live off the land, strike the enemy hard and disperse before they could hit back. We might not achieve a resounding victory, but we could hurt the invader for every step he took into the Delta."

"To what end?" the king asked. "I don't want to just hurt the enemy with little pricks of thorns; I want to hurl him out of the Delta."

"Who can say what the future holds, Majesty? The gods may smile on us, but that divine beneficence will be useless if we are not here to receive it. I believe this plan would give us the best chance of survival."

"And we have four senior commanders," Menkare pointed out. "Twelve hundred apiece. We could do it."

"Five commanders," Djedenre corrected his friend. "We have the king as well."

"Thank you, Commander Djedenre," Seneferenre said.

"We can't just live out in the open," Inkhare complained. "We need a base of operations. Occupy and fortify a city and defend it against the enemy's incursions."

"Then while we are locked in our city forts, the enemy picks us off one at a time," Djedenre said. "We should be mobile so we can support each other."

"But we could also have a city to fall back on," Menkare said. "Certain cities recommend themselves--Per-Bast, Djedu, Zau, Behdet, Per-Wadjet. Five cities, five commanders."

Seneferenre gave the idea some thought before nodding his acceptance. Being the king, he selected Per-Bast as his city, because it was closest to the enemy.

"It is only right that the king is foremost in the fight for the kingdom," he declared.

"And I will take Behdet," General Menenre said. "It too is in the forefront and close to the north."

"Per-Wadjet for me," General Inkhare said.

"That leaves Djedu and Zau for Menkare and me," Djedenre said.

"You'd better take Djedu," Menkare said with a grin. "It's almost named for you."

Seneferenre and Menenre selected the most warlike and aggressive soldiers for their commands, making no secret of their intention to carry the war to the enemy at every opportunity. Inkhare took most of the others, leaving only small commands of about five hundred men apiece for Menkare and Djedenre. They were happy with this arrangement as they preferred a small mobile force for what they had planned.

The two commanders took their men and moved to the northwest together travelling slowly while they worked out how they would cooperate militarily. Each unit would occupy and fortify their city, but would seldom spend time within its walls. The enemy would be making incursions into the central Delta and they were determined to meet them and inflict injuries.

"The only real problem I can see that will limit our mobility are the various arms of the river," Menkare said.

"Boats are the answer," Djedenre replied, "but how we manage to get sufficient in place when we need them is another matter. How many will we need for five hundred men?"

They arrived at Djedu first, where Djedenre informed Nebausir, the mayor of the city, that henceforth the city was under military rule. He showed him the orders under the seal of King Seneferenre, and although the mayor grumbled, he had no option but to obey his king. The mayor was also curious about the situation in Avaris.

"King Seneferenre is still king then? We have heard many rumours about the invasion of the *heqa khasut*, but it is hard to sift out the facts. Some say Avaris has been razed to the ground, others that the invader has been routed...even that the king is dead."

"Then let me put your mind at ease, Mayor Nebausir," Djedenre said. "The king is very much alive and is conducting the defence of his kingdom. Avaris still stands, but has been occupied by the invader, and I have no doubt that the king will liberate the kingdom in due course. What I require of you is your utmost cooperation as I intend to use Djedu as my base of operations."

Nebausir licked his lips. "Naturally, I shall obey all lawful commands from our king, but I fear for the people of my city. If you draw the enemy here, your men will not be sufficient to protect them."

"The invader will come anyway, Nebausir, whether I am here or not. You can either wait for him and kneel in submission, or you can help your king in opposing him."

Djedenre did not say that if the mayor refused to help, he would be removed from office and somebody else put in charge. He had several officers who could direct the fortification of the city. Nebausir was probably as aware as Djedenre, as he bowed his head in acquiescence.

"It would be an honour to assist the king in any way I can," he said.

Tradesmen and labourers of the city were pressed into service. Mud bricks were made by the thousand and, after drying in the sun, were used to rebuild the city walls and add observation towers. Ditches were dug and flooded from the river, with only narrow causeways left to allow access. Boats were pressed into service, and Djedenre's men practiced rapid crossings of the river. Word came from Menkare that Zau was being similarly fortified and, with both cities now a secure refuge, Djedenre's thoughts turned to wielding his small force against the enemy.

The opportunity arose a month later when a messenger arrived with the news that a large force of Amurru, together with a hundred chariots, had crossed the river and attacked Per-Bast. King Seneferenre, instead of employing the strike and retreat tactics agreed upon, attempted to attack the enemy face to face, with disastrous results.

"The king lives, Commander Djedenre," the messenger said, "but he was forced to flee. He bids you and your men come immediately to strengthen his army."

Djedenre swore under his breath. "Where is the king now?"

"He falls back to the south and west, Commander, but he is caught between two arms of the river and must soon have the water at his back. He says he will make a stand there and expects to see you fall on the enemy's rear."

"Tell the king I will come."

The messenger shook his head. "Of that there is no doubt, Commander, and I have no need of conveying that message. My orders are to find Commander Menkare and General Inkhare and seek their help."

Djedenre dismissed the messenger and turned his mind to the problem the king's summons presented. His understanding had been that the small units each commander controlled would be used to harass the enemy, rather than attack them as the king had done. Now Seneferenre was in retreat, likely from a superior force, and was likely to be trapped between two arms of the river. One thing was plain, he realised; he could not abandon the king. Seneferenre was more important than a thousand men, so he would have to attempt a rescue, though preferably without endangering his own men. The more he thought about it, the more he knew he needed Menkare's help, so he swiftly sent off a messenger of his own on the heels of the king's messenger, outlining what he thought was the best action to take.

He decided he could not wait for Menkare to reply so, hoping that his friend would agree with his plan, he marshalled his men and set out rapidly for the last known position of the invading force. According to the information supplied by the messenger, the king was retreating slowly into an ever-narrowing slice of land bordered by two arms of the river with about a thousand men. Opposing him was a mixed force of two or three thousand, mostly infantry, but with possibly two hundred chariots. The chariots alone, if they could find firm ground, would be enough to destroy all their opposition.

Djedenre fretted that he could not reach the enemy in time to help his king, and drove his men on, cajoling and encouraging extra speed from rapidly tiring limbs. He sent the fleetest of foot ahead to scout the way, and they returned with the news that the king had dug defences across a narrow strip of land and was defending it against the enemy. The good news was that the chariots could not engage the king's forces and were stationed in the rear while the main part of the invading army tested the defences.

Keeping his men back to give them a chance to rest, Djedenre ran forward with his scouts and crept within view of the enemy, noting their positions. They were more numerous than the messenger had indicated, and Djedenre almost despaired that he would be able to do anything. He had to try, though, so he sent the scouts back to bring the men up, dividing his force into five groups of about a hundred men apiece. A massed attack would serve no useful purpose as the enemy would turn and crush them, so he had to devise a strategy to inflict enough damage to give the king respite without endangering his own men. As his men came up on his position, Djedenre slipped back to talk to his officers.

"The king has dug in behind a ditch and embankment and is holding the enemy for now, but he will inevitably be pushed back. Then the chariots will pierce the defences and overwhelm him. We do not have enough men to give any effective help, unless we can neutralise the chariots."

"How can we do that, sir?" asked one of his officers. "We all saw what chariots can do, outside Avaris."

"I know; I was there. However, that was a chariot charge. Here, they are unaware of our presence. We must get close so that our archers can be sure of their targets. The axemen will run in and inflict as much damage as they can and then run, their retreat covered by the archers."

The officers grimaced, and the one who had spoken before, spoke again. "We will do our duty, of course, sir, but how effective can we be? The chariots are mobile and will turn on us as soon as we attack."

Djedenre grinned. "Did I not say? We attack the horses. If even one horse is hit in each pair, you render the chariot useless. Fifty archers, fifty horses, fifty chariots down. The axemen can surely take out another fifty horses and then the enemy power is halved."

He sent his men out into position, enjoining his archers to make their arrows count, and then took his own men forward. As he waited for everyone to get ready, he selected a chariot that looked as if it might belong to the commander. If he could strike at the commander it might demoralise the enemy. At his signal, the archers loosed their arrows, swiftly repeating their actions, and although only a hundred or so arrows arced into the enemy lines, the effect was sudden and bloody. Men shouted and horses screamed as shafts pierced hides and the stricken animals plunged and reared. Djedenre led his men in at a run, seeing other small groups heading for other sections, and then they were among the chariots. They ignored the men except where they interfered, concentrating on the horses. It pained him to strike at defenceless animals, but they were large, easy targets, and the life of his king was at stake.

Their sudden attack had caught the enemy completely by surprise, but now they were recovering. Men shouted orders and horns blew, alerting the main army to the assault in the rear. Already, soldiers were detaching from the attack on King Seneferenre's defences and streaming back toward the chariots. The chariot squadron was in chaos, with plunging horses and several beasts dead or dying, dragging down the animals yoked to them and tipping over chariots.

"Time to go lads," Djedenre yelled, gesturing to his men. "Back...for your lives."

There was just one more thing Djedenre wanted to do--kill the chariot commander. The man in question was rallying the chariots nearest him and his own driver had his horses under control. Djedenre ran toward the commander rather than with his men, but saw to his dismay that the commander was already bringing several chariots into line, facing the retreating men. Once he started the charge, nothing would save his men, so Djedenre uttered a despairing cry and hurled his axe.

The commander heard him and turned, then lurched to one side as the bronze axe flew by his head, burying itself in the driver's chest. Soundlessly, the driver fell from the chariot, the reins spilling from his lifeless hands, but the commander snatched them up as the chariot leapt forward.

Djedenre was now unarmed and could do no more. He turned to escape but found himself cut off by the enemy hurrying up in support. The chariot commander stood in his chariot unmoving and stared at Djedenre, watching as he ducked and weaved through the wreckage of chariots and dead horses. A soldier aimed a blow at him, missing, and Djedenre hit him with his shoulder, knocking him to the ground. He snatched up the fallen soldier's sword and just managed to parry a blow by another of the enemy, before running again.

Arrows slashed through the air close to him, and men were now ranging out on either side of him, cutting him off from where his men had fled. Ahead lay the river...his feet squelched through waterlogged grass and then mud...he splashed into the shallows as arrows zipped past him. Turning, he slashed at a soldier almost upon him, forcing him back before hurling his sword at another and throwing himself into deeper water. He started swimming, crying out as an arrow grazed his arm, and others fell close to him. Striking out strongly, he made it into the central current and beyond the range of all but the strongest archers, aiming for the opposite shore, when he heard shouts. He stopped swimming, treading water, and saw to his horror that men awaited him on the far shore. They were not armed with bows, but they were undoubtedly Amurru, and barred him from any safety on the eastern bank. Djedenre allowed the current to carry him for a minute or so before he realised the river was carrying him northward toward Iunu and into territory held by the enemy. Any hope he had of escape lay to the south, and that meant going against the current.

Djedenre started swimming but quickly realised he did not have the strength to fight against the current for any length of time. The water nearer the shores was slower, but put him in danger from the troops still lining either bank. Of the two shores, the eastern one was the least dangerous as the soldiers there had no archers, so he made his way into the shallows and swam slowly upriver, taking advantage of patches of slow-moving water and even some where an eddy aided him in his efforts. The soldiers kept pace with him on shore and if he came too close, they pelted him with rocks and the occasional spear. Nothing touched him, though the wound to his arm still bled. It was not until he felt the water swirl around him that he realised the danger he might be in from another source. Blood in the water would attract crocodiles and it felt as if one had found him already.

"O Sobek, great lord of the waters," Djedenre prayed, "O one of the pointed teeth, great splashing one who came from the thigh and tail of the goddess in the sunlight, hear me. Protect me from the denizens of the waters, Great Sobek, and I will sacrifice a bull to you."

A great swirl of water surrounded him once more and Djedenre gabbled his prayer again, sure in his heart that a crocodile was about to grip him with its pointed teeth and drag him down to his death in the green depths. The men on the eastern shore saw the eruption of water around the swimmer and cried aloud, but he swam on unscathed and they fell silent, certain that the gods had intervened. Their officers shouted and swore, but the men would go no further, steadfastly refusing to pursue the enemy soldier any further.

"We will be seen as opposing the gods if we do so," they said. "It is plain to see that if the crocodile of the river leaves him alone, then the gods favour him."

Djedenre swam on slowly, and now even the soldiers on the western shore turned back. A little later, he emerged onto the eastern shore, staggering up through the reeds and long grass to collapse with exhaustion on dry land. After a few minutes he rolled onto his back and shielded his eyes against the glare of the hot sun high in the blue dome of the sky.

"I'm alive," he murmured, feeling some amazement. He had skirted death at the hands of the foreign invaders and in the jaws of a crocodile and had made it safely to shore. Sitting up, he looked around, certain that the enemy on the eastern shore would be looking for him. Nobody was nearby, and even standing up he couldn't see anyone. He started walking south along the bank of the river, wondering if he dared swim across to the other bank. The king's men were over there somewhere and they would welcome him. He was reluctant to take to the water again, the memory of the nearness of the crocodile still too fresh. Sobek had intervened once, but would he do so again.

Half a day passed and Djedenre was starting to think about heading inland to find a village where he could perhaps rest and find something to eat when he saw sails upriver from him. He dropped to a crouch, wondering if he should try and hide, but someone had evidently seen him for the boats started angling in toward the eastern bank. Djedenre contemplated flight, but he doubted he had the strength, so he stood and waited to be captured. The boats came closer, about ten in all, and some sailed past him before stopping and the largest came in close to shore near where he stood. He started edging away, but a shout stopped him.

"Are you going to just stand there, brother? We don't have all day."

Djedenre stared at the man standing up in the boat.

"Menkare? Where did you come from?"

The man leapt overboard into the shallow water and waded ashore.

"Don't you remember? You're the one that suggested it. Gather up some boats and sail to the rescue of the king. Well, here I am."

"And the king?"

"Duly rescued, though we had to abandon most of his surviving men. There were just too many of them. It seems you allowed them just enough time to retreat down to the junction of the rivers where we waited. I heard you got in a spot of trouble so I thought I'd come looking for you."

Djedenre shook his head and embraced his brother-in-law. "I don't suppose you have a bull, do you?"

"A bull? No; but I dare say we can find one. Why?"

"A promise I made to Sobek." Djedenre put his arm around Menkare's shoulders and started toward the waiting boat. "So the king's really safe?" he asked.

Chapter 16

King Khasekhare died after a short illness contracted after drinking water from a well rather than from the healthful river. The servant who brought him the water was judged to be guilty of poisoning the king and was put to death. Ankh-Tawy and the neighbouring regions of Kemet were once more thrown into turmoil trying to decide on the new king. Bebi and Sobekhotep absented themselves from the capital city, being unwilling to enter into a contest that was becoming increasingly dangerous. A few families put forward scions that they thought might stand a chance, but after two of them died from illnesses that bore a strong resemblance to the one that carried off Khasekhare, the survivors withdrew, allowing an army officer called Mersemenenre to claim the throne. He was crowned and anointed as the new king, but apart from having his name carved on a few temple walls and scarabs made with his name inscribed on them, everything else continued much as before. Tjaty Aya kept his position and his son Ayameru continued to champion the construction and development of chariots under the leadership of Hori, son of Harrubaal.

King Mersemenenre was persuaded to back Hori's project too, as the news from the Delta was not good. The *heqa khasut* had recently cornered and beaten the army of the northern king Seneferenre, inflicting many casualties and sending the king running for his life. It was only the prompt and unorthodox actions of two military commanders that prevented the Delta from suffering a complete defeat. Mersemenenre could read the invader's intentions as easily as he could read the writing on temple walls and knew that something had to be done to counter the threat.

Orders had gone out to every *heri-tep a'a* of every *sepat* down the length of the Great River from the administrative area of the Knife Land, just south of Ankh-Tawy, to the Land of the Bow, bordering on the Kingdom of Kush. Only the area known as Great Land, around the city of Abdju, had refused to enlist men to counter the northern threat, and Khasekhare had been debating a suitable punishment for the Lords of Abdju when he had been divested of life. Mersemenenre decided to leave that problem alone for the time being as men were already arriving from the more northerly *sepatu*, and these men needed to be trained.

General of the Army Neferhotep had dared refuse the new king's command, and though Mersemenenre was angered by this refusal, he felt sufficiently unsure of his position to challenge the Commander of all the armies of Kemet.

"The men must be trained, General," the king said. "Most of these men are simple farmers who have never wielded anything more dangerous than a mattock or a hoe. The rest are tradesmen and city dwellers equally unused to warfare."

"In this we are agreed, Son of Re, but I am not some lowly officer that shouts at men and beats them with a stick when they disobey. I am General of the Army and it is an insult to ask me to do this training."

Mersemenenre forbore from pointing out that he had not asked the general to do it, but had ordered him instead. "Someone must do it, Neferhotep."

"There are a hundred junior officers capable of the task," he said.

"I'm sure there are," the king replied, "but I still need a senior officer to coordinate the training and make sure everything is carried out in the proper manner. You would excel at this."

"What about Commander Sewahenre?"

"General Sewahenre now. I promoted him."

"General Sewahenre then, Son of Re. He is still junior to me and more worthy of such a mind-numbing task."

"I have other tasks for him."

"Such as?"

King Mersemenenre bristled at the rudeness of his General. Perhaps he had been wrong about this man and he did not represent a danger to his newly acquired throne. After all, he had other generals and other commanders willing to obey him. All that was needed was a firm hand.

"I do not answer to you, Neferhotep. Now, are you going to accept this task or must I find myself another General of the Army?"

Neferhotep glared at the king for a moment, before lowering his gaze. He was General of the Army but he could not be completely sure of the loyalty of his men. Not yet, at any rate, though Neferhotep vowed that one day he would have revenge for the slights cast his way.

"If that is indeed your will, Son of Re, then I am happy to obey. But...may I humbly ask what General Sewahenre will be doing? I ask only that I may know what all my officers are doing."

"I have put him in charge of our chariot squadrons."

"What chariot squadrons? I wasn't aware we had any."

"Not yet, but soon. Commander Hori has built four chariots and trained horses to pull them. If everything goes well at the trials, then we will expand these few into a fighting force that can counter the northern invaders." King Mersemenenre smiled happily. "Who knows? Maybe we will win back the Delta as well."

"Four chariots? The invaders must be having nightmares." Neferhotep shook his head and left the king. He went to organise the first of the new men arriving from the southern *sepatu*.

Hori had continued with his work training the horses on his father's estate, while others in his team built chariot parts in Ankh-Tawy before bringing them down for trials. The best of the grooms on Harrubaal's estates learned to control the horses and to drive the chariots until Hori was reasonably satisfied with their progress. They displayed none of the skill and daring of the charioteers he had seen from the walls of Iunu, but that level of expertise only came after years of training. It would have to do because General Sewahenre had ordered horses and chariots north to the capital city for an exhibition of this new weapon. Ayameru had sent him a private message stressing the importance of this exhibition, saying that the future of the chariot force might depend on a successful showing.

The plains opposite the white-walled city, on the eastern bank of Iteru, were used to muster troops and allow them to train. Flat, firm ground, lightly grassed, was perfect for infantry practicing battle movements and it would provide an excellent venue for the chariot demonstration. Word had got around and instead of a small demonstration to selected viewers, hundreds of people streamed across the river, agog to see this new thing. King Mersemenenre was there with Generals Neferhotep and Sewahenre, Tjaty Aya and his son Ayameru, and every nobleman or high-ranking official who regarded himself important enough to attend. Wives attended, decked out in their finery, and servants thronged with them, bearing chairs and ostrich feather fans, jars of river-cooled wine and perfumes to ward off the stench of the common people. Such was the throng of onlookers that the soldiers in training were pressed into service constructing seating for the nobles and a raised dais for the more important personages.

"I don't like this," Hori muttered to Ayameru.

"Why not? You have a great audience for your triumph."

"We have never tested the chariots under extreme conditions. What happens if something goes wrong in front of the king and generals?"

"What do you mean, you've never tested them?" Ayameru asked, concern showing on his face. "I understood you had already done so on your father's estates."

"We've trotted them around and made sure the grooms can handle the teams, but I doubt the king will be satisfied with such a tame exhibition."

"You can't call it off now. Everyone is here and expecting great things."

Hori grunted. "Then pray to the gods that nothing goes wrong. At least we don't have and ditches to wreck us; just flat plains."

Hori hurried off to have some last words with the charioteers, beseeching them to drive safely and carefully, stressing the importance of getting through the afternoon without mishap.

The four charioteers saluted the king and climbed aboard their chariots, driving them in file before the king and nobles. Then, easing them into a trot, the chariots moved away for a space before circling back and coming to a halt before the dais. Mild applause greeted them, but General Neferhotep voiced what many were thinking.

"These are the much vaunted chariots? I've seen farm carts move faster and ox-drawn wagons look more menacing. This is all a waste of time."

"I am inclined to agree," King Mersemenenre said. "Tjaty Aya, how much gold has this exercise cost the treasury? I think we should be compensated."

"Son of Re, I am sure they can do better. Ayameru, see to it."

"Yes, father. Commander Hori?"

Hori bowed and ran out to the chariots, where he quickly spoke to the charioteers.

"We're going to have to do it now. Full speed, same manoeuvres, and in the name of all the gods, be careful."

The chariots wheeled and set off, the horses urged into a gallop. They raced past the crowd, away onto the plain, going through a series of turns before heading straight for the crowd and pulling up in a storm of dust. The applause was much louder this time.

"Better," General Neferhotep said. "I could almost believe they were instruments of war, but how effective are they going to be? I mean, what damage can they actually inflict? A hand of archers would be more dangerous."

"A chariot normally carries an archer into battle," Ayameru explained. "They carry them at speed and the damage to the enemy is inflicted speedily."

"Show us," Neferhotep challenged.

Hori groaned inwardly. "My lord General, we have not yet trained archers to loose arrows from a moving chariot."

"We have archers here amongst the recruits. Use them."

"They er...might find it hard to hang on and use a bow, my lord. They are untrained."

"All they need to do is stay upright," Neferhotep growled. "I'll take your word for it that archers can be trained to loose arrows from a chariot, but I want to see that a chariot can do those same manoeuvres with two men aboard."

Hori had no option but to order it so. Four archers were called out and they reluctantly climbed into the chariots, where they stood looking frightened, their hands gripping the guard rail beside the charioteers.

"Hold on tight and do not concern yourself with using your bows," Hori told them. "It will soon be over. Drive past the dais as before then turn away and speed up," he added for the charioteers. Do nothing fancy. Return and speed past the dais again, come to a halt and salute the king."

The charioteers saluted and did as Hori commanded, the four of them racing off into the distance before returning at speed, dashing past the crowd in a cloud of dust. One of the archers was grinning broadly and showing off by lifting his bow aloft in one hand and his sheaf of arrows in the other. His confidence exceeded his skill and he overbalanced, clutching wildly at the charioteer as he started to fall. The charioteer, startled, half turned and pulled back on the reins on one side. Obeying the commands transmitted through the reins, the horses turned as sharply to their right as they could and the sudden pressure snapped a segment of the rim in the left wheel. Between one breath and the next the wheel came apart, wood splintering and collapsing, spokes flying apart in splinters. The chariot flipped over, throwing its occupants out, the archer dying almost instantly but the charioteer, with reins still bound around his arms, was dragged with the wreckage until grooms could run out and bring the horses under control.

A cry of horror went up from the crowd, while Hori and his men ran to manage the situation, attending to the injured man until a physician could arrive. He looked back at the dais to see that the king, his senior nobles and the generals had all left, and that the crowd was dispersing. Ayameru came over to Hori, his face sombre.

"That was unfortunate," he said. "How is the charioteer?"

"He'll live...probably. A broken arm and a lot of cuts and bruises." Hori looked toward the now empty dais. "How did the king take it?"

"Not well, and Neferhotep was most scathing. If it is left to him, he'll end your project as a waste of time and gold."

Hori cursed. "I'd better try and get an audience with the king. See if I can persuade him this is just a setback rather than a disaster."

"Is it, Commander Hori? That wheel came apart very easily. How useful is a chariot if a sharp turn shatters the wheels?"

"We know that they are useful...and sturdier than our chariots, so there must be a reason. Perhaps we just need to make the wheels stronger."

"They're patterned on the fragments you salvaged from the north," Ayameru said. "If those were strong enough for the invader, why aren't they strong enough for you?"

"I don't know," Hori said.

"Well, you'd better find out the reason quickly, my friend, or that'll be the end for us."

"So much for that," General Neferhotep said. "That's what happens when you try to embrace something new."

"It was an unfortunate accident," Tjaty Aya said. "Nothing more."

"There seem to be a lot of accidents associated with these chariots," General Sewahenre commented. "I have a report that chariots were wrecked on the Harrubaal estate too."

"Doesn't surprise me," Neferhotep said. "That family is foreign. Harrubaal came from Hattush in Retjenu, if you remember. They're probably allied to the northern invader."

"Must I remind you, General Neferhotep, that both Lord Harrubaal and I married into the family of King Merneferre Aya? Royal blood flows in both of our families. Unless, of course, you are accusing me of being less than loyal to Kemet?"

"Of course not, Aya, but..." Neferhotep shrugged. "All I'm saying is that an army of axemen, swordsmen, spearmen and archers have served Kemet well for a thousand years or more. Why do we need to even consider something untried like these chariots? You have seen for yourself how unreliable they are."

"They're not exactly untried," Aya pointed out. "By all accounts the *heqa khasut* are using them to great effect against Seneferenre in the Delta."

"I think that says more about the poor quality of the Delta commanders than about the effectiveness of the *heqa khasut* chariots."

"You would gamble the fate of Kemet on your ability as a general?" Sewahenre asked.

"I know my capabilities."

"What if you're wrong? What if the *heqa khasut* chariots really are a superlative new weapon?"

"I'm not wrong," Neferhotep declared. "It's possible the chariots are effective against poorly led troops, but I'll back my men against them any day."

"And what do you say, Son of Re?" Sewahenre asked. "It is your kingdom that will fall if my esteemed colleague is wrong."

King Mersemenenre shifted uncomfortably on his throne, unwilling to commit himself on the topic. He had been excited and uplifted by the sheer innovation of the chariots, but after the accident disappointment had overwhelmed him.

"I think they could be useful, but also could be a liability," the king said.

"So do we continue with them?" Tjaty Aya asked.

Mersemenenre shrugged. "Maybe."

Aya sighed. "Then in the absence of a firm denial, Son of Re, I will instruct Commander Hori to continue his work."

"In the absence of a firm commitment to support them, I think the king is indicating we should reject them," Neferhotep said. "Is that not so, Son of Re?"

The king was obviously wavering, so Sewahenre stepped in. "Son of Re, before the accident, the chariots looked formidable, didn't they? All that went wrong today was the wheel shattering. If Hori can fix that problem, then should we not give them another chance?"

"They are expensive," Neferhotep growled. "A waste of time and gold."

"Yet having spent so much on them already, a little more won't hurt; will it, Son of Re?" Aya cajoled.

"Give Hori another month, Son of Re," Sewahenre said. "If he cannot solve it by then, then you can reconsider."

"That er...seems reasonable," Mersemenenre said. "What do you think, General Neferhotep?"

Neferhotep scowled but bowed to his king. "A month, Son of Re, and then we concentrate on building up our conventional army."

The king nodded. "Let it be so."

Hori sat down with his companions Ibi and Piye to ponder the problem of the wheel and how it might be solved. Ayameru joined them a little later with the news that they had a month to come up with a solution before the king shut them down.

"We won't need a month if we can identify the problem," Piye said. "It'll only take a few days for the carpenters to knock up another wheel built to whatever specifications are needed."

"Whatever specifications those are," Ibi said gloomily.

Hori picked up a piece of the shattered wheel and turned it over in his hands. "I don't understand it," he said. "This is exactly the same as the wheel we salvaged."

"Perhaps the only reason we were able to salvage it was because it was a faulty one in the first place," Ibi said. "The faulty wheels broke and were discarded, and that's what we found."

"If that's the case, then we stand no chance of success," Ayameru said.

"I find it hard to believe the *heqa khasut*, after so many years of building chariots, would still make faulty wheels," Hori said. "There must be more to it."

"I fail to see what," Piye grumbled. "Either the salvaged wheels were faulty and we have little hope of guessing what is wrong, or they are not faulty and we have no idea why our wheels are failing."

"Neither case helps us," Hori said. "Rather than dwell on past failure, let us search for a solution. We must clearly work with the wheels we have, so what do we know about what happened?"

"A spoke broke and the wheel shattered," Ayameru said.

"So what does that mean?"

"They weren't strong enough?"

"How can we strengthen them?"

"Thicker wood?"

"Thicker wood means heavier wheels. How much heavier can we make them before they are too heavy?"

"And besides," Hori said, "if they are supposed to be so much thicker and heavier, how is it that the wheels we salvaged were ever used in the first place? Surely the invaders would have rejected them immediately."

"So if not thicker and heavier...then what?"

Hori shook his head. "I don't know." He pondered for a few minutes. "Do we still have the pieces we salvaged?"

Piye nodded. "Some of them anyway."

"Have the fragments of wheel brought to us," Hori instructed. "Maybe we missed something when we examined them before."

Piye hurried off to find the pieces they still had and returned with servants carrying pieces of three different wheels. They set them down and the four men sat down to pore over them carefully, looking for anything they might have missed. Time passed, and Piye leaned back, stretching.

"I can't see anything different."

Ibi nodded. "Nothing we didn't see the first time."

Hori sighed and shook his head. "We're missing something. These wheels are identical to the ones used on their chariots, I'd swear to it. How is it that theirs work and ours don't?"

"Are we perhaps blind to something?" Ayameru asked. "Something that might mean nothing to us, so we disregard it?"

Hori nodded. "All right. Take a piece of the wheel, Ayameru, and describe what you see. We will listen and look as you do so."

Ayameru picked up a segment of the rim and turned it over. "A curved piece of wood about a fist thick and a cubit and a half long. The inner surface has a hole about two finger thicknesses across...probably where the spoke fitted in. The outer surface is smooth for the most part, and the sides also with only two blemishes...narrow holes that appear to be quite deep. Aside from that, each end is splintered but...there is nothing else."

"Did anyone see anything of interest?" Hori asked. "Anything that appears out of the ordinary?"

Piye and Ibi shook their heads, and Ayameru went on to the next piece, describing it in similar fashion. This piece was shorter and lacked a spoke socket and the outer and side surfaces were completely unmarked. He was about to pick up another fragment when Ibi stopped him.

"Isn't that a curiosity?" he asked. "The outer surfaces are smooth and unblemished."

"Why should that be curious?" Hori asked. "I'm sure the *heqa khasut* have carpenters every bit as skilled as ours."

"That is not what I meant, sir. Why are these rims so smooth when surely they should be dented and scratched from going over rocks? These are as smooth as if they just came out of a carpenter's workshop."

"Perhaps they weren't driven over rocks," Hori said.

"Even sand would scratch the wood," Ibi pointed out. "I've seen our own wheels after being driven over sand and soil. They are stained and scratched, quite unlike these."

"They do have holes in them, though," Ayameru said. He picked up the first piece again. "See, these two narrow, deep holes in the sides of the rim. Presumably, rocks caused those. And I've seen other pieces with similar holes."

Piye examined one carefully. "Rocks wouldn't make these holes," he said. "You'd need something sharper like...like an awl or a knife."

Ibi laughed. "What are the chances of running over one of those?"

"They were in a battle," Hori pointed out. "A stray weapon could have been run over, causing the holes. Something metallic, anyway."

"That would be the cause, I'm sure," Ayameru said. "I seem to remember seeing a fragment of metal caught up in one of these pieces." He started searching through the bits of wood. "Ah, here we are."

The section of rim had the two deep holes in the side found in other pieces but in this case one of them was plugged with bronze and had a tiny scrap of thin bronze, no bigger than a little fingernail, caught in it.

"The chariot wheel ran over this piece of bronze?" Ibi asked. "What are the chances?"

Hori examined it more closely. "I think it's a nail or a peg, but why would you put one in a wheel rim? It's not opposite a spoke, so it can't have anything to do with that. Nor is it joining two pieces of wood together. Dig it out, Piye. Let's see if it really is a nail."

Piye took to the timber with a knife and a chisel and soon freed up the metal. He laid the bronze pieces on the table in front of the others.

"It is a nail," Ibi said, "but why would you put a nail there? It's not holding anything together."

Hori turned the flat piece of bronze over in his hand. "I think it is holding something together," he said slowly. "It's holding this beaten bronze to the wheel rim."

"Why?" Ayameru asked.

"I believe a sheet of beaten bronze covered the wheel rim entirely. This little piece is all that is left. Bronze nails helped hold it in place."

"We would have seen bronze sheets if that was the case," Piye said.

"Not if they removed them. The bronze would be the most valuable part of the wheel and would be reused, even if the wheel itself was shattered."

"Why would you encase the wheel in bronze?" Ibi asked. "Ah, yes, of course," he added as the reason suggested itself. "It strengthens the wheel and protects it from damage."

"Would the nails be enough to hold it in place?" Ayameru asked. "There aren't many holes in the rim."

"I wondered about that," Hori said, "and then I noticed a few places where the wood was slightly charred, particularly on the sides. Could they be part of the same reason?"

"I fail to see how," Ayameru murmured.

"Nor I," Hori said. "We need the advice of a bronze worker."

Ayameru, using the power his father the Tjaty had given him, sent out for an experienced metal-worker from the city armoury. The man arrived post-haste and bowed to Ayameru and Hori.

"I am Amentep, a worker in copper, bronze and other metals. You sent for me, sirs?"

Hori explained the problem, telling Amentep that the wheels of a chariot appeared to be cased in bronze, the metal sheets being held in place by a handful of short nails.

"Is that feasible?" Hori asked. "Based on your experience?"

Amentep examined the fragments of wheel and also an intact one from the spares they had. "If this is an accurate representation of the wheel, sirs, then no. These nails would not be sufficient."

"What about the scorch marks?" Hori asked. "Could they be relevant?"

"Indeed they could, sirs. If hot metal was used."

"A sheet of beaten bronze affixed to the wheel rim and held in place by nails?" Hori asked. "How easy would that be to make?"

Amentep thought about this, torn between wanting to please these lords, but also worried that they would want him to make the bronze sheets.

"It could be done, sirs, but with difficulty. There would be a lot of work involved."

"But it can be done?"

"Yes, sirs, but if you require a simple strengthening of a wheel so it does not come apart easily, there are other ways. Easier ways, sirs, and quicker."

"Such as?"

"Wet leather, sirs. Bound around the wheel rim, it shrinks as it dries, holding the whole thing together. Also, strips of sinew binding bundles of reeds, or cured leather held by copper nails. These are all methods used for strengthening the wheels of farm carts and ox-drawn wagons."

Hori looked at Ayameru, and then at Ibi and Piye. "Well, we do need something quickly."

"And cheap," Ayameru said. "My father says the Treasury is already complaining about the cost."

"We need it within a month," Hori said. "Amentep, can you do it in that time?"

"Leather and sinews, sir, and...well, possibly beaten bronze."

"We need it sooner than a month, Hori," Ibi said. "We have to have at least two of them, we need to try them out and perhaps make adjustments if needed."

Hori muttered some choice imprecations. "Very well, it appears we have no choice. I will see you are supplied with what you need, Amentep. Make two wheels with wet leather and two with cured leather, sinews and copper nails. Have them ready within ten days."

Amentep grimaced, but nodded and saluted. "I'll do my best, sir."

Chapter 17

Following on from King Seneferenre's escape by boat, the remnants of his army, together with the survivors of Djedenre's force and Menkare's waterborne army, retreated into the city of Per-Bast and prepared to withstand a fresh assault from Samuqenu's army. Djedenre and his men had inflicted some damage on the enemy chariots between the rivers, but with the land drying out, the fields of the Delta became better suited to chariot warfare and fresh units were sent for from Avaris.

Neferit was among the chariot squadrons sent down to assault Per-Bast. Although she was still only a trainee, Anas-Har the Superviser of Chariotry felt that a little in the field training would prove beneficial. She was excited to be part of the expedition and did not give much thought to the fact that her brother Djedenre was somewhere among the king's men in the Delta. Her room-mate Sadiki was to lead a double hand of chariots and despite not having yet had experience driving a team, Neferit was included.

"What can I say, young Neterre?" Sadiki had said. "We are friends and I will put opportunity your way where I can. What you make of it is in your hands."

Neferit slipped out of the barracks the next night to visit her parents and tell them of her part in the expedition. If she thought her father might be excited and proud of her achievements, she was disappointed. Merybaal nodded and enjoined her to take care, but offered no congratulations on having achieved so much in such a short time.

"Our family is under stress, Neferit," he said. "I know you must follow your heart, but remember Djedenre and Menkare fight for the anointed king. If a family divided was not enough to bear, Rait is very sick with a flux and I fear she will not survive."

"I had not heard, father. The news grieves me as she has always been like a sister to me. Is she here? Can I go to her?"

Merybaal shook his head. "She is in her own house and your mother tends to her. I will convey your sisterly love to her."

"Does Djedenre know?"

"How can he? We are wracked by war and messages seldom cross the lines. I have sent letters, but I have no way of knowing if he has received the news. Even if he has, what can he do?"

"He should at least know that his wife is sick, so he can pray to the gods. What of Amenre? How is he taking it?"

"As you might expect of a young man who loves his mother. The family will look after him. You look after yourself, daughter, and come home safe to us."

A hundred chariots left Avaris the next day under the command of Anas-Har, driving down the Royal Road to Iunu. Neferit drove one of them, both excited and nervous, but the journey was uneventful, on a well-made road, and she felt a lot more confident by the time they arrived at the City of the Nine. Special broad-beamed boats awaited them at Iunu, and the chariots and horses were loaded aboard and carried over the river to the flat pastures beyond. A road had been constructed on the far side, one of several that now pushed across the Delta. It was not as firm and well-made as the Royal Road, but it served its purpose of conveying troops and chariots to where the Amurru pushed back at the forces of the Delta king.

Neferit continued to guide her team down this road, and the presence of armed men around her and the detritus of war that littered the farmlands exhilarated her. It was as if she drove a chariot into war herself. They arrived at another branch of the dividing river, a narrow stream where the latest floods had carved out a new channel, and more boats awaited them. On the far side, Neferit was chagrined to find herself relegated to a support function and someone else was tasked with driving what she had come to regard as 'her' chariot.

"Chin up, young Neterre," Sadiki said. "You'll get your chance, but for now there is a very real possibility that the enemy could attack us, so they want more experienced men on the reins."

"What? Attack chariots?"

"Apparently so. One of their leaders did so a little while ago and inflicted some damage. I doubt they'll be able to do the same thing again, but it's better to be safe."

The Amurran chariots made their approach safely and joined the camp outside the defences of Per-Bast. Anas-Har reported to Samuqenu, made his obeisance, and was made aware of the current situation facing them.

"Seneferenre is inside the city, along with some of his commanders and about fifteen hundred men," Samuqenu said. "I hope to entice him outside the walls and destroy him with my chariots, but I think he will be too afraid to do so. Instead, he will stay within the city walls and hope to outlast us."

"A siege then, my lord?" Anas-Har said.

"Regrettably, no. Per-Bast has access to the river and the king has a fleet of sorts that can resupply him as necessary."

"Our own ships...?"

"Are almost non-existent. We are not exactly a naval power, but I hope that will be rectified in time. I have sent for vessels of the Sea Peoples Confederation, and when they arrive, we can drive their ships from the river branches."

"So their access and resupply will only be temporary, my lord?"

Samuqenu scowled. "The Confederation says they will not be here for six months. I do not intend to wait that long for Per-Bast to fall. We will assault the city immediately."

"Of course, my lord...and the purpose of my chariots?"

"A direct assault on the city will be costly, so I hope I may yet entice their king to come out. If he does, you will fall upon him and destroy him."

"With great pleasure, my lord."

Djedenre was standing on the city walls of Per-Bast, watching the arrival of a contingent of chariots when Menkare arrived. He turned to greet his brother-in-law warmly, not having seen him for close on a month.

"You're here? I had not thought to see you for at least another half month. How was Zau?"

Menkare embraced the brother of his wife and then held him at arm's length, frowning at the pale complexion and sweat on his brother's brow.

"You do not look well. Have you been working too hard?"

Djedenre waved a hand to dismiss Menkare's concerns. "A touch of river fever; nothing more. It comes and goes. You are well? The war prospers elsewhere in the kingdom?"

"Well enough. Menenre faces a small army outside Behdet but has fought them off so far. Inkhare is...well, he is Inkhare; cautious to the point of cowardice. He collects men and supplies but refuses to do anything with them. I do the same in Zau, but I use them. I have brought another two hundred men and ten boat-loads of supplies with me."

"Good man." Djedenre clapped his brother on the shoulder. "They will be needed soon, I think. More chariots have arrived."

"You're not thinking of challenging them like you did before?"

"The thought had crossed my mind, but I lost too many men that time. Besides, the situation is completely different. I'm locked up in a city instead of wandering around behind..." Djedenre broke off as a coughing fit took hold. He wheezed and gasped for a few minutes, waving away Menkare's concerned intervention. "I'm all right...no, as I was saying, I no longer have the freedom I had being behind enemy lines. The only options left to us are to defend the city or go out and fight them man to man."

"I know what I'd rather do," Menkare said. "Waiting within city walls is no life for a soldier."

"I agree, but it would be death to step out..." Djedenre broke out in another fit of coughing. He doubled up and then sank to his knees, leaning against a wall as his vision blurred.

"This is not a simple river fever, brother," Menkare said, bending to support Djedenre. "You are coming with me to see a physician immediately."

"I'm all right," Djedenre wheezed. "There's really no need..."

He gave in as Menkare would not leave him, and in truth he felt like he would just like to lie down right there on the ramparts and sleep. Supported by his brother, he made his way to one of the city's physicians who examined him, listened to his symptoms, and tut-tutted at every phrase.

"Well, of course I can dose him up with a variety of things designed to counter fevers or aches and pains, light-headedness and nausea, but what he really needs is rest...about half a month's worth. I fear he won't find that in a besieged city."

"Nor would I take it if I could," Djedenre said. "I have a duty to the king and I intend to fulfil it." He started coughing again.

"We'll see about that," Menkare said. "Give him something for that cough, good physician."

The physician mixed a concoction of poppy and honey, together with a few other unidentifiable substances and Djedenre drank it down obediently. Within minutes, he felt his limbs relax and soon he slept. Menkare left him in the care of the physician and went in search of the king, to whom he explained the situation.

When Djedenre awoke, he found himself on one of the boats in the middle of the river. He sat up groggily and called out, whereupon the boat's captain explained matters to him.

"King Seneferenre has ordered you to be taken to Zau, sir."

"Nonsense. I have a duty to the king. Put me ashore."

"Sorry, sir, but my orders are plain. I was told to give you this if you proved difficult." The captain handed him a small piece of paper.

It read... 'Djedenre my brother, the king orders you to Zau to take over my duties when you have recovered from your fever. Do not try to come ashore or return until you have orders to that effect. The king has ordered it so and you will be arrested and taken forcibly to Zau if need be. Your brother, Menkare.'

Djedenre cursed and crumpled the paper, throwing it aside. The captain shrugged and walked off, issuing orders to get the boat under way. Within moments, the boat's sail rose and caught the northerly breeze, pushing out into the current and forging slowly upriver. Per-Bast dropped behind slowly, and Djedenre wished he was still there, defending the city and his king. It did not seem right that he should be forced into temporary retirement just because of a minor ailment, but he knew that if he tried to disobey the express orders of the king, he might suffer more. So instead, he resigned himself to a period of relative inactivity in Zau. At least he would be able to make himself useful by rounding up men and supplies for the defence of the kingdom.

Samuqenu launched an all-out attack on Per-Bast a few days later, his men storming the gates of the city initially without success. The recently erected walls were high and sturdy enough to make it difficult to climb them, and the gates thick enough to withstand a battering. Men of the city poured down a barrage of missiles from above that discouraged the attackers, but Samuqenu allowed his men no respite. When the first wave was thrown back, the Amurran commander made an example of a score of his own men, stiffening the resolve of the others, and for a time it seemed to work.

Neferit was in the rear, watching the fighting with the rest of the chariot squadrons. Men rushed the walls, trying to scale them, while others carried tree trunks against the wooden gates, but with little effect. Chariot commanders chafed at their inactivity in the rear and implored their superior officers to let them attack.

"What would you attack?" Commander Anas-Har said. "Are your chariots capable of flight that they can surmount the city walls?"

"We desire to fight, my lord," said one of the bolder officers.

"And fight you shall, but at a time of our General's choosing."

The battle beneath the city walls went on, halted only by nightfall. Daylight brought resumption of the assault, but without success. On the third day, the chariots were ordered away, out of sight of the city and Samuqenu called off the attack at noon, withdrawing his forces to their camp. The day passed in inactivity, with the Amurrans seemingly licking their wounds. On the fourth day, the number of Amurrans seemed to be less, and on the fifth day even less. One of the soldiers decided to try some fishing in the reed beds a little upriver from the city and was captured by some alert guards. The man was hauled before King Seneferenre and questioned. Under duress, he revealed what was happening in the enemy camp.

"The chariots have been sent away, there being no use for them in the attack on a city. Now the men are losing the will to fight and deserting."

King Seneferenre smiled at these words. "The flood of these invaders has reached its peak and will recede. Already the resolve of their king is weakening."

"Do not listen to the words of this man, my lord," Menkare said. "He tells you what you want to hear."

"You heard him, General Menkare. Their army grows smaller by the day as men desert. Do you deny there are fewer camp fires than yesterday? Or the day before? That is evidence that they have failed."

"This man is an enemy soldier, my lord. He says what he has been told to say."

"He has been tortured and after denying he had any such knowledge, now admits it. We had already seen fewer fires and now we know the reason."

Menkare bit back a harsh reply. Other officers and officials asked the king what action should be taken, offering up advice that ranged from attacking the enemy to staying inside the walls, or even evacuating the city.

"We have been given a respite, my lord," said the deputy mayor of Per-Bast. "Let us flee from the city to safety deeper within the lands of the Delta. There you can gather your scattered armies into one overwhelming force and utterly defeat the invader."

"Do you suggest I am a coward to run in the face of my enemy?" Seneferenre demanded.

While the official went pale and bowed abjectly, Menkare spoke up again.

"We all know your bravery and wisdom, my lord, and rather than fleeing, you should remain within the city and wait to see what the enemy will do. It is possible Samuqenu has terminated his attack because he is bringing up reinforcements."

"One counsels I flee and another tells me I should hide in the city and do nothing. I say we should attack the enemy at once and end this immediately. We have a chance to destroy Samuqenu and should take it." Seneferenre looked round at his army officers and city officials. "Is nobody here brave enough to follow their king?"

There was a chorus of protests from the gathering, all vying with one another to declare their loyalty and bravery. Menkare waited until the hubbub died down before declaring his own thoughts.

"My lord king, there is not one of us here who would not count it an honour to follow you into battle, and if it is your desire that we do so, then you will hear no protest from any of us. I count it my duty to advise you, my lord, and I would be remiss if I failed to point out my misgivings with the intelligence we have been offered by this enemy soldier. I have done so, thereby fulfilling the first part of my duty. Now I will fulfil the second part by following you into battle, and I pray to all the gods that they will give Your Majesty the victory."

"Well said, General Menkare," the king said. "I was minded to relieve you of your command, but you have set my mind at rest. You will accompany me into battle and hold my standard aloft for all to see."

"You do me a great honour, my lord king," Menkare said, bowing.

The attack started on the seventh day, just as Samuqenu was starting to believe his ruse had not worked. He was considering sending for the five thousand men who had appeared to desert, and the chariot squadrons, once more trying to force the gates of Per-Bast, when rams' horns blew and messengers came running to report that the city gates had opened and that King Seneferenre was coming out arrayed for battle.

"General Kanak," Samuqenu said. "Draw up your men in defensive lines and prepare to fall back slowly before their onslaught."

Samuqenu also sent messengers on horseback to bid General Yannass to return with his five thousand men, and Supervisor of Chariots Anas-Har to bring his squadrons up. Then he quickly donned his armour and went to join his men.

King Seneferenre led about six thousand men from the city, augmenting the regular soldiers from his army with citizens of Per-Bast pressed into service. General Menkare strode beside his king with a hundred picked warriors. His duty was keeping the royal standard aloft and exhorting the men around them to noble efforts, but he fully intended to fight. Other commanders led their own detachments of men into the fray, the soldiers shouting to keep their spirits up and hopefully to strike fear into the hearts of the enemy.

Seneferenre's men were running hard, their lines falling apart into a disorganised mob by the time they collided with the front ranks of the Amurrans. The force of the collision threw the Amurrans back several paces before they could collect themselves and push back, the charge dissolving into hundreds of individual conflicts. Swords stabbed and hacked, axes rose and fell and rose again in bloody sprays, while flights of arrows arced overhead, plunging down into both armies, thumping into leather shield or solid flesh, killing men in swathes. Screams arose, and cries of pain, and not a few tried to turn and run from the slaughter, but the press of men behind prevented them. They swiftly learned courage or died where they stood.

Menkare planted the king's standard in the dirt and stood by it with his khepesh sword, striking at the enemy and blocking their blows with his shield. Seneferenre fought beside him while the warriors of his guard killed and were killed all around. It slowly became apparent that although the numbers in each army were similar, the Per-Bast men were gaining the upper hand, pushing back the Amurrans. They were heartened by the belief that so many of the enemy had deserted in the past few days, while the Amurrans, though they knew the desertions were simply a ruse, now started to wonder if their comrades would return in time. When the orders came for them to fall back as had been Samuqenu's plan, it was not the orderly retreat the generals had hoped for. Within minutes, the retreat was showing signs of turning into a rout. It was only the personal intervention of Samuqenu, fighting fiercely in the front line that staved off a collapse and allowed the Amurran army a breathing space.

General Yannass at the head of his fresh five thousand sent a shock through the right flank of Seneferenre's men. Scores died and the advance of the Per-Bast men came to an end. They were now outnumbered and enormously disheartened by this sudden arrival of men they thought had vanished. Forced back from the positions they had held, the Delta men started falling back to the city, though Seneferenre and his select warriors still tried to rally them.

"We must fall back," Menkare said. "Our position is no longer tenable."

"Never," Seneferenre replied. "I have not come this far to give up now."

"Our men are already in retreat, my lord. We run the risk of being cut off." The king showed no sign of listening to him, so he tried again. "Retreat is not defeat, my lord. Preserve our army and your royal person within Per-Bast and we shall have another opportunity."

Seneferenre scowled but after quickly appraising the state of the battle, nodded his assent. Menkare rapped out orders and the warriors of the guard closed about the king and started to fall back. The Amurrans saw this withdrawal and took heart, pressing their pursuit and closing in on the king's standard from three directions. Menkare directed soldiers to either flank to stiffen the resistance there while the king retreated back toward the city and was taken by surprise when the Amurrans in the centre stopped and thinned away.

"What is happening?" Seneferenre called out. "Why have they stopped?"

Menkare leaned on the standard he carried and stared past the Amurrans. The ground trembled slightly and he knew what it meant. He had experienced it before and despair gripped him.

"Get back, my lord! On your life. The chariots are upon us."

Sadiki ran to his chariot in great excitement when the summons came for the chariot squadrons. Neferit already had the horses yoked and ready, and was talking idly with Aanu the charioteer when Sadiki arrived.

"At last," he cried. "Samuqenu has called for his squadrons and I ride into battle." Sadiki saw the look of intense disappointment on Neferit's face. "There will be other battles, young Neterre." He hesitated before coming close to the Ribu youth. "It means that much to you? It will be dangerous."

"Let me drive you, Sadiki," Neferit said. "You know I can do it."

"If I thought for one moment you were less than capable, I would not let you. Aanu, let Neterre take your place."

"It is my place to drive you, sir," Aanu said.

"Not this time."

Aanu reluctantly stood aside and Neferit leapt up into the chariot as the horses stamped and snorted, infected by the excitement of a hundred other teams preparing for battle. Sadiki climbed up alongside her and checked the arrows in the quiver at the front of the vehicle. He strung his bow and checked the foot straps that allowed him to remain upright and use his bow even at full gallop.

"You are ready, Neterre? Then let us be off to victory and great glory."

Neferit urged the team into motion, and guided her chariot into line with the others in their squadron. Excitement filled her at the thought that at last she was to be part of this glorious war machine, that soon she would know the thrill of riding into battle in support of her king. She had a moment's hesitation as she realised that the ones she rode against were truly her people of the Delta and that her brother might even be fighting on the other side--but she thrust the thought aside. Instead, she offered up a prayer to the gods that they would guide her and also protect her brother.

The chariots had withdrawn quite a way from Per-Bast in order to persuade any who saw them withdraw that they were genuinely doing so, but the return journey was swift. Pastures had dried out since the flood and the ground was firm beneath hooves and wheels as they thundered toward the battle. They caught sight of the city walls and then the battle beneath them, and Anas-Har had his signaller sound the code blasts for the spearhead formation. Every charioteer had practiced this, though Neferit had only performed it twice. Still, by copying what others were doing she could take her position and hold it. Her chariot eased into the second inner rank as the most experienced charioteers former the outer part of the spear.

"Look!" Sadiki cried. "See how our army fades away from in front of us. They knew of our approach. Now we will see some killing."

Neferit, peering over her own horses' heads and those of the rank in front, saw the Amurran standards move to either side while those of the Delta stayed right in front. She recognised the standard of King Seneferenre and shouted out the fact to Sadiki; though she never knew if he heard. He drew back his bow and loosed over the heads of the horses...one, two, three...and then they were among the bodies strewn over the landscape. Horses leapt forward and chariots bounced over bodies, and both Neferit and Sadiki had to hang on, their feet firmly in the leather straps.

Neferit found herself yelling with excitement, the horses' hooves mowing the enemy down and the wheels of the chariots crushing the bodies. Her horses balked at a pile of bodies and she jerked them aside, narrowly missing another chariot whose driver cursed her as it flew past. Urging them on again, Neferit and Sadiki followed in the wake of the squadrons, and now, as the chariot charge's momentum faded, they saw knots of men still upright and fighting. One such knot fought around the royal standard, and Neferit turned her team toward them.

"The enemy king, Sadiki," she yelled. "Straight ahead."

"I see them, Neterre. Hold our course steady."

Neferit eased her team to pass the standard on the left, giving Sadiki, who stood in the right-hand position, a clear view of the enemy. He loosed an arrow, missing, and then another that struck a soldier. At the last moment, the enemy caught sight of the chariot bearing down on them. Amurrans scattered, and a figure wearing a blue leather war crown stood and stared, while another man who held the standard tried to pull him away. Sadiki loosed, and the crowned figure staggered and fell, while the other figure threw himself down. The chariot wheels threw up dirt over them as they passed, and then they were out of sight behind them.

"Was that the king?" Sadiki yelled. "Have I just killed their king?"

Neferit trembled, not because of the death of Seneferenre, who meant nothing to her, but because of the man beside the king; the man bearing the royal standard. She could not be sure, as she had only a brief glimpse as they swept by, but she thought it had been her brother-in-law Menkare. To be responsible for the death of her sister's husband was bad enough, but her brother Djedenre was seldom far removed from Menkare. If the one had fallen on the field of battle, had the other also? Unashamedly, Neferit wept.

Chapter 18

D jedenre recovered from his fever and was hard at work in Zau when the news of the capture of Per-Bast and the death of King Seneferenre reached him. He was stunned at the news, and panic filled the city as it was imagined that the victorious invader was now marching toward them. Men who had flocked to the royal standard in defence of their kingdom now deserted in droves. Supplies that Djedenre had collected for shipment to Per-Bast sat on the docks at Zau, now lacking a destination. Djedenre ordered the soldiers at his disposal to restore order in the city using whatever means were necessary. As days passed, more messengers arrived from the disaster in the southeast, with more details of what had occurred.

"General, I was there when the king fell in battle," one said. "He fought valiantly to the end, only going down under a chariot charge."

Djedenre cursed the news, knowing the Delta armies had no real answer for the chariots. They might destroy a few, kill horses if they took them by surprise, but once massed chariots began their charge, there was nothing they could do except hope to survive.

"What of the men with the king?" he asked.

"Few escaped, General. I made it into the city and hid there until I could make my own way here."

"You chose your own life over that of your king?" Even as he said it, Djedenre knew he was being unfair. The battle had probably been lost as soon as the chariots charged, certainly when the king died. "Forget what I said, soldier. I am glad you escaped with your life. What of General Menkare? Do you know his fate?"

196

The man's face told him, the words being superfluous. "He was given the honour of bearing the king's standard into battle. I saw it fall when the king died."

Djedenre grieved for his brother and turned away from the messenger lest the man see tears in his eyes. "What possessed them to leave the safety of the city?" he muttered.

"I don't know, sir. I was not party to the meetings that decided that."

"No. No, of course not."

The messenger stood in silence for a few moments before coughing gently. "Sir?"

"What?"

"Er...who is king now that Seneferenre has fallen? He had no son."

"I don't know. Perhaps he had other relatives...or one of the generals."

"You, sir?"

"Gods, no. That is not something I wish for." Djedenre turned to face the man again. "You are dismissed with my thanks, but do not spread rumours about what has happened or what may happen in the future. The fight against the invader will go on, whether a king leads us or not."

The messenger saluted and left Djedenre to his thoughts. If Seneferenre was dead, then so was Menkare; somehow he would have to send news of that home. Grief threatened to overwhelm him, but he thrust it aside. Such luxuries would have to wait. He had sent out scouts as soon as the news reached him, but they reported that the invaders had merely occupied Per-Bast and were making no attempt to move toward any other Delta city. They had time to work out what to do next, but that was not something he could do on his own. Messengers would have to be sent to Inkhare and Menenre immediately; messages to follow up the bald facts of the king's defeat and death with a plea for a meeting to decide the future.

General Menenre in Behdet had furthest to come, yet he arrived only a little later than General Inkhare from Per-Wadjet. Inkhare had been cautious again, not wanting to commit himself to a course of action. His first words to Djedenre upon his arrival in Zau reflected this.

"How dare you, a junior general, command me to come south?"

Yet you came, thought Djedenre. "I deemed it necessary, sir. The king is dead and we must decide what to do."

"We carry on the fight, of course; you in your city, me in mine."

"That strategy may need to be reconsidered, sir. It did not work too well in Per-Bast."

Inkhare grunted. "You have some other idea, I suppose."

"No sir, and I think we should wait for General Menenre's arrival before we discuss it." Djedenre hesitated a moment. "Do you know if the king had any close relatives? Anyone he would consider his heir? The kingdom needs a successor, even if only to act as a focal point for the resistance."

"He had none that I know of," Inkhare said. "Menenre may know."

Menenre's arrival shocked everyone. His army appeared on the far bank of the river and was ferried across by a fleet of boats from Zau. He entered the city in full royal regalia even down to the false beard attached by a strap.

"I have assumed the throne," he informed the other generals.

"By what right?" Inkhare demanded.

Djedenre looked troubled but said nothing, waiting for Menenre's answer.

"By right of strength," Menenre said after a brief pause. "There is nobody else as capable."

"That is a matter of opinion," Inkhare grumbled. "You should not have claimed the throne without discussing it with your equals."

"What equals...?" Menenre started to say.

"Seneferenre had no surviving son, I know," Djedenre said, "but what about other relatives? Shouldn't we approach them first?"

"The days are long past when the kingdom was ruled by a dynasty," Menenre said. "Now it is the purview of the strongest, and that is just how it should be. The kingdom will need strength to counter the enemy."

"I am the senior general," Inkhare said. "If anyone should be king, it is me."

"You?" Menenre laughed. "If you had your way you'd lock yourself up in Per-Wadjet and sit there doing nothing in the hope that the enemy would go away."

"Have you done any better?" Inkhare retorted. "You're stuck in Behdet and the enemy still roams free."

"As a matter of fact I have. I've been conducting raids in the north with some success. I am at least engaging the enemy as we agreed."

Inkhare shrugged. "Djedenre here has done the same. Why should he not claim the throne?"

Menenre turned to stare at the younger man. "You desire the throne?"

Djedenre returned the stare for a few moments. "No, but such an important decision should be taken by all the generals."

"Quite right," Inkhare said. "Now, having raised your claim, Menenre, let us discuss it."

"Too late for that," Menenre replied. "I am already crowned. I am king, just as Seneferenre was."

Inkhare scowled. "Crowned...but not anointed?"

"The priest of Amun in Behdet offered the god's blessing."

"That may not be accepted elsewhere," Djedenre pointed out. "The Amun temple in Behdet is small and lowly ranked. Zau has a major temple of Amun."

"You are saying I need to be anointed in Zau to be accepted?" Menenre asked.

"I believe it would help."

"Then I shall do so."

"If you are not yet properly anointed, then we should discuss the whole matter," Inkhare said.

"Make no mistake, General Inkhare," Menenre said. "I am king and I have an army to back my claim. I am willing to be anointed here in Zau before everyone, but I don't need it...do I?"

Inkhare glared at Menenre, but dropped his gaze after a few minutes. "Oh, very well, be king then. Much good may it do you."

"My congratulations, Son of Re," Djedenre said.

Menenre looked askance at the young general. "That is not the usual title for a king of the Delta."

"True, but it seems to me that you need all the titles you can get to shore up your claim. Son of Re has a nice ring to it, don't you think? I'd insist on it, if I were you."

Menenre ordered Djedenre to organise a sumptuous coronation in Zau and Djedenre, conscious that the population of the Delta felt anxious about the invaders knocking on their collective gates, decided to give them something that would lift their spirits. He opened the city granaries, allowing bakers and brewers access to the precious grains to make bread and beer for free distribution. Priests were brought together and instructed to arrange complex and ostentatious ceremonies for the official coronation.

"Kings are never crowned in Zau," the priest of Amun objected. "We don't know what ceremonies are correct."

"Then make them up," Djedenre said. "Just make sure they are spectacular, involve every god, and are something to be remembered."

"But they will be meaningless," the priest of Min whined.

Djedenre sighed. "Who knows what the gods will think of it? Whether they actually bless Menenre is up to them. What I want is that every person who sees the ceremony or hears about it from someone else believes that Menenre is the legitimate king of the Delta. If we are to free our kingdom from the hand of the invader, we must stand firm with our king, and that king must be perceived as chosen by the gods."

The priests conferred, and Amun spoke for them all. "We shall do as you ask, General Djedenre."

The day of the coronation arrived and Menenre underwent a series of ceremonies in which priests of a score of gods, major and minor, subjected the man to anything their minds had dreamt up. Menenre bore it all patiently, and the population of Zau and the surrounding towns and villages lapped it up, viewing the complex and colourful ceremonies wide-eyed. The generous gifts of beer and bread helped, and Djedenre had secured a small herd of cattle to supply the people with meat. By the day's end, every man in the city cheered themselves hoarse, praising King Menenre.

Djedenre was not with them at the end as a letter reached him from his father Merybaal, bearing news that tore his world apart. He read it quickly and then, stunned, more slowly, not wanting to believe it.

'My son,' it read, 'I would give anything to save you this distress, but if you got any of my previous letters you will be prepared. If not, then I pray your brother-in-law Menkare can offer you such comfort as I cannot because of our separation. Alas, there is no easy way to tell you this--your wife Rait has died of an illness. She succumbed to a flux that washed through Avaris, taking many people with it. Know that she was not alone at the end, being surrounded by the love of her family. I have given her a sumptuous funeral here in Avaris. Be assured your son Amenre is well, as are the rest of our family. Ah, my son, it grieves me deeply to have to break this news to you in this way. Your whole family loves you and will pray to the gods for your safety, and that you may soon be reunited with us all. Your loving father, Merybaal.'

Djedenre wept openly, remembering happier times, the grief tearing at his throat and his heart, the pain almost more than he could bear. He took himself off, excusing himself from the coronation celebrations, hiding himself in his rooms in the Governor's Palace. The separation from his family was like a great weight on his shoulders as it was at times like this that he had most need of support and comfort. His father had written of the comfort that Menkare could provide, but he too was gone, struck down in battle defending his king. He wept anew for his friend and brother, and then again for Rait, crying aloud his grief and not caring who heard him. Eventually, exhausted, he fell asleep and dreamt of happier times.

He awoke the next day, smiling from the dream he had had, but reality washed over him and he felt despair. His servants attended to his needs and gave him the message that the king desired his attendance at a meeting that morning. Djedenre could find no enthusiasm for such a meeting, but knew he had to attend. Grief might claim his heart but he had a duty to the new king. Thrusting his feelings from him, he went to find Menenre.

Menenre took his new status seriously, and greeted his generals in full state panoply in the audience hall of Zau's Governor. Courtiers were gathered together, made up mostly of resident nobility and officials of the local administration. Little was required of them beyond putting in an appearance and giving support to the new king. General Inkhare was there already and he nodded pleasantly enough to Djedenre when he walked in.

"I heard your news, Djedenre," Inkhare murmured. "My commiserations. Will you be able to function?"

"Of course."

"I can advise the king alone if need be."

"There is no need. I know my duty."

A senior scribe on the Governor's staff was acting as Tjaty, and he called upon those present to hearken to the words of King Menenre, Great King of the Delta, Ruler of Avaris, Son of Re. The court cheered his words and Menenre waited for the applause to die down before speaking.

"For too long has our kingdom suffered under the foot of the invader from the north, but like the flooding of the Great River reaches its peak and then ebbs, so too we shall see the invader recede and fade away. I give you my word on this, the word of a king, for this the gods have told me. They raised me to the throne for this purpose, that I should restore their worship to the Delta, and rid our holy land of the false gods brought down from Amurru."

Djedenre raised an eyebrow at this. Certainly, this land was part of ancestral Kemet, but the blood of the inhabitants of the northern kingdom had mixed thoroughly over the last hundred or so years with the blood of those from Kanaan. The kings, the officials, and many army officers had more northern blood in them than Kemetu blood; their gods were equally of north and south. Even his own father bore the name of the god Baal in his name.

"Our previous king, Seneferenre," Menenre went on, "failed in this sacred duty and paid the price for this failure, but I will not. Seneferenre decided on a course that divided our forces and allowed the enemy to pick us off one at a time. No more. Starting in this, my first regnal year, I will bring together the massed might of the Delta and deal the northern invader such a blow that he will never recover. He will flee for the safety of Amurru like a kicked dog, his tail between his legs. This I will do, for I have the blessings of the gods."

"What about the chariots?" Djedenre wanted to scream, but dared not. "You were there in the north when the chariot squadrons first destroyed us, and again outside Avaris. And what about at Iunu? And now at Per-Bast? Have the gods clouded your eyes that you refuse to take note of this greatest flaw in your plan? We have no real answer for the chariots, and until we can successfully counter them, we cannot win a battle, let alone drive them from our lands." Djedenre wanted to say all these things and more, but dared not in open court. Perhaps he would have the chance when he and Inkhare alone had the ear of the king, for surely he would be making battle plans.

King Menenre continued in much the same vein for a few minutes longer, but his utterances were mere repetitions of what had gone before. The Tjaty called for more praise and the king basked in the adulation afforded him by men who had no real conception of what faced them all. When the court was dismissed, the Tjaty called on the generals to remain behind, and as the hall emptied, Djedenre and Inkhare exchanged looks.

"My lord king," Inkhare said as soon as they were alone. "I know you made promises in front of the court that were designed to raise the spirits of our people and give them courage against the struggle that we face, but perhaps we could now make more reasonable plans."

"I am not aware of having made promises I cannot fulfil," Menenre said coldly.

"My lord king, we cannot just simply mass an army and drive the invader out. He outnumbers us, and has chariots besides."

"This is what I was afraid of; that I had generals with weak stomachs. You always counselled caution, Inkhare, so much so that I suspected cowardice. I see I was right; you have no stomach for this fight."

"That is not so," Inkhare declared. "You know as well as I that I have faced the enemy alongside Seneferenre."

"Without discernible result."

"If it comes to that, my lord, then must I remind you of the army that faced the chariots in the north? An army commanded by you. What was the result, my lord? Did you drive them out of the kingdom or were you soundly defeated? Djedenre, you were there...how successful was our new king?"

Menenre leapt to his feet, his face pale and his fists clenched. "You dare? By the gods, you will go down on your knees and beg my forgiveness."

"Forgiveness for pointing out the truth, my lord? Do you want men beside you who utter the truth, or ones who will only tell you what you want to hear?"

"I do not want you beside me!" Menenre yelled. "You have always chosen the easiest path."

"Not so, my lord," Inkhare said. "I have tried to wage war against the invader while preserving the lives of the men in my care. As have the other generals. Though Menkare is no longer with us to back me up, Djedenre is here. Ask him."

Djedenre groaned at being dragged into this acerbic argument. "My lord king, no-one doubts your courage and determination, nor that of General Inkhare..."

"Well, I doubt his courage," Menenre said, "and if you take his part over mine, then I doubt yours too."

Djedenre looked at Inkhare and shook his head. "You are my king, Son of Re, duly crowned and anointed as monarch over our kingdom. Your word is law and my life is yours. Do with me as you will."

"Fool," Inkhare said.

"Not so," Menenre said. "I shall keep you with me, General Djedenre, for you I trust. You, Inkhare, I dismiss from the army and my service. Return to your estates and be thankful I leave you alive."

Inkhare glared at his king and at Djedenre, his mouth quivering as he bit back the retort that threatened to rise to his lips. Mastering himself, he bowed, turned on his heel and strode from the audience chamber.

King Menenre watched him leave and then turned to Djedenre with a smile. "Now perhaps we can plan our campaign."

"It will be costly, my lord king," Djedenre cautioned. "The enemy is strong."

The smile vanished from the king's lips. "Were your earlier words just air, Djedenre? You seem to be slipping back into Inkhare's error."

"No, my lord, but I am mindful of the task we face. It would be an error to dismiss the enemy as weak."

"I do not dismiss the enemy, but neither do I tremble in fear. We have good men in the Delta, and we are fighting for our very existence. What greater incentive can we have? A man will fight to the death for his gods, his king, and his family. Properly led, we cannot lose."

Menenre had a scribe bring in a sketch of the Delta region with the river arms and main cities on it, and he pointed out the salient aspects of the plan that was in his mind.

"Samuqenu is here in the south at Per-Bast with a large army and many chariots. Agreed?" Djedenre nodded and the king continued. "They will know that we are in Zau here in the west, because their spies will have told them. So, if their army is here, then we hit Avaris hard."

Djedenre frowned, trying to comprehend the details of the king's sketchy plan. "They are closer to Avaris than we are, my lord. How can we get there before them?"

"We must fool them into thinking we are still here, even after we are on our way. We will put it about that we are strengthening our position in the west and north, around Per-Wadjet, before striking down to recapture Per-Bast, but in reality we will strike fast and hard for Behdet and beyond, sweeping down on Avaris from the north before they even know we are no longer here."

Djedenre found himself in an unenviable position. He doubted that the enemy spies could be so easily fooled, and feared that Samuqenu's army would be waiting for them at Avaris, but how could he phrase his objections and still keep his command?

"May I suggest we send our men to Behdet in small numbers, my lord? And perhaps send them there by roundabout routes?"

"Why?" Menenre looked at him with suspicion. "Are you trying to break up my army for some reason?"

"My lord king, enemy spies will notice large troop movements but will more than likely overlook small ones. Further, if they see our troops moving to the northwest, they may guess our intentions and plan accordingly."

Menenre grunted. "You may be right. I will think on it."

The king considered Djedenre's words for the next two days, until he became convinced that the idea had been his. He issued his commands and small groups of men, numbering anywhere from a score to two hundred were sent off in all directions with secret orders to make for Behdet once they were out of sight of Zau. Meanwhile, Djedenre had worked to identify possible Amurru spies within the city and thought he had found three. He did not have them arrested but spun them tales, hinting at another army waiting to the south, and of the king's army preparing to defend Per-Wadjet until this other army could join up with them. The putative spies took the information and disappeared, so Djedenre hoped Samuqenu would soon hear of it and reach the wrong conclusions. Half a month later, the splintered parts of the king's army were nearing Behdet while Samuqenu's army was still ensconced in Per-Bast. Menenre's plan was coming to fruition.

Chapter 19

The army of King Menenre gathered in Behdet and the surrounding countryside, denuding the farmland of all food and livestock. River fish were about the only things left for the common people to eat and after most of the men had been forced to join the army, women and children went hungry. Djedenre tried to persuade the king to be less rapacious, but he dismissed his concerns.

"Who has the greater need?" Menenre demanded. "I need a well-fed army if I am to defeat the enemy."

"And what of the people, my lord? You have taken all the food and now you take all the men, leaving nobody to even fish the river. Women and children will starve."

"It sorrows me, Djedenre, but we must all make sacrifices for the common good. Once I have defeated the enemy, the men can go back to the land. A month or two will be all it takes."

"In a month or two, most of these children may be dead, my lord."

Menenre waved his hand dismissively. "They will find something to eat if it is the will of the gods. It is not my concern."

Djedenre was forced to accept the king's decision, though he made sure his own men shared the food they had with the people. Menenre ate well, Djedenre noted, and those of his newly created court also enjoyed the best things that could be stripped from the land.

This is hardly kingly behaviour, he thought. *What sort of a king will he make if he cares nothing for the lowest in his kingdom?*

The army swelled to nearly five thousand, not nearly enough to face Samuqenu's men, but from the latest reports they were still in Per-Bast. What size army was in Avaris was unknown, but Djedenre suspected it was not much smaller than their own, and there was always the problem of chariots. Even a few hundred could shatter the king's dreams.

"Send trusted men to scout out our route and the city," Menenre instructed. "I also want to know the mood of the city. Are the people still loyal to the Delta, or have they sold themselves to the enemy?"

"I am sure that most are loyal, my lord, and even those that are working with the enemy only do it to protect their families. They will welcome you when you are victorious."

"Loyalty is worthless if it bends like a reed in a storm. If the people of Avaris oppose me in any way, I will stamp them into the dust, along with the men they have allowed to conquer them. A man who works for the enemy in even the meanest way is a traitor and deserving of death. Send your spies to find out, Djedenre. It may be that blood will flow in the streets by the time the traitors have all been accounted for."

And what of my family? Djedenre asked himself. *My father has remained Treasurer so that he can make the lot of the people easier. Will the king count him a traitor and make him suffer for that? Will Menenre kill my family if he takes Avaris?*

Djedenre sent out his scouts and performed his other duties as a general of the king's army, but now doubts assailed him. Did a self-declaration count with the gods? Was Menenre truly the chosen man to claim the throne or was he just seizing power for his own ends? He needed to talk this over with someone, but his brother-in-law Menkare was the only one he trusted--and he was dead at Per-Bast. There was no-one else. His father Merybaal would know what to do, but could he risk a letter to him? If such a letter was discovered, he would be accused of treason and the penalty for that could be impalement, a gruesome and painful death.

The scouts returned and reported to Djedenre that there were no more than a thousand men in Avaris and perhaps a hundred chariots. Nobody seemed to have any suspicion that the Delta army was in the north, believing them still in the south and west. They also told him of the mood of the city and of how so many citizens had thrown in their lot with the conquerors, from the meanest street sweeper to the Treasurer himself. Djedenre knew he could hide some of this from Menenre, but that the scouts would eventually talk and word was sure to get back to the king. Omitting any mention of the Treasurer's lack of loyalty would condemn Djedenre, but mentioning him would have much the same effect.

"What choice do I have?" he groaned. "Menenre will sweep down on Avaris and take it, and then he will execute my family as traitors. My parents, my sisters Tiamen and Neferit, and my dear son Amenre. I cannot allow that."

He took himself off that evening to sit beside the northern reed beds and watch the flocks of ducks, geese and other waterbirds wheel and descend to their roosts. Thousands of birds darkened the sky and filled the pastures and reed beds, their very presence bringing him a measure of calmness. He listened as they called and honked and twittered, settling down for the night, and he relaxed, smiling. They had no real worries, he thought, beyond finding a place to sleep alongside their companions.

Do birds have families? he wondered. *Are they concerned for parents and children, brothers and sisters, like men?*

A little way off, Djedenre saw a few men armed with bows creeping closer to the roosts. He watched as they eased themselves through the twilight, at times up to their knees in water, but just as one of them drew back his bowstring, one of the birds honked a warning and those around it took to the air in a clatter of wings. The arrow loosed by the hunter arced high but fell harmlessly in the water. As the hunters returned, cursing, Djedenre considered what he had just seen.

Was this sent by the gods? Danger threatened and a goose sounded the warning, saving the lives of his family. Is that a lesson for me? Are the hunters the king's army creeping closer to Avaris and I the goose that sees their approach? Are the gods telling me to sound the warning and save my family?

Wishing more than ever that his brother Menkare was alive so he could talk to him, Djedenre walked further away from the army lines and found the pastures where the horses were grazing. He leaned on the enclosing fence and addressed a stallion he had ridden before. He had named him Seweh, for his speed was like the wind. Seweh came up to him, snuffling at his hand in the hope that he had brought him a treat, but all Djedenre could do was stroke his forehead and muzzle.

"Ah, Seweh, what am I to do? This king is not what I hoped he would be."

Djedenre found himself waiting for a reply and chuckled. "I wish you could talk, Seweh, or better still that you were Menkare, for he would certainly have good advice for me." He stroked the horse's forehead again, the great head dipping for him. "What would Menkare say? Let me think...ah...*well, brother, Menenre is your anointed king and you owe him your loyalty.*"

"What right does he have to be king? He was a general, and not a very good one at that. Now he looks to be a worse king."

"*Worse in what way?*"

"He cares nothing for the common people. They will starve as his army passes."

"*Can he win back the kingdom?*"

"Possibly. It depends on who faces him. He could probably take Avaris right now."

"*Then isn't that what you would expect of a king?*"

"But at what cost, Menkare? Seweh? The king means to kill all traitors."

"*Traitors deserve death.*"

"Is a man who tries to keep his family safe, provide bread and shelter, a traitor? And what of our own family? My father was treasurer to the Delta kings and has retained his position under the invaders, making sure that Avaris and its people survive. Does this make him a traitor?"

"*No.*"

"Yet if Menenre takes Avaris he will kill all those he sees as traitors, our family included. Is that just?"

"*No.*"

"So what do I do?"

"*You must warn our family. They can escape the city before the army arrives.*"

"If I send a letter, it could be intercepted."

"*Then you must go yourself.*"

"If I do that, Menenre will call me a traitor too. My life will be forfeit."

"*Better that than the lives of all our family.*"

Djedenre pondered the 'advice' but knew his mind had reached the truth of it. Whatever happened to him, he could not stand idly by and allow his family to suffer.

"Will you carry me, Seweh?"

As he asked the question, he stroked the horse's forehead and the stallion's head dipped as if assenting. Djedenre climbed over the fence and, opening the gate, led Seweh out into the darkness. He could see the camp fires and hear the sounds of the grooms and guards in the distance, but knew they would not hear him leave. Closing the gate, he thought better of it and left it open. If, in the morning, they discovered the horses straying, they would not immediately see that his horse had gone. They would discover his absence all too soon, but any time he could gain would be to his advantage.

Djedenre vaulted up onto Seweh's back and gripped his mane as he stamped and blew. He had been ridden by this man many times before and if this time he wore no bridle, then it did not matter. The pressure of the man's thighs, the gentling pat on his neck and the man's murmurs reassured him and he responded to the movements of legs and hands, setting off at a slow pace in the darkness.

Djedenre headed east, using the stars as guidance, letting his horse walk at his own pace in the uncertain footing of fields and ditches. He came to a stretch of water flowing sluggishly, an arm of the river that had almost silted up, choked with weed. Dismounting, Djedenre led Seweh into the water and swam alongside him for a few minutes, emerging on the far side untroubled by any crocodiles that may have inhabited that stretch. They rode on, into a night where the eastern stars were starting to disappear with the approach of dawn. He picked up the pace as the ground around them became more visible, and reached another arm of the river by mid-morning.

The riverbanks were not deserted as he had hoped, but the men there were peasants and fishermen and he doubted anyone would question him. There were no boats large enough to carry a horse, so he would have to swim across again. The river was wider here, but slow moving as it approached the sea and neither he nor Seweh had any problem with the crossing. Resting on the far bank, Djedenre noticed the approach of soldiers back on the western bank and knew that his escape had been detected. He saw them pointing at him and a few arrows arced high into the air, falling well short of him. Other men ran to commandeer fishing boats, so he realised it was high time he left.

The road north from Avaris ran not far inland, and Djedenre turned Seweh's head south as soon as he found it, urging his horse into a gallop. Looking back, he saw that a few soldiers had been ferried across the river, and a few boats were sailing upriver with the northerly wind in their sails. He urged his horse onward though, and his pursuers rapidly fell behind. When night fell, he felt secure enough to camp, though he took the precaution of leaving the road for the shelter of some trees. This precaution seemed unnecessary, for the next dawn revealed no pursuit behind him. The walls of Avaris appeared before him a day later, and plenty of armed men and a handful of chariots were present. Djedenre was stopped twice, but each time he told them he had a message for the Lord Treasurer and they let him through.

The streets of the city were busy, with people thronging the markets. Djedenre looked around avidly as he walked his horse through the crowds, interested to see how Avaris seemed just as it had been before the invasion. There were more foreigners about, and soldiers stood on every street corner, but the people seemed content, the women unmolested, and children still ran in the streets, laughing and playing.

How can I bring ruin on all this? Menenre would see this as evidence they were all traitors.

Djedenre dismounted and knocked on the courtyard gate of the family home. A servant opened it, gaped at the sight of his master's son, before letting him in and running to find Merybaal.

"By all the gods, my son, what are you doing here? I thought you far in the west with Seneferenre. Has he marched on Avaris? What is happening?"

"Father, I greatly fear that my brother Menkare is dead. He fell at Per-Bast, fighting against Samuqenu's army."

Merybaal groaned. "That is ill news indeed. It is certain?"

"No," Djedenre admitted.

"Then I will not grieve him until it is certain. Nor will I tax Tiamen with the news until we have evidence. Don't you do so either."

Djedenre nodded and Merybaal suddenly looked at him appalled. "Oh, my son, I was forgetting...you received my messages concerning Rait?"

"I did, father, thank you. My heart still hurts but...Amenre is well? Is he here?"

"He is well, but he is not here just now. Youth is resilient, but you might consider taking him back with you when you go. He thirsts to follow Seneferenre, like you, and I fear if he stays here he will get into trouble. Being in the loyalist army might be dangerous, but at least he would be with you."

"Seneferenre is dead in battle, father, and General Menenre has made himself king in his place."

Merybaal looked pensive. "Change follows upon change, it seems. In the absence of an heir, that is to be expected, I suppose. He was not a very effective general; we can only hope he will be a better king."

"He shows no signs of being so."

"Where is he? And why are you here?"

"Menenre has gathered his army in Behdet and means to strike at Avaris while Samuqenu is busy in the south. He'll probably be here in a few days."

"I see...but you came early?"

"I came to warn you, father. Menenre believes that any man that does not oppose the invader in everything is a traitor deserving of death. He will not look kindly on you."

"I have only ever tried to bring stability to Avaris and the Delta. The common people would suffer if I abandoned my post as Treasurer."

"I know, but Menenre does not see it that way, father. Please, take our family and flee Avaris so that they all might live."

"Where would we go? If he succeeds in retaking the Delta, then nowhere will be safe."

"You could go to Hattush. Our family came from there and...and King Baalbek would give us sanctuary."

Merybaal sat down and hunched his shoulders, his face screwed into a frown as he considered his son's words.

"What of yourself, Djedenre?" he asked after a few minutes. "Does Menenre know you have come to warn us?"

"No. I think I might have to flee with you."

"All right. Rest here and partake of food and drink. Let me make some enquiries as to our best course."

Merybaal waited until Djedenre was asleep before leaving the house. He made his way to the palace, where he sought audience with his grandfather's son, King Baalbek. The king made him wait, but eventually saw him.

"What is this about, Merybaal?"

"I have news that will affect everybody."

"All right, I'm listening."

"King Seneferenre is dead and General Menenre has assumed the throne. He is in Behdet with his army and is marching on Avaris."

Baalbek raised his eyebrows. "How is it you know all this?"

Merybaal took a deep breath and released it. "My son Djedenre brought the news."

"You say 'brought' rather than 'sent'. He is in Avaris?"

Merybaal cursed his slip, but nodded. "Please do not betray him."

"He is kin," Baalbek said simply. "Now tell me, why did he bring this warning?"

"He wants his family to be safe. He thinks you might give us all sanctuary in Hattush."

"If I did that, we would all be dead at the hands of King Anep-Aper. No, flight is not the answer."

"Then what is? Menenre has sworn to take Avaris and he is already talking about the vengeance he will take on the people for surrendering. From what I know of the troops and chariots available, he just might be able to do it."

"The answer is to make sure Menenre cannot take Avaris. If we lack sufficient troops to ensure that, then I must send for reinforcements."

"You cannot do that," Merybaal gasped. "I came to you in confidence. The life of my son could be endangered."

"His life is endangered if we do nothing," Baalbek pointed out, "to say nothing about the rest of our family and the population as a whole."

"You cannot offer us refuge?"

"I would, willingly, but it would do no good."

"Then I must tell Djedenre to flee immediately."

"Better to persuade him to change sides officially."

"Betray his oath to the Delta king?"

"Hasn't he done that already by warning you? Do you imagine Menenre will welcome him back?"

Merybaal sighed. "I suppose so."

"And you," Baalbek added. "You have already changed your allegiance. Oh, I know, you did it with the noblest of intentions, but the result is the same. Anep-Aper honours you, and Menenre will execute you if he catches you. Djedenre is the same--Menenre will kill him, but Anep-Aper may yet honour him if he swears loyalty to Amurru."

Merybaal shook his head and groaned. "He will never do it."

"He must. Persuade him." Baalbek smiled grimly. "He doesn't have much choice. Look, have him swear loyalty in my presence and I'll present it to Anep-Aper in the best way. He'll be saving his family too."

Merybaal could see no alternative, so agreed to speak to his son. "Too many bad things have happened to our family of late," he said. "First, my son's wife Rait died of the flux, and now it seems as though my daughter's husband Menkare has died in battle...and I don't know what has happened to my other daughter Neferit."

"I am sorry to hear it, cousin," Baalbek said, "but let no other tragedy happen to your family. Whatever you might wish, Amurru is unstoppable. Fix your family firmly on the side of the victors."

Merybaal took his leave of Baalbek and made his way home. He called together all the members of his family in an inner room, and after they had greeted Djedenre, he let his son tell them of recent events, though Djedenre omitted any reference to the presumed death of Menkare. Then Merybaal addressed them all, telling them of his meeting with the Hattushi king.

"He cannot offer us refuge, so we must find another solution to the problem."

"Why must we?" Amenre asked. "We are all loyal to the Delta kingdom and Menenre is our new king."

"I explained that," Djedenre said. "Menenre regards anyone who made their peace with Amurru as a traitor. If he takes Avaris, he will punish us all."

"I don't see why, father," Amenre said. "I can see that he might not look kindly on you as you abandoned him, but the rest of us are loyal."

"And what of me?" Merybaal asked gently. "I went from being Treasurer to the kings of the Delta to being Treasurer for Amurru. What will be my fate?"

Amenre shrugged and said nothing.

"And of your mother, your sisters? They are of my household, as are you."

Amenre said nothing.

"As I see it, we have three possible courses of action," Merybaal went on. "We either flee ahead of Menenre's advance, or we convince him we are not traitors, or we ensure that he cannot win."

"We must convince him we are not traitors," Amenre said at once.

"Not possible," Djedenre said. "I know Menenre from when he was a general and he's no different as a king. He is a man of narrow vision and once he has an idea in his head he hangs onto it tenaciously, even if evidence to the contrary is presented. He believes anyone who does not fight Amurru to the death is automatically a traitor."

"Then we must flee," Amatia said. Tiamen nodded her agreement.

"The problem is to where," Merybaal said. "Nowhere in the Delta is safe, and Baalbek has refused Hattush as a refuge. The only other place is Kemet, but that means travelling through a war zone."

"That only leaves your third option--making sure Menenre cannot win," Djedenre said. "I don't see how we can do that."

"Nor would we want to," Amenre said hotly. "I'd rather be dead than a traitor."

Merybaal shook his head wearily at this adolescent fanaticism. "I have already taken the first step on this road by agreeing to remain as Treasurer in Avaris. I am largely trusted by Anep-Aper, but there must always be an element of doubt when members of my family continue to fight for the Delta kings. If we swear our loyalty to Amurru, and reveal Menenre's plans, then we can encompass his defeat and our safety."

"I don't like it," Djedenre said.

"Nor I," Amenre added.

"If it means our safety, then it seems a small thing to do," Tiamen said.

"Well, I'm not doing it," Amenre declared.

"I can declare on behalf of the women," Merybaal said, "but you must declare for yourself and your son," he told Djedenre.

"What about Menkare?" Tiamen asked. "We don't know where he is and even if he'd agree to it."

"Menkare can make his own declaration," Merybaal said, not wanting to reveal the possibility that he was past doing so. "You are my daughter, though, and a member of my household."

"And what of Neferit," Djedenre added. "Can you declare for her if she hasn't consented?"

"She has already consented."

Merybaal revealed that Neferit had disguised herself as a man and was an apprentice charioteer in the Amurran army. His family was shocked at this revelation, but the news of her acceptance eased their own misgivings. Amenre was the only one to still object.

"I do not consent," he said, "and I never will."

"You are a member of my household," Merybaal said, "and will do as I say. We are making the declaration of loyalty to Baalbek as the representative of Amurru...agreed?"

Amatia and Tiamen nodded, while Djedenre murmured his assent. Amenre glowered and was ignored.

"That's settled then. Djedenre, you will accompany me to the palace immediately, and we will swear loyalty to Amurru."

Baalbek sent for his son Aribaal as soon as Merybaal had left, and revealed what he had learned about the approach of King Menenre. The young man grinned.

"I'll alert the garrison. We'll soon take care of this upstart."

"Menenre has an estimated five thousand men, more than we can handle. No, you must alert Samuqenu in the south. Recommend to him that he sends his chariots back here immediately."

Aribaal looked disappointed. "If you insist, father. I'll prepare a despatch at once."

"Do so, and I'll add my seal...but you carry it."

"Me? My place is here in Avaris."

"Your place is where I say it is," Baalbek said. "I had hoped to be in the front line of the invasion, my son, but I have been relegated to administrative duties. I want more for you than that."

"By running away from a battle?"

"Menenre will take days to get here, and even then he has to force the walls before he can take Avaris. By that time, you'll have ridden all the way to Iunu or beyond, alerted Samuqenu, and returned with the chariot squadrons."

"I don't want to miss it."

"You won't...and what's more, you'll be with the relieving army. You are my heir, Aribaal, and it is fitting that you should be in the front ranks."

Chapter 20

The gods of Kemet were clearly in two minds as to whether the southern kingdom would survive in its present form. For a kingdom to flourish, it needs stability, and stability of leadership is paramount. Kemet, though, suffered through a surfeit of minor kings who rose up out of obscurity, reigned for a short time, and then disappeared. King Mersemenenre was just the latest in a string of inconsequential monarchs.

Mersemenenre had withdrawn from public life after only a few months, preferring to enjoy the luxuries available in his palace in Ankh-Tawy rather than deal with the problems facing Kemet from the north and from within. The problems found him out and a few hours later, his servants found him dead of poison in his private chambers, flies already buzzing around the stiffening corpse. News of the death flew outward and men of influence started regarding each other with suspicion and interest. Two questions were uppermost in their minds-- who had killed the king, and who would succeed him. It was quite possible that these two men were one and the same. Whatever the truth of it, a strong contender for the throne emerged from the city of Waset in the deep south--Mershepsesre, who took the throne name Ini.

There were other contenders of course, notably Sewadjare Montuhotep who set up his own court in the south for a short time, and Mersekhemre Neferhotep, who claimed to reign in the north, though he rarely strayed from his estates in the west. Mershepsesre Ini ignored both of these, and others who tried to carve out some power in these troubled times. He had the backing of the army, and that was all-important. Tjaty Aya supported him too, which made the transfer of power seamless. Ini left the self-proclaimed kings in the south and west to their own devices and set about strengthening the kingdom for the onslaught he knew was coming. The *heqa khasut* were too formidable to ignore; their chariots seemed unstoppable, and something had to be done to neutralise this threat. Ini was surprised to find that his predecessors had already started to copy the enemy chariots. He sent for Hori, the newly appointed Overseer of All Chariots of the King.

"Is this true?" Mershepsesre Ini asked. "We have chariots of our own?"

"Yes, Son of Re," Hori said. "A few."

"How many is a few?"

"About twenty, Son of Re. Completed ones, that is. We have parts to make perhaps another thirty."

"Then why haven't they been made? This is important."

"Thank you for that, Son of Re. Nobody has ever acknowledged my work as important before."

The king inclined his head in recognition of Hori's words. "You haven't answered my question."

"We had some ongoing problems with the strength of the wheels, Son of Re, but that has been solved satisfactorily. While that was happening, the carpenters continued their production of parts."

"Have the parts made up into chariots immediately. I want all fifty chariots ready for use."

"I can make up the chariots, Son of Re, but there is another problem. Horses need to be trained to pull the chariots, working as a team. My father's estates have provided most of them so far, but we need other sources. Fifty chariots means a hundred horses and not every horse can be properly trained. Drivers must also be trained with them."

"I shall have gold released to expedite this," Ini said.

"Thank you. Son of Re."

Hori went off to set things in motion, asking his friend Ayameru to have the promised gold released from the treasury. Piye had been made Overseer of Chariot Construction, while Ibi became Overseer of Horses; both positions given as reward for their long service to Hori and the development of chariots. Another man had been brought in to become Overseer of Charioteers, one Ptahhotep, who had been one of the first charioteers of the Kingdom of Kemet.

As was expected of a man of his standing, Hori had admitted friends and relatives to the upcoming prestigious positions within the chariot squadrons. His own son Sekhem had asked to be made a charioteer, having fallen under the spell of the speedy and beautiful vehicles of war. Hori's wife Ayat, a daughter of Tjaty Aya, had remonstrated, saying Sekhem was but a boy, and Hori had bowed to her will, making him a groom instead.

"You are only twelve summers," Hori told his son. "Learn the care of horses and in three years I will let you become a charioteer."

Two other youths belonging to Hori's family also pestered him for inclusion in the cadre of charioteers. These were the brothers Bebi and Sobekhotep, sons of Hori's sister Iset, being sixteen and fourteen respectively. He could not exclude Bebi on the grounds of age, and having included him, could not deny Sobekhotep. Their inclusion would make Sekhem unhappy, he knew, but that was a problem that could be faced later.

Ayameru partially solved the problem of lack of horses. Far-flung enquiries revealed the presence of other breeders of horses in Kemet, though there were not many. Horses were not used much in the southern kingdom as oxen were stronger at pulling sleds and large wagons. If speed was a requirement, a messenger might risk life and limb by climbing on a horse's back, but runners were used for short distances, and small boats on the river that ran the length of the kingdom for longer distances. Consequently, there were not many horses in Kemet and few people went to the trouble of breeding them. Ayameru arranged for all available horses to be bought and transported to Hori's estate south of Ankh-Tawy.

Hori's father Harrubaal had died six months before, old in years and with his wits failing. His wife Init, sister-in-law of Tjaty Aya, was much younger than her late husband, but of course Hori inherited the estate. Close to the road south, a tomb was constructed on a low hill overlooking the river, high enough in elevation to keep it above all but the highest floods. Hori had harked back to older times and built a small Per-Djet out of mud brick, a flat-topped, rectangular 'house for eternity' with the tomb itself lying beneath it. Out of consideration for more modern sensibilities, Hori also caused a small chapel to be built beside the Per-Djet, where sacrifices and prayers could be offered up to his father.

The horses from the south, gathered into a herd numbering over two hundred, were driven past Harrubaal's tomb, their hooves drumming on the packed earth of the road, dust rising in a great cloud that drifted out over the waters of the Great River. Harrubaal would have been pleased to see so many horses, and Hori hoped his father's spirit was aware of them.

Overseer Ibi was on hand to oversee the arrival of the horses, and had his men sort them as to quality, quickly rejecting those that were too small or had some defect that might affect their ability to draw a chariot. He was left with about a hundred and fifty animals, and had these entered into the next phase. Trained charioteers examined every horse and paired them with another horse of the same height and strength. They had learned how important it was that the horses pulling a chariot were properly matched. Then the pair was stabled together where they were cared for by two grooms and a charioteer. A groom would have responsibility for a single horse, caring for all its needs, while the charioteer's duty was to form a bond with the team that would draw his chariot into battle.

Overseer Piye was now responsible for production of the leather and copper tack that would bind and harness the horses to the chariot yoke, and these were being sent down from the Ankh-Tawy artisans by the wagon load. These straps and reins would then be selected by the grooms and adjusted for the particular horses as their training began. After the first few pairs of horses, the trainers had learned from their mistakes and no longer pushed the horses too hard, letting them learn at their own rate. Although this slowed the rate at which teams were passed as fit to draw chariots, they were calmer and more malleable when they did finally pass, and with the extra horses now entering the system, Hori judged that progress was satisfactory.

"Slow, though," Ayameru commented. "Twenty chariots is not much with which to face *heqa khasut*."

"Twenty-four now, but yes, you are right," Hori replied. "If we had to face them now we would be swept aside like dust before a broom, but they will not come yet."

"You seem very sure of that."

"Look at the situation in the Delta. Their king sits behind city walls and his generals are spread out across their kingdom fighting the invader, who only holds Hut-waret and Iunu and a few minor villages in the east. They won't risk attacking Kemet with an unconquered army sitting at their backs. We could have years in which to prepare."

"I pray you are right." Ayameru shuddered. "These men of the north scare me. They are followers of Set."

"Set is a Kemetu god," Hori pointed out.

"True, but Set is a storm god and so is their main god Baal. I doubt the heavens hold two storm gods, so it follows that these followers of Baal are followers of Set. Violent men all."

"Not all. My father Harrubaal is named for that god, as is my brother Merybaal in Hut-waret, and neither of them are bloodthirsty and violent."

"Two exceptions then," Ayameru admitted.

"And even Baalbek, my kin who is king of Hattush," went on Hori. "He is a warrior, but he loves his family and is not a monster."

Ayameru regarded Hori thoughtfully. "One might suspect you of favouring these *heqa khasut*."

"You think that of me?"

"Not really, Hori, though others might. You might be advised to be careful to whom you utter such thoughts."

"It's only the truth, but I take your point."

"So how many chariots do we need to be a credible threat to the invader?" Ayameru asked. "And how long will that take?"

"Now you're asking difficult questions. It's possible they can muster as many as a thousand chariots, so we'll need comparable numbers. That could take us ten years, but I doubt we have that long." Hori considered the problem for a few moments. "Say we're granted two years to prepare...we could have two hundred chariots."

"That won't be enough."

"They might be if they were used judiciously, rather than just thrown at their chariot squadrons. There is another more pressing problem, though."

"More important than numbers?"

"More important to Mershepsesre Ini, I think. It is costly to build and equip chariots, and then maintain them, particularly if you're only making them for a future threat. How long will it be before he calls a halt to production?"

"He wouldn't be that short-sighted, surely?"

"Kings have many expenses," Hori said gloomily. "It's only a matter of time before he thinks of something he'd rather be spending his gold on."

"I will plead with my father to support chariots when talking with the king," Ayameru said. "Kings listen to their Tjaties."

Aribaal drove a chariot swiftly down the Great Road to Iunu and then took a ferry across the river to find Samuqenu's army in the captured city of Per-Bast. He arrived just as the General was preparing to push north and west to Djedu, where he believed the remnants of the defeated Delta army had taken refuge. Samuqenu's anger at the news that Menenre was threatening Avaris from the north was monumental, and the courtiers and army officers gathered with him feared for their lives. Aribaal offered up his father's advice in a shaky voice, and sighed in relief as Samuqenu calmed down and nodded his agreement.

"Anas-Har, you will take the chariots back to Avaris. Once you have relieved the city, continue to push northward and drive this upstart king back across the river. I will bring my foot soldiers round behind him and crush their army once and for all."

There was some confusion while several hundred chariots and their horses were shipped back across an arm of the river where they had been marshalled in preparation for the push north. Neferit had proved her worth in the battle for Per-Bast and Sadiki kept her on as his personal charioteer. They were part of the force returning to Avaris, though a small number of chariots were to stay with Samuqenu.

Neferit was a little nervous about the presence of Aribaal, who would also be returning to Avaris. She had met him when the city had fallen and King Baalbek had put a guard on their house to prevent the Amurru army from looting it. Her father had kept her in the background, but she had been face to face with him once. She doubted the young man would recognise her as she had worn a dress then and had obviously been a daughter of the household; whereas now she was an outlandishly dressed charioteer. Still, she thought she would rather not put it to the test, so she took pains to avoid Aribaal. All went well until the chariots were mustering outside Iunu, ready for the swift journey north. Aribaal had obviously heard about this Ribu prince in the service of the Amurran army and sought her out. She could not avoid the meeting.

"So you are the famous Ribu charioteer I have been hearing about?" Aribaal said.

"Yes, my lord," Neferit said. She kept her head lowered and hunched her shoulders.

"Just Aribaal. We are both the sons of kings and have no need of empty honorifics."

For a moment, Neferit was taken aback, and then she remembered that she had taken on the identity of foreign royalty. She inclined her head in acknowledgement. "I have little experience with chariots, my...Aribaal. I have only just started my training."

"Yet you have already guided a chariot into battle. That is more than I have done. I was in the original attack on Avaris, but my father forbade my active participation. I long for the day when I can drive a chariot against the enemy."

"May that day soon arrive, my lord."

"I told you, call me Aribaal. There should be no difference between us."

"You are the son and heir of the King of Hattush, whereas I am only a younger son of a minor king of Ribu."

"Even so, I have had my fill of men bowing to me and..." Aribaal broke off and stared at Neferit. "What was your name again?"

"Neterre."

"There is something familiar about you. Have we met?"

"I think I would remember that."

"And I. I'm sure I would remember a Ribu prince as I've never met one before...but there is something about you that puzzles me."

"There are other Ribu in the Delta army," Neferit said. "Perhaps you saw them during the battle for Avaris. We all wear much the same apparel."

"That...that could be it," Aribaal said, though he did not look convinced.

Luckily, for Neferit's peace of mind, Aribaal took his leave and departed without further probing. She returned to her unit, keeping well away from Aribaal, and an hour later the chariot squadrons were racing north along the Royal Road. There was urgency now as reports came to them indicating that Menenre had crossed the river and was approaching Avaris from the north. The good news was that he had no chariots, only an estimated five thousand foot soldiers. Anas-Har and the other officers of the chariot squadrons were confident that they could easily defeat the enemy.

They came to Avaris and found Menenre had not yet arrived so without stopping, they circumvented the city and continued north to intercept the Delta army. Chariots from Avaris joined them, raising their numbers to around eight hundred, while many foot soldiers trailed after the more mobile squadrons. Then Anas-Har called a halt when the enemy was no more than half a day ahead.

"The horses are tired. Water and groom them and everyone eat a meal and rest. I want the squadrons fresh for the battle."

Neferit dismounted from her chariot and together with Sadiki, tended to their horses. She felt tired and dirty, her face, hair and clothes thick with dust and she would have liked nothing better than to strip off and swim in the cool river waters as so many of the other charioteers and warriors were doing. Sadiki encouraged her, but she shook her head, muttering some excuse about Ribu being a private people not given to public nudity.

"Nor are the Amurru," Sadiki said, "but we are all soldiers together here."

"You go on, then. I will stay dressed and just wash my hair."

Neferit did so, and the feel of the cool water on her skin encouraged her to splash more water over herself, letting it trickle down beneath her clothing. She even waded into the water and let muddy water stream out of her clothing before wading ashore and lying down in her wet tunic and leggings to dry out in the sun. Closing her eyes, she drifted on the border of sleep, lulled by the sounds of men splashing and laughing on the banks of the river. Then a shadow fell over her and she opened her eyes to see Sadiki standing over her, staring down.

"What?" she asked, struggling up onto her elbows. "Are we summoned?"

"I never noticed," Sadiki murmured. "It never occurred to me."

"What are you talking about? You're not making sense."

"You're a woman."

Neferit sat up, hunching her shoulders and tucking her hair into her damp cap. "Don't be ridiculous."

"It's easy enough to disprove," Sadiki said.

"No. I told you; the Ribu are a private people."

"Are you even Ribu? Is it all a lie?"

Neferit got to her feet, her heart hammering and stared at Sadiki, wondering what to do. If he laid hands on her he would know the truth at once...and then what? Would she be thrown out of the squadrons or...or worse? She had heard the ribald remarks and stories the men told around the camp fires or in the barracks and feared what they might do to her.

"I suppose if I was interested in women, I might have seen it sooner," Sadiki said. "Your beauty is rare in young men, but I saw what I thought was there."

"What are you going to do?" Neferit asked.

"Ah, you admit it then?"

Neferit felt like crying, mostly out of frustration, but refused to give in. "I cannot disprove your assertions."

"This concerns the whole squadron. I should notify Commander Anas-Har," Sadiki said.

"Is there anything I can say...or do...that will dissuade you?"

"Tell me why I shouldn't."

Neferit looked at Sadiki, thinking about what might possibly sway him. She decided the truth--or at least close enough to it--was the best.

"You are a man, Sadiki. When you decided you wanted to join the chariot squadrons there was nothing standing in your way..."

"I still had to apply and be accepted."

"Yes, but there was little doubt that you would be. I, on the other hand? I'm a young woman; I'm supposed to get married and have children. As a member of the nobility, I have some say over what will happen to me, but only if I fit in with society's expectations...do what my family say. If I want to do something completely different, like fighting in a war or becoming a charioteer, I'm not allowed to. Well, that is what I want to do...but how can I? I have to be someone I am not."

"But you're a beautiful young woman." Sadiki grinned. "Even I can recognise that, though I'm not in the least attracted to you. Why don't you embrace who you are, get married, and rule your household?"

"Because that's not who I am. I don't like men...not in that way." Neferit looked hard at Sadiki. "What would you do if there was something you desperately wanted to do, but couldn't, just because of who you were? Would you just accept your fate or would you look for a way to do what you wanted anyway?"

Sadiki considered her words and nodded slowly. "I'd do what I needed to do."

"We're the same, you and I. You're a man who doesn't like women; I'm a woman who doesn't like men. Neither of us really fit in, but shouldn't we be allowed to do what we want?"

"How long do you think you can get away with this deception?"

"How long will you give me?"

Sadiki shook his head. "If I hadn't discovered the truth about you?"

Neferit shrugged. "As long as I could. Until the Commander recognised me as a superlative charioteer and allowed me to remain one, even knowing my gender."

"You think you're that good?"

"Yes, I do."

"You might be right."

"So what will you do?"

"I don't know. What's your name...your real name? You said you were nobility...who's your family?"

"I am Neferit, youngest daughter of Lord Merybaal, Treasurer of Avaris."

"Gods above and below! Do you realise how much trouble I could get into by aiding you?"

"So don't turn me in and nobody will even know."

"It will have to come out sooner or later. Nobody would believe I didn't know and...and they'd believe we were...well, that we'd been...you'd be dishonoured, even if just by implication."

"I don't care; and it's not as if I'm in any danger from you."

"The other men in the squadron..."

"They'll believe I'm your partner and stay away. How many men are there in the squadron who prefer men to women?"

"Not many," Sadiki admitted. "In fact, I don't know of any."

"But they know you are?"

Sadiki nodded. "I don't boast about it...but yes, they know."

"And they don't mind?"

"Why should they? I'm good at what I do."

"That's all I ask for myself," Neferit said. "To be left alone because I'm good at what I do."

"Ah, so we're back to that again," Sadiki said with a grin. "You think you're that good?"

"You tell me."

"Then no, you're not...but you could be. I think you have it in you to be an excellent charioteer one day, and had you really been Neterre the Ribu prince, I'd have said you could one day be the king's charioteer."

"And as a woman?"

Sadiki shrugged. "I honestly don't know. I wouldn't have said a woman could be a charioteer. Women don't have the strength to control a team..." He reached out and gripped Neferit by the upper arms as she drew back in alarm, "but you've developed somewhat. You have a rapport with the horses anyway, so perhaps you don't need raw strength." Sadiki released her and regarded her thoughtfully. "You could be my personal charioteer."

Neferit grimaced. "Thank you, Sadiki, but must I really aim that low?"

Sadiki threw back his head and laughed, so that heads turned among the men bathing close by. "Oh, you'll go far, young Nefer...young Neterre. Stay with me until you have qualified, at least. Then we'll see about finding you a prestigious position."

"You won't betray me, then?"

"No. This decision might return to stab me, but...no. I'll keep your secret for as long as I can, and then we'll see."

"Thank you, Sadiki."

Anas-Har took the massed chariot squadrons northward when they were rested, and his scouts reported the presence of Menenre's army not far ahead. It amused him that the Amurran chariots were once more meeting an army under the command of Menenre close to where they had met before, and he looked forward to a similar outcome.

"There are five times as many soldiers facing us today than there were then," one of his senior officers said. "And we have fewer chariots today."

"Then it will take us as long as an hour to destroy them," Anas-Har replied.

It took a bit longer than that, if only because Menenre had faced chariots before and knew what to expect. As soon as the dust of the chariots came in sight, he halted his advance and organised his men into tightly packed formations with spear holders on the outside and archers in the middle. These formations were not easy to crack, but eight hundred chariots could unleash a storm of arrows as they swept by the stationary soldiers and the return volleys from Menenre's archers were less effective against moving targets. Chariots ranged closer and closer, taunting Menenre's men until one formation broke, men surging out in an effort to overwhelm a few chariots. As soon as the packed lines of men shattered, other chariots changed course, charging the gaps, and the formation came apart, the soldiers scattering in the face of flying hooves and thundering wheels.

Soldiers in the other formations quailed when they saw one fail, and as they lost cohesion, the chariots made further inroads, the disorganisation compounding until King Menenre's stand became a rout. His men streamed away, most to the north, back the way they had come, but others seeking refuge in the marshlands where the chariots could not easily follow. Here, the chariots disgorged archers who ran after the fugitives and killed them as they struggled through mud and swamp or took to the water to escape their foes. By the time Anas-Har called his chariots back, Menenre's men lay scattered in death like a field of barley laid flat by a sudden storm. Only a handful of horses had been killed, and a few more chariots broken.

Over the next half month, the survivors of Menenre's army, including the king himself, limped back toward Behdet, but there was no refuge to be found there. General Samuqenu had brought his own army north from Per-Bast, swept through Djedu, and then turned northeast to catch Menenre in the rear. He hoped to destroy the Delta army completely, but Anas-Har had been too successful and there was no cohesive army for Samuqenu to engage. Instead, he had to be content with mopping up remnants of the army as they scattered into the Delta lands. Samuqenu himself led his men across all branches of the river and followed Anas-Har's chariots back to Avaris.

Chapter 21

Samuqenu stopped off in Avaris intending to stay only long enough to ask after the health of his father Anep-Aper, before moving back into the field. The king was thin and looked a lot more infirm than his son remembered; frail of body and his mind wandering. Seeking out the palace physicians, Samuqenu learned that they thought he would be assuming the throne of Amurru, Lebanon, Syria and Kanaan sooner than anticipated. Samuqenu cancelled his move south and sent Commander Anas-Har in his place. Then he sent out swift messengers to all parts of the Delta, calling together his generals for a meeting with them and other officials to discuss the progress of the war.

"As you will no doubt have heard, palace gossip being what it is, my father Anep-Aper is in poor health and it falls to me to make decisions about the future conduct of the war. Before I can do that, I need to know how we are faring militarily. I need your reports, gentlemen."

General Kanak spoke first, bowing to the heir. "My lord, I have an army group in the northwest, where the enemy has taken refuge in their city of Per-Wadjet. The enemy seems reluctant to meet me in battle and I am pressing him hard. It will only be a matter of time...a month or so at the most...before I can destroy resistance there."

General Yannass was next, but his message was similar. "The enemy has retreated to their city of Zau in the west. Their resistance is weak and I anticipate being able to encompass their destruction within a very short time."

General Siaan saluted his Commander. "As you know, my lord, resistance was fierce in Djedu, and after you left with your army to attack their king Menenre, I continued to wage war against mobile forces that used the rivers to move about. I have not yet been able to bring them to a final battle, but I will."

"How are they using the rivers, Siaan? As barriers...or with boats?"

"Boats, my lord. We are not a seafaring people and have little experience with water."

"Then you must learn, Siaan. Kemet is a land dominated by one great river, and when we push south we must be able to dominate them on water as well as on land."

"It will be done, my lord," Siaan assured him.

"General Qub-Har, you are my Chief of Spies. What have you to report?"

"The Delta is all but conquered, my lord," Qub-Har said. "The people just don't realise it yet. It may be months...or even years before we achieve full peace, but that will not prevent you pushing south with the army, if that is what you want."

"Of course. I have never made any secret of the fact that I mean to take the river valley as well as the fertile Delta. I would like to take their northern capital by the end of the year."

"Ankh-Tawy will be difficult to take, my lord, without inside help."

"You can get this for me?"

"I am working on it, my lord." Qub-Har hesitated a moment. Bad news was never an easy thing to bring before a king. "There is one other thing, my lord. Kemet has chariots."

"I thought this was something the Kemetu did not possess. You told me this Qub-Har. Were you lying?"

"No, my lord. At the time, it was the truth, but since our invasion of the Delta, the southern kingdom has been building chariots in anticipation of the threat our army would pose when we turn to face them."

Samuqenu scowled as he pondered this unwelcome news. "We shall have to rethink our strategy if the enemy has chariots. How strong is their force? Do they match us?"

"No, my lord. My spies report no more than fifty chariots."

General Anati burst out roaring with laughter. "Forgive me, my lord," he said, wiping his eyes on his sleeve. "I was imagining fifty chariots...or even a hundred...facing our squadrons. We will roll over them without even noticing."

"I am glad to hear it, Anati. Your squadrons are in good health then?"

"Never better, my lord. Our training program is progressing well and we have a number of very promising native charioteers taking shape. We are up to full strength again despite our losses."

Samuqenu sat pensively for a few minutes. "You see, Anati, this is what concerns me. We faced an enemy lacking chariots entirely, yet a number were destroyed. Now you are always telling me that our strength lies in our chariot squadrons--we have a thousand, and the enemy has none. Based on your claims, we should have been able to conquer the Delta in months, yet it has been three years since we invaded. If it has taken this long...and we have not yet entirely subjugated them...then how long will it take to conquer Kemet if they do have chariots? Even only a hundred?"

General Anati paled at the threat in Samuqenu's voice. "My lord, the Delta has proved a difficult land to conquer, with its soft pastures, its rivers and canals, irrigation ditches and swamps. Chariots do not fare well on such land, but when we reach the dry lands bordering the river in the south, my chariots will sweep all before them."

"I hope so, Anati, for your sake. I have others who can command if you fail me. Your kinsman Anas-Har for one. He proved competent enough in the most recent campaign against Menenre."

Anati grovelled, and after a few moments, Samuqenu allowed him to resume his place in the king's Council.

"On the whole I am satisfied with the conduct of this war," Samuqenu said to his generals. "However, I look for its speedy conclusion. You will return to your units and bring the remaining enemy to heel. Take their surrender and their oaths of loyalty if possible; if not, kill them. I want to move against the south next year."

The generals saluted and took their leave of Samuqenu, but he signalled for the other two officials to remain behind. Merybaal glanced at Baalbek, managing to convey anxiety wordlessly. The heir of Anep-Aper was a savage man and unpredictable, and both men knew they could be counted as foreigners and thus automatically suspect.

"Now, I intend to lead my army against the south and take their capital...what is its name?"

"Ankh-Tawy, my lord," Merybaal said.

"Very well. I will take this Ankh-Tawy next year, but this means the bulk of my forces must be away from Avaris for some time. A year or more probably. That means I must secure the rear before venturing south. You are my Councillors. Counsel me."

Merybaal and Baalbek looked at each other, and then the young king shrugged. "My lord, to secure your rear you must have a strong force in Avaris, commanded by someone who knows the area well and commands respect."

"What else?"

"A strong economy, my lord," Merybaal said. "Work for all, and a fair return for investment. Poverty breeds discontent, and discontent spawns rebellion. Fortunately, you already have a prosperous city populated with people who know that your rule is a fair one."

Samuqenu grunted. "Protecting your position as Treasurer, Merybaal?"

"I believe I have served Avaris well for the last thirty or more years, my lord--Delta and Amurru both. You know I will continue to serve the people faithfully, and that is to your benefit as well as mine."

"Yes, you have served Avaris well," Samuqenu conceded. "That is the economy taken care of, then. What about the military side of things? Should I appoint one of your family members to the post as reward for your services?"

The offer surprised Merybaal and it was on his lips to accept, perhaps nominating Djedenre, but then it occurred to him that Samuqenu, known for his suspicious mind, might believe Djedenre to be less than trustworthy. He had only recently changed sides, having been a general under Menenre, and putting him forward might make Samuqenu suspect a plot against him. It was safer to let the heir make up his own mind.

"No, my lord," Merybaal said. "I can think of no member of my family who would be right for the position of Commander of the Avaris garrison."

"Can't you? I can."

"A member of my family?"

"Yes."

"I... I can't think who, my lord."

"Baalbek, King of Hattush. You are related, aren't you?"

"Er, yes, my lord. Baalbek is half-brother to my father Harrubaal."

"And yet I trust him where I would not trust another member of your family."

"Yes, my lord." Merybaal thought that agreement was the safest course.

"You I trust, Treasurer Merybaal," Samuqenu said. "The women are inconsequential, but you have a son who has just changed sides and a son-in-law who perhaps died in defence of King Seneferenre. A grandson too...son of your son. None of these men are trustworthy, or perhaps I should say have yet to prove their trustworthiness. Is this a fair assessment, Merybaal?"

"I believe my entire family to be trustworthy, my lord, but...but I can see why might think so."

Samuqenu grunted and turned his attention to the other man. "What of you, Baalbek of Hattush? Are you trustworthy? Is your son Aribaal?"

"It pains me that you would think otherwise."

"Come now, it can't be that much of a surprise. You rule the kingdom of Hattush and you must surely wonder about the loyalty of the men who serve you. How many serve you through love, Baalbek, and how many because you reward them for their service?" Samuqenu lifted an eyebrow interrogatively, but when Baalbek said nothing, continued. "With the possible exception of a family member, I would hazard a guess that nobody loves you for who you are, but rather for what you can do for them. Am I right?"

"Even a man who serves out of love deserves recompense," Baalbek said.

"Of course," Samuqenu said. "But a man who does not serve out of love requires a greater reward...or a greater fear...to keep them loyal. You agree?"

"I have generally found that justice and mercy are useful tools for a leader. If a man is treated fairly and with honour, he returns the favour."

"Then you are a paragon among men, Baalbek...and an exception. In fact, so exceptional that I hesitate to believe you." Samuqenu shrugged. "I am not such a man, and have never pretended to be. I rule--and here I speak of my father Anep-Aper and me as one--through reward and punishment...and the threat of punishment. You might have noticed that I have many sons of kings among my staff? They are hostage to their fathers' continued good behaviour. The fathers enjoy gold and land and the good things that flow from my rule, and in most cases nothing else affects them. Just occasionally, though, a king steps out of line, decides he can find a better ally elsewhere, and then he finds he is wrong. First his son dies, then my army arrives on his palace steps and his family is exterminated and he dies painfully. It doesn't happen often. I find the threat is enough to ensure their compliance. Now, King Baalbek, Treasure Merybaal...why am I telling you all this? Why am I sharing the details of my methods of governance?"

"Because, my lord, you have rewarded us well for our service but now you want a threat hanging over us to remind us of your benevolence?" Merybaal asked.

Samuqenu smiled. "And why now?"

"Your father the king is dying and you cannot remain in Avaris to govern the land in his place," Baalbek said. "You are going to lead the army against your enemies and that means that Merybaal and I will remain behind in Avaris to govern in your name. To do that, you must ensure our continued loyalty."

"Very good. Yes, I must be sure of your continued loyalty, and to that end your sons will accompany me south. I will find places for them on my personal staff. You need not be worried for their safety as I shall keep a close eye upon them."

"Thank you for the honour you show me, my lord," Merybaal said, striving to keep any hint of irony out of his voice.

"My son Aribaal will be pleased," Baalbek said. "He is forever asking when he can fight the enemy."

King Mershepsesre Ini died of what might be described as an unfortunate accident, but might as well have been murder. While inspecting the troops training on the vast fields across the river from Ankh-Tawy, a stray arrow from an archer practicing nearby pierced his chest and killed him almost instantaneously. The archer was from the town of Henen-nesut and under the command of one Lord Seheqenre who had estates in those parts. He might have been able to shed some light on his motives for killing the king had he lived, but in the horrifying moments following the act, the archer was hacked to death by his comrades, all of whom came from the same town.

The situation threatened to slide out of control, so Lord Seheqenre took charge of the dead king's body, transported it back to Ankh-Tawy for burial, and set up martial law in the city to quell any disturbances. By the time other army officers worked out what was going on, Seheqenre controlled the City Treasury, the local barracks, and had bought the loyalty of the city militia. He announced that, for the peace of the kingdom, he was assuming the throne and, even before Mershepsesre Ini was ready for burial, had crowned himself king of Kemet, taking the throne name of Seheqenre Sankhptahi.

Strength was ever an admirable quality in the eyes of the common people of Kemet, and this seemed to be an attribute the new king held in abundance, as evidenced by his swift and ruthless grasp of the vacant throne. Nobody whispered too loudly the rumour that the archer who had released the fatal shaft had been one of Seheqenre's own men, and had been acting under orders. The men who had hacked the killer to death were rewarded with gold and sent off to man a distant outpost where nothing they said could trouble the consciences of the people of Ankh-Tawy.

Seheqenre Sankhptahi then set about making changes within the army. He was a firm believer in the efficacy of large armies, and decided that the gold spent on other aspects of the armed forces would be better spent on boosting the numbers of the infantry, and supplying them with basic copper axes and cowhide shields. The gold for this expansion came at the expense of the growing chariot force as Seheqenre saw these vehicles as unnecessary and expensive. Within a month of his accession, the chariot workshops and horse estates were shut down and the men who staffed them employed elsewhere. Hori immediately complained to Ayameru who took it up with his father Tjaty Aya.

"What can I say?" Aya said. "We live in uncertain times."

"But chariots are essential to the defence of Kemet," Ayameru said.

"Not in the view of the new king."

"Can't you persuade him otherwise? As Tjaty you have his ear."

"I have done that already," Aya said, "pushing it to the limit. He is adamant chariots are a waste of resources."

"Then how can we change his mind?"

"I can think of no easy way, short of a defeat in the field to the *heqa khasut* chariots."

Ayameru reported back to Hori who raged against the king's stubbornness. When he calmed down, he realised that whatever course they took would have to accommodate the king's wishes.

"What are we going to do?" Hori asked. "We can't just give up."

"I'm not sure what we can do," Ayameru replied. "We have lost all funding."

"That doesn't necessarily mean we can't do anything; just that we don't have the support of the king or treasury. For instance, what happens to the chariots already constructed? Are they to be broken up?"

"What would be the point; it's not as if you can use the parts for anything else?"

"So we could just store them against future need?"

"I suppose so," Ayameru admitted.

"And the horses? What happens to them?"

"Horses have other uses. Messengers can use them."

"Not that many." Hori thought for a few moments. "Perhaps we could release our second-string horses for the messengers, the ones that cannot draw chariots. Our trained ones need to be kept for that purpose only."

"Why?" Ayameru asked. "What's the point if there are no chariots for them to draw?"

Hori looked around carefully to make sure they were not overheard. "We all thought Mershepsesre Ini was going to deliver a fully fledged chariot force, but he was...ah...he died before that could happen. Seheqenre Sankhptahi is the opposite, but..." Hori lowered his voice to a whisper, "but who knows how long he will last? The next king may once again favour chariot production."

Ayameru looked alarmed. "Hush, Hori...even to think about such sentiments is dangerous. Do not voice them, I beg of you, for the listener as well as the speaker would suffer for it."

"I will say no more on that, my friend, but consider...let us say the king changes his mind and wants chariots in a year or two...or five. Wouldn't it be better to have horses and vehicles ready to go?"

Ayameru nodded. "What about charioteers? Chariots are useless without them, but drivers need the most training."

"We keep the ones we have; find them other duties."

236

"What could we find for them to do that would be half as satisfying?"

"They'll still work with horses. Not as charioteers, it's true, but it would be something."

Ayameru shook his head. "I doubt that will be enough."

"Many will fall away," Hori agreed, "but some will stay. I can think of...six? Eight? Not enough to man a chariot squadron, but enough to serve as a nucleus for future training."

"So, you have eight men, thirty chariots and several wagon loads of parts, as well as what...a hundred horses? Where are you going to keep them all that won't attract unwelcome attention? If the king thinks you are disobeying him, you'll suffer for it."

"I know, but remember, Ayameru, I have a large estate south of the city. We've always bred horses there, so taking on another herd won't be suspicious. I'll need men to work them, so why not use men already trained for that? Our ex-charioteers."

"And the chariots and parts?"

"Who would want them? I'll send them down quickly before anyone gets any other ideas."

"The king...or rather, Mershepsesre Ini...paid good gold for the horses and chariots. Do you think he will just give them away?"

"No, I'll buy them. I think that given the surfeit of horses the king will have, I can probably get a hundred of them cheaply, and the chariots for a fraction of the cost. They have no other use, after all. It'll be expensive, I grant, but worthwhile."

"I'll try and get my father to put me in charge of sales," Ayameru said. "That way I can get you a good deal."

Chapter 22

King Menenre fought on, but his army had disintegrated, leaving him with splintered groups who warred amongst themselves almost as much as they fought Samuqenu's army. Menenre went to ground in the city of Zau, building up his defences, but he suffered from desertions. Some of these men fled back to their former lives as peasants, fishermen or artisans, but some favoured another king to rule over the Delta. General Inkhare attracted many, as did General Menkare when it became known that he had survived the battle at Per-Bast. A few even called for Djedenre to claim the throne, ignoring the fact that he had surrendered to the enemy.

"He is the descendant of kings," these men claimed. "Kings of Hattush and the Delta are in his lineage, and that is more than you can say for the other claimants."

"Menenre is king," contested his supporters. "He was crowned and anointed and is the rightful king."

"Crowned quickly in a rural town without benefit of the Hem-netjers of the gods. Look at his lack of success--doesn't that speak of the gods having forsaken him?"

"Is Djedenre any better? He surrendered to Samuqenu, having deserted Menenre in his time of need. Far from being a king or descendant of kings, he is a traitor."

Often, by this point, the two groups came to blows, or else, if there were supporters of Inkhare present, joined forces to sneer at "General Caution" as they called him.

Samuqenu brought a large army to invest Zau, determined to capture or kill the Delta king, but the gods had not yet completely forsaken him. The Great River rose in flood and such was the volume of water it submerged farmland and towns, leaving only the cities untouched. Unable to maintain his army in the field, Samuqenu retreated to the margins of the Delta where the land stayed above the encroaching waters. If the invader could do nothing with the flood waters covering everything, then neither could the defenders of the Delta. The enforced stay within the city walls engendered more dissension that threatened to flare into violence.

A local lord, Muthotep, thought himself a worthy successor to kings and raised the flag of open rebellion in Zau. He was prosperous, and his estates had so far been untouched by war, so encouraged by sycophants and backed by servants and mercenaries, he sought to overthrow the king. Menenre, however, had chafed at the inaction forced upon him by the flood waters and a superior army outside the walls, and flew into a rage when Muthotep confronted him. Supported by his soldiers, he ordered the arrest of the rebel, whereupon his supporters fled and his mercenaries surrendered. A trial was unnecessary, so Menenre proceeded immediately to the execution, determined to stamp out rebellion once and for all. Muthotep was impaled and left to die screaming in the city market, and after he died his body was burnt to ashes and scattered into the flood waters. His estate was confiscated and his family cast out.

News of this rebellion and the support garnered by Generals Inkhare and Menkare reached the ears of Samuqenu camped with his army near Iunu, and it pleased him. He called Djedenre into his presence and apprised him of the information.

"I rejoice that my brother Menkare has survived, my lord," Djedenre said. "I thought him dead at Per-Bast."

"You know the man," Samuqenu said. "Will men support his claim?"

"I find it hard to believe he claims the throne for himself. It is more likely others claim it for him. As for his support, I would judge it minimal. He has no legitimate claim on the throne."

"I want you to reach out to him. Persuade him to surrender and bend his knee."

"I will try, my lord."

"What of Inkhare?" Samuqenu asked.

"He is an able general, my lord, but has no greater claim on the throne than Menenre. More will follow him, but he is unlikely to pursue an active role. He will sit in Per-Wadjet and sue for peace, hoping you will confirm him as a subject king."

"He will wait a long time then."

"It might be no bad thing to offer him that, my lord," Djedenre said. "The Delta kingdom is almost yours anyway, and if it will bring about peace..."

"You could be right; I will consider it. Now, there is one other name that has been put forward as king--yours, Djedenre."

"Mine?"

"Have you betrayed me, Djedenre? Have you conspired with your family to subvert my rule?"

"My lord, no. On my honour, my lord. This is the first I have heard of it."

"Why would people claim the throne on your behalf then? They must have reason to believe you could be king."

Djedenre shook his head. "I don't know, my lord. I have never given any indication that I sought the throne. All I ever wanted to do is to be a soldier, later a general, and the gods blessed me with an opportunity to serve my king well. Nothing more than that, I swear."

Samuqenu grunted and considered Djedenre. "You realise, of course, that just as you are hostage to your father's good behaviour, so too is he for yours. If you played me false, I would have no hesitation in ridding myself of your relatives."

"It will not happen, my lord. I have given an oath of loyalty to you."

"As you gave it to Menenre and before him to Seneferenre. That is the problem with a man who switches loyalties--can one ever trust him?"

"That is for you to say, my lord, but I only ever gave my oath to Menenre under duress. He claimed the throne for himself, not for the people. That is why I turned from him."

Samuqenu turned away from Djedenre and looked out of his command tent at the vast sheet of water that was the Delta in flood. The water was starting to drop at last, the tips of reeds poking through the surface and here and there where the land was slightly higher, farmers were moving about, splashing in the shallow water as they started to dig out the irrigation ditches.

"I said that I would consider your suggestion to support Inkhare as king. Well, I have considered and I reject it." Samuqenu turned back to face Djedenre.

"As you will, my lord. It was only a suggestion."

"The idea has merit though, so I will support one man as king over the Delta kingdom--you, Djedenre."

Djedenre stared, sure that he had misheard.

"What do you say, Djedenre?"

"I...I don't understand."

"Come, you know how things work. Menenre has a splintered army and loses support daily. Inkhare would like to become king but has no real ability to attract supporters; likewise Menkare. You, on the other hand, would be popular. If you claimed the throne, many would support you."

"But I don't want to be king, my lord. I have no ambitions in that regard; I'm quite satisfied to serve you."

"Well of course you are, and I would expect nothing less, but if you were to claim the throne, my opposition would fall apart. Support for Menenre would vanish, as it would for Inkhare and Menkare and any others out there. You would be the only possible king in the Delta, and all men would follow you. With you as king, all fighting stops when you bend your knee to me as your sovereign lord. Your father was brother to a king of the Delta and you are related to a king of Hattush, so it is not a ridiculous idea."

Djedenre shook his head, his heart hammering in his chest. *I don't want to be king*, he thought. *This is madness...or is it a test? Is Samuqenu testing my loyalty?*

Samuqenu smiled as if Djedenre had spoken his thoughts aloud. "I understand, Djedenre. You think I am testing you, but I am not. You are a child of the Delta and these are your people; you don't want to deceive them. But think...if war continues, many more will die, but if you become king, then the fighting ceases and lives...the lives of your people...will be saved."

"You would really do that for the people of the Delta, my lord?"

"Don't be naive, Djedenre. I would do it to bring the fighting to an end. I thought the Delta would take me a year at most to subjugate, and it is already closer to four. I want Kemet, but I can't move against it until the Delta is at peace. You can help me achieve that and if it saves lives, well and good."

Djedenre looked unhappy. "I wouldn't even know how to go about becoming king," he said.

"Whether you actually become king is immaterial. All you need to do is be a reasonable alternative to Menenre and the rest. I'll send you into the Delta once the water dries up. You'll have some good officers in support and enough men to show the populace you are a serious contender. I'll have craftsmen make some official seals in your name, have a few inscriptions carved, a handful of statues commissioned." Samuqenu smiled mirthlessly. "I can even get the priests of Iunu to anoint you if necessary."

Djedenre had misgivings but realised he would have to obey the word of the heir of Amurru. While he waited for the flood to recede, he got to know the officers who would accompany him and quickly realised they had another purpose besides supporting him. They were strong men of Amurru, owing sole loyalty to Samuqenu and he doubted they would hesitate in bringing him to heel if he stepped out of line. The men were a different matter, being drawn from Delta natives. They would be seen as men who had already freely offered up their allegiance to him. With luck, no fighting would be necessary, only persuasion.

He found out one other thing while he waited. His sister Neferit served alongside him in Samuqenu's army, albeit in the chariot squadrons. It was startling news, and he was nonplussed to find her garbed in men's clothing and in the company of a known homosexual.

"Have you taken leave of your senses, Neferit?"

"Neterre, brother. I am a young Ribu man now...as you see." She smiled and held out her arms, twirling to show off her clothing.

"You are my sister still, despite being garbed in such a ridiculous fashion."

"Not so ridiculous if you are a woman trying to live in a man's world. I am suitably disguised and thus protected from unwanted attention."

"You do yourself no favours, Neferit. One day you will want to marry, and who will want you if it's known you consorted with low men?"

"I have no intention of marrying, brother. Other women may desire men; I do not. All I want is to be a charioteer."

Djedenre turned on Sadiki, who had been standing to one side, pretending not to listen. "I suppose you are the one who has filled her head with such nonsense, though I cannot conceive why. You don't even like women."

"It was nothing to do with me, my lord," Sadiki said. "I did not even know her gender until recently." He hazarded a tentative smile. "I would have preferred she was a man..." His smile slipped as he saw the expression on Djedenre's face. "You need not fear for your sister's virtue. She is in no danger from me, as you rightly point out, but being with me protects her from other men. No man will even look at her as long as she is known to be my companion."

"That is true, brother," Neferit said. "No-one pays me any attention in that regard, and...and Sadiki is like a brother to me."

"What is your interest in all this?" Djedenre demanded of Sadiki. "What are you getting out of it? Nobody is that selfless."

"I enjoy her company," Sadiki said. "Is that so hard to imagine? And she has the makings of a good charioteer."

"You are leading her on for some purpose of your own."

"Why is it hard to imagine I might be a charioteer?" Neferit asked. "Is it just because you think of me as your young sister and cannot see me as an adult in charge of my own destiny?"

"In truth, my lord, she is a passable charioteer already, having guided me into battle at Per-Bast," Sadiki said. "She will get better."

Djedenre stared at them both. "Our father will have a fit when he hears of this."

"He already knows and has accepted it, even if he doesn't approve."

Djedenre shook his head. "It is your life, I suppose."

"It is, brother. And what of yours? You were a rebel not so long ago, yet here you are in Samuqenu's army."

"I think of myself as a loyalist, if you don't mind," Djedenre said stiffly, "as you were when you broke me out of prison, if you remember. Yet you quickly transferred your loyalty. I remained loyal to Seneferenre, only changing sides after Menenre seized the throne." He shrugged. "Samuqenu will win, so if I want to survive and protect my family, I must cleave to him."

"But that's not all, is it, my lord?" Sadiki said softly. "If the rumours are true. You are to become king of the Delta kingdom."

Djedenre nodded. "That is Samuqenu's intention."

"What is this?" Neferit demanded. "How can that be?"

"It is only a nominal office, designed to bring an end to the resistance. If I can get men to accept me, I can formally surrender and hand over the Delta to Samuqenu."

Neferit whistled. "And you accuse me of forsaking my former loyalty? How will you be remembered by generations to come if you do this?"

"I hope I'll be remembered for saving lives."

"King Djedenre," Neferit said, unable to keep the mockery out of her voice.

Djedenre scowled. "Sister," he murmured, before taking his leave.

He grieved for the strain that had come upon their relationship, believing that she was fooling herself if she thought she could maintain her deception for long. She would be discovered and her plans would come to nothing; whereas his own could bear valuable fruit for everyone.

As soon as the waters had receded and the sun dried out the black soil sufficiently, Djedenre led a column of men, numbering no more than two hundred, into the Delta farmlands. His mission was to talk to people, to persuade them, to garner support for his claims. The soldiers with him were only to prevent violence, not instigate it. They were largely successful in this as the farmers and villagers tended to flee as soon as soldiers appeared. When that happened, Djedenre would send most of his soldiers away and, keeping only a handful of men with him, set up camp and wait for the villagers to reappear. As soon as they saw the intruders were peaceful, they crept back, whereupon Djedenre was able to address them.

He told them who he was, that he was of the royal families of Avaris and Hattush, and that he came to bring peace to the Delta. Seneferenre had been the last legitimate king, he told them, and Menenre was a usurper seeking only his own benefit. Others were raising their standards, but none of them had a legitimate claim to the throne--except him. Support me, he told them, and I will bring peace. When he was king, he would recognise the authority of Samuqenu rather than trying to fight him. No armies would march the lands of the Delta; no man would see his house burn, his flocks butchered and his crops plundered. Their women would be safe too, their children happy. Djedenre was received well. People had had enough of war and wanted only to get on with their lives. Power and wealth was all very well for the elite, but all the common people wanted were food, shelter and safety. Anyone who promised that would get their support.

Djedenre moved on; deeper into the Delta, moving faster as the land dried. Near Zau, he was surprised by a small force of soldiers flying the standard of Menenre. They erupted out of the darkness in the cool before the dawn, axes swinging, and cut down several of Djedenre's men before a proper defence could be organised. He led the counterattack himself, and such was the ferocity of his men that the attacking soldiers faltered and melted away into the growing daylight, leaving their dead and wounded behind. Djedenre ordered the wounded be attended to and sent messengers to Zau requesting embalmers be sent to attend upon the dead. They came, and it was as they started preparing the bodies that Djedenre discovered the corpse of King Menenre.

He viewed the body, commenting that Menenre had risen from obscurity to become a general, and then a king; had done nothing of note during his short reign, and in death had sunk back into obscurity.

News of the death of the king spread rapidly, and by the time Djedenre returned to Iunu and Samuqenu's court, General Inkhare had made himself king. As expected, he took his small army to the remote city of Per-Wadjet and shut the gates against the world. There he remained, though an army camped outside his gates. The flood came again, isolating him still further.

Menkare surrendered to Samuqenu and the Amurran heir insisted on him making obeisance to the new king of the Delta. Djedenre was uncomfortable with his brother-in-law prostrating himself and raised him up, welcoming him. He sent him back to Avaris to be with his wife, asking him to keep an eye on Amenre who was now approaching manhood. Menkare sent a letter back almost immediately with some alarming news. Djedenre's son Amenre had become incensed at the idea that his father should claim the throne of the Delta as a gift from the invader, and had run away a few months before. His avowed intention was to join Inkhare and fight against Samuqenu.

There was nothing Djedenre could do except inform the troops laying siege to Per-Wadjet that his son was in or near the city. He offered a reward for the boy's safe return, and hoped that that would be enough to protect him. Beyond that it was with the gods.

Within twelve months of Inkhare's retreat and Djedenre's formal accession to the throne, though only recognised by a small ceremony in

Iunu, peace came to the Delta. Inkhare surrendered and was imprisoned, and his soldiers dispersed back to their farms and trades. Of Amenre there was no trace, despite a thorough search being made. Nobody in the city knew the name, and Djedenre could only surmise that he was going under another name. He refused to consider the other possibility; that his son was dead and lying in some unmarked grave.

Samuqenu was inordinately pleased that his scheme had worked, and decided to reward his puppet king. "A man should not be alone," he told Djedenre. "Take as many women as pleases you from Iunu...or elsewhere in the Delta if you prefer."

"Thank you, my lord, but I have no need in that regard."

"You are married? Or you have a consort? I know you have a son."

"Amenre, my lord. His mother died of the flux last year. He...he was with Inkhare, but has gone missing."

"The will of the gods, eh? I'm sure he will turn up and you can keep him with you; give him some proper guidance. A boy needs a mother though. You should consider marrying again."

"He is a grown man, my lord, and I could not remarry. I still love my wife Rait."

"Love is good; the memory of love not so good," Samuqenu said. "You are a king now, Djedenre. You should set an example for your people and marry."

"I would rather not, thank you all the same, my lord."

"I wish it, Djedenre."

Djedenre kept silent, hoping the conversation would not develop further.

Samuqenu frowned. "You have no regard for my wishes?"

"Of course, my lord, but if it is all the same to you, I would rather not take another wife."

"You have performed well in bringing peace to the Delta and I want to reward you. You're not going to throw that reward back in my face, are you?"

"No, my lord, but...perhaps gold? Or an estate? Those would be suitable rewards."

"You already have gold and land. As king, those are yours by right. I would give you something you do not have."

"But something I do not need, my lord."

"Nevertheless, you will accept it. I have made up my mind."

Djedenre could see there was no escaping it, but the acceptance of Samuqenu's reward need not interfere with his private feelings. He would always love Rait, and never love a substitute.

"I serve you, my lord, in all things. Command me and I will obey."

"Good man," Samuqenu said, his bearded face relaxing into a satisfied smile. "When you see the lady I have in mind, you will welcome her. She is Ishat, daughter of Aliyan, one of my kinsmen...although not close." He grinned. "Do not think I will make you my heir just because you too will be my kinsman."

Djedenre was not amused by any of the banter, but knew he must appear grateful. "You honour me greatly, my lord."

"You deserve it, King Djedenre. Now, do not concern yourself with the details. I will organise everything."

"Yes, my lord. Er...when...?"

"Not for a while. Aliyan is still in Amurru and unaware of my generosity on his behalf. Naturally, Ishat will do as she is told, but I must break the news to her father." Samuqenu mistook the look on Djedenre's face for anxiety and hurried to reassure him. "Never fear, Aliyan will accept your hand for his daughter. You are a king after all."

Chapter 23

Amenre had had no standing in Inkhare's army when he joined it, not wanting to claim any familial relationship with his father or grandfather--both traitors to the Delta in his eyes. He arrived, muddy and bedraggled from his solitary journey across the breadth of the kingdom, slipping through the enemy siege lines at night. His arrival was not heralded in any way and he was drafted into one of the units guarding the walls. Days passed and he became disillusioned with Inkhare's strategy of just sitting within his fortress city. This was not the glorious struggle against the hated invader that he had envisioned while sitting at home in Avaris. He found himself grumbling to another youth while on guard duty.

"This is not what I hoped for, Zhu," Amenre said in a low voice, careful not to let the officer overhear him.

"What's wrong with it?" Zhu asked, scratching for lice in his hair. "We get fed and there's not much work to do. Just stand here and watch that the enemy doesn't get up to anything."

"That's just it; we don't do anything. This is supposed to be a war of liberation."

Zhu shrugged. "Who knows what the king and his officers are doing? Let them worry about it. I'm content just to obey orders."

"They don't seem to be doing anything."

"That's just because they don't tell us. If we need to know, they will."

"I suppose so," Amenre said, "but wouldn't you like to do something worthwhile?"

"Like what?"

"Fight the enemy? Strike a blow for freedom?"

"We're doing our bit," Zhu said.

"What, standing around on guard duty? We should be leaving the city and attacking the enemy in their camp out there." Amenre pointed out toward the tents and camp fires of the encircling Amurran army.

The officer saw his expansive gesture and walked over.

"What are you two doing? This is guard duty, not a discussion over a cup of beer."

"Yes, sir. Sorry, sir," Zhu mumbled.

"Just tired of doing nothing, sir," Amenre grumbled.

The officer stared at the youth and his lips smiled though his eyes did not. "You want something to do, eh? Well, you'll get what you want--both of you. Report to me when your watch ends; there are some middens that need cleaning out." He stalked away, back to his post.

"Thank you, I don't think," Zhu whispered.

Amenre just shrugged, his anger building but now directed at the officer. "Son of a whore," he muttered.

When their watch ended, the other guards made for the taverns and a welcome pot of beer and food, but Amenre and Zhu joined a small group of others also on punishment detail at the officers' latrines. Armed with buckets and mattocks, the men entered the pits that were almost overflowing and scooped up the faecal matter, carrying the buckets up to the top of the wall and emptying them into the arm of the river that flowed nearby. If the city had not been under siege, the faeces would have been carried out to the fields and dug into the soil.

By the time the pits were empty, Amenre and Zhu were covered in filth, and though they scrubbed themselves with sand and doused themselves liberally with water, a stinking miasma accompanied them when they crawled exhausted into their barracks.

"Get out, you stinking bastards," men yelled at them, throwing anything at them that came to hand. "Get out or we'll throw you out."

Under a barrage of objects, the two men retreated, seeking lodging for the night in the shelter of the wall. The stink of their still-soiled bodies was bearable in the open air, but Amenre felt humiliated by the knowledge of what he had been forced to do.

"I'm going to get that son of a whore back for this," he muttered.

"Don't be a fool," Zhu said. "We were talking on duty and while I hated what he made us do, we deserved punishment."

"I didn't join up to clean out middens; I came to fight."

Zhu grinned, his teeth showing faintly in the gloom. "If it's a fight you're after, you should have stayed in the barracks...ow!" He shifted away as Amenre landed a punch on his arm.

"I mean it. I came to fight."

"The king will get around to it eventually. He's probably just waiting for the right time."

The flood came, the water rising until it seemed as if the city stood in the midst of a shallow lake. As the water rose, the besieging army withdrew to higher ground to the west, while a small fleet of boats kept watch over the city. After a time, the waters fell again, leaving a thin layer of black mud over the fields. The encircling army returned--and still King Inkhare hid within Per-Wadjet. It was now the season of planting, but nobody tended the fields around the city and the food stores that had been gathered after the previous harvest ran low.

"Now we have hunger as well as boredom to contend with," Amenre grumbled.

"The king will have to do something soon or we'll starve," Zhu observed. "You may get your wish."

"Can't happen soon enough."

Although the common soldiers were not party to the determinations of the King's Council and senior officers, gossip leaked downward and rumours abounded. The army was going to break out of the city, pierce the encircling Amurrans, and try to capture Avaris; King Inkhare was close to death; Samuqenu had died; a new king had made himself ruler of the Delta and was calling men to his standard; the city was surrendering. These and a score of other rumours had them all guessing.

Amenre hoped it was going to be the first of these and prepared himself as best he could by repairing his sandals and sharpening his copper spearhead and axe. There was little more he could do except hold himself in readiness. Rumours swirled anew and then settled, dominated by the fact that the troops were to assemble in the streets near the main gates at dawn the next day.

"It's true," Amenre said. "I heard the Troop commander issuing the orders. We're going to attack at last."

Zhu grimaced, but said nothing. He hoped nothing would come of it, but was afraid of seeming a coward by voicing his misgivings. His concerns were unnecessary as discipline seemed to be slipping in the remains of the Delta army and many others openly hoped they were not in for a fight. Soldiers all around them were voicing complaints as they stood in their companies, waiting for orders.

Inkhare came out of his residence but his appearance was not encouraging. He was obviously better fed than his men, but his shoulders were slumped, and the regalia of his kingdom seemed too heavy to bear. His expression was one of pain and Amenre wondered if the rumour concerning the king's health was true. Inkhare turned to his Chief Adviser and spoke with him briefly. The Adviser then took out a scroll and read loudly so as many as possible should hear the king's words.

"It is over. I hoped that the gods might support me in my just endeavour to keep the Delta kingdom out of the clutches of the invader...but it is not to be. Samuqenu has offered generous terms for my surrender, and I have accepted them..."

"No, it cannot be," Amenre muttered. "Are we to just meekly surrender without striking a blow?"

"Shh," Zhu said. "I want to know the terms."

"As for me," the Adviser continued on behalf of Inkhare, "I will accept house arrest in Avaris, while other senior officers in my army will be similarly imprisoned in other cities of the Delta. They, and all junior officers above the rank of 'Fifty' will be required to swear an oath of loyalty to Amurru and to Samuqenu personally. Anyone refusing to do so, or who later goes back on their word will be summarily executed."

"What about us?" a man called out when the Adviser started to roll up the scroll. "What is to happen to the ordinary soldiers?"

The Adviser glanced at the king and then shrugged. He called out in reply. "There are no provisions in the surrender for ordinary soldiers. You are to hand in your weapons, then disband and return to your former occupations. If any of you want to join the Amurru officers, you will have to take it up with their officers. Your service here is at an end."

"Just like that," Amenre muttered. "Not even a word of thanks...and you can bet we won't be getting any pay we're owed."

"At least we get out of it with our lives," Zhu said.

The gates opened and King Inkhare, with his court officials and senior officers walked out and formally surrendered, handing over the emblems and symbols of the rank and power, laying them at the feet of Samuqenu. Each man then swore the oath of loyalty and was taken away, though Inkhare was offered wine by his conqueror and sat with him while his army now surrendered their arms.

Amenre hated the thought of handing over his weapons. He had not yet used them to extract the life from any of his enemies, so debated how he could retain them. His axe was too conspicuous to hide, but he broke the copper point off his spear and just handed in the staff. He also picked up a dagger that another man had dropped and slipped that into his loincloth. The Amurran soldiers were overwhelmed by the numbers of men surrendering, so were cursory in their examination. Zhu and Amenre were able to walk away unsearched and unmolested.

"You're not going to join them?" Zhu asked.

"I'll die first," Amenre said. "The king may have surrendered, but I haven't. I'll continue the fight while there's still life in me."

Refusing to look at the Amurran soldiers, Amenre kept his head down as he passed through their lines, but had he looked up he might have been amazed to see his aunt in an enemy chariot. Neferit was there with Samuqenu's army when he took the surrender that effectively brought the war in the Delta to a close.

Hundreds of soldiers dispersed into the broad lands of the Delta and returned to being fishermen, farmers, carpenters, brick makers, bakers, and a host of other professions. Zhu wanted to, as he enjoyed being a fisherman, but Amenre would not let him; instead insisting he accompany him south toward the borders of Kemet.

"We can seek refuge among the enemies of Samuqenu," Amenre said. "The invaders are sure to attack Kemet next, so we will be welcome there. They will need all the help they can get."

"I'd really rather not," Zhu said. "I mean, I survived the war and I don't want to tempt the gods by taking up arms again. If I stay at peace I can go back to fishing."

"You took an oath of loyalty to the king," Amenre pointed out.

"Inkhare is no longer king."

"It doesn't matter. Your oath was to the throne, not any particular king. Until you're released from it, you must remain loyal to whoever is king."

Zhu frowned, trying to make sense of the argument. "All right, but who is the king?"

"I don't know, but somebody must be. We'll just have to stay strong until we find someone we can follow."

They made their way cautiously south, avoiding towns where they could, taking menial work on the farms in exchange for food. It was at one of these farms that they heard a startling piece of news. Amenre had returned to their camp with a measure of grain and a pot of beer as their wages, while Zhu stayed back to try and wheedle a couple of eggs from an itinerant trader. He came hurrying back without the eggs, but bursting with the news the trader had voiced.

"We have a king, Amenre. The trader said so...in fact, he's been king all along. Properly anointed and everything. We can go to him now instead of fleeing south."

"Who is this new king?"

"Djedenre, the trader said."

Amenre went pale. "It...it couldn't be...did the trader say anything else? About whom this man is?"

"Only that he has a greater claim to the throne than anyone recently. He is the son of Merybaal the Treasurer and is even related to the King of Hattush. He has the support of Samuqenu too, so there won't be any more fighting."

"Oh...the traitor...how could he lower himself so?" Amenre groaned.

"What is wrong?" Zhu asked, puzzled at his friend's reaction.

Amenre hesitated, at first not wanting to reveal his connection. Then he shook his head, desiring only to distance himself from such treachery.

"Djedenre is my father, but I renounce him completely. If I never see him again, I will be content; and if I am dragged into his presence I will kill him with my bare hands."

"Amenre," Zhu said, shocked to his innermost parts. "If he is your father, you owe him the respect of a dutiful son, what...whatever his actions."

"I could forgive him many things," Amenre said, "but not that. He is no longer my father, but an enemy of the Delta Kingdom."

"But you told me we had to be loyal to the throne, no matter who sat upon it."

"In that I was wrong. I would not be loyal to Samuqenu or any puppet he puts upon it; only to the rightful king."

"So who is the rightful king?"

"He will appear when the time is right."

253

Zhu thought about that for a while. "All right. If that is so, then we will find out. Now I suppose we'd better be going if we're to get to Kemet."

"No; I have changed my mind. We're not going."

"We're not? Good. I didn't really want to fight any more."

"Oh, we're fighting, but not in the south. I'm going to take the battle to Djedenre and make him rue the day he ever decided to turn against the Delta kingdom."

Zhu groaned. "How? You're only one man..." he saw the look on Amenre's face and added, "...only two men."

"There will be others similarly disgusted with this traitor. We shall find them and enlist their help. Together we shall drive that usurper from the throne and the invader from our land."

"Whole armies weren't able to do that," Zhu pointed out.

Amenre looked hard at his companion until Zhu started to feel uncomfortable. "We have only recently witnessed the cowardly behaviour of Inkhare when he surrendered without a fight. This disgusting display may have tainted your mind, so I shall overlook your words which could also be construed as displaying cowardice. We will remain faithful to our vows to the Delta, to our rightful king, and our vow to resist the invader. Is that clear, Zhu?"

"Yes, Amenre," Zhu said meekly. "Er...where do we go then?"

"We go north, back into the wide lands of the Delta, looking for allies. There must be others who believe as we do, so we shall join with them in our ongoing fight."

The two men turned and headed back into the pastures of the Delta, determined to fight for a non-existent king.

King Anep-Aper died and Samuqenu ascended to the throne of Amurru, Syria, Lebanon and Kanaan...and now claimed suzerainty over the Kingdom of the Delta through his client king Djedenre. The body of the old king was dried in salt, packed into a gilt coffin and taken back to Amurru to be laid in a tomb alongside his ancestors. Samuqenu, as surviving son and heir, accompanied the king's body on its last journey. He was gone for nearly three months, during which time his army consolidated its hold over the Delta kingdom and continued to pick away at little pockets of resistance that still held out.

Rumours of a fanatical leader surfaced, though nobody could be certain as to his identity. He was sometimes known as 'Ustjennu' which the Amurran troops were told meant 'freedom'. This leader was troublesome, but only as a wolf might be to a flock of sheep--more nuisance than truly dangerous. Local troops tried to find him but he had the habit of melting back into the wide Delta lands, so their efforts came to nothing.

Samuqenu returned from burying his father and brought with him fresh troops and his son Aper-Anati, who as heir needed experience of warfare. The southern kingdoms would yield riches in abundance once they had been properly pacified, and the youth should have a share in the process.

Another new member of Samuqenu's entourage was his kinsman Lord Aliyan and his daughter Ishat. The new king had not forgotten his promise to Djedenre amidst the troubles surrounding his father's death and burial and his own formal accession. Djedenre was less than enthusiastic when he heard of Ishat's arrival in Avaris, but answered Samuqenu's summons a few days later.

"King Djedenre, this is my kinsman Lord Aliyan. Aliyan, your future son-in-law Djedenre of the Houses of Avaris and Hattush."

Aliyan, a tall, thin man with a neatly trimmed beard and piercing gaze bowed to the client king of Avaris, careful in the depth of his obeisance and the gestures he made to convey the idea that though only a Lord of Amurru, he judged himself every bit the equal of a foreign king. Djedenre, less versed in the etiquette of court life, accepted his future father-in-law's assessment without realising it, by bowing deeply and addressing him first.

"Lord Aliyan, you are welcome in Avaris."

"Thank you, Lord Djedenre. My kinsman Samuqenu, the Monarch of Amurru and the Delta and all lands between, has told me much about you. Your father is Merybaal, who was the Treasurer of Avaris under the tribal kings of the Delta, I understand. Forgive my seeming ignorance of such matters, my lord, but how is it that the mere Treasurer can claim kinship to the royal house of Avaris?"

Djedenre became aware that Aliyan believed himself superior in rank, but was determined to be polite.

"My father Merybaal was the adopted brother of King Asehre Nehsy and adopted son of King Maaibre Sheshi of the Delta."

"And your connection to the House of Hattush, one of the minor kings in my noble kinsman's stable of clients?"

Djedenre bristled, but remained polite. "Merybaal was grandson of Arimawat, a former King of Hattush."

Aliyan grunted. "Well, a tenuous connection is better than none, I suppose."

"And what of yourself, Lord Aliyan? How are you related to my illustrious Lord Samuqenu, King of Amurru, Lebanon and Syria?"

"My sister was married to King Anep-Aper's cousin."

Djedenre smiled. "Well, as you say, Aliyan, a tenuous connection is better than none."

Aliyan scowled, and it was left to Samuqenu to make the peace.

"Come, your two families are soon to be joined. Let us have no more bickering and jostling for position. You are both dear to my heart and I would bind the Delta Kingdom closer to Amurru. Aliyan, when will we see your daughter Ishat? I imagine Djedenre is eager to see his new bride."

"Then he must wait a while longer, my lord king," Aliyan said. "As you know, it is not our custom to flaunt our womenfolk before strangers."

"A custom that is not always observed," Samuqenu pointed out. "I am hardly a stranger, being your kinsman, and Djedenre will soon be her husband."

"Nevertheless, my lord king, I must hold fast to our customs in a foreign land."

Samuqenu turned to Djedenre and shrugged, smiling. "What can I do?" he asked. "It is a custom, and while I think it unnecessary, Aliyan is her father."

"I do not mind, my lord," Djedenre said. The thought of marriage to this foreign woman filled him with sorrow, for it felt like a betrayal of his vows to Rait. He would be happy if the marriage never took place.

"At least describe your daughter for us, if we are not permitted to see her," Samuqenu said.

Aliyan bowed. "She is tall, my lord king, with hair long and lustrous, dark as the night. Her face is well-formed and her features fine; she is reckoned a beauty by all who know her. She is well-proportioned, and knowledgeable, skilled with the needle and in music."

"A paragon indeed," Samuqenu said. "What do you think, Djedenre?"

"Indeed, my lord, she sounds like everything an Amurran lord could wish for."

"Everything that any man could wish for," Aliyan snapped. "She is too good for an Avaris man."

"What is it that she lacks, Djedenre?" Samuqenu asked. "In your opinion."

Djedenre sighed. "My lord, I have nothing to say against the daughter of Lord Aliyan. I have neither met her nor even seen her, so how can I judge her?" He stood pensively for a few moments. "My wife Rait was of humble stock and though in all honesty she was not a beauty that would turn heads, yet she was beautiful in my eyes. She was always laughing, hardworking, and was a wonderful mother to our only son Amenre. There was this funny little thing she used to do..." He shook his head. "Forgive me, I stray into matters of a personal nature. Just let it be said that I loved...that I love...her very much. I find it hard to accept another woman while I still love Rait."

"Well, I would be happy to call off this marriage," Aliyan said. "I do not want Ishat to feel as if she is unwanted."

"No, no, it will happen," Samuqenu said. "Djedenre and Ishat will grow to love each other. Djedenre...isn't it true that your father arranged your marriage to your wife? That you only met her on the day you married?"

"That is so, my lord, but I fell in love the moment I saw her."

"Then let us pray that you will likewise fall in love with Ishat when you see her."

Djedenre sighed again. "Forgive me, my lord, but it is hard to concentrate on such matters when the only son of my marriage to my beloved wife is gone. He went to join the Delta loyalists and disappeared. Now I have lost not only my wife but my son as well."

"Through the good offices of Aliyan and me, you will gain a new wife whom you will come to love," Samuqenu said. "As for your son, it may be that not all is lost. This man they call Ustjennu bears a resemblance to your son, I am told."

"Amenre? He is Ustjennu?"

"I'm told by men who have seen him and that know your family, that there is a resemblance."

"Who could possibly know Amenre? He is only a youth of seventeen."

"I don't know his name, but he was a servant in your father's house in Avaris before he joined the army."

"I must see him...talk to him myself."

"I will have my aides find the man."

"And what about your marriage to my daughter?" Aliyan demanded. "Your behaviour is already bordering on an insult, and if you now reject her, I...I will have satisfaction with sword or spear."

"He will not reject her...will you, Djedenre? He will talk to this servant and once he knows his son still lives, he will marry your daughter."

It took only three days to send word out and for the servant to return to Avaris. He was brought before Djedenre and the man collapsed in front of him, shivering with fright and apprehension. Not only was Djedenre his previous master's son, but he was now King of Avaris, and he was bringing the king news that could be construed as unwelcome.

"I have seen you in my father's house," Djedenre said. "What is your name?"

"She...Shere, my lord."

"You are familiar with my son Amenre?"

"Y...yes, my lord. I s...saw him many times."

"You joined Samuqenu's army?"

"Yes, my lord. I...other men I knew were doing so, and...and..."

"I understand you have seen Amenre since you joined up. Tell me about this."

"Yes, my lord. We was near Zau, doing patrols and...and we was attacked by some men. Just a few, like, and they didn't kill no-one, just a few wounded. Their leader looked like I had seen him before and...and when I thought about it; I knew it was the young master."

"Amenre? You're sure?"

"He has a beard now, and long hair, but yes, my lord king. I'm sure."

"You say he was the leader of these men. Bandits were they? Or army?"

"They was disciplined, my lord, like they was army, but like no army I seen. Scruffy, young mostly, with all sorts of weapons. He was this man they is calling Ustjennu, my lord."

Djedenre dismissed the man and thought about the information he had received from his father's former servant Shere. He talked to his father and learned that Shere had been a trustworthy servant not prone to lying. On the face of it, it seemed that Shere was telling the truth and that Amenre was still alive, even if he was living the life of a bandit. Djedenre did not even want to contemplate the alternative, that Amenre had set himself up in opposition to his father and was fighting to bring about his downfall. With a weight lifted from his shoulders, he reported what he had found out to Samuqenu, but of course the King of Amurru already knew all of it.

"Don't worry," he told Djedenre. "My men have orders to capture this Ustjennu Amenre alive. You will have the opportunity to talk to him."

Now that he had found out about his son, Djedenre knew he would have to face the subject of his marriage. Samuqenu had made it clear that he wanted the marriage to take place, and Aliyan would consider it an insult if he backed away, so he would have to go through with it. He did not love the girl, but many marriages took place without that ingredient and he hoped it could just be an appearance of marriage, not the real thing. It would be hard on the girl if she was expecting more, but this had been forced on him.

The marriage was a simple affair that took place a few days later. Ishat was represented only by her father and Samuqenu, and Djedenre by his parents. Water and hearth fire were given as tokens of the change of habitation of the woman from her father's household to that of her husband, and the priests of Baal and Amun recorded the union in their respective temple scrolls. A wedding feast took place with only a few guests, and it was here that Ishat finally unveiled herself.

Aliyan had not lied that his daughter was tall and dark haired, nor that she was well-proportioned. Her skills with needle and music would be revealed in due course, but in one aspect Aliyan had described her as seen through a father's eyes. She was not what Djedenre would have called beautiful, but because he had not set any store on her being so, it did not matter. He saw a plain face, but one that showed character and what he thought might be humour and intelligence. Perhaps, he thought, she might provide companionship at least, even if there was no desire on his part and perhaps none on hers. They exchanged only a few words during the feast and not many more when they were alone together.

Djedenre had insisted that they occupy a new residence rather than one that he had lived in with Rait. His former house was nowhere near grand enough to be the home of a king, though that did not matter in the slightest to him. What did matter was that he was not bringing another woman into the home that had belonged to his beloved wife.

"I have had rooms set aside for you, Ishat," Djedenre said when they were alone. "I know you will be tired and understandably nervous about the circumstances of our marriage."

"You will not take me to bed, husband?" Ishat asked.

"There is no need to rush into these things. We have only just met, and we should take time to get to know each other."

"You do not desire me?"

"You are a desirable woman, Ishat, but there is plenty of time for such things." Djedenre bowed to his new wife and left her alone, taking himself off to another part of the house where he lay awake most of the night, remembering Rait.

Chapter 24

King Seheqenre Sankhptahi came to the throne of Kemet in violence and he ruled the same way, removing anyone he judged to be a threat to his life. His suspicions fell on court officials and army officers, nobles and commoners alike until the very fabric of life in the southern kingdom started to come apart. The only thing to hold firm was the army, for if there was one thing Seheqenre hated more than his fellow Kemetu, it was foreigners. He was convinced the *heqa khasut* were preparing to invade Kemet and spent every deben of gold that came out of the mines in the southern deserts on strengthening the army. Every noble that survived his persecutions was pressed into service and thousands of peasants were required to leave farms and workshops and wield an axe or a sword in defence of Kemet.

Hori was one of these nobles. Though he was related to Kemetu royalty through marriage, his blood was judged to be too attenuated to be a threat to Seheqenre, so he let him live. His nephews Bebi and Sobekhotep, being the sons of a former king, were another matter and they were forced to flee ahead of the king's assassins. They disappeared, with Hori's help, into a small fishing village three days upriver, where they lived simply without attracting notice. Of course, their very disappearance spoke of their guilt to Seheqenre, and he redoubled his efforts to find them.

Hori became an officer in one of the newly formed infantry legions, rising swiftly to become a Troop Commander. His rank allowed him to have an aide and he chose his young son Sekhem. Though only twelve years old, Hori believed it was safer for him in the army than left at home on the family estate. Sekhem treated it as an adventure, revelling in the squads of armed men everywhere, of living in tents, and the deference shown him as the son of an officer.

"You need to find a path for yourself, Sekhem," Hori said. "I brought you with me to protect you, but also that you may find what is important to you."

"The men cheer me and smile because I am your son. That is important. I have no need of anything else."

"Do not view yourself as important because of your birth, Sekhem," Hori chided. "Every man must make his own way in the world."

"I will be an officer in the king's army then...like you."

"That would please me greatly, but you must work for it instead of standing around expecting the men to do things for you."

"But that's what you do, father..." Sekhem broke off as he saw the expression on Hori's face. "I mean, men fetch and carry for you, obeying your orders."

"That is because I have earned their respect. I did not rely on who my father was, but went out and learned how to lead men, how to fight with spear and axe, sword and bow. I learned about horses and worked out how chariots are made. The more I learned, and the more I proved myself capable of achieving, the higher I rose in rank. As I rose within the army, I took on more responsibility, and proved myself worthy. That is what you must do, my son. Respect is earned, not given."

"I know horses."

"Yes, you do, but only as a groom knows them, having tended to them on our estate. The king has made it plain he has no use for chariots, so if you want to further your education with horses, you will have to become a proficient rider."

"To ride them into battle?"

"I've never heard of that being done, but you could prove valuable as a messenger."

"I suppose so." Sekhem looked doubtful. "It doesn't sound glorious."

"Not all that is necessary is glorious," Hori reproved.

"How do you mean?"

"You like eating, I know, so think how important a good cook is...or the man who grows and harvests the grain with which bread is made. Or the man who hunts the goose that graces the dinner table. None of these are glorious professions, but necessary all the same."

"I'd rather be a general conquering the enemy."

"Even a general has to eat. How can he win a glorious victory if he is starving?"

"Hmm."

"Or you could learn the use of a weapon. I know you can already use a bow for hunting birds. Perhaps you could train as an archer."

"I want to lead men into battle."

Hori sighed, wondering if anything he said was getting through to his son. "That will come in time, but for now you must become proficient is some aspect of warfare. How else will the men respect you?"

"They'll respect me because I am your son."

"In this Troop perhaps, but what if you are sent to another army group? One where my name is not known? Then you would have to make your own path."

Sekhem thought hard about his father's words, though he sulked for a few days. Then he made his decision and sought out his father.

"Father, I have thought about what you said and I want to make you proud of me. We have no horses here, so I would like to become an archer."

"I am glad to hear it, my son, and I think you have chosen well. I will arrange for an instructor to tutor you."

"If you do that, he will still treat me as your son rather than as a man in my own right. Let me learn elsewhere, in another legion."

"I swore to your mother that I would look after you. How can I do that if you are under another's command?"

"I am twelve years old, father; no longer a boy."

Hori smiled to himself and said that he would see what could be arranged. He went to see a man he knew, Anaken the Captain of Archers in a legion stationed south of the capital city, though on the eastern bank. It was not ideal, but Hori hoped it would be far enough away from any possible conflict to protect Sekhem. The regimen of training necessary would also keep him from the front lines.

"Hori, old friend," Anaken rumbled, his voice deep and reverberating, "what brings you to see me? Actually, who cares? It has been too long. You'll share a cup of wine? Or would you prefer beer or water?"

Hori embraced the towering man of Kush, his dark almost purple skin marred by lines of cicatrices. It had the effect of making him look fierce, but Hori knew Anaken was gentler than most men. He had joined the Kemetu army twenty years before and had risen to his present position through his skill with the bow. Knowing Hori's father had not hindered him either as Harrubaal still had influence at court.

"Wine would be good, my friend." Hori accepted a cup of inferior wine and sipped, his face involuntarily puckering.

Anaken laughed. "That's all our commander will provide. Vinegar would be sweeter. Have a seat, Hori and tell me the news. How is your father?"

"He passed into the west two years ago."

Anaken dropped his wine cup and thumped his chest with his right hand, his face screwed up into a grimace of grief. "Ah, my friend, I grieve for you. Your father was a great man and will be sorely missed."

Hori thanked him and proceeded to tell him about the rest of the family and how they fared. "That brings me to my son Sekhem, a boy of only twelve floods, but one who thinks himself a man."

"I know how he feels," Anaken said. He picked up the wine cup and wiped the sand from it before filling it from the jar. "I was ten when I fought my first battle against a neighbouring tribe."

"Different customs, my friend. I have tried to protect my son from such things."

"Understandable, yet he must fret at being left behind while you go to war."

"That's just it; I couldn't leave him behind." Hori got up and looked out of the tent flap, making sure nobody was close enough to overhear them. "The king has left my family alone so far, but I cannot be sure he always will."

"So you have him with you? You will be able to protect him."

Hori nodded and sipped again from his cup. "He is still a boy though, and mindful of his position as son of the Troop Commander. I want him to learn a military skill, but not where his status might hinder him."

"You want me to take him under my wing and teach him to be an archer?"

"Would you? I would deem it a great favour."

"It would bring me joy to serve the grandson of the great Harrubaal," Anaken said.

Sekhem stared at the huge Kushite warrior when Hori brought him, but Anaken knew how to put him at ease and soon had him chattering away as he investigated every part of the archer's unit. He hardly noticed when his father left, and Hori felt a bit put out. The sadness he felt at leaving his son in the care of another was mitigated by the knowledge that there was probably nowhere safer in the king's army. Anaken would look after Sekhem; teach him what he needed to know, and offer protection as far as he was able.

Hori returned to his unit where he continued with his duties, training the men under his command for upcoming battles with the *heqa khasut*. He feared these battles would prove disastrous for the Kemetu, but as he had no control over that, he did the best he could. His Troop, of which he was the Commander, numbered about six hundred men armed for the most part with copper axes. Some had swords or spears, and there were some fifty archers. Training was rudimentary. They were taught how to hold their weapons and practiced wielding them against leather and straw models using a few basic strokes. Archers loosed all their arrows at targets that stood no more than fifty paces away, and the instructors were satisfied if one in ten struck home.

"It hardly matters," the chief instructor told Hori when he took him to task over the lack of accuracy. "In a battle situation we loose off all our arrows into the enemy ranks and perhaps three in ten find their targets. If an archer can drop an arrow in the general vicinity of the enemy, I'm satisfied."

The battle tactics for the infantry was just as unsatisfactory in Hori's eyes. Prior to a battle, the men lined up in ranks and files, their weapons shouldered, and gave the appearance of being disciplined, capable of fighting together as a unit. When battle was joined, however, the men would charge forward, rapidly losing all cohesion, and engage the enemy one-on-one. Then it became six hundred fights in which individual strength and skill led to a very limited victory. Hori asked the overall commander why no effort was made to teach the men how to fight together.

"It's not worth the time and trouble. They are peasants who have only ever held a stick or a mattock before. Their idea of cooperation is to wait until their comrade's back is turned and take what they want. It's cheaper and easier just to throw them at the enemy and press more men later."

Hori groaned at the waste of life this represented. "Do you mind if I train my own men, sir?"

"As long as you can do it without using more resources...and still have them ready to go if they're needed."

Hori went back to his Troop eager to train his men further, but it proved to be a harder task than he envisaged. The men just could not be made to see any advantage in looking out for each other or working together.

"Begging your pardon, sir, but what's in it for me?" one of them said. "I starts watching out for the man next to me and next thing I know, some beggar sticks me from behind."

"The man next to you would be looking out for you too."

The man looked uncomfortable and dragged one foot in the dirt, not wanting to meet Hori's eyes.

"Go on, say what you want, I won't be angry."

"Well sir, if I'm watching him and he's watching me...well...wouldn't it be better if we just looked out for ourselves? I mean, I got a lot more interest in looking out for me than any other beggar."

Hori kept trying to persuade this man and others, but the only change he could make was to encourage them to stick together longer in a charge rather than meeting the enemy as a disorganised mob. He tried different arrangements of the men, putting spearmen together, or swordfighters or axemen, but if he moved them they tended to wander back to a preferred position with other men who hailed from the same village or district. The only change he could effect was to put his spearman in a tight defensive grouping, kneeling or standing, and presenting a bristling hedge of copper points to an attacker. Even this fell apart though when they had to charge. Hori despaired of getting his men to cooperate, so had to resign himself to increasing their fighting abilities. He set them rigorous programs that had them complaining, but after a month he thought he could see some improvement.

More time was needed, but they were called to action prematurely. The *heqa khasut* were probing southward in small numbers, testing the resistance rather than attempting conquest. Hori's Troop was dispatched toward the border to counter an enemy numbering no more than three hundred men.

"Any chariots with them?" he asked.

Thankfully, none had been reported, so Hori moved his men out quickly, taking them north at a trot. His scouts reported on the proximity of the enemy by the next day and Hori arranged his men in a defensive posture. They outnumbered the enemy, so Hori knew they would probably withdraw as soon as they perceived his strength. To counter this, he dropped half of his men back a few hundred paces and hid them in a fold of the land. Then he watched as the enemy marched up, hesitated, and evidently decided they could tackle his men, for they spread themselves out in a line opposite him. The enemy stood and waited, inviting an attack by drumming their swords on their cow-hide shields.

"Very well," Hori growled. "If they want it, we'll give it to them. Signal the attack," he told his aide.

The message was passed along and a banner dipped. With a roar, the soldiers broke ranks and charged toward the enemy, losing any semblance of order. In vain, Hori ran with them, shouting for them to remember who they were, to guard their comrades as they fought, but few paid any attention to their commander. The charge broke on the enemy line like a wave on a rocky shore, shattering into bits that fought fiercely but without coordination, each man picking out another and struggling to kill him.

Dust arose all around as the mass of men fought, but Hori hung back, trying to see how the battle was progressing, rather than taking part. The two sides were evenly matched and a slight advance in one area was matched by a retreat in another. It was time; he gave the command and the banner dipped and rose. Although he could see nothing because of the churned up dust, he could hear the rest of his men charging into the fray. The crush of men shuddered as the full Troop impacted and weight of numbers threw the enemy back. One moment a hundred individual contests surrounded him, the next the invaders were streaming away, leaving dead and wounded behind them. His own men tended to just stand and watch them go, so Hori had to shout at them, encouraging and threatening them until they set off in pursuit, dealing more destruction on the fleeing enemy.

After a while, he called them back and set about making a tally of their losses and the enemy dead. The enemy lost twenty dead and the same number badly wounded. There was no real point in wasting resources on the fallen, so they were despatched where they lay. The

Troop lost about an equal number, but in their case the wounded were treated and carried back to camp for proper treatment.

Hori was praised by the commander of the legion for his successful battle and more recruits were sent his way to make up for losses sustained. Then he was sent north again to patrol the border region with orders to pursue and destroy the *heqa khasut* wherever he found them.

"Hit them hard and hit them repeatedly," the commander said. "That's the only thing these foreigners understand. Make them realise they cannot win against us."

"Until they bring up their chariot squadrons anyway," Hori said.

"Chariots are overrated."

"I have seen them in action, sir. They are a fearsome weapon."

"If they were that fearsome, the king would have created our own chariot squadrons," the commander said. "The fact that he hasn't indicates they are no match for enthusiastic men."

Hori knew there was no point in arguing with his commander. Any words he might use could be construed as criticism of the king, and he knew that Seheqenre Sankhptahi reacted badly to criticism. So he saluted his commander and went back to his Troop thinking about how he might counteract the inevitable chariots. From what he had seen, there was little hope of surviving a full chariot charge, but it would be extremely unlucky if they encountered the massed squadrons of the *heqa khasut*. Far more likely it would be a patrol of only a few chariots, and they might choose to avoid battle.

He took his time organising his men for another border excursion, delaying so that his new recruits would have plenty of time to become accustomed to the Troop. Once more he tried to get his men to work together, but while they were amenable to follow instructions in a training situation, he saw no real enthusiasm for the concept. It would have to do, as the commander ordered them north. Raids had been occurring on farms within the borders of Kemet and Hori was ordered to stamp out the raiders. Naturally, he sent out scouts and was heartened when they returned with reports of only a few foot-soldiers.

Hori's Troop travelled quickly, giving little warning of their presence, and thus managed to surprise a group of raiders. They saw the smoke of burning buildings from afar and sped toward it in two groups, spreading wide to come upon them from two directions. Surprise was complete, the soldiers erupting upon the scene while the raiders were still engaged in driving off the livestock. Several were slaughtered with their arms still full of crops they had plundered, and while most of them grabbed their weapons to try and defend themselves, a few dropped everything and fled. The ones that stayed were killed, and though Hori sent men in pursuit of the ones that fled, they failed to catch them.

Hori could not be certain whether the raiders were part of a larger group, now alerted by the uncaught fugitives, so he set out guards and used the rescued produce and livestock to feed his men. They were undisturbed that night, but the next morning they saw a small dust cloud to the northeast. Hori sent out scouts who failed to return, and then others who reported a group of horse-drawn vehicles moving slowly toward them.

"How many?" Hori demanded.

"Not many," the scouts reported. "Fifty, maybe, which means only a hundred men."

"We can easily dispatch a hundred men," said one of Hori's officers.

"It's only a hundred men if they fight on foot," Hori said. "They won't, of course. Fifty chariots are worth far more than a hundred men."

"These are the chariots you have told us about, sir?"

Hori nodded. "They may not attack, but we'd better prepare all the same."

He gathered the men together and reiterated his warnings about chariots and how they would be likely to attack.

"If we are scattered they will just charge into our midst and we will lose men beneath trampling hooves and crushing wheels. Their archers will pour arrows into us before turning and retreating faster than we can follow. They'll repeat this until we can stand no more; then we die or flee."

Hori saw the dismayed looks on the faces of his men, so followed his words of warning with hope.

"Not all is lost though, providing you can maintain discipline as I have tried to instil in you. Horses do not fear individual men, but they will balk at men gathered together. If you remain in tight groups, shoulder to shoulder, with your weapons at the ready, they will not trample you. Rather, they will sweep around us on all sides, seeking to pour their arrows into us. This is our opportunity. Our archers must

269

loose their arrows, not seeking to hit the men, but the larger target--the horses. A man may press home an attack even when grievously wounded, but a horse will not. They will flee, and when they do so we attack any chariot whose horses are crippled. We will have a victory today, I promise, if you hold your nerve."

The men cheered Hori, hesitantly at first, and then with growing vigour. Hori encouraged their cries, working them up into a fury. Then, as the dust cloud loomed closer, he and his officers formed the men into three defensive squares. Spearmen formed the outer ranks, kneeling and standing, with spear hafts firmly grounded, and interspersed with them axe and sword bearers with their shields lifted high. Archers stood in the middle of each square, arrows stuck into the ground beside them for easy access.

"This will work, won't it, sir?" asked one of his junior officers.

"It should do," Hori replied.

"I...I mean, you've seen it work?"

Hori smiled and spoke loudly so many men could hear him. "Of course. Do not doubt yourselves and we will deal these *heqa khasut* a mighty blow."

Then there was no more time for talk as the dust cloud resolved into a swarm of chariots. They heard shouted commands and the chariots spread out, forming into groups and halted a few hundred paces away. For several long minutes the enemy stared at them and Hori could imagine them working out how to attack.

"We have the easier task," Hori murmured. "All we have to do is wait and react to whatever you do." Louder, he called out, "Stand firm, men. Remember what I told you..."

His words trailed off as the chariots surged into motion, splitting into three groups, one to each of their defensive squares. Hori wondered at that, thinking that less than a score of chariots attacking a square of two hundred men could not possibly succeed, whereas if they all attacked one square they might have a chance. Then he had no more time to think as the chariots raced toward them and the arrows started falling from the sky. Men fell with cries and screams and were hauled back into the centre of the square, the remaining men bunching up. Shields sprouted a crop of arrows and his own archers sent a flurry back. He saw two horses hit. Neither fell, though the chariot they were hauling slowed and broke formation.

Shouts erupted from behind him and he whirled to see the square to his left come apart as the men lost their nerve under the sustained assault of a score of chariots. At once, the enemy wheeled and charged back, smashing into the now loose formation of men, throwing them to the ground and trampling them. Many others fled, and a flurry of shafts from the enemy archers sought them out and harvested them. The slaughter of their companions sent a shudder through his own square and Hori called out to them.

"Take heart; your own steadfastness is a lesson to others. No harm will come to us if we remain strong."

The chariots that had destroyed the left square now joined forces with the others and redoubled their efforts. Hori saw the right square starting to panic, and as it started to come apart had his men yell to the men to join forces. Many of them fled toward Hori's square and the square opened to receive their comrades, strengthening the only defensive position remaining. The situation was not good though, and Hori started to wonder how he was going to extricate his men. If he had needed a demonstration of the power of chariots, this was it. He only hoped they would remain alive to tell others about it.

There was little possibility of striking back at the enemy with only a fraction of their archers surviving and those running out of arrows, so Hori had the men hunker down under the cover of shields with only the copper-tipper spears warning off the attacking chariots. Now concentrating on survival, Hori had time to look at the squadrons, taking note of everything, hoping that something he saw might prove useful in future. He marvelled at the men in their flying chariots, their long hair spread out behind them, and the skill with which the charioteers managed their horses, the reins seemingly an extension of their arms. The charioteers guided the vehicles, leaving the other occupant to harass the enemy with arrows or spears.

One charioteer in particular caught Hori's attention, a slim youth garbed in a strange tunic and legging, and his long hair streaming behind. Unlike the other warriors, the youth's face was shaven...or possibly *he is too young to shave*, Hori thought. He decided that was unlikely, given the skill with which he guided the chariot. There was something familiar about the youth, but Hori could not imagine what. The only place he could have seen him was from the walls of Iunu a few years back, but he thought that unlikely. Despite this, the sense of familiarity persisted. A shouted command sent the chariots wheeling away to the north while the beardless youth brought his chariot to a halt facing the surviving men of Hori's Troop. For several long minutes, the charioteer and the commander beside him stared and Hori stared back.

"It isn't possible," Hori muttered. For some reason, the only thing he could think of was that he had seen the youth in Avaris many years before...but that had been before the *heqa khasut* invasion. The youth had the look of Merybaal, impossible as that was, unless... *What was his name? The son of Djedenre? Or is there another son I know nothing about? Could it possibly be, and why would they side with the invaders*? Hori pushed through the ranks of his men and faced the chariot, and that much closer, the resemblance to the old Treasurer of Avaris was even stronger.

"Who are you?" Hori yelled. "Are you of the family of Merybaal?"

The youth appeared to stagger, and the man beside him said something. A nod, and the horses were in motion again, turning and trotting past Hori and then away to the north, picking up speed. Hori let out his breath in a ragged gust, unaware he had been holding his breath. The youth had not answered and he supposed he would never know the truth of it now.

The battle had proved calamitous for the Kemetu. Close to six hundred men had defended their position against just fifty chariots, and though the chariots had withdrawn from the field of battle leaving the Kemetu in possession, there was no doubt as to who had won. Over a hundred of his own men lay dead, and another hundred nursed wounds of varying severity, while on the enemy side only five horses lay dead and no men, and two chariots lay in pieces. The only positive aspect to the battle, in Hori's mind, was that there could now be no doubt as to the efficacy of the chariot squadrons and of a need to counter them somehow.

"The king will have to listen now," Hori told his commander. "He has to change his mind about chariots."

The commander shook his head. "You haven't heard, of course. King Seheqenre Sankhptahi has died and a man called Senebmiu has claimed the throne."

"What? How?"

"Senebmiu was Captain of the Palace Guard and cut the king's throat." The commander grimaced and lowered his voice. "Nobody was sorry it happened and Senebmiu immediately proclaimed himself king by the will of the gods."

"And people accepted that?"

"Seems so. Anyway, such things are out of my experience. I just do as the generals tell me and leave politics to the men at court."

Hori shook his head. "What will it mean for us? For the army? Does this mean they'll take more account of chariots?"

"Who can say? We'll just have to wait and see."

Senebmiu had himself crowned king of Kemet, taking the throne name of Sewahenre, but his time on the throne was brief. The sanctity of the kingship had been devalued in recent years, and men took notice of the fact that murder went not only unpunished, but sometimes was rewarded. Sewahenre Senebmiu died by violence only a month after his accession, though this time the man who killed him was himself struck down by a guard. A distant relative of Hori, through his mother's side, a court official called Heru, was persuaded to take up this increasingly dangerous position and became king. Perhaps because he had not sought out the throne for himself, Mersekhemre Heru proved more popular.

The new king was popular with Hori too as he reinstituted the program of chariot building, having read the account of Hori's battle with chariots and taken notice of it. Hori welcomed the change in policy, but feared it was too late. How much longer would the gods allow Kemet before the *heqa khasut* came against them in earnest?

Chapter 25

Djedenre may have been king in the Delta and monarch of Avaris, but he had no real power. Samuqenu was overall king and made no secret of the fact that Djedenre was there solely to provide a local and familiar face to keep the populace quiet. The last thing he needed was for disenchanted groups to focus their grievances on someone prepared to rebel against the new power in the north. As long as Djedenre was there, sitting on the throne in Avaris, ostensibly ruling, dissidents found little support.

Being little more than a figurehead, Djedenre found himself with time on his hands. He could ride out into the countryside or take a boat out onto the river, but Amurru guards accompanied him every time. They stayed close to his person, telling him that they had orders to protect him, but he suspected it was as much to prevent him enjoying too much freedom as anything else. He went hunting a few times; taking bow and arrows into the estuarine swamps after wildfowl, but the constant presence of armed guards destroyed what enjoyment he could extract from the expeditions. About the only pastime they allowed him to enjoy uninterrupted was the company of his family.

Merybaal was old, nearly seventy summers, and had recently retired from his duties as Treasurer of Avaris. He had remained in good health, having served the kings of the Delta for fifty years, his control of the wealth of the kingdom firmly in his grasp no matter who was king. Nearly forty kings had reigned in that time, many for only a few months and in one case at least, for only a few days. Merybaal had provided the stiffening, the continuity, which allowed the kingdom the ability to survive such lack of leadership.

He had been hard at work in his office in the palace, working through the latest information on the cost of the war when he found his vision blurring, the figures and words on the scrolls becoming indecipherable. Pressing his fingers against his eyes to try and clear his vision, he called to his chief scribe, but his voice came out slurred. The scribe, a look of intense concern on his face, immediately called the palace physician. He examined him at length, his expression grim.

"Any headaches, sir?"

Merybaal nodded slowly and pointed to the right side of his head with a shaking finger.

"Dizziness?"

"Noo."

"Difficulty speaking?"

"Noo... no r'lly."

The physician grunted, and reached out to Merybaal, touching his face and pressing the skin. He grunted again and recommended that Merybaal lie down in a darkened room.

"You can prescribe something?" the scribe asked anxiously.

The physician shrugged. "For now, just rest. I will see him in the morning."

He would not be drawn on what might be wrong with the Treasurer, so the scribe called for servants to help Merybaal to a bedroom, and someone to watch over him during the night. The next morning, the physician re-examined his patient and was alarmed to see that Merybaal's face had sagged on the right side, the flesh drooping and not responding when Merybaal tried to talk. Djedenre was informed and he hurried to his father's side.

"He is suffering from a paralysis on one side, my lord king," said the physician. "I have seen it before."

"You can cure him?"

The physician looked uncomfortable and avoided looking directly at the king.

"Tell me," Djedenre said. "The truth."

"Once, I saw a man who lived a little while and seemed to recover his functions somewhat, my lord king, but...but mostly the paralysis is a sign that death approaches."

Djedenre ordered his father to be taken home and arranged for the Chief Scribe of the Treasury to take over his father's duties until a replacement could be found. Merybaal remained in his home with his wife Amatia looking after him, and Djedenre visited him as often as his duties would allow. He consulted other physicians but they told the same story--death was approaching--and it was only the rate of approach that was in question.

His father's impending demise made Djedenre think about his family and its continuation. Merybaal was dying, his sister Neferit was throwing herself into danger and did not look like starting a family, his other sister Tiamen was married but without children, and his own son Amenre was estranged and in danger daily. It looked as if the family of Merybaal was in danger of dying out along with its head. Djedenre was the only one with even a hint of a future. He had a new wife, at least, and she could prove fertile, if he chose to pursue that possibility.

After months of paying her only formal attentions, Djedenre relented and opened up personal negotiations, trying to get to know her better. Ishat was suspicious at first, wondering what her husband desired of her after months of neglect. Amurru women were brought up to be subservient to their men, but also to be forthright in voicing their complaints, particularly if justified.

"What is your will, husband? We have been married for months now and yet we are as strangers to each other."

"I have neglected you," Djedenre admitted. "I did not want a wife, but Samuqenu insisted."

"It was the same for me," Ishat replied. "I was not looking for a husband, but I could not disobey my father or my king."

"I am sorry you have been subjected to an unwelcome marriage."

Ishat looked at her husband thoughtfully. "The marriage itself may be unwelcome, but not necessarily the husband."

Djedenre looked surprised. "You have feelings for me?"

"I did not say that. How could I when I do not know you? What I meant was that if my father was going to force me into a marriage, at least he chose a king as my husband."

"Only a client king," Djedenre pointed out.

"A king nonetheless, and more importantly, a decent man from what others tell me."

Djedenre flashed a quick smile. "I try to be," he murmured.

"What are your intentions, husband?"

"We are husband and wife, yet we are strangers. That should be rectified."

"I see...you mean to claim your husbandly rights?"

"My husbandly rights? What do...ah...no, that is not the way of Kemet, nor of the Delta."

"I have been properly brought up and will submit to the demands of my husband."

"You do not look as if you are willing, Ishat."

"I can do my duty by my husband without being willing."

"That is not right," Djedenre said, frowning.

"By the laws of Amurru a wife must submit to her husband."

"In Kemet, a woman is her own person and is not required to submit unwillingly."

"I am a woman of Amurru, not of Kemet."

"And you are now the wife of a Kemetu man. I do not require submission. I want you to willingly...ah...enter into a...ah...union."

"If it is the will of my husband."

Djedenre frowned, feeling as if his words bounced off a high wall, his arguments turning in circles. What could he say that would break through the wall and allow a discussion to take place--a discussion that would hopefully lead to proper relations between a husband and wife?

"When I was a youth of no more than seventeen, I met Rait, who would become my wife," Djedenre said. "She was the daughter of a prominent trader in Avaris, and when I first met her she disdained me, refusing to even talk to me."

Ishat raised her eyebrows. "How then did she become your wife? Did her father command her? You were the son of the Treasurer, after all, and an important man in your own right."

"Her father would not have tried to command her and she would not have listened in any case, for neither father nor daughter liked me. I was a proud young man, full of my own importance."

Ishat smiled. "I find that hard to believe."

"It is true. Anyway, Rait would not even talk to me, yet I could not just walk away for I loved her."

"Love? Without knowing her? I am told that a man and a woman may come to love one another after a time, but never when they do not know each other."

"Yet that is how it was," Djedenre said. "I saw her and I knew the gods had put her there for me, and I was determined that she should know I was there for her."

"So how did you convince her?"

"I courted her. Constantly. She had other men interested in her, but I devoted myself entirely to her and gradually the other men became convinced they could not win her."

"And so she came to accept you?"

"No. She still didn't like me, but I took the time to get to know her father, her mother, her brothers and sisters, even the family servants and gradually they warmed to me. I brought them all gifts...but not Rait. She could not understand it and it piqued her interest. Why, she asked herself, did I approach her family and not her? Why did I ignore her? It ate at her until finally she stopped me in the street and asked me."

Ishat smiled again. "What did she say?"

"She asked why I ignored her, why I no longer courted her."

"And what did you reply?"

"I told her that I did not think she liked me, and out of respect for her wishes I did not want to bother her with my words of love, though my feelings were unchanged."

Ishat laughed. "And so she fell into your arms."

"Not immediately, but her attitude toward me changed. She let me court her again and gradually I won her over. We were married a year later and in due course she gave me a son, Amenre."

"It sounds as if you were very happy."

"We were." Djedenre sighed. "Then she died and Amenre left me. He hates me now."

"I'm sure he does not," Ishat said. "All young men seek to find their own way in life, often believing their fathers are wrong. He will come to his senses again and embrace you as a father."

"I wish I could believe that."

"Believe it, husband. The gods are good and they will not let a good man suffer."

Djedenre forbore from pointing out that good men suffered all the time, and nodded. "It hurts, though," he murmured.

"I would make it hurt less if I could, husband."

"You are a good woman, Ishat."

"I would be a good wife if you would let me."

It did not happen then, nor the next day, or even that month, but Djedenre came to see Ishat in a new way, so he started to court her. She did not give herself immediately, even though that was his right, but allowed him to move at a pace that satisfied his sense of honour, and in the fullness of time they lived together as man and wife rather than just as king and consort. They found joy in each other, and more when she gave birth to a son, whom they named Melqart.

Merybaal held his grandchild only three days before he died, never having fully recovered from the sickness that struck him down. Samuqenu gave him a grand funeral, honouring a man who had held Avaris together for fifty years, and buried him in a newly built mausoleum in the foothills east of the city. He was mourned by much of the population, and Samuqenu even went out of his way to send directives to the principal cities of the Delta, instructing the Governors to have offerings made to the gods on his behalf. The honour paid to his father overwhelmed Djedenre, and any remaining reluctance he felt in acknowledging Samuqenu as overlord, were washed away.

News of Merybaal's death filtered out from Zau to the towns and villages within its sepat, and eventually came to the notice of a small group of brigands in the far north. They did not call themselves brigands, but clung to the notion that they were Delta loyalists; something the local population would have disputed had they dared. Members of the gang took what they needed from the villages, and it was on one of these foraging trips that one of their number, Zhu, overheard the news. He questioned the bearer of the news at length and then hurried back to share it with his leader, knowing it would affect him personally.

"Merybaal, the Treasurer of Avaris is dead, Amenre. The news is even in the smallest villages."

"Tell me everything you heard," Amenre demanded.

"It is said the gods struck him down with the one-sided sickness a month before and he has just died," Zhu said. "Samuqenu gave him a royal funeral and buried him with full honours."

"The honours of a northern barbarian are as nothing," Amenre said. "But he was a decent enough man even though he sided with the invader. I shall miss him."

"There is other news," Zhu said hesitantly. "News that concerns your father."

"I have no father. Do you perhaps refer to the traitor Djedenre that styles himself king over the Delta?"

Zhu nodded. "Yes, sir."

"Tell me."

"The man Djedenre has married a noble lady of the invaders and...and has a son by her that he has named Melqart."

"He dishonours my mother," Amenre muttered.

"But surely there is no dishonour if..."

Amenre turned on Zhu and gripped him by the throat, thrusting his face close and glaring into the eyes of the other man. "Never make excuses for him. He is a traitor to his rightful king, to the kingdom, and to his family."

Zhu managed to break free from Amenre's grip and retreated a few paces, rubbing his throat. "Forgive me, sir, I meant nothing by it. Only that men...that men often remarry and...forgive me."

"What do you know about this northern whore that has married the traitor?"

"Her name is Ishat, and she is the daughter of an Amurran noble, reputedly of the family of Samuqenu..."

"The traitor aims high. Go on."

"There is little else to tell, sir. They have married and have borne a son...er...your brother, sir."

"I deny any relationship, Zhu. How can I have a brother when both of my parents are dead? No, this Melqart is just another invader child and means nothing to me...less than nothing."

"What will you do, sir?"

"Do? What is there to do? I will continue to raise an army against the invader and the traitors that support them, and one day we will drive them from our land."

"Yes sir. In...in the meantime, perhaps we should think of moving on. The people in this region are growing troublesome and resent our taxes."

"Ungrateful sons of whores. Don't they realise we fight for them?"

Zhu said nothing, knowing that in truth they were little more than thieves preying on the peasants of the Delta. Amenre still seemed to believe he was doing this for a higher purpose, and Zhu still hoped they might achieve something, but most of the men they had attracted merely looked for a better life without having to work for it. Their band numbered twenty, which was about as many unproductive mouths as a village could support. The villagers would have liked Amenre's men to move on, but lacked the ability to make them. Amenre's gang was made up of soldiers who had killed before and would not hesitate to do so again.

"Perhaps you are right," Amenre said. "We should move east and challenge the invader closer to Avaris. People must see that we are fighting for them."

"We are only twenty strong," Zhu pointed out. "We lack the strength to challenge anyone."

"What we lack in numbers, we more than make up for in zeal."

Amenre knew the truth of it, no matter how he might try to deny it, and when they left the vicinity of Zau they moved northward, toward more sparsely inhabited regions where the invader was thin on the ground. His men followed reluctantly, preferring the villages in the Delta's heartland where the crops were plentiful and the livestock fat. They went though, not willing to challenge Amenre.

There were other men wandering the land, alone or in small groups, also seeking a living by robbing others. Mostly, they were deserters from one or other army, or peasants dispossessed by the continual warfare, and it was inevitable that Amenre and his gang should meet up with some of them. Handfuls of men were absorbed into the gang, a few who did not wish to join were killed and occasionally, if a larger group was encountered, bloody fighting broke out. Attrition of the original gang was more or less matched by the addition of new recruits, and Amenre's group grew slowly. This was to change in the north, where they stumbled upon a gang of equal strength. A fight to the death would be in nobody's interest, so Amenre and his opposing number, a burly, one-eyed man named Pitahkhare met to talk.

"This land is big enough for both of us," Amenre said. "I suggest you take your men and move away."

"I was here first," Pitahkhare pointed out. "It is for you to leave."

"I do not move for any man."

"Then you must learn to or face the consequences," Pitahkhare said with a gap-toothed grin. His grin faded as he saw the intractable expression on Amenre's face. "Come, Amenre, fighting me would be stupid. We would both be the losers."

"Perhaps, but I am not going to back down. You must ask yourself how much you are prepared to lose to make a point."

Pitahkhare shrugged, and glanced at Amenre's men who sat some fifty paces away, fingering their weapons. "How long have you lived this life, Amenre?"

"Since the fall of King Inkhare. Why?"

"Pickings were good at the start, but no longer, eh?"

"What is your point?"

"Tell me if this story is familiar to you. My men and I wander the Delta seeking out villages too weak to defend themselves, taking what we want from poor people, but unable to take what we want from towns or even well-defended estates. There are times when I would slit the throat of my closest companions for a decent meal of roasted beef and a cup of good wine."

Amenre nodded. "Your tale is a familiar one, though I have been luckier than you in that we have feasted on beef recently."

Pitahkhare grunted. "My point is that we are too weak to take what we want. Alone, we could never succeed, but together..."

"It is a pleasant dream, Pitahkhare, but are you just going to hand over leadership of your band to me? Or do you expect me to bow to you?"

"I hear you, Amenre, but I believe an accommodation is possible. We just need to work out a working relationship that is mutually beneficial."

"You use high-flown words. What are you, a priest or something?"

Pitahkhare shrugged. "I was an acolyte of Ptah at one point, until I found I could get rich quicker by working for myself rather than for others. And you?"

It was Amenre's turn to shrug...and pick his words with care. "My family is noble, but my father betrayed his king and I decided I would rather prey on traitors than bend my knee to unworthy men."

"So who is your king now that Inkhare has fallen? Djedenre or Samuqenu? Or someone else?"

"Never those two. Until a rightful king presents himself, I will strive to keep the banner of an independent Delta flying."

"Very noble sentiments, Amenre. Do they stand in the way of you making a decent living?"

"No.

"Then I think we could work together," Pitahkhare said. "We just have to find a way to trust each other, don't we?"

Chapter 26

Mersekhemre Heru, the new king of Kemet who ruled from Ankh-Tawy, was a sensible man who recognised he had little experience of the army, never having strayed far from the court in his forty years. He was not so arrogant as to think that being king made him a great commander, so he called his generals to him to advise him on the nature of the *heqa khasut* and whether they were truly a threat to the southern kingdom.

"They had all but conquered the Delta a year ago," Mersekhemre Heru said. "They could easily have come south then but they did not. Are they content with what they have or will they seek more?"

General Neferhotep was the senior army officer and the other commanders deferred to him. Neferhotep was not popular with the men and officers under his command as he seemed unable to decide upon bravado or caution. He sought to please both trains of thought and inevitably pleased neither.

"The *heqa khasut* are strong," Neferhotep said, "but strong as they are, we are stronger."

"You are certain of that?" Heru asked.

"Why else would their king hold back? If he believed himself capable, he would have attacked by now. He has no more than ten thousand men and he would have to hold the Delta as well as invade us."

The king nodded sagely, looking pleased, but Hori broke in on his thoughts, unable to contain himself.

"Son of Re, General Neferhotep speaks nonsense and any officer in the army would tell you the same..."

Neferhotep flushed and tried to shout Hori down, while several senior officers tutted or looked outraged.

"Commander Hori is the least amongst us," Neferhotep spluttered. "Do not listen to him."

"That is so," Commander Ankhhenre agreed. "Be quiet, Hori, and let your betters speak."

"I will keep silent if the kings bids me do so," Hori said, "but I ask him to hear me out. I may be junior, but I have had experience fighting the *heqa khasut*, which is more than most of you can claim."

The other officers erupted in outrage once more, but the king raised his hands, commanding silence.

"I will hear your words, Commander Hori," the king said, "but if they lack substance I will punish you for insulting your superior officers."

Hori bowed to the king. "Son of Re, General Neferhotep is misinformed if he believes the enemy has only ten thousand men. He has at least twice that, and a much stronger weapon besides. Have you all forgotten the war chariot that the *heqa khasut* wields with such devastating force?"

"Chariots are overrated," Commander Ankhhenre said. "They are nothing but wagons that haul soldiers into battle."

"Have you ever faced a chariot charge?" Hori asked.

Ankhhenre muttered, but had to shake his head.

"Anyone else?"

Nobody said anything, so Hori continued.

"Well, I have. I saw them several years ago, going through their paces outside Iunu, and I read the reports of the chariot charges that destroyed the Delta armies. A month ago, I faced them myself."

Hori spoke of how his Troop had faced fifty chariots and that although his Troop had been left in possession of the field; it had left him in no doubt as to who had won the battle.

"Fifty chariots against a Troop of nearly six hundred. Imagine what a thousand chariots could do."

"All that tells me is that you completely mismanaged your men," Neferhotep said. "Six hundred should have surrounded and overwhelmed a mere fifty."

"You've never faced chariots. They don't just sit and wait for you to attack, but charge and burst through any formation of men, scattering and trampling them."

284

"How does this--if true--relate to General Neferhotep's contention that the enemy does not have enough men to hold the Delta and attack Kemet?" Heru asked.

"Son of Re, I believe they can call on an army of twenty thousand men and a thousand chariots. The chariots alone could shatter our armies, but backed by even five thousand men we could not hope to stand against them."

"Thus speaks a defeatist," Ankhhenre muttered. "A coward too, no doubt."

"I do not fear them, nor do I talk of defeat," Hori said. "But we must be realists. The normal way of fighting--two armies fighting with hand weapons--won't work. We must counter their strongest weapon somehow."

"If half of what you say is true," Commander Montu said, "we have nothing that will counter their chariots."

"So what is your advice?" Mersekhemre Heru asked, looking round at his military men. "Do we fight conventionally; do we sue for peace, or what?"

"To sue for peace is to surrender," Neferhotep growled. "We must fight them to the death."

"I agree," Ankhhenre said. "At least we will die honourably."

"Better if we could survive," Montu said. He looked at Hori. "You, at least, are with me on this?"

"If we fight army to army, we may die honourably, but we will die and Kemet will swiftly fall to the invader," Hori said. "Surrender would be worse."

"Then what is left?" the king asked.

"Fight them with their own weapons--with chariots."

"And where do we get chariots?" Neferhotep sneered. "By going to the *heqa khasut* and asking nicely?"

"Didn't we have chariots at one point?" Heru asked.

"We did, Son of Re," Hori confirmed, "but one of your recent predecessors ordered them scrapped. Too expensive, apparently."

"How long to build them again?"

"Too long, I suspect," Montu said. "I remember seeing your chariots, Hori, and thinking how long it took to put together even the handful you had."

"Actually, not that long," Hori said slowly. He frowned as he tried to recollect just what resources he still had on his estate. "I stored the few chariots we had, a lot of parts, most of the horses and even some of the trained charioteers were employed on my estates. I think I could have...ten chariots in a month."

The king's face expressed his disappointment. "That few? We cannot face a thousand with only ten."

"That would only be the start, Son of Re. Now that I know how to build them and train horses and men, production would be faster...perhaps twenty a month...or more."

"Then it rather depends on how long we have," the king said. "If we have six months, then we have something that might delay the enemy, a year and we might be able to face them successfully." Heru considered for a few moments. "I will make Commander Hori a General, in charge of chariots. He is to build up a squadron as fast as he can. Gold will be made available from the treasury."

Hori thought it would take a lot longer to build a chariot force capable of facing the enemy, but kept that thought to himself. With chariots, Kemet might survive, without them, they were doomed. He would take what he could get and praise the king.

"On the other hand," Mersekhemre Heru went on, "we cannot neglect our army. General Neferhotep retains overall command of the Army of Kemet and is charged with protecting our borders from any enemy incursions. Gold will be made available...whatever is needed."

"Thank you, Son of Re," Neferhotep said. "Rest assured that while my army guards the northern border, no-one shall pass uninvited."

"If I may offer a word of advice to the General..." Hori hesitated, until the king nodded his permission.

"Build defences against the northern chariots," Hori said. "Ditches, embankments, even piled rocks. Horses and wheeled vehicles need fairly smooth ground on which to operate. My advice is to make our border difficult to cross."

Neferhotep scowled. "They will not cross our border."

With that, King Mersekhemre Heru dismissed his officers and they each went their separate ways, to carry out the king's dictates. Hori hurried off to gather his friends together for chariot production, while Neferhotep and Ankhhenre took a boat back to the army which was camped on the eastern plains across the river.

"You will take Hori's advice?" Ankhhenre asked.

"Never. He has limited experience and does not realise the potential strength of a well-equipped and determined army."

"A thousand chariots sound formidable though."

"When he says it, maybe, but I doubt they are anywhere near as dangerous."

Samuqenu was also calling for a meeting of his generals in Avaris. As well as King Baalbek and King Djedenre, he called upon his General of Chariots Anati, and the senior commanders of the other Amurran forces, Kanak, Yannass, Siaan, and Qub-Har. They each reported on the forces under their command and the reports were gratifying to Samuqenu as the strength of the army had increased rather than decreased after the conquest of the Delta.

"As soon as the kings of the Delta were conquered, the men of the Delta came flocking to our banners," General Kanak said. "We have more men under arms now than five years ago when we crossed the borders."

"Excellent news," Samuqenu said. "And you are satisfied they will remain loyal?"

"They are under military discipline," Kanak said grimly. "If there is any back-sliding, a few examples will sort them out."

"And the Delta is at peace? We were having some problems with brigands and bandits."

"They were mostly renegades from the disbanded Delta armies," General Yannass said. "They have been dealt with...mostly."

"Mostly?"

"There are one or two still holding out, one in the north particularly. He goes by the name Amenre."

Djedenre went pale, but told himself there could be others of that name.

"I want him stamped flat before we move," Samuqenu said. "I can't have troublesome groups in my rear."

"He's hardly worth worrying about, my lord," Yannass said. "A hundred men; no more."

"King Djedenre will remain in Avaris, won't he?" General Qub-Har asked. "That will be his job; to maintain order."

Samuqenu nodded. "Are you capable of doing that, Djedenre?"

"Yes, my lord." Djedenre glanced at Baalbek who shook his head slightly.

"I could remain in the Delta too, if it pleases you, my lord," Baalbek said.

"No, I'm giving you command of my fleet. You will provide backup and ferry troops from one side of the river to the other as needed."

"I have no experience with boats, my lord."

"You don't need experience," Samuqenu said testily. "I'm not asking you to sail one, only have overall command. Do I need to get someone else? Someone with a bit more enthusiasm?"

"No, my lord."

"Good. Now, the army will gather at Iunu for the invasion and strip it of men and resources. General Kanak, you will lead the push south along the Great Road with five thousand men. Your job is to probe the enemy defences and clear the way for the chariots under General Anati. Hard on his heels will be General Qub-Har with another five thousand men. When the chariots shatter the Kemetu armies, as they will, you Qub-Har will mop up any resistance and send prisoners back to General Siaan who will be responsible for incarceration and processing of captives. It would be useful to know what the enemy plans are and their proposed troop movements. I give you free rein on the methods you employ to extract that information.

"I will lead the main army of ten thousand men, and General Baalbek's fleet will keep pace with me. Overall, we will strike down the Great Road, but if there is greater than expected resistance, the fleet will convey men to the west bank and attack their capital of Ankh-Tawy. Any questions?"

"My lord king...you have left me out of your battle plans," General Yannass said. "What are my duties?"

"Your job will be the final pacification of the Delta. I cannot have armed men in my rear, so you will hunt down and destroy this Amenre and any other bands of thieves who may raise their heads. You said he has a hundred men, so I will give you a thousand, but by the time I have taken Ankh-Tawy, I want Amenre's head."

"You shall have it, my lord, but...may I then join you in the conquest of Kemet?"

"You may. Any other questions?"

"What do we know about the strengths of the Kemetu army?" Siaan asked.

"My spies report an active army of ten thousand men under arms, but no chariots. If they scoured the cities and towns they could possibly enlist another ten thousand, but they would be ill-equipped and poorly trained."

"No real threat then," Kanak said.

"I don't expect we shall meet with much resistance," Samuqenu confirmed, "but it would not do to become complacent. It took us five years to placate the Delta after all. We know what the northern part of Kemet has in the way of resources, but the long river valley is an unknown quantity. My spies have not been able to penetrate very far south."

The meeting broke up and Djedenre caught Baalbek's eye, motioning him aside. They waited until they were alone before Djedenre spoke of his concerns.

"My son is in great danger. What do I do?"

"You don't know that this Amenre is your son," Baalbek said. "It could be another man of that name."

"I think it is...and if it is, he is in danger. Yannass has orders to take his head." Djedenre shuddered and shook his head. "I cannot just stand by and see that happen."

"There is nothing you can do."

"You wouldn't say that if your son Aribaal was the one in danger. You would do anything to help him."

"You are right, but are situations are very different. My son fights beside me, while yours is a rebel."

"He is loyal to the Delta, rather," Djedenre said. He shrugged. "It amounts to the same, though. I must find a way to warn him."

"That would be a dangerous course to take," Baalbek said. "Samuqenu would have your head as well as your son's. You have risen to the throne of the Delta, but you can fall just as fast."

"Nevertheless, I must. He is my son."

"A son who has chosen a path that puts him in conflict with you and your overlord, I might point out." Baalbek hesitated before continuing. "Look, my friend, don't take this the wrong way, but Amenre has made himself your enemy, and bears full responsibility for what happens to him. You...you have another son, you know."

"Amenre is my only son by Rait."

Baalbek sighed. "But now you have another wife and another son. Ishat and Melqart need you. What do you think would happen to them if something happened to you?"

"Nothing's going to happen to me."

"Unless you put yourself in danger by warning Amenre...who may not even be your son."

Djedenre was silent a long time and Baalbek let him think, hoping that he had provided a sufficient argument to counter his friend's foolish desires.

"I cannot abandon him," Djedenre said.

"Even if he has abandoned you?"

"Even then."

"So what will you do?"

"I don't know. Get a message to him somehow."

Baalbek shook his head, knowing now that nothing he said would sway his relative from his course. "Be careful. Just...be careful."

Djedenre went home to think about what he could do. He knew that Amenre had effectively rejected him as accepting the enemy's rewards, so anything he said might well be similarly rejected.

General Yannass is coming after you with a thousand men. He has orders to take your head.

'What is that to me?' he could imagine Amenre saying. 'You are a traitor and will say whatever pleases you.'

I am your father. Whatever you think of me, I only want what is the best for you.

'So you say. I think this is all falsehood. Why should Samuqenu bother with me? I have only a hundred men. I may want more, but I know I can be no more than a nuisance to him.'

Djedenre wondered what would convince Amenre that he spoke the truth. He would not accept his unsupported word, but what could he give in support? What truth could he speak?

There is only one thing that will convince him. I must tell him what I know of Samuqenu's plans.

He shivered at the thought. Such an action would be regarded as the rankest treachery if his warning was intercepted, but really, what else could he do?

Amenre is my son.

Djedenre called for a blank scroll, a quill and ink, but he refused the services of the royal scribe. Then he sat down and thought about what he needed to say, then carefully penning the necessary words and phrases. His hand shook as he wrote, but the writing was legible. He spoke of the coming invasion of Kemet, of the troops that would be leaving from Iunu and the stripping of the city's resources and defences.

When he verifies that fact he will know I speak the truth.

He spoke of Yannass's orders and how he was to continue until all opposition was dead. It would do no good to resist Yannass--he must flee for his life, either ahead of the invasion into Kemet and beyond, or try for Ribu in the west, or seek him out in Avaris. He could probably prevail upon Baalbek to offer him refuge in Hattush.

It took several attempts before he was satisfied with what he had written. He discarded the early attempts and rolled up his letter, binding it with cord. The next problem was how to get it to Amenre, but on considering the problem, there was only one answer. He sent for the soldier who had once worked in his father's house, and who had seen Amenre only a few months before.

"You remember you saw my son Amenre?"

"Yes my lord king," Shere said, kneeling before his king.

"Get up. Now, you still have a loyalty toward my family? To me? To Amenre?"

"Yes my lord king."

"Could you find Amenre again?"

"I... I suppose so, my lord...I mean, he'll have gone from where I saw him, but I suppose I could ask. Most people have heard of Ustjennu."

"Would you be willing to find him and deliver something to him, Shere? It might be dangerous."

"You are my king," Shere said simply.

"I will reward you for this service."

"No need, my lord, except...well, a bit for expenses?"

"I will give you silver. Can you read?"

"No, my lord. Never had the need."

"Good, then take this." Djedenre handed Shere the scroll. "Hide it; let no-one see it, and give it only into the hands of Amenre. If it looks like you might be captured, destroy it."

Shere looked alarmed. "Is...is this scroll what's dangerous?"

"Not to you, Shere. I'm trying to save Amenre's life, but if the wrong people saw it they might take it the wrong way. Any danger you

291

might face is only from wandering the countryside looking for him."
Djedenre looked at the soldier, remembering him when he was only a
servant in his father's house. "Will you do it?"

"Yes, my lord, seeing as how it's you and master Amenre at risk."

"When you deliver it into his hands, wait to see if there is an
answer. Even if there isn't, I would like to see you again, Shere. You
can tell me how he looks, whether...whether he has any kind words for
me..." Djedenre looked away and brushed at his eyes. "You know the
sort of thing a father wants to know about the son he loves."

"I know, my lord, and I will obey you faithfully, bringing back
word of Amenre, even if not his actual words."

Djedenre gave Shere silver and another scroll that identified the
bearer as performing a special task for the king, and that anyone
reading it should offer the bearer any assistance he asked for. Shere
changed his clothes from military uniform to that of a lowly ranked
court official, and set off for the interior of the Delta.

One of the other palace servants watched him go and wondered
why the king had called a man out of the army and sent him off on an
errand. He noted, too, the scrolls Shere bore and wondered if they were
related to the scraps of papyrus he had found screwed up in the king's
chambers when he went to clean them. The scraps had writing on
them, some scratched out, but others in neat lines. He could not read
what was written there, but that was not why he took them. Only one
side was marked, and the other side would serve well enough for lists
if he could interest other more highly ranked servants who could read
and write. There might be a few copper pieces in it for him. Carefully,
folding the scraps of papyrus, he tucked them inside his tunic and
resumed his duties.

Chapter 27

Over a hundred men moved quietly in the pre-dawn darkness, spreading out and surrounding a small village in the middle of the Delta. If the village had a name, nobody cared, and soon it would not matter. Five days previously, the village elders had refused to hand over their pitiful belongings to the local bandit gang, pleading poverty, and now the leaders of the gang were determined to teach the villagers a lesson. The village would cease to exist, huts burned and goods plundered, men killed or pressed into service, young women taken for the use of the gang members.

Not everyone in the gang supported these violent attacks on the people, but they were in a minority. Theoretically, the gang had two leaders wielding equal power, but in reality Pitahkhare was dominant, holding a hundred men in his hand, while Amenre held only Zhu and perhaps twenty others. Pitahkhare viewed the Delta as a resource to be plundered at will, while Amenre believed it should be held in trust for the rightful king when he would reveal himself. The new king's reluctance to do so had led to a weakening of Amenre's position, and his followers drifted off looking for a strong leader.

The eastern sky grew light and the first stirrings in the village carried to the men crouched in the fields. A dog barked, a baby cried out, and a murmur of women's voices spoke of the hearth fires being stirred into life. Pitahkhare stood and lifted his sword, waving it in a circle. His men leapt to their feet, limbs chilled by the night air and eager to get to grips with their task. Amenre was slower to make a move, his feet reluctant to join in what was certain to be an unnecessary slaughter. The men moved inward, weapons drawn.

A man relieving himself on the edge of the village called out in surprise as armed men emerged from the fields, his cries turning to alarm and then a shriek as an axe claimed his life. Secrecy was abandoned now as the men raced into the village, yelling war cries to confuse and disturb the inhabitants. Men staggered out of their huts and were swiftly cut down. Cries of alarm split the early morning air, children screamed in terror, and women wailed. Axes and swords rose and fell, spraying blood and drenching the dry dust between the huts. Pleas for mercy were disregarded as the old people were killed, until the sounds of death were stilled. The only sound now was of terrified children sobbing and the panting of the killers as they leaned against huts or squatted, regaining their breath. One of the village elders survived, though grievously wounded. Pitahkhare stood over him, the blade of his sword dripping blood onto the elder's chest.

"All of this could have been avoided," Pitahkhare said, "all you had to do was accede to our very reasonable demands."

The elder coughed and struggled for breath, blood dribbling from the corner of his mouth. "We...we are poor...you...asked...too much."

"And now you are poorer still and we will take what we want." Pitahkhare squatted down beside the man and leaned closer. "Tell me, was it worth it?"

The elder did not answer, any such capability having fled with his life. Pitahkhare got to his feet and called out to his men. "Strip the village of anything of value. If you want a woman, take her, and kill the rest..."

Amenre, who had not taken part in the killing, remonstrated with his fellow leader. "There is no need to kill the other women. Leave them alive to care for the children."

"Why should I care what happens to them?" Pitahkhare demanded.

Amenre shrugged. "Let them live and men will join them. In a year or two the village will be productive again and perhaps willing to pay tribute."

"You are too soft," Pitahkhare sneered. However, he gave instructions that nobody else was to be killed.

The huts were stripped of valuables and torched. Young women were raped or taken with them when the gang left, but there were no further deaths. The gang moved off, heading south, laden with supplies from the village. These were mostly a few sacks of grain, some vegetables, a few head of livestock and assorted pottery or wooden utensils. A few copper mattocks rounded out the wealth of the village. Amenre groaned inwardly at the thought that these spoils had cost the lives of a score of men and the liberty of as many young girls.

"This is wrong," Amenre said to Zhu as they made their way through the farmland. "We should be protecting the villagers instead of preying on them."

"What can we do?" Zhu asked. "We are few and Pitahkhare's men are many."

"We could go our own way."

"I'd follow, and so would some of our men...but not all. And how would Pitahkhare react? He might kill us rather than let us go."

Amenre walked on in silence, and Zhu left him to his thoughts. In the end, Amenre did nothing, and his inaction caused him pain. Increasingly these days, he felt depressed, as nothing he did matched the high-flown aims he had entertained when turning back from refuge in Kemet.

"I owe my loyalty to the king of the Delta," he muttered, "but who is the king? It is not my father who licks the buttocks of Samuqenu in Avaris; nor is it Inkhare who is now in captivity somewhere. We need a new king...but where do I find him?"

If Amenre hoped the gods would answer him, he was disappointed. The gang moved south, the news of their recent depredations moving ahead of them. Poor villagers gave up what little they had and cursed the Delta men who were worse than the northern invaders. Faced with a choice between hard work and little to show for it, and threats and enough to eat, many men joined Pitahkhare's gang, and as they neared the eastern arm of the river and the city of Iunu, a man sought out Amenre.

"Greetings, Ustjennu," the man said. "I am Shere, and I once worked in your grandfather's house."

"You are welcome, Shere, though calling me Ustjennu only adds to my pain. I once thought to represent 'freedom' in the Delta, but I have seen just what a foolish notion that was."

"I am sad to hear that, Amenre." Shere glanced around and saw they were unobserved. He took out a scroll from his tunic and held it out. "I was asked to give you this."

Amenre looked at the scroll but made no move to take it. "Who asked you to?"

"Your father King Djedenre."

"I don't want it. Take it back to him."

"Your father told me to take back any message you might have."

"I have none. He is dead to me."

"Please don't say that, sir. I know he grieves that you are estranged, and I honestly think he wants the best for you in these troubled times. Particularly now that the invasion of Kemet is starting."

"What? You have news of that?"

"Only what I have seen, sir. And your father's letter." Shere held it out again, and this time, after a brief hesitation, Amenre took it and unrolled it.

"He wants me to flee the Delta," Amenre said after a few moments. "Is what he says about troop movements accurate?"

"I don't know, sir. I can't read and even if I could I wouldn't. All I know is that troops and chariots have moved through Iunu on their way south."

"I should tell Pitahkhare. He should know that we are being hunted. Thank you, Shere. You may report to my father that I read his letter and will act upon it."

"Just that, sir?"

"Just that."

Amenre went to find Pitahkhare and told him about the letter and its contents. The gang leader demanded the scroll but turned it this way and that. It was obvious that despite his former position as a priestly acolyte, he had left before learning to read.

"We are becoming great men if one of the generals is looking for us," Pitahkhare said.

"And dead ones if he finds us. We should disperse so he can't."

"Perhaps, but there is another piece of news that interests me. If Iunu has been stripped bare of men, then it is ripe for plucking. We could live like rich men from that plunder."

"Are you mad? Iunu is a city, not some village defended by farmers."

Pitahkhare scowled. "I will not stand for insults from any man; even you. I have well over a hundred warriors, quite capable of handling anything left behind in Iunu. I intend to take what I can and then we will scatter into the vastnesses of the Delta."

"It is a mistake," Amenre said. "Possibly even a trap."

"We'll scout it out first. Now let's move. It won't stay undefended forever."

Amenre shook his head. "I want no part of it."

Pitahkhare stared. "There will be no reward for you if you don't join me."

"I don't want anything."

"Then you shall get nothing." Pitahkhare started to walk away and then turned back. "I have had my fill of your weakness and cowardice, Amenre. Don't let me find you when I return. I will display no mercy."

"Give me back my letter then."

Pitahkhare laughed as he tucked it into his tunic. "I said you would get nothing."

Amenre was dismayed to find that apart from Zhu and a handful of others, every man followed Pitahkhare as he moved off toward Iunu. He followed at a distance, curious to see what would happen. Pitahkhare moved his men across the river on commandeered boats and moved into the city in small groups. From Amenre's viewpoint there seemed to be nothing happening for a time, and then he saw a dust cloud to the north as a body of armed men approached.

"It was a trap," Zhu said.

"Possibly...or else these are just another part of the army that is moving south. Or even Yannass's men come to move against us."

"What do we do?"

"What can we do? We can't cross the river in time to give a warning. We can only hope they extricate themselves in time."

Evidently, Pitahkhare had not forgotten the basics of warfare as he had set guards who raised the alarm as the armed men reached the city. Fighting must have occurred within the streets, but Pitahkhare's men were outnumbered and few broke free of the city and ran for the boats. Armed men pursued them and archers sent volleys of arrows after them, cutting them down and leaving bodies littering the riverbank. A handful made it to the boats and cast off, though Pitahkhare was not among them. Back on the relative safety of the far bank, the gang headed inland, but a few men approached Amenre and knelt before him.

"Forgive our doubt," they said. "We should have listened to you."

"You will follow me now? What of Pitahkhare?"

"He fell, sir, along with all but a score of men."

"We should go, sir," Zhu said. "The soldiers are starting to cross the river."

As they moved away at a trot, the followers of Amenre looked to him for security. Some recognised in him a nobler spirit than that of their previous leader, while others saw him as just a strong leader who offered them relative safety. As they travelled, they talked amongst themselves and one or two called him king.

General Yannass looked at the pile of bodies with satisfaction. He had brought his men south to Iunu in the wake of the army, ready to head into the Delta from that city in pursuit of the bandits and rebels. Instead, as he entered Iunu he had found them there, wild lawless men engaged in murder and theft committing their acts of barbarity upon the populace in broad daylight. Their destruction did not take long, for Yanass commanded professional soldiers and the rebels, though they might once have been the same, had lost discipline.

"How many escaped?" Yanass demanded of Arib-Har, his second in command.

"Fifty made it out of the city, but all but a score died trying to get to their boats."

"Send men after them. I want them totally destroyed."

While Arib-Har gave the orders, Yannass contemplated the speedy resolution of the task he had been given. If he could kill the last of them in the next few days, he could rejoin the army for the attack on Kemet. There was glory to be found in battle, but little in hunting down thieves and murderers. Arib-Har returned and saluted.

"I found this on one of the bodies, sir." He held out a scroll, torn and stained with blood. "I thought it might be important."

Yannass took it gingerly and unrolled it, scanning the writing. It was in Kemetu script and he did not understand all of it. There seemed to be references to troop movements and if that was so...

"By the gods, these rebels had warning. We have a spy at work in Avaris."

"Sir?"

"Find me your fastest messenger, Arib-Har. This scroll must be put in Samuqenu's hands without delay."

Yannass added a note of his own explaining the circumstances under which the scroll had come to light and sent it off by messenger.

Having done that, he paid his respects to the governor of Iunu and waited to hear back from the men who had crossed the river in pursuit of the fleeing rebels.

Samuqenu was with the main army, marching slowly southwest on the Great Road not very far from Iunu when the messenger caught up with him. The king took the stained scroll and handed it to his scribe while he perused the note from Yannass that accompanied it.

"What does it say?" Samuqenu asked the scribe.

"My lord king, it...it describes your battle plans, outlining every unit and general and...and that Iunu would be stripped bare of men. This must surely be the work of a traitor."

"To whom is it addressed?"

"To Amenre, my lord king."

"Who is he? Who wrote the letter?"

"The writer does not identify himself, my lord, but...his concern for this Amenre is evident. He tells Amenre to flee to Kemet or Ribu or Avaris...or...my lord, he says King Baalbek might give him refuge. One must surely assume a blood relationship between the writer and recipient."

"Baalbek is implicated? Show me the letter."

Samuqenu read the letter slowly and carefully, concentrating on the sentence that mentioned the king of Hattush.

"It says that the writer might prevail upon Baalbek to offer refuge, not that he has already," Samuqenu mused. "Send for Baalbek, he has some explaining to do."

It took a little while to contact Baalbek on the fleet that shadowed the main army, but he arrived in Samuqenu's command tent looking a little puzzled by the guards that had brought him unarmed into the king's presence. Saying nothing, Samuqenu handed Baalbek the letter and watched him as he read it.

"My lord," Baalbek gasped as the full import of the words sunk in. "I know nothing of this. Nobody has approached me asking me to offer such...I would never...I am appalled by this."

"Do you know this Amenre, to whom the letter is addressed?"

"I know of a man called Amenre, my lord, but I cannot say if it is the same one."

"Who is he?"

Baalbek groaned inwardly, knowing he was caught. Unless he was very careful, he would be implicated in this plot by Djedenre. He could not imagine what he had been thinking of...but actually he could. If it was Aribaal in peril, he would probably... possibly...do the same. Even so, this was open treachery and the king would certainly react strongly.

"The Amenre I know is the son of King Djedenre, my lord."

Samuqenu grunted. "It seems I made a mistake trusting him."

"My lord, Djedenre may not be at fault."

"How not? The writer was a man who knew our battle plans and Djedenre has a son called Amenre who is somewhere in the Delta."

"Others could have heard the plans, my lord, and if one of them knew an Amenre..."

"Unlikely, but I take your point. I shall have Djedenre arrested and held pending an investigation. After Kemet is taken I will return to Avaris and sort this out. But what do I do about you, Baalbek?"

"My lord?"

"Are you party to this treachery?"

"No, my lord. On my honour."

"If you are it was extraordinarily foolish to have your name in the document."

"That is so, my lord. It only says that I would be approached after the event. If King Djedenre was indeed the writer then...then he has been very foolish, but I believe he only did so in protection of his son."

"Yet because of his actions, men have died. Some good men of Iunu died in the raid on the city, according to General Yannass. The raid that was precipitated by the letter."

"Let me return to Avaris and confront Djedenre, my lord. I will find out the truth of it."

"No, King Baalbek; you have your duties with the fleet. Return there now, and send your son Aribaal to me. I will keep him with me."

Baalbek knew that the king did not fully trust him and was going to keep Aribaal hostage to his continuing good behaviour. There was no gainsaying the king and his son would be safe enough, but that did not stop him roundly cursing Djedenre when he was alone.

Samuqenu called his own son and heir Aper-Anati into his presence and showed him the letter, giving him instructions.

"Return to Avaris immediately, isolate and question King Djedenre. I don't want him harmed, but I will have the truth of this. Incarcerate him if you have to and have him guarded by trusted men."

"What am I to ask him?"

"About this letter. The only thing that ties him to it is a supposed relationship with an Amenre. See if you can find out whether he wrote it and whether his motive was solely to protect his son or whether he is trying to bring us to ruin."

"I'll do what I can, father, but unless he openly admits it..."

"Do what you can. The most important thing for now is to remove him from any power he might have. We can't afford an uprising behind us."

"Do you want me to stay on and rule Avaris?" Aper-Anati asked.

"No, I want you here with me. You will be ruling Kemet after me and should be instrumental in its conquest." He thought for a few moments. "Install Apepi as king for the time being."

"The Governor of the Avaris Barracks? He's..."

"Not exactly capable? I agree; but he is loyal if nothing else and he will stop any of Djedenre's followers from causing trouble."

Commander Arib-Har reported to General Yannass the next day with news of the pursuit of the rebels.

"Fifteen right hands taken sir."

"Any escape?"

Arib-Har knew better than to lie. "A few, sir. There was a group of eight or ten men who held together and turned at bay when pressed too closely. Our soldiers lost two to none of theirs, so they withdrew. I can send more men after them."

Yannass considered the worth of ten men against his ambitions. As long as he was pursuing rebels across the Delta, he could not truly say he had obeyed his orders. The longer he spent on the pursuit, the longer it would be for him to join the main army and win glory.

"What are ten men?" he muttered.

"Sir?"

Yannass waved a hand dismissively. "Never mind; I'm thinking aloud. Ten men can achieve nothing and it could take us months to find them now. No, we have smashed this gang, obliterating them as ordered. Yes...yes indeed. Commander Arib-Har, have the men ready to march south tomorrow. We will join the king's army."

If Aper-Anati was expecting his questioning of King Djedenre to be awkward or difficult, he was pleasantly surprised. As soon as it became known that he was in Avaris, and before he had even taken Djedenre into custody, the Royal Chamberlain Mutkhare came to see him.

"My lord Aper-Anati," the chamberlain said. "I have news of great import."

"Can it wait? I have a task from the king that must be carried out immediately."

"I fear not, my lord, for if my news is correct, the king faces treachery in Avaris."

"Speak then."

Mutkhare proceeded to relate how a palace servant, tidying the king's chamber, had come upon some pieces of papyrus with writing on them. Being unable to read, he had taken them innocently, intending to sell the pieces for a few copper scraps as only one side was written on. The man he sold them to was a scribe in the city who, being a loyal supporter of the king, was aghast when he read the writing and had brought them to the palace.

"My lord, the pieces of papyrus appear to be rough drafts of a letter addressed to a man called Amenre..."

"What?" That caught Aper-Anati's attention. "Show me these pieces."

Mutkhare handed them over and stood biting his lip as the heir read them, and then took out a torn and stained scroll and compared them.

"These came before the scroll that was delivered. Mutkhare, where were these pieces found?"

"In the king's chamber, my lord."

"You are certain of this? There could be no mistake?"

"No, my lord. I... I have made a few discreet enquiries. Just before, the king sent for writing materials but did not request a scribe. A soldier was admitted to the king's presence and then left. After the king went to his meal, the servant went in to clean up and found the pieces of papyrus."

"Do you know who the soldier was?"

"No, my lord."

"Or whether he carried anything away with him?"

"No, my lord."

Aper-Anati considered the evidence and smiled grimly. "You have done well, Chamberlain Mutkhare. Leave these with me and speak of this to no-one. Can the scribe and the servant remain discreet?"

Mutkhare nodded. "I will make sure of it, my lord."

Chapter 28

Rams' horns sounded in the night, the urgent notes bouncing off walls and reverberating through the streets of Ankh-Tawy and quickly tapers were lit from the hearth fires in every house and soon the mellow glow of oil lamps was seen everywhere and people poured out into the streets, voices raised in interrogation. The palace was roused too, and King Mersekhemre Neferhotep called for his advisers, alarm and sudden fear making his voice high pitched.

"What is happening? Why have the horns sounded?"

Tjaty Ayatep tried to calm him, sending for food and wine and telling him that messengers had arrived from the army in the north.

"It is probably nothing, Son of Re..."

"How can it be nothing? The whole city is in an uproar."

"I will send for the garrison commander."

Garrison Commander Sobekemre was at the palace almost immediately and was ushered into the king's presence to explain why the alarm had been sounded.

"Son of Re, a messenger has arrived from the army. The *heqa khasut* are on the march."

"How long before they get here?"

"Not for a long time...or never, Son of Re. Our army awaits them and if it is the will of the gods, we shall destroy their army at the border."

Neferhotep calmed down at this thought, and dismissing the Commander, partook of the food and drink that servants had brought.

"It will be all right, won't it, Ayatep? Our army is strong, isn't it?"

Ayatep reassured the king and watched him eat, thinking how much the man had changed in the last month. No more than a month and a half ago, Mersekhemre Heru had been the king, and Neferhotep the leading general in the king's army. Then Heru had died when an abscess in his jaw had become suddenly inflamed. Heru died in agony within days, and Neferhotep had seized control of Kemet, using his army connections to make himself king. He had taken the same throne name as Heru to provide continuity, especially as the common people would now know him as Mersekhemre, not Neferhotep the General.

And then there was the mystery, Ayatep thought, of how a martial and belligerent General turned into a timid king almost overnight. It was almost as if he drew strength from physical contact with the army and losing touch with it had drained him of his courage. Ayatep hoped he would recover it quickly, as Kemet needed a strong king on the throne more than ever.

Neferhotep yawned and threw down the crust of bread he had been chewing. "I think I'll go back to bed; it's still the middle of the night." He got up and then frowned at the noise from the city drifting in through the wide windows. "Can you tell them not to disturb me?"

"I will send word, Son of Re, but I think the people will be worried about what the horns signalled. They don't know, as you do, that the danger is not imminent."

"Well, have somebody tell them. It's too noisy."

The city quietened down in its own time, and soon messengers were running back and forth between the palace and the army, sending reports of enemy movements southward and often contradictory commands northward. Commander Ankhhenre had been promoted to General, and Commander Montu was his second in command. Commander Hori, only technically a General, was in command of the tiny but growing chariot squadron. Still not battle hardened, he had thirty chariots now, but more were drifting in daily as fast as his officers could build the vehicles and train men and horses.

Neferhotep as king was just as much against the use of chariots as was Neferhotep the general, and Ankhhenre as general in command of the northern army shared his beliefs. However, Ankhhenre was not about to turn anyone away who could have some positive effect on the outcome of the coming confrontation. Spies revealed the *heqa khasut* to be moving southward, with a small infantry force in the lead, their massed chariot squadrons seemingly relegated to a support function.

305

The general had taken Hori's advice and had the land at the end of the Delta's Great Road dug up, with pits and rocks speckling the landscape. Where Ankhhenre failed was in making the barrier deep enough and long enough. It stretched from the marshland bordering the river, across the road and petered out about a thousand paces beyond, where they encountered a patch of naturally occurring rock. The barrier was less than fifty paces deep even at its widest, and while it would slow the passage of chariots to a crawl, it would not keep them out. Hori had remonstrated when he saw the barrier, but Commander Montu had pointed out how vulnerable the foreigners would be as they traversed the rough ground.

"Our archers will cut them to pieces," Montu boasted.

"I hope you are right, but they won't just stand by and let you do it. They have archers of their own and many more men."

"That is not what our spies say. Five thousand in their advance unit, followed by a thousand chariots. We number well over ten thousand."

"And how many follow the chariots?" Hori asked. "At least as many as we have."

Montu would not be swayed, and continued to follow Ankhhenre's orders to set up men to strengthen the rock and soil of the barrier with the flesh of his men.

"With their blood you mean," Hori muttered when he heard these commands.

He mustered his small chariot force behind the barrier and sent urgent messages back to his estates to accelerate the provision of new chariots.

"I want another twenty within five days, and fifty more within ten days."

His officers shook their heads. "Can't be done, sir. We might have ten in ten days and another twenty in a month."

"We'll be overrun in a month. I don't care how you do it, but get me those chariots. Use half-trained horses if you must, and let the instructors act as charioteers, but if we are to have any effect on the enemy, I must have a hundred chariots of my own."

Hori knew that even a hundred would not stem the onrush of enemy chariots unless the gods were on their side. Still, one never knew; perhaps the enemy commander would split his forces and allow them the chance to fall on them piecemeal.

The Kemetu army still only had some forty chariots at their disposal when the *heqa khasut* appeared, the dust of their passing rising high in the gentle north breezes. Horns sounded, rousing the men from their camp and horses were swiftly harnessed. Meanwhile, archers ran to take up their positions. General Ankhhenre and Commander Montu climbed a low hill a little inland and surveyed the oncoming army anxiously.

"Still only five thousand, sir," Montu said. "They haven't been reinforced."

"Bring the axemen up in support," Ankhhenre said. "If the archers can't contain them, we'll push them back by force."

There was no way Hori's chariots could engage the enemy unless they broke through the barrier, so he withdrew him men a hundred paces and watched developments. The northerners advanced slowly now as they could see the barrier ahead of them and the men waiting. They halted fifty paces shy of the broken ground and raised their shields, just as Montu gave the order to his archers. Arrows arced overhead, descending on the enemy with a sound like a sudden hailstorm. Cries arose where a soldier had not guarded himself sufficiently, and then as the last arrows thumped into shields, the enemy archers prepared their response. This was not as effective, as the Kemetu bowmen were spread out and took advantage of the rocks and pits that formed the barrier, but numbers fell and cursed as they clutched at wounds.

More volleys were exchanged, but now the enemy pressed closer under cover of their shields, and some soldiers grabbed mattocks to shift soil or just used their hands, pulling at rocks and casting them aside. Now it became apparent that the barrier was insufficient in both depth and structure, for the enemy pushed deep into the barrier, levelling the ground over a broad front.

Ankhhenre ordered troops into the barrier, the archers now falling back, and the clearing action halted as the enemy soldiers were forced to take up arms again in defence. A battle ensued, degenerating into a general melee with swords and axes striking shields, spears stabbing. More Kemetu troops were committed and gradually the enemy were pushed back out of the barrier. They withdrew, breaking off the action, and when the Kemetu poured after them, uttering cries of victory, Commander Montu called them back.

"Why did you do that?" General Ankhhenre demanded in fury. "Go back, go back. Close with them immediately while we have them on the run."

For a few moments there was utter confusion as conflicting orders from Ankhhenre and Montu had the soldiers trying to obey all commands.

"There, sir...look," Montu yelled, pointing. "Their chariots. We must fall back."

Unnoticed during the battle, a dust cloud had arisen in the north, and this now resolved into chariots which approached at a steady pace.

"Fall back, fall back," Ankhhenre ordered, pulling back his men behind the barrier, where they formed up in ranks to face the oncoming chariots.

Hori stared at the enemy force, avidly noting the details of what the chariots looked like, how the horses were hitched, and how the men in them rode. He had seen them once at Iunu being put through their exercises and once in battle, but neither instance had involved many chariots. The sight that confronted him now was very different-- terrifying even--and the prospect of meeting them in battle was daunting. From his vantage point, the army of the *heqa khasut* was a sea of stamping horses and as many men standing high, bristling with spears and bows. Even General Ankhhenre was silent in the face of that threat.

"Orders, sir?" Montu asked.

Ankhhenre shook his head and cleared his throat as the dust cloud churned up by hooves and wheels drifted over them. "Stand firm. Let them come to us if they dare."

Several chariots came closer, the riders scouting out the approaches to the barrier, and where their men had started to clear a path through the pits and rocks. Even this gouge in the barrier had only advanced some twenty paces, with at least as much again intact. One of the chariots probed deeper and the charioteer, filled with daring, evidently thought he could pass through the barrier. He shook the reins, urging his horses forward, and the spearman beside him crouched down, holding tightly as the chariot started to buck and slide over the obstacles.

Hori watched the enemy chariot surge closer, and he started to wonder if the barrier was sufficient protection. Then he saw the left wheel strike a large rock, the chariot leapt into the air, lurching sideways, and as it came down again, the wheel shattered. The spearman was thrown out, landed awkwardly, rolled over a few times and lay still, but the charioteer hung onto the broken chariot even as it was dragged across rocks by the frightened horses, the vehicle disintegrating beneath him.

The remains of the chariot burst through the last few paces of the barrier into the clear space in front of Ankhhenre and men ran forward with knives to grab the horses' bridles, cutting them loose from the wreckage of the chariot, and to kill the charioteer.

A cheer went up from the Kemetu army, but the enemy host was silent. As Hori's men ran out to claim the horses, the chariots wheeled and divided. A few raced down the edge of the barrier in either direction, but the bulk turned back and drove north, with their foot-soldiers following more sedately. Another cheer erupted from the Kemetu and General Ankhhenre smiled at Commander Montu.

"We have neutralised the threat and seen them off." He looked over at Hori standing with his chariots. "Chariots are overrated I think. At the first sign of a reverse, they flee."

"I hope you are right, sir," Hori said, "but I think they will return soon enough."

"They'll bring their main army up now," Ankhhenre predicted. "Then we'll see a proper battle where man is matched against man and the strongest army wins."

"Indeed, sir," Montu agreed. "The Delta army could not contend with the *heqa khasut*, but we shall halt their progress right here. They will be no match for us."

General Anati called a meeting of his squadron commanders and senior officers as soon as they had withdrawn far enough to remain unobserved. Captain Sadiki, as an up-and-coming chariot commander, attended the meeting, though he was not senior enough to be allowed to voice his opinions. He told Neferit about it when he got back from the meeting.

"It was incredible. There I was, in the presence of the General and all his senior officers, being briefed on the coming battle."

"And what words of wisdom did you impart?" Neferit asked.

"Well, I wasn't there to give my opinion, but I had to agree with the plan they decided upon."

"Are you allowed to tell me?"

"Not really, but I will. If I can't trust my pretend Ribu prince, who can I trust?"

"Hush...you said you would keep my secret."

"No-one can hear us, and besides, you not being Ribu is nothing--imagine what Anati would say if he was to learn you're a woman."

"I'd rather not think about that, if you don't mind, so just tell me the plan and stop teasing me."

"But I enjoy it, little Neferit," Sadiki said, smiling. "Only one thing would make your presence more enjoyable, and that's..."

"Yes, I know. As you've often said, if I was a young man. Well, I'm not, so get over it." Neferit saw her companion's grimace and added, "Don't think I'm not grateful for your silence; being a charioteer is all I've ever wanted to be."

"Well, you're good at it and getting better every day. Seriously, much as I like you, and despite how exciting it is to see you put one over on the Commanders, I'd turn you in if you weren't so good at what you do."

"Flatterer," Neferit said, but looked pleased. "Now, tell me the plan."

"All right. Look, you've seen the barrier the Kemetu have made--rocks and pits across our path--and you know it's just about impassable for chariots..."

"Poor Khayan and Anakri. What a way to go."

"Yes, but they were fools to try it. Anyone could see those rocks were too large."

"It was brave, though."

"Yes it was brave," Sadiki said, "and I honour them for it, but it was lives thrown away for no good purpose."

"They showed us the barrier was impassable."

"We already knew that," Sadiki said. "The barrier extends from the swampy land near the river to a patch of rocks about a thousand paces inland. Swamps and rocks are equally impassable, but what those fools seem to have ignored is that further east, out in the wasteland, maybe ten thousand paces on, there is decent ground. A thousand men are out there even now, clearing away anything that might hinder us."

Neferit grinned. "So we're going around the barrier, rather than through it?"

"Exactly."

"Imagine their faces when they see us coming, on their side of the barrier."

General Anati moved a hundred chariots back toward the Kemetu, having them drive closer and away again, while the foot soldiers made feints, probing at the barrier as the southern army made repairs to the barrier. While this was going on, the main part of the chariot force headed east in small groups so the dust they kicked up would not signal their presence. It took a day and a half to slowly work their way around the rocky waste that had become the eastern flank of the barrier, and they camped well out of sight of the Kemetu.

"Tomorrow at dawn," General Anati said. "We attack with the sun behind us and obliterate their army once and for all. As we do that, the infantry will charge the barrier and take possession of it, levelling it and allowing the other hundred chariots through."

"What about the main army under the king?" a senior officer asked. "Will they be taking part?"

"I plan on presenting our king with a complete victory when he joins us." Anati looked round at his officers grimly. "Don't disappoint me."

"We're on the left wing," Sadiki told Neferit.

"Is that good or bad?"

Sadiki shrugged. "I don't know. We'll be the furthest from where our scouts have seen, so we don't know what the terrain will be like, unlike the right wing which will be skirting the rear edges of the barrier."

"We'll manage. When do we attack?"

"We leave an hour before dawn and move into position for an attack just after the sun rises. They won't be able to see us coming with the sun in their eyes."

That night, as the chariot force rested and prepared for the coming battle, Neferit lay beside their small cooking fire and unfolded a scrap of papyrus that had found its way to her from her mother Amatia. The letter was addressed to Neterre, Prince of Ribu and a family friend, and the contents gave little away to any other reader. Neferit blessed her father for allowing her to learn at the least the rudiments of reading and writing the common script of the Delta, for it now meant she could find out how her family fared in Avaris and other places.

She had grieved when her father Merybaal had died, and sorrowed to learn that her nephew Amenre was a fugitive from the king's men. On the brighter side, her mother was well, as was her sister Tiamen and her husband Menkare had returned unharmed. Amatia could say little else except to say that the last she had heard, Neferit was safe and well, and that she prayed to the gods that Neterre was also safe.

'You have been a good friend to our family, Neterre, Prince of Ribu,' Amatia said. 'I pray that the gods will keep you safe until you can return to friends and family.'

Neferit shared the news with Sadiki, murmuring in a low voice so they would not be overheard by others in the chariot squadrons. "No news on my brother Djedenre, though no doubt he still enjoys being king."

Sadiki shook his head. "I still find it hard thinking of you as sister..." Neferit hissed at him and he amended his words. "As friend of a king."

"And as I have told you before, I am just plain Neterre. If Djedenre is king it is more than he deserves, even if I do love him dearly. I am friend and ally of Amurru now...just another man in Samuqenu's army."

"Unfortunately not just any man, but a man I cannot have." Sadiki smiled wryly and looked around at their neighbours before continuing in a low voice. "Already, men are wondering why we are not lovers. They know my proclivities, yet here I have a personable and beautiful youth to share my quarters, and yet nothing happens."

"Poor Sadiki. Is your reputation suffering?"

"A bit," he admitted. "The worst of it is...I can't even go looking for another partner. If others saw me forsaking you for another..." Sadiki shrugged. "The men like you, Neferit. I would be soundly chastised for being unfaithful."

"Am I being selfish, Sadiki? Should I own up to whom I am? Once they know I'm a woman, you can go out looking for men again."

"Don't be foolish. If you do that, you'll be thrown out of the chariot squadrons and I'll probably be punished for covering it up. Nobody will believe I didn't know. And they'd be right...I did know."

It seemed they had barely fallen asleep before they were aroused. Neferit was glad for the woollen garments she wore in her Ribu persona as it offered some protection against the crisp night air. They readied their chariots and horses for moving out, leaving their other gear behind. It could be collected later or not at all; and all Neferit kept was the letter from her mother, tucking it into a pouch at her belt. Mounting her chariot, she held it in readiness for Sadiki and when he climbed in beside her with his bow and quivers of arrows, urged the horses into a walk as they joined a column of chariots heading westward.

Scouts had reported back all through the night that the Kemetu army was camped behind the barrier they had erected, and as far as the scouts could tell the only guards they had set were facing the hundred chariots and few thousand men beyond the barrier. New scouts arrived, reporting the same, but the chariot commanders knew it was only a matter of time before someone became aware of the danger closing in on them from their flank, so they issued quiet orders for the pace to increase.

Nothing could make the approach of a thousand chariots quiet, but they were in sight of the Kemetu army, the first rays of the sun illuminating them, before the alarm was given. Horns sounded and the army campsite fell into chaos as orders were shouted to turn the army to face the sudden threat on their flank. The chariots, approaching in a column, now spread out on a broad front, and Neferit found her chariot being ordered into a position near the extreme left flank. Anati ordered the pace increased to a gallop as they charged the Kemetu line, the soldiers still scrambling for position.

Neferit concentrated on controlling her horses, guiding her chariot to keep a space between it and its neighbours, and to avoid any obstacles on the ground. Every now and then she would glance up at the rapidly approaching enemy and was astonished to see chariots facing them.

"I didn't think they had chariots," she yelled.

"Forget them," Sadiki yelled back. "Straight for their line."

Neferit urged her horses on and they leapt forward as the two lines came together. There was a crash of wood and metal, horses screaming as the front lines of both armies went down. Neferit's chariot was thrown up in the air and came down with such force that she wondered how they had survived; then they were through the enemy chariot wall and into the milling infantry still extricating themselves from their camp. All around her were other chariots of her squadron, racing

313

through the camp and trampling any opposition, while Sadiki and others loosed arrow after arrow into the enemy soldiers.

The din of battle was deafening and Neferit thanked the gods for her training. She did not have to think, being guided by Sadiki's murmured words or touches. They and a hundred other chariots burst through the Kemetu camp and wheeled round in some confusion. Now, as they viewed the melee of the battlefield, they could pick their targets, and Sadiki pointed out the banners of the Kemetu General in the centre of the line. As a chariot Captain, he commanded more than twenty and he ordered them to follow him. Neferit whipped up the horses and they thundered toward the rear of the Kemetu command.

Many soldiers had clustered around the General and Anati's main charge had foundered on the massed men around the standards. Now he tried to extricate his chariots from the confusion while the Kemetu soldiers struggled to overwhelm them. Chariots were only useful in motion and limited the ability of their occupants to be effective when panicked horses stamped and reared.

"Straight at the standards," Sadiki yelled.

All his chariots and many others that had recognised the peril that threatened their commander followed him and the massed chariots bit deep into the rear of the enemy. Sadiki and others loosed volleys of arrows, while the infantry around the enemy General shuddered and turned to face this new danger.

Anati and many other chariots broke free and withdrew, and now the Kemetu turned their attention to Sadiki's squadron. Arrows and spears found many targets, horses plunging in death and men collapsing or falling to the ground. An arrow whispered by Neferit, tugging at her clothing as she strove to maintain her chariot's impetus.

"Away again," Sadiki ordered. "Keep moving."

Fifty chariots had followed Sadiki in, but scarcely more than thirty followed him out. Their charge had fulfilled its purpose however, as Anati had drawn away over a hundred chariots and now hurled them back at the Kemetu command. Sadiki grinned and pointed, and his men followed him back.

Neferit could not see how the rest of the battle was going as a choking cloud of dust obscured details, and the shouting and screaming, clash of wood and metal and leather, squealing of wounded horses and cries of dying men drowned out everything else. Sadiki ran out of arrows and leapt to the ground, unsheathing a sword and laying about him. Neferit was terrified that something would happen to him and used all her skill to keep her chariot close. The soldiers around the enemy General had thinned considerably and now this person turned to where Sadiki was carving his way through the Kemetu foot soldiers.

Sadiki turned to meet him, but was at an immediate disadvantage as he had no shield. The General blocked Sadiki's strokes with his own shield and struck back, pushing Sadiki back a few paces. Other fighters interposed themselves for a few moments, forcing both men to defend themselves, and then the way was clear once more. The General snatched up a spear and launched it at Sadiki who stumbled as he tried to evade the missile. Missed by the copper point, the wooden shaft clipped him on the side of the head and he went down, his sword falling from his hand. The Kemetu General ran forward and lifted his sword over Sadiki.

Neferit uttered a cry of horror and tugged the horses' heads round, bringing one wheel very close to where stunned Sadiki lay. She yelled and dragged back on the reins and the horses reared up, hooves flailing. The proximity of the horses distracted the enemy General and his downward blow missed Sadiki, but he ducked and moved closer, preparing another one. Neferit hurled herself over the railing of the chariot, colliding with the General and sending him staggering back. Other Kemetu men surged forward and Neferit snatched up a spear and swung wildly at them, defending Sadiki who still lay stunned. Chariots came to her aid, and the Kemetu men turned to counter this new threat, surging onto the chariot and stabbing at charioteer and commander. Neferit impaled one on her spear and clubbed another over the head, enabling the man in the chariot to evict the last of his attackers. One fell against Neferit, knocking her over while another fell into the path of Neferit's still-rearing horses. A hoof thumped into his chest and he fell with an agonised cry, before the hooves came down again, silencing the stricken man.

Neferit lay next to Sadiki for a few moments before pushing herself to her knees and bending over him. He was stunned, a huge welt marring the side of his head, but seemed unhurt otherwise. After a few moments he groaned and Neferit helped him up, sitting him in the back of their chariot. The fighting had ebbed from around them as the Kemetu fled from the rampaging chariots and the infantry now streaming through the barrier. Neferit heard wheels and hooves and looked up to see General Anati staring down at her from his chariot.

Their own General had been she man she had rescued from the Kemetu attackers.

"I saw what you did, charioteer," he said. "Do not think I will forget it. What is your name?"

"Neterre, General, and this is Captain Sadiki."

Anati nodded. "I know Sadiki and value him, and now it seems I must value you too. Follow on when you are able, Neterre. The enemy is in full flight and I do not intend they should stop before they find the river."

Anati ordered his chariots onward, bumping over the body-strewn battlefield, as the remains of the Kemetu army streamed southward, disorganised and fearful.

Chapter 29

Amenre, Zhu, and a handful of followers ran westward for their lives as the soldiers of Yannass hunted the remnants of Pitahkhare's gang. The only reason they escaped where the other gang members were tracked down and killed was because these men had feelings of loyalty toward each other and to the kingdom of the Delta, supporting one another and holding fast to a set of beliefs. They all believed that the invaders could be defeated and ejected from the kingdom if only a strong king would arise to lead them. This led them to defend each other and in particular their leader whom some already referred to as their king.

"I am not your king," Amenre protested. "I have no special standing, even among the nobility of Avaris."

"Your father Djedenre is king in Avaris," one man pointed out.

"That man is not my father. He sided with the enemy against the rightful king of the Delta, proving himself a traitor."

"In what way was Inkhare the rightful king?" Zhu asked. "In truth, Amenre, he was just a General who seized the throne for his own selfish purposes, like Menenre before him. We don't have any surviving sons of previous legitimate kings, so why shouldn't we choose one of our own?"

The other men murmured agreement. "Amenre should be our king," said one.

"King over what?" Amenre demanded. "The Delta has been conquered and the general population accepts it. There is nobody left."

"That is not what you have said before," Zhu pointed out. "You've always said that the fight isn't over while even one man resists the invader. Well, here are seven who resist. Lead us, Amenre."

"How do you expect me to lead you? We are powerless, having only the clothes we wear and the weapons in our hands. How can we resist the invader who numbers in the tens of thousands?"

"When the annual flood comes, it does not come all at once," Zhu said. "First, there is a slight discolouration of the water. It rises less than a finger width. But that keeps on and after a time the flood waters submerge the land and bring new life in their wake. So too will it be under the rulership of King Amenre. He will be the creeping flood that brings new life to the Delta kingdom."

The other five men applauded and called out to Amenre to accept the throne. He shook his head wearily and looked from man to man.

"Is this truly what you want?" he asked.

"It is," they chorused.

"Then I will accept. I will be your king, but..." Amenre held up his hand, "only until such time as I can hand over the throne to a man more deserving of the title."

The men cheered and Zhu called out loudly, "Hail Amenre, King of the Delta, Lord of Avaris, Son of Re."

Djedenre languished in a prison cell attached to the barracks in Avaris for a month before being dragged before King Apepi. He further suffered the indignity of having to kneel on the hard tiled floor of the audience chamber, before the throne which he had so recently occupied, and bow to a man who had recently provided him with horses. His robes were soiled and crawled with vermin; he was unshaven and dirty and his mind was troubled as to the safety of his family. He looked up at the man on the throne and thought he detected compassion in his eyes.

"Where is my family, Apepi?" he croaked. "What have you done with them?"

"You will address me as King Apepi, my lord king, or exalted one."

Djedenre shook his head. "Where is my family, King Apepi?"

"They are well, prisoner. I do not punish women and children for the sins of husbands and fathers."

"May I see them?" He saw the frown on Apepi's face and quickly added, "King Apepi."

"I will consider it. You may rise."

Djedenre got painfully to his feet and scratched himself through his ragged clothing.

"They are well, my lord king?"

"If you mean your mother and sister of the House of Merybaal, then they are well enough considering they have displayed little loyalty to the new rulers of the Delta. If, on the other hand, you mean your Amurran wife and infant son, then they are as well as can be expected after finding out that you are a traitor. They have suffered nothing at our hands, for they are loyal to the Great King."

"I never meant to be disloyal, King Apepi," Djedenre said. "I have another son, as you know, and I merely wanted to ensure his survival."

"You mean the traitor Amenre?"

"He is still my son, King Apepi."

"A son who has turned against you and clings to an outdated loyalty to dead kings."

"A son who has lost his way and whom I hoped to lead back to a straight path."

"By inciting him to treason."

"Not treason, my lord king."

"As I understand it, you relayed the invasion plans to our enemies, even telling them that Iunu was unguarded. How is this not treason?"

"I wanted him to believe what I said. I hoped he would see it was so, believe me, and see how hopeless his situation was. I wanted him to surrender."

"Instead, he attacks Iunu and kills innocent people. Well, you will be interested to know that General Yannass was close at hand. They fled his righteous wrath and he hunted them down, killing them all. Over a hundred right hands were taken as trophies."

Djedenre staggered and collapsed to the floor, his face screwing up in grief and he wept.

Apepi waited and watched Djedenre as he howled his grief on the floor of the audience chamber. At last, he signed to the guards to bring the prisoner to order. They hauled him to his feet and wiped his face with a cloth, smearing the dirt with his tears and mucus.

"I am not a hard-hearted man, Djedenre," Apepi said. "I do not believe you have any further cause to be disloyal, so I am inclined to be merciful. Instead of returning you to your prison cell, you will be placed in plain but comfortable surroundings in a secure house in Avaris. You will not be allowed out, but your wife Ishat and son Melqart can visit you...if that is their wish." Apepi waited for a response, and when none was forthcoming added, "I can send you back to prison if you prefer, or send you to slave in the mines, or even execute you."

"No... I... I thank you, King Apepi. I will accept your generous offer."

Baalbek was the king of the small nation of Hattush in southern Kanaan. It was situated in the hilly country inland, and though it extended down to the Great Sea, it did not possess a navy. The king himself had never ventured on board a ship before being given command of the fleet assembled by Samuqenu to support his army as it invaded Kemet. He was not at all at home on the swaying decks of the boats adapted from fishing vessels to carry troops and supplies, but he gritted his teeth and applied himself. The quickest way to anonymity and the end of a career was to refuse an assignment given by one's overlord.

His son Aribaal joined him on the fleet and the young man actually enjoyed the experience, much to his father's mystification. Water flowing strongly and deeply beneath the wooden hulls did not alarm Aribaal, and he quickly became a competent swimmer, whereas Baalbek could barely swim to save his life. Luckily, when Baalbek went headlong into the river not long after taking command, Aribaal was on hand to fish him out, coughing and spluttering.

Baalbek knew he would have to rely on the expertise of local fishermen and traders if he was to manage the several hundred small boats in his fleet, and organised these boats into several sub-fleets, each commanded by a Delta man respected by his peers. When Amurrans, or sons of court officials, demanded positions of importance within the fleet, he gave them grand sounding titles but made sure they realised they had little real power.

"But my father is Lord Zuppath in the king's court," one young man objected. "You cannot make me subservient to a mere fisherman. Why, he still stinks of fish."

"Rahotep has fished these waters for thirty years," Baalbek replied. "He knows more about boats and the different arms of the river than you or I will ever know. Are you telling me you have greater experience, Zuth-Har?"

"Well, no...but he is a commoner. A lord should command."

Baalbek cursed beneath his breath at the stupidity of a society that held birth to be more important than knowledge and experience, but he was caught up in the folds of his society and had to work within it.

"I agree," he said, "and you will be titular head of a squadron. You will be paid in gold and honours as long as your squadron successfully completes its assignments. Now, Rahotep knows exactly how to do this, so you would be advised to let him do the actual work, while you supervise him and reap the rewards."

"What if I want to give him a command?"

"Then command him," Baalbek said, "but bear in mind that if your squadron fails because of one of your commands, you will bear the blame, not him. If you will take my advice, you'll ask him for his thoughts on everything, and if your ideas differ, go with his."

"That doesn't sound like I'm in command."

"You have a choice, Zuth-Har, accept that Rahotep knows what he is doing and his actions will bring you gold and glory, or try and do it yourself. If the latter, it means a lot of hard work for little reward." Baalbek regarded the young man. "As I said, it is your choice."

Zuth-Har accepted, but not in his heart, and soon tried to command Rahotep, issuing orders that resulted in chaos. When Rahotep tried to restore order, Zuth-Har brought him up on charges, and Baalbek was forced to overrule the young nobleman.

"You are to blame, Zuth-Har, not Rahotep. I am removing you from your position..."

"I am a nobleman, son of Lord Zuppath. You cannot do this."

"I think you'll find I can. However, I have another assignment for you, more suited to your abilities. The fleet needs rope, so take an oxcart and five men and scour the fishing villages for spare rope."

"That is menial work. I won't do it."

"Then go, Zuth-Har. You are dismissed from my service."

The young man left, cursing, and went straight to his father, who in turn complained to King Samuqenu, but he got no joy from it. Baalbek had his confidence, he said.

When the fleet sailed from Avaris in support of the army, it was in several small fleets, there being too many to manoeuvre as they used the northerly breezes to carry them against the current. Aribaal was given the command of the vanguard, his boats forging ahead of the army into territory still possessed by the Kemetu. He was there in the middle of the river when the army encountered the barrier across the Great Road, and glimpsed the battle that erupted two days later. As the Kemetu fled southward in confusion, his boats resupplied the army before shadowing them as they pursued the enemy.

Baalbek, on hearing that battle was joined on land, sped south to join his son and caught up with him where the last of the river arms came together in one great expanse of green water.

"I would not have guessed there was so much water in the world," Baalbek murmured.

"Only the Great Sea has more," Aribaal agreed.

To the south and west, Baalbek glimpsed the peaks of very regularly shaped mountains, gleaming brilliantly in the rays of the sun and pointed them out to the captain of his command ship.

"They are manmade tombs, Excellence," said the captain.

"What? They are...are huge."

The captain nodded. "And even more imposing when you stand at their base. It is easier to imagine they were created by gods than put together by men, one block at a time."

"What are they called?"

"I have never heard that they have a collective name, but they are named after the kings who had them built. Khufu's Horizon, Menkaure is Divine, and Khafra is Great."

"I would like to see them up close."

"Perhaps you shall, Excellence, when we have conquered Kemet."

The fleeing Kemetu had gathered on the plains of the eastern shore, reassembling themselves into an army as they prepared to turn and face their enemies. Hard on their heels rose the dust of Samuqenu's army and his chariots, ready to deal a death blow. Across the river from them stood the gleaming white walls of Ankh-Tawy, and in the shadow of its walls, numerous boats lay moored.

"Do we attack?" Aribaal asked, staring avidly at the enemy.

"Our orders are to wait," Baalbek replied. "However, you may ready our forces and make certain none of their boats can flee north."

Hori's wife Ayat managed the estate while he was away with the army, but his sister Iset often disputed her rule. Iset had once married a man called Sobekhotep who years later had briefly reigned over Kemet under the name Merkawre. As the wife of a former king, she believed she should hold precedence over the daughter of a mere Tjaty. It was only her love for her brother that restrained her. She only wanted what was due to her sons, Bebi and Sobekhotep, after all. They were the sons of a king, and despite numerous other kings claiming the throne since the death of Merkawre, she still hoped that they would one day be in a position to claim their birthright. It irked her therefore to see Sekhem the son of Hori and Ayat given precedence even though he was younger. And it irked her even more that neither Bebi nor Sobekhotep regarded themselves as superior to Sekhem.

Since the chariot making and training enterprise had been reinstated by the king, the estate had become a hive of activity. The parts that made up the chariots and leather and brass tack was made in Ankh-Tawy and sent south almost daily by oxcart. Meanwhile, horses were drawn in from up and down the river valley and grooms set about training them. Young men flocked in, though not in sufficient numbers, and learned how to control a team of horses. The young princes, Bebi and Sobekhotep, were in the forefront of this activity as they had taken to charioteering as if born to it. Sekhem, at twelve years, was still judged too young to control a chariot, though if he got the chance he would hitch up a team when nobody was looking and race it around one of the distant fields.

"I can drive a chariot as well as you," he claimed, when confronted by the princes.

Sobekhotep smiled in a superior manner. "You show promise," he admitted. "Another year or two and you'll be ready to join us on the battlefield."

"What do you mean, join you? Has father called for you?"

Bebi, as the eldest, nodded. "He wants as many chariots as we can produce, as soon as possible."

"Then he will want me too."

"He wants fully trained teams," Bebi said. "Sorry, cousin, but that excludes you."

Sekhem stamped off in a temper, leaving the princes at their work checking over the leather tack on one of the chariots.

"What did uncle Hori really say?" Sobekhotep asked.

"Just that."

"Come on, brother, I know you. There was more."

Bebi looked round to make sure they were not overheard. "All right, but speak of it to no-one. Ten days ago, his message was that he wanted chariots as quickly as possible. He was in the north with the army with forty chariots and..." Bebi dropped his voice to a whisper, "he says the preparations to defend Kemet are greatly lacking. He fears there will be a battle soon and that it will not go well with us."

"So that was ten days ago," Sobekhotep said. "You've heard more?"

"There was a battle."

Sobekhotep dropped the copper tool he used to punch holes in leather strips. "And?" he demanded.

"We lost."

"What? How? What happened?"

"I don't know the details," Bebi said, "but we were crushed by their chariots and the whole army is retreating in disarray."

Sobekhotep stared at his brother in disbelief. "What about Uncle Hori?"

"He's alive...or he was, but all our chariots have gone. The army is retreating to the eastern plains where General Ankhhenre plans on facing them again. He has petitioned King Neferhotep to bring across every man he can from the city."

"We must join him."

"Of course. We'll take all the men we can and cross the river on fishing boats."

"And the chariots and horses. We'll need larger boats."

"No, we leave them. We can't take them. There's no point anyway. How can ten chariots face a thousand?"

"Is it...is it really that hopeless, brother?"

Bebi nodded. "If they could not stand against them in the north, how will they do so on the eastern plains?"

"The sight of Ankh-Tawy and the presence of the king will fortify their hearts," said Sobekhotep.

"I pray it will be so," Bebi replied gravely.

Chapter 30

If General Ankhhenre could have taken his defeated army farther south he would have done so. His men were dispirited and rebellious, and he feared that if he tried to breach the desert fastness to the south, his already fractured army would totally fall apart. The only alternative was to stand and fight again, no matter how hopeless the prospect. A stand on the eastern marshalling plains across the river from Ankh-Tawy promised the best outcome, so with the help of his officers, he managed to halt the flight of his men. Forming them up roughly into their units, he addressed them.

"Men of Kemet, we stand at the cusp, when our actions today will decide if our beloved nation survives to claim once more its preeminent place among the other nations, or whether we kneel before the *heqa khasut* and let them put their feet on our necks.

"Now, I know you are feeling tired and dispirited, but if any man tells you we are defeated, throw that lie back in his face. Look around you, proud Men of Kemet; look around at the thousands of men gathered here and recognise that you are the best fighting men every gathered together for such a great purpose.

"Shortly, we will fight the *heqa khasut* once more and this time we will beat them, send them running back to their homes like whipped dogs with their tails between their legs. You ask why that did not happen north of here at the barrier? I will tell you, Men of Kemet. We were betrayed. A vile traitor gave away our positions and invited a sneak attack on our camp. That traitor has died by my hand, so there is no possibility of it happening again. This time, when Kemet meets the enemy, we shall prevail, because right is on our side, the gods of Kemet fight with us and will not let foreign gods rule our land of Re.

"And there is one more vital weapon in our arsenal, men of Kemet. Here, on this field, under the gaze of our sacred city of Ankh-Tawy, we shall be joined by our glorious king, Mersekhemre Neferhotep, who will lead every able-bodied man from the city to our side and will fight with us, shoulder to shoulder, until we achieve final victory."

The men cheered, sporadically at first, and then louder and continuously as each man strove to find his courage in the eyes of his comrades. Ankhhenre walked aside and gathered his Commanders to him where they could view the white walls of the city across the stretch of green water.

"A beautiful sight, gentlemen," Ankhhenre said. "It is fitting that we should fight for our lives beneath our city's walls."

"A traitor?" Montu asked. "I wasn't aware of one."

Ankhhenre shrugged. "There may as well have been one, in which case I would have killed him. I could scarcely tell the men we were just fooled by a superior enemy."

"And the king's presence today?" Hori asked. "Is that going to happen?"

"The thought encourages the men, but I think our beloved Neferhotep has lost his nerve. I sent word to him that he should lead his army, but he prevaricates and will not commit himself."

"Then we must lose the coming battle?" Hori asked.

"Look there," Ankhhenre said, pointing downriver. "The enemy fleet covers the waters to the north, and there..." his arm swung round, "to the northeast are the storm clouds that spell our deaths. Do you imagine that if we escape one, we shall escape the other?"

Hori looked at the huge cloud of dust raised by the oncoming army and shook his head.

"If it gives you any comfort, General Hori, you were right," Ankhhenre went on. "Chariots are a fearsome weapon and we should have invested more gold in building them a year ago."

Hori nodded wearily. It was too late now to think about what might have been done.

"Did any of your chariots survive?" Montu asked.

"Two, and both were damaged."

"Then we have no possible defence against their chariot attack."

"Yes we do," Ankhhenre said. "The stout hearts and strong arms of our brave men."

The three men looked at each other, knowing those words were mere bravado. Truly that day would see the power of Kemet fall unless the gods stepped in to save them.

If Ankhhenre had found it difficult to control his fleeing army and persuade it to make a stand on the eastern plains, Samuqenu had a similar problem with his victorious army. When the enemy had fled, Anati's chariots had pursued them, pressing hard on their heels for thousands of paces before his officers managed to catch up and instil some sort of order into them. The main army under Samuqenu's direct command poured through the barrier, leaving a few hundred men to restore the ground, but the rest pressing on at a steady pace. They were in high spirits, wanting to close with the enemy and end their resistance.

Samuqenu finally managed to restore order on the northern boundary of the great plain that stretched along the eastern shore of the river. The enemy could still be seen in the distance, milling around in confusion, so he organised his infantry into thick wedges and divided his chariotry into two, one unit on each wing. Anati retained control of the larger unit on the right wing, but he made a field appointment that surprised a few people by making Captain Sadiki the officer in charge of the left wing.

Sadiki was puffed up with pride, and Neferit praised him as she guided his chariot into position at the head of three hundred chariots on the left.

"It is no more than you deserve," she told him.

Sadiki nodded, looking round at the faces of the men in nearby chariots. He noted many friendly faces; men who recognised his worth; but also others whose expressions were resentful.

"Not everyone thinks so," he murmured.

"Then into the middens with them," she replied. "Anati promoted you, so who cares what they think."

"We must be sure to give a good account of ourselves then."

"We will, I know. The gods are with us today."

The great army lurched into motion, thousands of feet churning up the dust in the centre, while horses' hooves and chariot wheels raised more on the flanks. Dust towered above them as Samuqenu's invading army bore down on the army of Kemet.

Neferit lifted her head and snatched off her cap, letting her long hair flow free. She gave a great cry of joy that had other charioteers lifting up their voices in cheers. Their advance held almost a holiday atmosphere, the bright sun shining down on them from a great blue bowl of sky, the wall of dust behind them, the dark ribbon of the river far to their right and beyond it, growing slowly more visible, the gleaming walls of Ankh-Tawy.

"This is what I was created for," Neferit cried. "To ride into battle at the head of a host."

Sadiki laughed with her. He pushed aside the immense responsibility of his new command, determined to enjoy himself. The plain was flat and grassy, without many emergent rocks or holes and was almost perfect for chariots. It was tempting to urge the horses into a gallop but a glance to his right saw Anati's host in their measured advance and held himself in check.

A strand of Neferit's hair flicked across Sadiki's face. He glanced at her and found himself wondering at this woman who was so unlike any other woman he had come across. Examining his feelings, he knew he had no sexual interest in her, yet there was definitely an interest of some sort there. He had never considered a woman as a friend and marvelled that he could do so now. What was it about her that piqued his interest? Could it be that very lack of desire, or was it more? Did it have anything to do with her desire for excellence, for wanting to drive his chariot and share some aspects of his life? Or was it that she had saved his life that morning? He had an image of himself as a strong self-reliant man and it irked him that he owed his life to anyone, let alone a woman.

"Well, why not?" he yelled suddenly.

"What, Captain?"

"Nothing...never mind. No, I want to thank you for saving my life this morning."

"It's what friends do," Neferit murmured.

For several minutes there was silence in their chariot, both feeling a measure of embarrassment, and then Neferit tossed her head.

"We're getting close."

Ahead, the mass of the Kemetu army had resolved into figures of men, weapons glinting in the sun. Sadiki looked to his right and saw Anati's standard dip, releasing his squadrons.

"Go!" he yelled, waving his own men forward.

Neferit needed no encouragement. With a shout she urged her horses on and they leapt forward even as the whole line of chariots surged toward the enemy. The chariot forces swept down on the waiting army in two unequal waves, converging slightly as they outpaced the running men of their infantry. A wall of men faced them as they hurtled on and in the last moments before they came together, Neferit saw expressions of terror and panic on the faces of the men.

The two armies collided with a shock that was unlike anything Neferit had ever experienced before. Horses and men screamed as the chariots bit deep into the line, trampling soldiers underfoot and crushing others between horses and vehicles. Cries rose to a crescendo as the momentum of the chariot charge carried them deep into the enemy lines, and then their forward motion slowed...and stopped. The crush of men was too great for the charioteers to extricate the chariots. Soldiers slashed at men in the chariots, and the men there hacked downward, stabbing and slashing, arrows snatching lives away, and the cloud of dust caught up with them and mingled with the spray and gouts of blood from men and horses.

The Kemetu army pushed back, using sheer weight of numbers, and Neferit actually felt her chariot shifted back. Hardly had that happened than another shudder was felt as Samuqenu's army arrived, pouring into the gap between the two chariot wings, carrying all before them. The crush around the chariots eased and Neferit was able to extricate them, limping back to open ground, followed by most of the chariots in the left wing. Others lay wrecked and several could not move, hampered by a dead horse or two. If the charioteer and commander still survived, they dismounted and fought on foot.

Sadiki ordered his chariots back into the attack, but this time reverting to their harassing tactics, swinging close to the mass of fighting men, loosing volleys of arrows and veering away before repeating the manoeuvre. Time and again they charged, until every arrow and spear had been used up. Now they sped closer, using horses and wheels to knock men down, slashing at others with sword or axe, continuing until horses, chariots and men were speckled and smeared with blood, exhausted and breathing hard as the slaughter continued.

Then between one breath and the next, the Kemetu army fell apart. Men streamed away to the south and east, into the desert, while others fled westward hoping that boats would carry them to the safety of the city. Anati's chariots had cut a swathe through the enemy on the right flank, leaving the plain a carpet of mangled bodies. Kemetu seeking sanctuary in the city found themselves clambering over windrows of bodies to the riverbank, where they found themselves deserted by the fleet. Some of the boats were fighting in the north, but more were scudding back to Ankh-Tawy or heading upriver.

Samuqenu let his men pursue the routed enemy for an hour and then called them back, not wanting to risk a sudden resurgence. He had the men strip the dead, carrying his own fallen back for burial and cutting the right hands off the enemy fallen and piled in front of his command tent. Then he let his men make camp and plunder the supplies the enemy had left behind, while he and his principal officers drank beer and wine and watched a drama unfolding on the water between them and the city.

King Mersekhemre Neferhotep had watched the battle from the highest point in Ankh-Tawy, the Hem-netjer of Ptah's rooms atop the Great Pylon of the temple. He had resisted any suggestion to join his men on the eastern plains, or even to show himself to his people. Instead, he shivered and drank wine, biting his lip as the enemy chariots carved chunks out of his army, as the horde of foot soldiers overwhelmed his men, finally sending them running for the dubious safety of the desert.

"It is all over," he whimpered. "Nothing can stop them now."

"We still have the city, Son of Re," the Hem-netjer of Ptah said. "The walls will hold them for a time."

"Not without men to defend them. No, it is over. What will become of me?"

"It seems you have two choices, Majesty, since you have already rejected dying with your men. You can either surrender and throw yourself on Samuqenu's mercy, or..." The Hem-netjer shrugged. "Or you can flee to the south. The two cities of Abdju and Waset are as yet untouched by war. You could raise another army and retake what you have lost here in the north."

Hope blossomed in Neferhotep's eyes. "Yes...yes, I could, couldn't I?" His face fell. "How, though? They have those chariots and they can travel faster than a man on foot. I'd be overtaken."

"By boat, Majesty. A swift messenger boat that can carry you upriver with the wind at your back."

"Hmm." Neferhotep turned away from his view of the unfolding disaster on the east bank and started considering the possibilities. "I'll need guards, courtiers, attendants...and my treasury of course. You'll come too?"

"My place is here at the Great Temple of Ptah, Majesty. As for everything else, you will have all you need in the southern cities. They are part of Kemet, after all, and will be delighted to host their king."

"Yes, I suppose that is true."

"You should leave immediately, Son of Re, before the *heqa khasut* find a way to cross the river and capture Ankh-Tawy."

Neferhotep hurried back to the palace where he called Tjaty Ayatep to him and ordered a swift boat to be made ready.

"I'll need fifty guards, my favourite women and at least a hundred deben of gold from the treasury. The rest can follow later."

"Son of Re, we do not have a swift boat large enough for all that. You have a choice between a barge which moves slowly and could perhaps accommodate twenty guards and your women and gold, and a fast messenger boat which could take five people at most and some gold."

"I have to have my gold," Neferhotep said. "I am a king and I need to appear one to my people. I need my crowns and my robes, my guards and..." He broke off and grimaced. "Several boats then. A fleet of ten boats at least--one for me and my gold, another for my women, the others for my guards. Get them ready at once, Ayatep. I want to leave today."

Ayatep bowed and went to see what he could do. The king was not the only person contemplating flight from the city in the face of the *heqa khasut* and many boats had been bought up by nobles and rich traders. There were still a few messenger boats available, as they were the property of the government and could not be sold without permission. They would have to do, so he notified the Captain of the Palace Guard to detail twenty of his best men for this special duty. Ayatep also drew out a hundred deben of fine gold from the treasury and packed it into boxes.

Neferhotep had difficulty deciding on which women to take with him as there were a number of women he had inherited from the previous king and had not yet had time to enjoy. They all wanted to bring their maidservants with them, limiting the space in the boat, so he finally settled on three, allowing them one servant apiece and a few essential items of clothing. He was not happy when Ayatep informed him he could only take twenty guards.

"There aren't the boats, Son of Re. All the fishing boats have gone and there are only six messenger boats available. One for you, one for your ladies, and four for guards."

Neferhotep grumbled, but there was nothing to be done. If he was to seek safety in the south, he would have to leave at once. Waiting even a day to try and find more boats would multiply the danger. Ayatep supervised the loading of the gold and women, the selected guards and essential stores, while many more guards kept everyone else at a distance. When all was ready, Neferhotep arrived and took his place in the lead boat. Crowds had gathered round to see what was happening, and when they saw the king was preparing to flee the city, murmurs of outrage grew to cries of anger, and people even dared to throw missiles at the king and his small entourage.

"Cast off, cast off," Neferhotep cried.

The sailors who captained the little messenger ships expertly guided the tiny craft away from the docks and into the current, the king's boat in the lead and the more heavily laden boats wallowing as they tried to follow. Sails were raised and the boats turned their heads upriver, the northerly breeze driving them against the current. Neferhotep started to breath more easily as the city walls slipped slowly by, but then one of the guards in the last boat gave a cry of alarm and pointed to the north where many sails could be seen bearing down on them.

The command came from King Samuqenu for Baalbek on his flagship to guide his fleet down to the environs of Ankh-Tawy, there to facilitate the transport of the army across to the west bank in preparation for taking the city.

"At last," Aribaal cried. "Here we've been sitting doing nothing while our army wins honours in the field. Now maybe we can do something useful."

"Useful, yes, but I fear not very honourable," Baalbek said. "We'll only be ferrying men across the river."

"There might still be some of the enemy to contest our passage. There could yet be some fighting."

Baalbek considered this. "Yes, you could be right. I will send a force of archers to clear the way."

"Send me, father," Aribaal pleaded. When his father hesitated he added, "Please, I desire a taste of war, a chance to command in your absence."

Baalbek smiled. "Very well, my son. Take your first independent command and make me proud."

Aribaal shouted for his officers and swiftly organised fifteen boats with six archers apiece and ordered them south, the fast boats drawing away rapidly from the bulk of the fleet that slowly started upriver, sails billowing and oars threshing the green water. His little command rapidly closed on the eastern plains where the carnage of battle could be glimpsed, and the high, white walls of Ankh-Tawy on the western bank. As they neared, Aribaal's helmsman, Aku, pointed to where six small boats were leaving the city docks and turning south.

"Looks like people are fleeing the city, sir."

"Cowards. Let them go."

"I think they have weapons with them, sir. I'm sure I saw the gleam of spear points."

"Can we catch them?" Aribaal demanded.

Aku watched the small boats for a few moments. "They seem to be heavily laden. I think we could, sir."

"Then let us do so. If they carry soldiers, then we must neutralise whatever threat they represent."

Aku shouted out their commander's wishes to the other boats and they altered course slightly to bear down on the six boats ahead of them.

"How soon?" Aribaal asked.

"Within the hour, sir."

The time passed frustratingly slowly as the gentle northerly breeze barely gave them headway against the current. Aribaal stood in the

334

front of his boat, staring hungrily at the six boats ahead of them, trying to decide how much of a threat they really represented.

"Only four of them have soldiers," he called out to his helmsman. "And by the gods, one of them is filled with women. What do you think that means?"

"Nobles trying to escape the city perhaps," Aku called back. He trimmed the sail to catch more of the fitful breeze and altered course minutely.

"Could be. There's a man alone in the lead boat. Maybe he's someone important."

"We'll know soon enough, sir. They'll be in arrow range."

When the first arrows fell, Aribaal could hear shouted orders carry across the water and the four boats loaded with soldiers dropped back, interposing themselves between the other two boats and their pursuers. Four boats with soldiers armed with spear and sword were no match for fifteen with archers, however, and within minutes the four boats were adrift, filled with dead or dying men. A few men survived that deadly onslaught of arrows, and rather than sit and wait for death, they threw aside their weapons and armour and leapt into the water, striking out for land.

Three of Aribaal's boats turned aside, the archers laughing and making bets as they picked off the swimmers one by one. Aribaal led the others toward the remaining boat, rapidly overhauling the one with the women aboard. He ordered two boats to take the women into custody and escort them to the eastern shore, before setting off after the last boat--the one with a single man and a helmsman. The helmsman yelled something to his passenger and pointed to the shore. There was a short exchange and the boat abruptly changed course, heading for the western shore. A few minutes brought it closer.

Seeing their prey escaping, Aribaal ordered his archers into action again, and shortly the helmsman fell inboard and with his hand no longer on the steering oar, the boat swung about, sail flapping as it lost way. The passenger stood up, making the boat rock violently and shouted something that Aribaal could not hear.

"What's he saying, Aku? Can you understand him?"

"Something about gold I think, sir."

"Close with him. We'll capture him and then we'll see about his gold."

Aku eased his boat toward the one drifting in the current and Aribaal's other boats followed. The man looked round wildly and then opened a box at his feet, holding up jewellery and golden chains, proffering them at the oncoming boats. Aribaal's men laughed and pointed, and the man dropped the gold, looked toward the nearing shoreline. With a despairing cry, he jumped overboard, striking out strongly for the western bank which was now very close. Aribaal shook his head and ordered the archers into action, telling them to wound the man if at all possible.

"A finger of gold for the man who puts an arrow in his arm."

Arrows plunged into the water all about the swimming man as the archers laughed and joked, each wanting to claim the reward but no-one wanting to risk killing him. The water shallowed and the man found his footing, staggering up in waist deep water by the reed beds. He started wading ashore, faster and faster as the water became shallower, but now the archers risked everything and an arrow scored a path across the man's back and another took him in the shoulder, followed a moment late by one in the thigh.

The man fell forward with a cry, blood streaming from his wounds, but was up in moments, staggering onward through the reeds. He was almost to the long grass bordering the river when the reeds and lily pads erupted and the man fell with a scream. Water and plants churned wildly and a scaly tail thrashed the water to foam, before vanishing beneath the water. Ripples sped outward from where the man had disappeared.

"I wonder who he was," Aku said.

"Someone rich by the look of it, though much good it will do him now," Aribaal said. "We'll question his women. Turn the boat, Aku, and set a course for the eastern bank."

Chapter 31

When Kemetu resistance collapsed, the army had scattered in all directions, harried by the *heqa khasut*. Most fled south with General Ankhhenre unsuccessfully trying to rally his troops. Commander Montu fell in the early stages of the retreat, and Hori was left, as senior surviving officer, to gather men around him as they fought their way to the riverbank. He had some hope that boats from the city might be on hand to rescue them, but his hopes were dashed when he reached the river and saw only the invading fleet. Looking around the exhausted, dispirited and blood-smeared faces of his companions, he knew there was only one course to take--surrender; if the enemy would accept it.

As the enemy closed in on the hundred or so weary men that now made up his last command, he instructed them all to cast aside their weapons and to kneel with arms stretched out in supplication. He walked out in front of them and as a squad of chariots rolled up at the head of enemy infantry, he threw aside his own sword and knelt. The lead chariot drew up only a few paces from him and he looked up into the implacable face of a man with General's insignia.

"I am Anati, Chariotry General of King Samuqenu," the man barked. "Tell me why I should spare you and your men."

"I am Hori, sometime General of Chariots in the army of Mersekhemre Neferhotep. It would be dishonourable not to spare men who have laid down their arms."

Anati grunted. "For a chariot general you have been singularly inept, Hori. We hardly noticed your presence."

"Chariots are new to us. Perhaps if we had had another year we might have made a better showing."

"Perhaps." Anati considered the kneeling men and shook his head. "We will never know now, for I cannot let you live."

"My lord General," called a voice from the chariot ranks behind him. A chariot pulled out from among the others and came up alongside Anati. "I ask a reward of you."

"Lord General, forgive my charioteer. He is headstrong and not always mindful of his superiors. Leave it, Nef...Neterre," he added.

Anati glowered at the two men in the other chariot. "Captain Sadiki, isn't it? And I remember your charioteer from the earlier battle. Why should I reward you, charioteer?"

"I doubt I saved your life in that battle, General Anati, for you are a formidable warrior, but I think I provided a distraction that enabled you to get the better of an enemy."

"Your action might be interpreted that way. What reward do you seek of me? Gold? Advancement?"

"The life of this man, Hori son of Harrubaal."

Anati frowned. "You know him?"

"He is my uncle, General Anati."

"Careful," Sadiki hissed. "You are on treacherous ground."

"You are the Ribu prince, the lover of our good Captain Sadiki. How is it that you are kin to this Kemetu?"

"I cannot let him die," Neferit whispered to Sadiki before squaring her shoulders and facing Anati. "My lord General, the man Harrubaal who took up residence in Kemet had two sons. One was Hori, whom you see kneeling before you; the other was my father Merybaal of Avaris."

"Merybaal who was Treasurer of Avaris?"

"Yes, my lord."

"I understood him to only have one son--Djedenre, who was made king before he proved to be a traitor."

Neferit took a deep breath, aware that everything was about to come tumbling down around her. "I am not Neterre the Ribu, but Neferit, the youngest daughter of Merybaal."

"What? That is impossible...Sadiki?"

"General, my apologies for the insane utterances of my charioteer. I can only plead exhaustion...the hot sun...she...he is temporarily devoid of reason..." Sadiki drew her aside and whispered, "You will be thrown out or...or worse. You will never become a great charioteer."

"I must, Sadiki. Hori is family; that matters more than my ambition." Neferit turned back to Anati. "I am who I say I am, General Anati." She undid her tunic and drew the garment aside, exposing her breasts for a few moments.

Anati stared and then guffawed, slapping his thighs with mirth. "Did you know about this, Sadiki?"

"Not immediately..."

"I deceived him too, General," Neferit said.

"And why?" Anati demanded. "Why this deception? Are you following your husband or your lover into the army?"

"I follow no man, General, and need no man. I am my own woman."

"Then why?"

"I love horses, and ever since I first saw chariots in action, where your squadrons smashed General Menenre in the north, I knew that I had to become a charioteer. There is nothing I want more in life than to be a charioteer in your squadrons, General Anati."

Anati shook his head, eyeing Neferit with interest, though she had refastened her tunic. "A woman cannot be a charioteer."

"I have already proven you wrong, General."

Sadiki and others nearby hissed their disapproval.

"Have a care, Neferit or whatever your name is," Anati said. "One does not contradict a General with impunity."

"Nevertheless, I have shown by my actions in several skirmishes and battles, including today's that I am a competent charioteer. If you doubt me, ask those in Sadiki's squadron who have seen me in action."

"Is this true, Sadiki? On your honour."

"It is, General. She took to it as if born behind a team. She is a good charioteer now and has the ability to become a great one."

"Only if I allow it," Anati said. "It is unheard of...well, almost unheard of. Do you have Amazu blood in you, woman? The warrior women of the far north? It is said that they ride horses and chariots into battle."

"I don't know, General."

Amati mused for a few minutes, stroking his beard while all around him men viewed the General and the woman with interest.

"Much as I might hate to admit it, this woman did save my life this morning, and I am minded to reward her for that despite the deception she has played on me. I will give you a choice, Neferit. You may continue to be Captain Sadiki's charioteer, or you may have the life of your Uncle Hori as your reward."

Neferit's shoulders slumped. She looked at Sadiki and then at Hori who still knelt on the ground, his mouth open in amazement.

"Being a charioteer means more to me than life itself, General, yet Hori is family. I will take his life as your gift."

"Very well, let it be so." Anati nodded to his driver to take him away, but Sadiki called out to stop him.

"Grant me a gift too, my lord General."

"Let me guess; you want the woman. And here I was thinking you only liked men."

"I only want her as my charioteer. I have no use for women in any other way, but she is talented--worth encouraging. Let her remain as my charioteer. I promise you will not lose by it, my lord."

Anati guffawed again, and several men joined in. "We have won a great victory today and I am feeling generous. Let Captain Sadiki who only likes men be driven around by a woman who only likes women. It is a fine jest."

Bebi, eldest son of Merkawre Sobekhotep and Iset, sister of General Hori, had spent an exhausting few days searching for a pair of horses that had escaped from the estate and fled into the western desert. He had tracked them, quite enjoying this break from routine, until he discovered the half-eaten corpse of one of them. It was evident from the tracks that lions had happened upon them, killing one outright. Bebi cast about cautiously with his bow at the ready, but the tracks of the lions--three if he read the signs correctly--led into an area of thick scrub. He was not foolhardy enough to follow them, so instead he tracked the other horse which had fled farther to the west. Blood spots indicated it had been wounded in the attack, slowing its pace, and it was only a day later when he found it standing in the shade of a thorn tree, head down and shaking.

He soothed it as he approached, and was dismayed to see deep gouges ripped in its flanks, already flyblown and crawling with maggots. It flinched when he touched its sides and he knew it could not survive. Bebi's bow was powerful and he selected an arrow with the sharpest flint head. Then he positioned himself behind the beast's left foreleg and, with a prayer to the gods, released the animal from its agony. The arrow thumped home, driving through the ribs and into the heart.

Bebi turned from the body of the horse and started back the way he had come, but remembering the presence of the three lions still somewhere close by, he set off at an angle, heading toward the river. Once he found that, he could head northward and reach home. The day was hot and as the sun rose higher he sought out a scrap of shade beneath a gnarled tree. He drank from his water skin and, tired from his exertions, fell asleep.

He awoke with the feeling he was not alone, and his first thought was that the lions had tracked him. Opening his eyes just a crack, he saw his bow beside him and he eased a hand out to grasp it.

"You will not need the bow, Bebi son of Merkawre."

Bebi's head snapped up and he stared at the figure sitting on its haunches on the sand in front of him, no more than ten paces away. It was a huge baboon, and Bebi felt a frisson of fear course through him as it yawned, revealing long canine teeth. Then his fear fell away as he discerned the intelligence in the beast's eyes, and he recognised the god. Without getting up, he twisted his legs around and knelt, touching his fist to his forehead in submission.

"A'an of Djehuti, I see you. What do you want of me?"

"Kemet has lost its balance, its equilibrium, Bebi son of Merkawre."

"You...you mean the *heqa khasut*?"

"Now is the time for those who can to step up and come to the aid of their kingdom."

"Me? I am just a youth with no military skills and no name. What can I do?"

"You will have a name and men will follow you...if you desire it."

The baboon leaned forward and started making marks in the sand. Bebi shifted closer and squinted to make out the marks as they appeared.

"Sekhemre Sementawy," Bebi muttered. "The might of Re which establishes the Two Lands. What does it mean, O Great Djehuti? Whose name is it?"

"The name of one who will fight back against the invader."

Bebi heard a distant call and he looked round, spying two men in the distance. When he looked back at the god, he had disappeared as if he had never been there. Even the marks in the sand were filling in as the light breeze blew sand grains over it. He rose to his feet and went to meet the two men, who turned out to be his brother Sobekhotep and cousin Sekhem.

"Did you see him?" Bebi demanded. "Did you see the god?"

Sekhem and Sobekhotep looked at each other. "What god?" Sekhem asked.

"Djehuti...in the form of a baboon. You must have seen him. He was right in front of me when you called out."

"We saw you kneeling under the tree," Sobekhotep said, "but there was nobody with you."

"Nothing," Sekhem added. "We would have seen if there was anything."

"There was," Bebi said. "It was Djehuti in the form of a baboon. He spoke to me..."

"Spoke to you?"

"And wrote a name in the sand--Sekhemre Sementawy."

"A royal name," Sobekhotep said.

"Can you show us the name that he wrote in the sand?" Sekhem asked.

Bebi shook his head. "The wind took it away...but it was there and the god wrote it."

"Brother, you dreamt it," Sobekhotep said gently.

"No, it was real..."

"The gods speak to us in dreams too," Sekhem said.

"Maybe the god spoke of you, cousin," Sobekhotep said smiling. "You already own part of the name. Is it such a jump from Sekhem to Sekhemre?"

"The god spoke to me," Bebi said. "If he had meant Sekhem he would have spoken to him."

"Besides, I have no royal blood in me," Sekhem said. "The god would not speak to me." He shrugged. "Did you find the horses? We were worried about you."

"Lions got them," Bebi said. "And there was nothing to worry about. I was on my way home."

"That wasn't the only reason we came to find you, Bebi," Sobekhotep said. "There has been a battle...two, actually...and our army has been destroyed. The king is dead, as is Commander Montu, and General Ankhhenre on the run."

"What of Uncle Hori?"

"He lives. He surrendered and was spared."

"Thank the gods for that but...what happens now?"

Sobekhotep shook his head. "My guess is that the enemy will capture Ankh-Tawy and press on southward."

"I'm going to fight them," Sekhem said.

Bebi grunted, thinking. "You should join your father. If Hori has offered up his surrender, he will be allowed to live, but the enemy might change their minds if you are seen to be fighting against them. Go to your father and be guided by what he says."

"What will you do?"

"I have been thinking about that ever since the god spoke to me. He came to me for a reason and gave me the name Sekhemre Sementawy. He means me to be the one who once more restores order and establishes the Two Lands."

"You want to be king?" Sobekhotep cried.

"Djehuti wants me to be king," Bebi said. "And why not? My father was king, and now who else is there?"

"King over what?"

"King of Kemet, of course. And the Delta. He wants me to restore order to both kingdoms."

"The kings of Kemet haven't ruled both kingdoms for a hundred and fifty years."

"Then it is time for them to do so again."

"You're mad," Sobekhotep said.

"Touched by the god, anyway," Sekhem said.

"Yes, and I'm going to change my name in recognition of being chosen by him."

"You can't take on Sekhemre Sementawy," Sobekhotep objected. "That's a royal name. Only an anointed king can take it."

"I meant my common name. No longer Bebi, but Djehuty."

"You would use the god's name?" Sekhem asked.

"Yes, he was the one that called me."

Sobekhotep looked at his cousin Sekhem and shrugged. "Well, it is all one to me. If the god truly spoke to you, then use his name and aim for the throne. What else can you do?"

"Will you help me brother?"

"Of course. We are the sons of Merkawre, aren't we?"

"The *heqa khasut* won't let you be king," Sekhem said.

"They do not have a say in it," Djehuty growled. "They think they have conquered Kemet, but all they've done is defeat one army, maybe captured one city. Kemet stretches southward for many Iteru with many cities and many men. I will raise armies and bring them against the invader. I will fight them until the *heqa khasut* have been expelled from the two kingdoms."

"And I alongside you, brother," Sobekhotep said.

"And I," Sekhem echoed.

"No, you return to your father."

"I can fight too."

"I'm sure you can, and you will in your way, cousin. We will have need of a spy within the enemy camp."

Sekhem did not like it but allowed himself to be persuaded. The discomfort of being on the run was less than glamorous when compared to the thrill of being a spy anyway, he thought.

"When will you leave?"

"We'll return to your father's estate and harness up two chariots," Djehuty said. "Then we'll head south."

The three young men returned home and the brothers spoke their farewells to their mother, before taking supplies and harnessing up the chariots. Some of the other men on the estate declared their allegiance to Kemet and went with them, so as night fell, Sekhem watched as a troop of seven chariots drove southward. He turned back when he could no longer see them, but vowed that one day he would join them in their fight against the *heqa khasut*.

The story of the Hyksos continues in Book 3: Two Cities

About the Author

Max Overton has travelled extensively and lived in many places around the world--including Malaysia, India, Germany, England, Jamaica, New Zealand, USA and Australia. Trained in the biological sciences in New Zealand and Australia, he has worked within the scientific field for many years, but now concentrates on writing. While predominantly a writer of historical fiction (Scarab: Books 1 - 6 of the Amarnan Kings; the Scythian Trilogy; the Demon Series; Ascension), he also writes in other genres (A Cry of Shadows, the Glass Trilogy, Haunted Trail, Sequestered) and draws on true life (Adventures of a Small Game Hunter in Jamaica, We Came From Königsberg). Max also maintains an interest in butterflies, photography, the paranormal and other aspects of Fortean Studies.

Most of his other published books are available at Writers Exchange Ebooks, http://www.writers-exchange.com/Max-Overton/ and all his books may be viewed on his website:
http://www.maxovertonauthor.com/

Max's book covers are all designed and created by Julie Napier, and other examples of her art and photography may be viewed at www.julienapier.com

If you want to read more about other books by this author, they are listed on the following pages...

A Cry of Shadows
(Paranormal Murder Mystery)

Australian Professor Ian Delaney is single-minded in his determination to prove his theory that one can discover the moment that the life force leaves the body. After succumbing to the temptation to kill a girl under scientifically controlled conditions, he takes an offer of work in St Louis, hoping to leave the undiscovered crime behind him.

In America, Wayne Richardson seeks revenge by killing his ex-girlfriend, believing it will give him the upper hand, a means to seize control following their breakup. Wayne quickly discovers that he enjoys killing and begins to seek out young women who resemble his dead ex-girlfriend.

Ian and Wayne meet, and when Ian recognizes the symptoms of violent delusion he employs Wayne to help him further his research. Despite the police closing in, the two killers manage to evade identification as the death toll rises.

John Barnes, the detective in charge of the case, is frantic, willing to try anything to catch his killer. With time running out, he looks desperately for answers. Will John get them before it's too late?

Publisher: http://www.writers-exchange.com/A-Cry-of-Shadows/

Ascension Series,
A Novel of Nazi Germany
(Historical: Holocaust)

Before he fully realized the diabolical cruelties of the National Socialist German Worker's Party, Konrad Wengler had committed atrocities against his own people, the Jews, out of fear of both his faith and his heritage. But after he witnesses firsthand the concentration camps, the corruption, the inhuman malevolence of the Nazi war machine and the propaganda aimed at annihilating an entire race, he knows he must find a way to turn the tide and become the saviour his people desperately need.

Series Page for all books:
Publisher: http://www.writers-exchange.com/ascension-series/

Adventures of a Small Game Hunter in Jamaica
(Autobiography)

An eleven-year-old boy is plucked from boarding school in England and transported to the tropical paradise of Jamaica. A shy and dreamy boy, he has one great love in his life--butterflies. He discovers that Jamaica has a wealth of these wonderful insects and sets about making a collection of as many as he can find. Along the way, he has adventures with many other creatures, from hummingbirds to vultures, from iguanas to black widow spiders, and through it all runs the promise of the legendary Homerus swallowtail, Jamaica's national butterfly.

Other activities intrude, like school, boxing and swimming lessons, but he manages to inveigle his parents into taking him to strange and sometimes dangerous places, all in the name of butterfly collecting. He meets scientists and Rastafarians, teachers, small boys and the ordinary people of this tropical isle, and even discovers butterflies that should not exist in Jamaica.

I was that young boy. I count myself fortunate to have lived in Jamaica in an age very different from our present one. I still have some of the butterflies I collected half a century or more ago, and each one releases a flood of memories every time I open the box and gaze at their tattered and fading wings. These memories have become stories--stories of the Adventures of a Small Game Hunter in Jamaica.

Publisher: http://www.writers-exchange.com/Adventures-of-a-Small-Game-Hunter/

Glass Trilogy
(Paranormal Thriller)

Delve deep into the mysteries of Aboriginal mythology, present day UFO activity and pure science that surround the continent of Australia, from its barren deserts to the depths of its rainforest and even deeper into its mysterious mountains. Along the way, love, greed, murder, and mystery abound while the secrets of mankind and the ultimate answer to 'what happens now?' just might be answered.

Series Page for all books:
Publisher: http://www.writers-exchange.com/glass-trilogy/

Fall of the House of Ramesses,
A Novel of Ancient Egypt
{Historical: Ancient Egypt}

Egypt was at the height of its powers in the days of Ramesses the Great, a young king who confidently predicted his House would last for a Thousand Years. Sixty years later, he was still on the throne. One by one, his heirs had died and the survivors had become old men. When Ramesses at last died, he left a stagnant kingdom and his throne to an old man--Merenptah. What followed laid the groundwork for a nation ripped apart by civil war.

Series Page for all books:
Publisher: http://www.writers-exchange.com/fall-of-the-house-of-ramesses-series/

Haunted Trail A Tale of Wickedness
& Moral Turpitude
(Western: Paranormal)

Ned Abernathy is a hot-tempered young cowboy in the small town of Hammond's Bluff in the Dakota Territories in 1876. In a drunken argument with his best friend Billy over a girl, he guns him down. He flees, and wanders the plains, forests and hills of the Dakota Territories, certain that every man's hand is against him.

Horse rustlers, marauding Indians, killers, gold prospectors and French trappers cross his path and lead to complications, as do persistent apparitions of what Ned believes is the ghost of his friend Billy, come to accuse him of murder. He finds love and loses it, he finds gold in the Black Hills and must defend his new-found wealth against greedy men. Finally, he comes to terms with who he is and what he has done. Ned confronts the ghosts of his past and returns to Hammond's Bluff, where a shocking surprise awaits him at the end of the haunted trail.
Publisher: http://www.writers-exchange.com/Haunted-Trail/

Hyksos Series,
A Novel of Ancient Egypt
{Historical: Ancient Egypt}

The power of the kings of the Middle Kingdom have been failing for some time, having lost control of the Nile Delta to a series of Canaanite kings who ruled from the northern city of Avaris.
Into this mix came the Kings of Amurri, Lebanon and Syria bent on subduing the whole of Egypt. These kings were known as the Hyksos, and they dealt a devastating blow to the peoples of the Nile Delta and Valley.

Series Page for all books:
Publisher: http://www.writers-exchange.com/hyksos-series/

Scythian Trilogy
(Historical)
Captured by the warlike, tribal Scythians who bicker amongst themselves and bitterly resent outside interference, a fiercely loyal captain in Alexander the Great's Companion Cavalry Nikometros and his men are to be sacrificed to the Mother Goddess. Lucky chance--and the timely intervention of Tomyra, priestess and daughter of the Massegetae chieftain--allows him to defeat the Champion. With their immediate survival secured, acceptance into the tribe...and escape...is complicated by the captain's growing feelings for Tomyra--death to any who touch her--and the chief's son Areipithes who not only detests Nikometros and wants to have him killed or banished but intends to murder his own father and take over the tribe.

Series Page for all books:
Publisher: http://www.writers-exchange.com/scythian-trilogy/

Winner of the 2006 EPIC Ebook Awards.

Sequestered
By Max Overton and Jim Darley
(Action/Thriller)

Storing carbon dioxide underground as a means of removing a greenhouse gas responsible for global warming has made James Matternicht a fabulously wealthy man. For 15 years, the Carbon Capture and Sequestration Facility at Rushing River in Oregon's hinterland has been operating without a problem--or so it seems.

Annaliese Winton is a reporter, and when mysterious documents arrive on her desk that purport to show the Facility is leaking, she investigates. Together with a government geologist, Matt Morrison, she uncovers a morass of corruption and deceit that now threatens the safety of her community and the whole northwest coast of America.

Liquid carbon dioxide, stored at the critical point under great pressure, is a tremendously dangerous substance, and millions of tonnes of it are sequestered in the rock strata below Rushing River. All it takes is a crack in the overlying rock and the whole pressurized mass could erupt with disastrous consequences. And that crack has always been there...

Recipient of the Life Award (Literature for the Environment): "There are only two kinds of people: conservationists and suicides. To qualify for this Award, your book needs to value the wonderful world of nature, to recognize that we are merely one species out of millions, and that we have a responsibility to cherish and maintain our small planet."

Awarded from http://bobswriting.com/life.html
Publisher: http://www.writers-exchange.com/Sequestered/

Strong is the Ma'at of Re Series,
A Novel of Ancient Egypt
{Historical: Ancient Egypt}

In Ancient Egypt, C1200 BCE, bitter contention and resentment, secret coups and assassination attempts may decide the fate of those who would become legends...by any means necessary.

Series Page for all books:
Publisher: http://www.writers-exchange.com/strong-is-the-maat-of-re-series/

The Amarnan Kings Series,
A Novel of Ancient Egypt

Set in Egypt of the 14th century B.C.E. and piecing together a mosaic of the reigns of the five Amarnan kings, threaded through by the memories of princess Beketaten-Scarab, a tapestry unfolds of the royal figures lost in the mists of antiquity.

Series Page for all books:
Publisher: http://www.writers-exchange.com/the-armarnan-kings/

TULPA
(Paranormal Thriller)

From the rainforests of tropical Australia to the cane fields and communities of the North Queensland coastal strip comes a tale of the horror than can be unleashed by playing with unknown forces.

It starts with a fairy story to amuse small children, but when four bored teenagers and a young university student in a North Queensland town become interested in an ancient Tibetan technique for creating a life form; all hell breaks loose...literally. A seemingly harmless experiment unleashes terror and death and soon the teenagers are fighting to contain a menace that grows exponentially. The police are helpless to end the horror, and it is left to the teenagers to find a way of destroying the menace, aided by two old big game hunters, a student of the paranormal and a few small children. But how do you destroy beings that can escape into an alternate reality when threatened?
Publisher: http://www.writers-exchange.com/TULPA/

We Came From Konigsberg,
A Novel of Nazi Germany
(Historical: Holocaust)

January 1945, and the Soviet Army is poised for the final push through East Prussia and Poland to Berlin. Elisabet Daeker and her five young sons are in Königsberg, East Prussia, and have heard the stories of Russian atrocities. They seek to escape to the perceived safety of Germany.

This is the story of their struggle to survive, of the hardships endured at the hands of Nazi hardliners, of Soviet troops bent on rape, pillage and murder, and of Allied cruelty in the Occupied Zones of post-war Germany. 'We Came From Königsberg' is based on a true story gleaned from the memories of family members sixty years after the events, from photographs and documents, and from published works of non-fiction describing the times and events that are described in the narrative.

Elisabet Daeker's sons, and subsequent daughters, all have families of their own, and have carved out meaningful lives for themselves in far-flung parts of the world. One thing they all claim, though, is - we came from Königsberg.

Winner of the 2014 EPIC Ebook Awards.
Publisher: http://www.writers-exchange.com/We-Came-From-Konigsberg/

Kadesh,
A Novel of Ancient Egypt

Holding the key to strategic military advantage, Kadesh is a jewel city that distant lands covet. Ramesses II of Egypt and Muwatalli II of Hatti believe they're chosen by the gods to claim ascendancy to Kadesh. When the two meet in the largest chariot battle ever fought, not just the fate of empires will be decided but also the lives of citizens helplessly caught up in the greedy ambition of kings.
Publisher: http://www.writers-exchange.com/Kadesh/

You can find ALL our books up on our website at:
http://www.writers-exchange.com

All our Historical novels:
http://www.writers-exchange.com/category/genres/historical/